PREY

L.A. LARKIN

Copyright © 2020 L.A. Larkin
The right of L.A. Larkin to be identified as the Author of the Work has been asserted by her in
accordance to the Copyright, Designs and Patents Act 1988.
First published in 2020 by Bloodhound Books
Apart from any use permitted under UK copyright law, this publication may only be reproduced, stored, or transmitted, in any form, or by any means, with prior permission in
writing of the publisher or, in the case of reprographic production, in accordance with the
terms of licences issued by the Copyright Licensing Agency.
All characters in this publication are fictitious and any resemblance to real persons, living
or dead, is purely coincidental.
www.bloodhoundbooks.com

Print ISBN 978-1-913419-45-5

To Lynne MacTavish. You are an inspiration.

1

BRIGHTON, UK

Parked outside a ground-floor Victorian terrace flat, he watches Sandra West through the bay window. It's been raining on and off all morning and the car windscreen is a blur, but he sees enough to know that she and her fiancé, Charles Powell, are arguing. Powell's are angry gestures: head jutted forward, staccato arm movements. She takes his hand. Powell yanks it away.

Their observer isn't interested in their argument. The less he knows the better.

'Fuck off, Charlie boy, and let's get on with it,' he mutters, staring longingly at the heater, which is off, as is the engine. A stationary car pumping out exhaust attracts unwanted attention. 'I hate this country.'

It was a last-minute job, and if it had been for anyone else, he would have refused. A smile spreads across his unremarkable face, remembering the text message *House clearance*, followed by a name and address. He'd done a double take, mistaking Buckingham *Place* for *Palace*, until he saw the Brighton postcode. It came through as he was dragging the Russian woman into a cold storage unit on the outskirts of Moscow. Distracted for a moment, the bitch had bitten his wrist. He'd almost gouged her eye out to force her to let go.

Peeling back a leather glove, he prods the swollen skin around the semi-circular teeth marks and inhales the pain, then exhales slowly as he folds the leather back into position. Eyes on his target again, Powell disappears from view, leaving the woman dabbing a tissue to her blotchy face. Maybe he's finally leaving.

No such luck. The pigeon-chested beanpole reappears, waving a phone in West's face. She takes it, dials, speaks. The call is over quickly. Must have gone to voicemail. Neither of them has looked out into the street, so he's pretty sure they haven't reported a strange man watching them from a Ford Fiesta.

Bored, he swipes his thumb across his phone's screen and finds the photos of the Russian, Marta Ramazanova. He enlarges them to get a better look. Nice work. Artistic. Shame West's death has to look like an accident. Takes all the fun out of it.

He looks up. The front door opens, and Powell appears in a beige mac. It's still pissing down, so he opens an umbrella and strides off towards the town centre.

'About bloody time.'

The assassin waits exactly five minutes to make sure Powell doesn't change his mind.

With the peak of his unbranded baseball cap pulled low over his face, he leaves the car in a standard black parka and strolls down a narrow path that leads to a back lane running the length of the terrace. He's average height and works hard at being forgettable. His only identifying mark is on his neck, which is why he always wears shirts with collars.

An elderly woman in a Barbour bucket hat and jacket passes him, clutching a stick in one hand and a lead attached to a shivering miniature poodle in the other.

'Number twos, there's a good boy, do number twos,' says the woman to her dog, and neither pay the stranger the slightest attention.

The ground-floor flat has exclusive access to a small rear garden. Running atop the fence is a lattice and through one of the little square holes he sees a waterlogged lawn and some wind-blown daffodils. The flats above are empty, their occupiers at work. The bedroom looks onto the garden and the ceiling light is switched on, which makes it easy for him to see she is packing a suitcase, moving back and forth in a dazed, mechanical way between a wardrobe and the case on the bed.

The garden gate has an easily picked lock. He opens the gate slowly, wary of rusty hinges, and moves hastily to the back door, taking care to step on the square paving stones so he doesn't leave footprints in the soggy lawn. The rear French door has an old-fashioned turn-key lock. He tests the handle and finds the door is unlocked. He sighs. She's making it too easy. He covers each boot with pale blue, plastic booties and enters. He notices Powell's forgotten Cabinet Office security pass on the workbench by the kettle.

Tempting. But he doesn't take it.

From the next room, he hears sniffing. Cranes his neck just enough to see West, her back to him, bent over her suitcase, reflected in the mirrored wardrobe. Out of sight, he pulls off his cap which he replaces with a ski mask. He readies the syringe of suxamethonium chloride and steps through the doorway.

At that moment, West looks up. In the mirror she sees a man behind her in a ski mask. She freezes. They often do. He moves quickly. Grabbing her from behind, he plunges the needle into her neck. She struggles, thrashes, kicks him, tries to pull the syringe away. Their eyes meet in the mirror, hers wide with terror. She's feeling it now, the gradual paralysis, her arms and legs turning to jelly. Too late, she tries to scream. Her tongue and jaw won't co-operate. A gurgle, nothing more.

He lays her on the bed next to the suitcase she will never use, then surveys the wardrobe. One side is filled with Powell's stuff; on the other, hers. His client's instructions were very clear. So instead of leaving his usual signature, he will have to be satisfied with a small theatrical touch: a suicide using the ties of the man who drove her to it. He picks out a navy-blue tie with diagonal stripes. Then a sky blue one with white spots, then red with navy spots, red and blue stripes, plain royal blue and, finally, a grey Prince of Wales check. He ties them together and creates a hangman's noose which he pulls over West's head and tightens around her neck. West watches, eyes watery, powerless, her muscles incapable of movement, her breathing so shallow she will be dead soon anyway.

Now for the tricky bit. West probably only weighs fifty-five, fifty-six kilos, but she can't support herself. He manages to get her on a chair, and, using one knee to keep her upright, he throws the other end of the makeshift rope through the ceiling light fitting, a wrought iron thing with candle-shaped lights. He pulls down hard. The light fitting holds. He keeps tugging at the rope until Sandra is dragged up to stand. She makes sucking noises. The next yank lifts her onto tiptoes. With the next, her feet are off the ground. Guttural choking, spittle dribbling. There's an unexpected flutter of her eyelids. Her face swells, turns puce.

When he has her raised a foot from the floor, he ties off the rope to the fitting, then pushes the chair away. It topples on its side, as if she has kicked it away. Stepping back, he admires his handiwork for a moment. He smooths down the duvet's surface, checks he's left nothing incriminating behind, and, having removed the ski mask and pulled on his cap, he leaves the way he came.

Inside his rental car he uses a burner phone purchased at Heathrow Airport to dial Powell's mobile.

'Charles Powell?' The assassin adopts a neutral British accent.

'Yes, who is this?'

'A word of warning. Tell anyone, particularly the police, what you *think* you know about the Chancellor, and you will be next.'

'Next?'

The killer cuts the connection. He drives away, dropping the phone into a public bin.

2

LONDON, UK

Investigative journalist Olivia Wolfe waits on a damp wooden bench in Kensington Gardens. Ahead is a winding path between cherry trees, their blooms battered by the heavy rain. In the distance, tourists in plastic ponchos mill around the ostentatious Albert Memorial, defying the weather. Pink cherry blossoms litter the glistening grass and float like confetti in a puddle at Wolfe's feet, until a little girl in wellington boots runs through it, trampling the diaphanous petals.

She's five minutes early, her Harley-Davidson Sportster 883 parked down a side street off Kensington Road. On her way out, Wolfe got caught in a downpour so heavy it was like riding through a car wash. Her sodden leather jacket and jeans are cold and heavy against her skin. On her lap is her retro three-quarter black helmet with chin strap. On her back is a waterproof day-pack which goes with her everywhere. It contains everything she needs to travel at a moment's notice, including her passport. But it's more than that. Sewn into the back is an ESAPI bulletproof plate she managed to get her hands on in Afghanistan, which has saved her life more than once.

Her line of work can be dangerous.

She raises cold fingers to the scar above her right ear, less visible now the hair around it has started to grow back. She'll never forget the rapid *fut fut* of a sniper rifle, then waking up in hospital to discover a bullet from an SR-25 had narrowly missed shattering her skull. At first, the headaches had been like a road crew at work inside her head day and night, but these days they're little more than a dull ache.

The fine hairs on the back of her neck prickle at the sight of Detective Superintendent Dan Casburn heading her way. Her spine straightens. For a blessed four months Wolfe hasn't had any contact with him. Then out of the blue that morning he phones her, insisting they meet. She almost refused. Then he mentioned a name.

Sandra West.

As an investigative journalist renowned for exposing the criminal and the corrupt, Wolfe gets lots of tips. More often than not, they're a waste of time. Some simply don't interest her. Many are fabrications. Recently, she's been getting a lot of prank calls because of her uncomfortably high profile – gained when a tabloid journalist splashed pictures of her and her Russian lover across a double-page spread of *UK Today* last year. But when she met Sandra West in a country pub nestled in the Downs behind Brighton, she knew immediately the woman was telling the truth, even though the topic, tax fraud by a member of parliament, was not normally Wolfe's bag. Then West unwittingly revealed who the MP was. That's when Wolfe started paying attention.

'My fiancé was Assistant Private Secretary to, um, a cabinet minister. Well still is, I suppose,' West had said, her eyes flitting nervously from the pub entrance to the bartender who was busy taking packets of crisps from a box. 'He's going to resign. Had enough, you see.' She had paused. Chewed her lower lip. 'He doesn't know I'm talking to you.'

'You are an anonymous source,' Wolfe had confirmed. 'But I need to know the name of the minister.'

West replied, 'For now, I want to keep it vague. At least until he's resigned.' As she took a sip of her coffee, her hand trembled. 'This minister has a brother. They're chalk and cheese. The brother is a loser. An alcoholic.'

Wolfe immediately knew the MP in question. 'You're talking about the Chancellor of the Exchequer, Harold Sackville, and his brother, William?'

West's shoulders sagged. 'How did you know?'

'"Wild Will" is a bit of an open secret. He's off limits except for the tabloid rags. The Chancellor tries to protect him.'

'Bloody hell!' said West. 'I'm making a hash of this, aren't I?'

'I would have worked it out anyway. Please go on.'

West had stared at Wolfe for a long while. 'Of all the journalists I could have picked, I chose you because it's said you're trustworthy. I hope I haven't made a mistake.'

'Your fiancé's name will stay out of anything I publish, unless he gives his consent for me to use it.' Olivia waited.

'Very well.' West took a deep breath. 'William phones the office. Won't be fobbed off. Charlie puts the call through, but instead of cutting the connection, he listens in. I should make it clear that he's never done anything like that before, but the brother's desperation piqued his interest. Will was drunk. Slurring his words. Anyway, he pleads with Harold. Said he owed money. "How much this time?" asks Harold. "Twenty grand," says Will, "and I promise this will be the last time." "It never is the last time, and I'm not doing it. Not ever again." Will then lays into him and threatens to tell the press about a tax-haven account.'

'Were those Will's exact words?' Wolfe asked. 'Tax-haven account?'

West nodded.

'Tell me about the account.'

West then looked down. 'I don't know about that.' Wolfe sensed she was lying. 'What I do know is my Charlie came home that night devastated. Said that he couldn't believe someone he revered, entrusted with the financial stability of the country, was dodging tax.'

Wolfe had closed her notepad. 'I'd like to look into this, but you haven't given me much to go on. I'm sorry.' She had stood up to leave.

West grabbed her wrist. Convinced her to stay. Told her what she knew about the offshore account.

The park bench shakes, jolting Wolfe back to the present. Casburn sits next to her, hands in beige raincoat pockets, jaw in perpetual motion. Nicorette gum, she guesses. He's never without it. Same flat-top haircut, shaved at the sides, as when she last saw him. He avoids eye contact. Just two people sharing a bench.

'Thought you'd be past the nicotine cravings by now,' Wolfe says.

'I've an addictive personality.' Casburn looks straight ahead.

'Addicted to your job, that's for sure.'

'Look who's talking,' he says.

She flicks him a quick look and swears she sees the hint of a smile.

Two mounted police officers, both female, in fluorescent yellow reflector jackets and riding muscular greys, go by.

'You've changed your hair,' Casburn says.

'Yeah, well, they shaved it to stitch my head. It looked daft, so I cut it short all over.' Her black hair is in a pixie cut.

'Suits you.'

Her brows knit. 'Now you're getting weird.' She leans forward, trying to catch his eye. 'What do you want?'

'What did Sandra West tell you?'

'Ah.' Wolfe clicks the stud in her tongue against her teeth, which she does when she's thinking.

Casburn places his hands behind his head and cricks his neck, first one way and then the other. 'Her boyfriend, Charles Powell, is bound by the Official Secrets Act. If he's betrayed government secrets to his girlfriend, who's then told you, he's committed a crime.'

'How is that of interest to SO24?'

Specialist operations units within the Metropolitan Police are assigned an SO number. The newly created Global Threat Taskforce is SO24. Casburn was appointed head of SO24 after he prevented a terrorist attack on London. Very few within the Met know that Wolfe paved the way for Casburn to capture the terror cell, or that she paid a heavy price for doing so: a man very dear to her was forced to leave the country. She hasn't heard from him since.

Casburn sighs. 'I ask a question. You answer with a question. We get nowhere.'

'Look, Dan. We've been through hell together. I've even grown to respect you.' Casburn snorts. He still doesn't look at her. 'Yeah, surprised me too. Thing is, we know each other. How we work. How we think. I'm guessing you had West's phone tapped, otherwise how else would you know we were meeting? And to bug her phone, somebody high up in government would have to approve it, which begs the question: why?'

Casburn doesn't so much as blink. He wears his face like an iron mask.

Wolfe continues, keeping her voice down. 'I'm also guessing you're investigating the Chancellor of the Exchequer, Harold Sackville?'

She leaves the question hanging, counting the seconds inside her head, determined to wait for an answer. She doesn't get one. She tries another tack. 'You owe me, Dan.'

He stops chewing his Nicorette. 'I owe you nothing. I gave loverboy his freedom.'

Casburn is trying to rattle her. He knows Vitaly Yushkov was more than just a 'lover-boy'. The not knowing where he is or what he's doing drives her crazy.

'Vitaly handed you Kabir Khan on a plate,' she said. Khan was the terror cell leader. 'And he did it because I asked him to, remember? As I said, you owe me.'

'Vitaly's a killer, Olivia. He should be behind bars.'

'He was innocent,' she snaps, glaring at him, forgetting their pretence at being strangers.

Two mums with prams stare at them. Wolfe hates herself for letting Casburn rankle her.

He stands. 'Let's walk.'

Casburn marches across the damp grass towards a clump of

London plane trees as though he's still in the SAS. She jogs to keep pace with him.

'I'm giving you a chance to tell me what West told you. And don't give me some bullshit about protecting your sources. We're beyond that.'

He stops. Tugs at his shirt collar. She's rarely seen him this tense.

'What's happened?' she asks.

He eyes her for a brief moment. 'This is off the record,' he says. A statement, not a question.

'Agreed.'

'Whatever she told you cost her her life.' His tone is sharp. Accusatory.

'*What*?' Wolfe's step falters. Casburn walks on, ignoring her obvious shock. Wolfe catches up with him. 'She was killed?'

Casburn stops walking and, finally, makes eye contact. 'Officially it's suicide. Hung herself at home yesterday, according to Sussex Police.' He looks around him, then back to her. 'Whatever she told you either pushed her over the edge, or someone murdered her because of it.'

'Oh God.'

She has lost sources before. It never gets easier. The guilt weighs heavily. So heavily, she often takes risks she shouldn't to protect them. Now Casburn is blaming her for West's death. Wolfe stares blankly at the ground, trying to process the tragic news.

'Olivia!' Casburn clicks his fingers in her face.

'I'm not your dog,' says Wolfe looking up, her large dark eyes angry. 'Sandra was a good person trying to do the right thing. I'll do what I can to help you. Listen to this. She left me a voice message yesterday.'

Wolfe rummages in her leather jacket for her iPhone, finds the voicemail and plays it so Casburn can hear. In it West tells Wolfe she made everything up about Sackville. It was done in spite, and to forget everything. Her voice is tremulous.

'Eleven fourteen,' Casburn says noting the timing of the message. 'What did West tell you at the pub, the day before?'

'That Sackville is stashing money in an offshore tax-haven account. British Virgin Islands.'

Casburn shows no surprise.

'Name of account?'

'ZIB Trading.'

'Account number?'

Is he testing to see if she has it, or does he want it?

He moves closer. She feels his breath on her skin. She instinctively puts her arm out and pushes him back. She hates people invading her personal space, and he knows it. At five feet eight, he's taller than her by four inches and uses his muscular build to intimidate. Sometimes she thinks there are two Dan Casburns, and it's rare for the nice guy to be in charge.

'Back off, Dan, or I swear to God I'll put you on the ground.'

'Butcher's a good teacher, but don't ever try anything like that with me.'

The threat in his voice incenses her. Casburn would be a difficult man to bring down, but she'd have a damn good go if he gave her no choice.

She was going to co-operate, but his bully-boy tactics are infuriating.

'I have nothing more to say,' she says, ducking under his arm.

He grabs hers. 'You have a chance to walk away. Forget Sandra West and whatever you think you know.'

'And if I don't?'

'There are people who will make your life hell.'

Wolfe yanks her arm free. 'Is that a threat?'

'Take it whatever way you like.'

3

Butcher Investigations is a two-person PI business run out of a shoebox at the back of an old-world, working-men's gym in Tooting. The entrance is at the back of the building, down a narrow lane littered with overflowing industrial-sized bins. A laminated printout stuck to the door with Blu Tack informs visitors – not that there are many – they are in the right place. Most of their work comes from referrals from Jerry Butcher's mates in the Met: jobs the over-stretched and underfunded police have no time for. The one-room office is just big enough for two desks which face each other, a small round table shoved into a corner, a kettle and mini fridge.

Balancing a cardboard tray supporting three takeaway coffee cups, Wolfe opens the door to find sandy-haired, craggy-faced Butcher standing behind the seated twenty-five-year-old hacker Jwala Ponnappa, with a hunting knife at her throat.

'Coffee's up,' Wolfe says, putting the tray down.

Ponnappa turns her head awkwardly and peers over Butcher's arm at Wolfe. 'I'm a bit tied up,' she says.

'Grab the pencil and stab his hand,' Wolfe suggests.

Butcher releases his business partner. 'Good call, Liv.'

Ponnappa, whose sylph-like physique makes even Wolfe look tall, gives her a wave, bangles jangling, and grabs one of the coffees. Ponnappa first met Butcher when working cybercrime for the Met. A few years later, they opened their PI business. 'Thanks for this.'

'What a lovely surprise,' Butcher says. 'We've missed you.'

He gives Wolfe a hug.

Wolfe doesn't hug, but Butcher is an exception. The retired Detective Chief Superintendent of London's Homicide and Serious Crime Command has been the one constant and positive influence in her life. Without him, she would have gone off the rails at fourteen when her world imploded. Nor would she have survived the last year and still have her job as a journalist. Wolfe holds him tight. 'Missed you too.'

'Take a look at this,' Butcher says, handing her the knife. 'Made entirely of plastic.'

'Not strong enough, surely?' She takes it.

'Test it.' He nods at an apple on Ponnappa's desk.

'Hey! That's my token healthy meal,' Ponnappa protests.

Wolfe thrusts the knife into the apple, expecting the blade to break or at least bow. It slices right through.

'And here's the sheath.' He hands her what looks like a comb. 'Slide it over the blade.' She does. A perfect fit. It now looks like a comb with a handle.

'Where did you get this?'

'A shipment arrived from China yesterday. Seized by Customs. Has them worried.'

'I can see why.'

'Take it. You might find it useful.'

'Thanks.'

'When are you moving back into the area?' Butcher asks.

'Not yet.'

'Well at least come back to the gym. You need practice. Got to keep your edge.'

'I'm using a gym near work. Keeping fit.'

'Who's training you?'

'Nobody. Me.'

'Lazy.'

Butcher teaches Kali stick fighting and Brazilian jiu-jitsu. He taught Wolfe everything she knows about self-defence, including how to use everyday objects like metal water bottles and key chains as weapons. Maybe he's right, and she has become lazy.

Butcher continues, nodding at her, 'And your stalker's disappeared?'

'So far so good. Looks like moving out of my flat worked. Which is why I'm not sure about coming back. He knows where I lived.'

'I go there regularly. No sign of intruders.'

Ponnappa chips in. 'No bugs or hidden cameras either, and when I last looked, your phone and laptop were clean. I'd say he's moved on.'

Wolfe isn't convinced. He invaded her home, spied on her through minute cameras in her smoke detectors, watched her through her webcam, even deleted her emails. That's why she moved to west London and set up a new mobile phone number. To this day, she still doesn't know who it was.

'I need your help with a story I'm researching,' Wolfe says, keen to change the subject.

'Take a seat,' invites Butcher.

She briefs them on her meeting with Sandra West two days ago, and her claims about the Chancellor. 'Sandra said the account was in the name of ZIB Trading and that Harold Sackville was the signatory.'

'How does West know this?' Butcher asks, taking notes in a small ring-bound notebook.

'Her boyfriend, Charles Powell, is Sackville's assistant private secretary. She claims he overheard an argument between Sackville and his brother, who's an alcoholic and a gambler. He wanted to borrow money. The brother referred to millions stashed away in the British Virgin Islands.'

'So, are you telling me the man who holds the government's purse strings is secretly defrauding HMRC?' asks Ponnappa, referring to Her Majesty's Revenue and Customs.

'I don't know yet. Powell sounds a bit naïve. He couldn't believe his boss would do such a thing. He did some snooping. Found Sackville had made calls to the British Virgin Islands.'

'That in itself doesn't mean anything,' says Butcher.

'Agreed. But ten days later, the Chancellor goes out, leaves his mobile behind. Phone rings. Powell answers. A woman says there's a problem in the Virgin Islands. Powell asks what problem. The woman realises she's not speaking to Sackville and puts the phone down. He calls back. It goes to answerphone. It's the office of ZIB Trading.'

'Which is?' Ponnappa asks.

'A company registered in the UK, supposedly importing carpets and floor coverings, with an address in Morden.'

'Sounds like a shell company,' says Butcher.

'Or a front.'

'Don't suppose West gave you the account number?' asks Ponnappa.

'I think she knew it, but wouldn't give it to me. Which could be why she died.'

'Died?' Ponnappa repeats.

Wolfe looks away, the guilt rising again like flood waters. 'She was found dead, hanging from her bedroom light fitting. Apparent suicide. But Casburn clearly thinks it's not.'

Butcher runs a hand across his mouth, a mannerism Wolfe has come to recognise. He doesn't like what she's just told him. 'Wait a minute. Casburn's involved in this?'

'Yes.'

'How?'

'Not sure, exactly.' Wolfe tells them about her meeting with Casburn and his warning to leave well alone.

Butcher shakes his head. 'I'd hoped that after last time, you two might at least be civil to each other.'

'I think we were pretty civil, right up to the point he tried to intimidate me.'

Butcher frowns. 'Did he threaten you?'

Wolfe stretches across the tiny table and squeezes his arm to reassure him. 'No, just made it very clear he wanted me to drop it.'

'Don't make Casburn your enemy, Liv,' Butcher says. 'His new role gives him a lot of power. If he wants to stop you, he will.'

Wolfe considers this for a moment. 'Him warning me off tells me this is about more than tax fraud. Something much bigger is going on, and I'm going to find out what.' She leans forward. 'Will you help me?'

Butcher and Ponnappa look across the table at each other. Ponnappa nods.

'We're in,' says Butcher.

'I'll get cracking on identifying the account,' Ponnappa says. She spins her wheelie-chair around, puts on hot-pink headphones and her child-like fingers tap her keyboard with lightning speed.

Wolfe heads for the door.

'Where are you going?' asks Butcher.

'Morden. See you later.'

4

The Assistant Commissioner of Specialist Operations beckons Casburn into his office at New Scotland Yard.

'Shut the door.'

Ex-military, like Casburn, Frank Sutton has a no-nonsense manner which some at London's Metroplitan Police, including the commissioner, occasionally find uncomfortable. Sutton has been sent on training courses in people management and media skills, and as a result his style is more diplomatic when addressing the public or his junior officers. But with his direct reports, like Casburn, he doesn't pussyfoot around, and Casburn prefers it that way. Their affinity has paved the way for Casburn's meteoric rise. Since joining the Met, he has hunted criminals like a man possessed. Refusing to settle for the low-hanging fruit, he's targeted the untouchables, the canny bastards who've managed to escape prosecution, including the terrorist Kabir Khan who's now incarcerated for life. There are plenty of rumours about the way he operates – suggestions of brutality and even darker whispers. But he's succeeded. Casburn suspects Sutton approves of his methods, not that he would ever admit to it.

Sutton sits rigid-backed, his perfectly pressed, crisp white short-sleeved shirt with shoulder epaulettes denoting his rank. Another quality Casburn identifies with. Tidy kit, tidy mind. Casburn's tie is always perfectly centred, his shirt is laundered, his leather lace-ups buffed to a shine. A discipline from his time in the SAS he chooses to maintain.

Sutton frowns at him through frameless glasses, which, the rumour goes, he was advised to wear so the media and the public can see his eyes more clearly, which enhances trust. Sutton denounced the idea as 'poppycock', but he bought the glasses none the less.

'What does Wolfe know?' Sutton asks, fingers interlocked and resting on his desk.

'She knows ZIB Trading exists and that Sackville is a signatory. She wouldn't tell me if she knows the account details.'

'Will she drop it?'

'From past experience, I'd say not.'

'Wolfe isn't easily...' Sutton pauses to find the right word, '*persuaded*, is she?'

'No, sir.'

'Buggeration.' Sutton's thumbs circle each other.

'Sir? I'm not clear why I've been instructed to do this. It's not a natural fit for SO24.'

The organisation was set up to protect Greater London from overseas threats.

'I was asked to use my most trusted man.'

'Thank you, sir.' Casburn's poker face masks his frustration. He's been told very little. 'But what am I looking for?'

Sutton removes his glasses and rubs the indentations either side of his nose. 'This is an awkward one, Dan.' Casburn notes they have reached the chummy point in their conversation. He is seldom called by his first name. 'I'm not entirely comfortable with this whole affair, but the commissioner wants a watching brief.'

Casburn guesses the PM or somebody else in the cabinet has asked the commissioner to do this.

'What about PaDP?' Casburn asks, referring to the Parliamentary and Diplomatic Protection unit, which also comes under Sutton's command. 'Are they in the loop?'

Sutton's glasses are back on his face. 'One officer only. Like you, someone I trust. If we're going to succeed, it's critical Sackville doesn't get a whiff of anything. Which is why we can't have that journalist poking around. Find a way to get her to drop it.'

Casburn considers this for a moment. 'If we could give Wolfe a bigger story than this one, an exclusive, then she might let it go.'

Sutton nods. 'Let me see what I can do.'

'Sir, can I speak plainly?'

'Go ahead.'

'Sackville has access to some of this country's most politically sensitive information. We don't know what the offshore account is for. If there's a chance he's selling State secrets, wouldn't it be advisable to have MI5 involved?'

'No need to involve the spooks. Not yet, anyway.'

'Is there something you're not telling me, sir?'

'That'll be all.'

5

Wolfe weaves her Harley through London's traffic, heading for the registered address of ZIB Trading. As far as she could tell, it has only one director: Zoe Blunt, South African. Wolfe couldn't find anything else about the company, or its director.

Her satnav brings her to a block of flats off Central Road in Morden. Wolfe parks around the corner so as not to draw attention to herself, then walks up a sloping paved path to the main entrance which has a buzzer entry. Through the glass door Wolfe sees key-locked mailboxes, from one to thirty-four. Rolled-up brochures stick out of most mailboxes, but not mailbox fourteen, which means that somebody has cleared the box in the last day or two. A man in his thirties leaves a ground-floor flat, a baby strapped to his chest and a black miniature schnauzer straining on a lead.

Wolfe pretends to search for her key. The man opens the main door. The dog lurches through the gap. Wolfe holds open the door.

'Looks like you've got your hands full,' she says, smiling.

'Thanks,' he says.

Wolfe slips through and takes the carpeted stairs two steps at a time. Flat fourteen is on the second floor. Pressing her ear to the door, she hears nothing. Wolfe knocks.

No response.

She knocks again, a bit louder this time.

Still nothing.

She is about to knock again when the door to number fifteen opens. A woman in her late sixties pokes her nose out.

'There's nobody there, love. Hasn't been for a while.' She frowns at Wolfe's leather jacket and biker boots. 'How did you get in?'

'A friend of a friend lives here. She's selling up. Said I could look around before it goes on the market.'

'They're selling it, are they? About time. Been vacant for at least six months. I don't like having an empty flat next door.'

'That's strange,' says Wolfe. 'I thought Zoe Blunt lived here.'

'There's a woman who comes to collect the post. I see her from time to time. Unfriendly. I say hello and she ignores me.'

'When does she collect the post?' Wolfe asks.

The old lady frowns again. 'Why would you want to know that?'

'Never mind,' says Wolfe. 'I'll see if I can catch her another time. Thanks for your help.'

Wolfe heads back down the stairs, convinced a legitimate company is not being run from flat fourteen.

6

Ponnappa is still glued to her computer, the music blaring through her headphones so loud even Wolfe can hear it. Butcher beckons Wolfe over.

'I got hold of Sackville's last tax return,' Butcher says. 'Salary... dividends... some interest... a couple of investment properties in Northumberland and London. No mention of income from overseas or any offshore accounts.'

'So he's a tax cheat.'

'If the account is his, which we don't yet know. How did you go with ZIB Trading?' Butcher says.

'An empty flat used to receive mail. It's a front.'

'Found it!' shouts Ponnappa.

'You're shouting,' mimes Butcher.

'Ah, sorry,' says Ponnappa, removing her headphones and switching off the music.

'What have you got?' asks Wolfe, peering over her shoulder.

'You're looking at the ZIB Trading account with the Bank of Tortola in the British Virgin Islands.'

'However did you do that?' Wolfe asks.

Ponnappa shrugs. 'It's what I do. Take a look at this.'

Wolfe's jaw drops. 'Bloody hell!'

'Am I reading this right?' says Butcher. 'Twenty million US dollars.'

Ponnappa nods. 'You sure are. Money comes and goes on a daily basis, but it seems to stay around fifteen to twenty million.'

'Can you find out where it's coming from and where it's going?' Wolfe asks her.

'That could take some time. Days. Maybe weeks. Depends on how clever they are.'

'I can't see anything linking this to Harold Sackville,' says Wolfe.

'I'm keeping the best till last,' says Ponnappa, scrolling down. 'Get a load of that!'

Wolfe leans in and stares at an almost illegible scribble. 'I can see what I think is an H, and an A, but the rest is indecipherable.'

'He was christened Harold Arthur,' says Butcher.

'Okay, we need to confirm this is his signature. Do you remember last year the Home Secretary walked out of Number Ten with Brexit costings visible and a photographer took a snap?'

'Yes, it was front page news.'

Wolfe searches for the article on her phone.

'Well, Sackville's signature was on it. Let me just find it… here we go.' She peers closely at the document in question. 'There it is,' Wolfe says, passing her phone to Ponnappa so she can compare the two.

'A perfect match,' says Ponnappa.

Butcher whistles through his teeth. 'Our Chancellor is an extremely wealthy man.'

'Where in God's name did he get that kind of money?' asks Wolfe.

'Ah, well, it isn't all his,' says Ponnappa.

'How do you mean?' Wolfe asks.

'The account has two signatories. Look.'

Ponnappa scrolls down her screen a little further. Wolfe scrutinises the second signature.

'At least this one is legible,' says Wolfe. 'But who on earth is Mazwi Ximba?'

'Good question,' says Butcher.

Wolfe taps the name into Google.

'Too many hits. It's too common a surname. Especially in South Africa and Zimbabwe.'

'Leave it to me,' says Ponnappa. 'I'll find him.'

'I'd better see Moz,' says Wolfe, referring to *The Post*'s editor, Mozart Cohen. 'This could be delicate, to say the least. I need him onside if we're going to take on a senior cabinet minister.'

7

Mozart Cohen, the six-foot-three, praying mantis-like editor of *The Post*, leans forward in his chair, bony forearms resting on his desk, eyeballing Wolfe as if he were about to spring forward and bite her head off.

'Turn that fucking thing off or get out of my office.'

Her phone is ringing. She switches it to silent and shuts his door.

'Seen the news?' Cohen asks. 'Your old mate Caroline Bloom has been made Secretary of State for Environment, Food and Rural Affairs.'

'Wow!. She's in the cabinet. She'll be so happy.'

Wolfe hasn't been in contact with Caroline for years. Time to put that right.

'She should be slashing her wrists,' says Cohen. 'It's a career killer. Even worse than Immigration, and that's saying something.' He raps his knuckles on the desk's surface. 'What have you got for me?'

Outside his office, the open-plan news floor is a hive of frenetic activity.

'Moz, I think I'm onto something,' Wolfe says, struggling to stay upright on a yellow monstrosity of a sofa which sucks its victims in like the carnivorous pitcher plant.

Cohen clasps his hands together and forms a steeple with his long middle fingers, examining her from beneath wiry grey eyebrows that twist and curl like antennae. 'Go on.'

Wolfe fills him in on what she knows about Harold Sackville, the offshore account, and suspicious death of her informant.

'How much money?' Cohen asks.

'Twenty million US dollars.'

'So, the penny-pinching Chancellor is secretly hoarding millions?' He grins. 'Are you absolutely sure it's Sackville's account?'

'I saw his signature with my own eyes. There's a second signatory. A Mazwi Ximba. I've no idea who he is, or how he's connected. Butcher and Ponnappa are looking into it.'

Cohen rolls his eyes. 'And I suppose they'll want to be paid?'

'Don't be such a tight-arse.'

'Times are tough, Liv.' Cohen exhales loudly. 'Tell me about your dead informant.'

Wolfe tells him what she knows, including what she learnt from Casburn.

'I agree with Casburn. If she died because she blabbed about Sackville, you too could be at risk. So be careful.'

'I always am.'

He snorts. 'Bollocks. Have you spoken to Powell?'

'Yes, he told me nothing. Sounded terrified. There's something else you should know. Casburn did his best to scare me off.'

'Okay, that says to me someone high up wants to hush this up. So, what do you want to do? Publish what you've got, or keep digging?'

'My gut says there's more here. It's dirty money, I know it.'

Cohen nods, deep in thought. 'This could be a dirty great big scandal.' He pauses. 'Okay, write me a millionaire Chancellor fiddling his tax piece. Today. If it looks like someone else is onto the story, we'll run it. If not, I'll sit tight. In the meantime, find out where all that dosh came from and where it's going.'

8

Wolfe is rarely in Notting Hill, but tonight she rides her Harley-Davidson along Portobello Road, dropping speed as she searches for the cobblestone mews where Caroline and Tom Bloom live. Wolfe hasn't been to their house for almost two years, so her memory is a bit hazy. How could she have left it so long?

Wolfe met Caroline when she was studying journalism at university. Caroline, not surprisingly, was studying politics. They became flatmates and then best mates. Wolfe started working at *The Post*. As Caroline's political career took off, their friendship came under strain. Politicians and journalists have an uneasy relationship and, if she was honest, she had been as single-minded as Caroline. Wolfe's appointment as foreign correspondent was the final nail in the coffin; she was constantly overseas, often in war zones or up to her eyeballs investigating some scandal or other. Their email correspondence dwindled and eventually stopped altogether.

So, when Wolfe took the plunge and phoned Caroline to congratulate her on her cabinet appointment, she was surprised her olive branch was so readily accepted, and even more surprised when Caroline invited her to dinner that night.

Wolfe spots an armed police officer standing to one side of a narrow, cobbled mews and pulls up. Through the stone arch are two rows of quaint terraced houses, five on each side. Hanging baskets of petunias, ivy-clad walls and stable-style garage doors give the mews a country feel. Caroline's is the house at the far end.

'Olivia Wolfe to see Caroline Bloom,' Wolfe says, voice raised, so the officer can hear her above the rumble of the Harley's engine.

'Take off your helmet and show me photo ID.'

Wolfe obliges. The cop compares her driver's licence to her face.

'Are you expected?' he asks.

'Yes, we're having dinner.'

The police officer makes a call, and Wolfe gets the all clear. She leaves her bike outside her friend's white-painted house. A dog barks on the other side of the door, which opens and a Cavalier King Charles spaniel rushes at her, tail wagging furiously.

'Lady B!' Wolfe says, kneeling down and giving the excited dog a pat. 'She was a puppy when last I saw her.'

'She remembers you.'

Tall and lanky, Caroline's wavy brown hair is cut to shoulder length these days, her green eyes framed by tortoiseshell glasses. Still the same charming smile that has, ever since Wolfe can remember, been able to disarm even the most combative of adversaries.

'It's been too long,' Caroline says, embracing Wolfe.

'It has.'

In black slacks, white business shirt and pumps, her make-up immaculate even after a long day, they make an odd couple, Wolfe thinks, who stands there in Harley insignia jacket, an old black T-shirt, lived-in jeans, lace-up biker boots, and no make-up.

'Come in,' Caroline says. 'I've got a bottle of your favourite tipple.'

Wolfe hangs her jacket on a hook by the door and leaves her helmet and gloves on the vestibule table, then follows her host up a flight of stairs to an open-plan kitchen and sitting room, the front of which has a large bay window with a view down the length of the mews. Lady B curls up on her dog bed and closes her eyes.

Wolfe sits on a tall stool at the kitchen's island bench where Caroline pours them each a glass of Côte-Rôtie.

'To you,' says Wolfe, clinking glasses. 'Congratulations! I'm so very proud of you.'

Wolfe sips her wine. Caroline puts the glass down, her drink untouched.

'I still can't believe it,' Caroline says, smiling, 'a cabinet minister at thirty-nine. *And* a woman. Not bad, huh?'

'Bloody brilliant. And you so deserve it. Tom must be very proud.' Wolfe looks around the room. 'Is he joining us?'

'Away on business.' Caroline looks down. Fiddles with the stem of her glass.

'Charlie? What's the matter?'

When they were close friends, Wolfe called her Charlie. It feels good to use the name again.

'Nothing. Just wish... Tom wasn't away right now.' She shrugs and drinks from a tumbler of water. Something is definitely not right.

'It means a lot, you inviting me here,' Wolfe reaches out and squeezes Caroline's hand. 'I want to clear the air. Tonight, I'm here as your friend, not a reporter. Let's relax and have fun, like old times.'

Caroline stares at her, as if performing long division in her head. 'I have to be careful. Especially now. You understand?'

'I do. But not with me. Not tonight,' Wolfe says.

Caroline abruptly turns her back on Wolfe and opens the fridge. 'How does lasagne and salad sound?'

'Sounds great.'

Caroline peers into the fridge, the chilled air spilling into the kitchen. She doesn't remove any food. Just stares. Wolfe sips her wine, waiting, but when Caroline doesn't say anything, Wolfe breaks the silence.

'So, when do you start?'

'Tomorrow. I'm flying to Geneva for UN climate change talks. Later in the week, an endangered species convention. In between, I'm reviewing our position on fracking, then environmental impacts of a new housing development, windfarms off the Sussex coast, and a whole load of stuff I haven't yet been briefed on.'

Caroline still has her back to her. Wolfe gets off her bar stool and stands close to her friend. Wolfe is startled to see she is close to tears and gives her friend a hug. 'What's wrong, Charlie?'

'You have to promise you won't tell anyone. This is so off the record it's not funny.'

'I promise.'

Caroline grabs a tissue from a box and blows her nose. 'You know Tom and I tried for a baby, and never had any luck?'

'Yes, of course I remember the IVF.'

'And the miscarriages?'

'I do. It was terrible, but you got through it.'

'We gave up trying. Moved on. I never thought...' her voice peters out.

'You're pregnant?'

Caroline nods. 'Thirteen weeks.'

'That's wonderful. Really wonderful.'

'But the timing, Liv. It couldn't possibly be worse. I'll soon be a very pregnant minister.'

'So what?'

'It's a lot all at once, Liv. I mean, what if I throw up in the House?'

Wolfe chuckles. 'You'll power on. You always do. Is this why you're all glum?'

Caroline nods.

'It's more than that, isn't it?'

'I want to be taken seriously.'

'And you think those stuffy middle-aged politicians can't handle a pregnant cabinet minister?'

'Of course I do. It's still a boys' club.'

'Don't let that bother you. You're at the pinnacle of your political career, have a lovely husband, *and* you're having a baby. You'll not only be the best mum, but the best environment minister too.'

Caroline wipes her eyes. 'I hope you're right. I've been so weary lately. Probably the pregnancy.'

'And the fourteen-hour days,' Wolfe says. 'Why don't you put your feet up? I'll do dinner, okay?'

Caroline allows Wolfe to shepherd her to a sofa from where she can see the kitchen.

'So nobody's guessed?' Wolfe asks.

'The PM knows. He wanted to announce my appointment first, then the pregnancy.'

'So stop worrying.'

'Stay the night, Liv. There's a spare room; the bed's already made up.'

Wolfe would rather sleep at home, but senses Caroline would like the company. 'I'd love to.' She switches on the oven.

'So, how's the man?' Caroline asks.

'What man?'

'You know, the big Russian.'

'Ah, you read about that did you?'

'Yes, and I'm so sorry I didn't get in contact as a friend. Your lot really gave you a pasting.'

Wolfe takes a bag of rocket from the fridge. 'I've put it behind me. I had to.' She starts slicing tomatoes. Then stops. Looks up at Caroline. 'He wasn't all those terrible things they said.'

'What was he then?'

'Someone I'd like to be with. But that can't happen.'

9

MAGDALEN COLLEGE, UNIVERSITY OF OXFORD, UK

Saneliso Simelane's unzipped jacket blows open in a gust of wind and he tugs it back around his skinny frame as he hastens along the barely-lit cloister. The sound of his footsteps on the centuries-old limestone is loud and lonely to his ears. He glances nervously across the immaculately grassed Great Quad which, at this late hour, is empty. In the moonlight, the ugly gargoyles peering down at him cast eerie shadows. Simelane is the last to leave Professor Allcomb's tediously boring book launch: he is failing miserably at his undergraduate studies and needs to garner some goodwill. To make matters worse, his father is visiting from Swaziland in two weeks' time expecting to hear his son's studies are going swimmingly.

A kick to the small of his back sends Simelane flying. He lands hard, flat on the flagstones, a shooting pain in his lumbar region. His attacker straddles him, and a powerful hand grips his mouth so he can't call for help. There is a sharp sting in his neck. He hits out with fists, each blow weaker than the last until his limbs will not obey him. A squeaky wheel. A blurred view of a rubbish cart used by the gardeners. He feels his consciousness slipping away from him as he is manoeuvred into the cart. His last sight is a stone gargoyle high above, part-pig, part-lizard, mouth wide in a salacious grin, mocking his terror.

~

Barely conscious, Simelane hears a whirring noise, then a metallic screech. Something cold touches his forehead and drips down his nose. The air is heavy with damp and the mustiness of mildew. And something else. Vomit. His vomit? He tries shifting his legs. Something stops him. A stabbing pain in his lower back makes him gasp. His eyes spring open.

In the gloom Simelane at first thinks he's still in the cloisters because before him is a wide arch, but when his vision adjusts, he realises the arch is bricked up with a wooden door at its centre. Above him, a bare bulb dangles from a high ceiling, generating the only light in a space that looks as if it was once an auto repair workshop. At one end is a four-post vehicle hoist. Simelane is vertical. He doesn't know how he is standing up, because his legs feel like jelly. His coat has been removed and the back of his long-sleeved T-shirt is sodden from the damp wall. He shivers. He looks down and sees vomit on his chest, but his movement is restricted by something pressing against his throat. He tries to call out, his voice feeble.

To his right, a clank. A man, only just visible out of the corner of Simelane's eye, has his back to him and leans over a workbench.

'No one will hear you.'

His abductor doesn't look around and continues with whatever he is doing. Simelane can hardly breathe as his panic rises and the metal restraint around his neck presses against his Adam's apple. He wants to tear at it, but his wrists are manacled. His legs are similarly restrained.

'Who... who are you?'

No answer. Just the rasp of metal on stone.

'Please, what do you want?'

That grating sound. Over and over again.

'You have the wrong person. Please. I am not important,' Simelane pleads.

'My client thinks you are.'

The man turns and walks towards him. He is Caucasian, wearing a green coverall and gloves, like the ones gardeners use. He has not bothered to hide his face.

'I do not know your client. Please! Let me go! My father, he will pay you.'

'Where I come from, this,' the man says, holding up a machete, the polished blade reflecting the bright ceiling light, 'is how we solve problems. Used to be, anyway. These days, it's guns. More's the pity.'

Simelane feels the warm wetness of his piss seeping down his thigh. If he wasn't held to the wall by his manacles, he'd have collapsed.

'Please,' he begs. 'My father! He has money. Whatever you want.'

His captor studies his skinny body as if it were a fascinating sculpture in a gallery. 'I am an artist.' He holds up the machete. 'I can achieve things with this no other man is capable of.'

Simelane blubs like a baby.

'Pathetic!'

He takes a photo with his smartphone, then walks back to the workbench. When the man returns there is no phone. He grips Simelane's thick hair and yanks his head back into the wall.

'This is less painful if you keep still.'

Simelane stares wide-eyed as the man raises the machete, then brings it down fast, slicing through bone. He screams, gags on the blood running into his throat. The pain is like fire on his face. The man lets go of his hair and Simelane instinctively hangs his head forward, as far as his binding permits, to ease the choking. Blood floods down his T-shirt and onto the floor. In the dirt, next to a crushed Coke can, is part of his nose.

He wails, a long wordless stream of shock and terror.

The man reappears and holds up a cheap circular handheld mirror so Simelane can see his face. There are two bony holes where his nose used to be and without an upper lip, his gums and upper row of teeth are exposed.

'Don't worry about your looks,' his torturer says. 'Your body will never be found.'

The man holds up his phone, close to Simelane's face.

'Smile for the camera.'

10

Ponnappa looks as though she has barely moved, wearing the same clothes as yesterday. Littering her desk are empty Red Bull cans and Thai takeaway containers, the congealed remains contributing to the stale smell in the office.

'I thought you might pull an all-nighter,' Wolfe says. 'So I've brought breakfast.' She holds up a bacon and egg roll and long black coffee.

'You're an angel,' says Ponnappa, swivelling in her chair. She sinks her teeth into the roll.

Wolfe opens a window a few inches. The air is bracing. 'Did you find anything interesting?'

Her mouth too full to answer, Ponnappa chews fast. Butcher walks in.

'I did,' Ponnappa replies. 'Look at this.'

Wolfe and Butcher stand either side of her chair. On the screen is a FirstRand bank statement belonging to Mazwi Ximba, which has his mailing address in Johannesburg, and the current balance of the account: a little over fifteen million rand.

'That's about eight hundred thousand pounds,' says Ponnappa.

'How do we know this is the same guy as on the ZIB account?' Butcher asks.

Ponnappa slurps some coffee, then divides her screen so they can see the signatures of Mazwi Ximba for both accounts.

Wolfe smiles. 'Identical. You're a genius.'

'There's more. This is where it gets really interesting,' says Ponnappa, opening an article on the *Soweto Urban News* website. 'Meet Mazwi Ximba.'

The article is about a secondary school in the impoverished Soweto suburb of Meadowlands West. In the two years Ximba has been headmaster, it says, the school's dismal academic record has improved to the point where three students have been accepted by universities. There's a photograph of a silver-haired man with a warm smile, aged mid-fifties, surrounded by boys and girls in blue school uniform, shot in the dusty playground. The tag under the photo says: Headmaster, Mazwi Ximba at Moeta High School.

'How does a headmaster get hold of that kind of money?' says Wolfe.

'Well, it's not his pay,' Ponnappa says. 'I checked. Nothing special there. But every week there's a big transfer from the Bank of Tortola to his FirstRand account, and the next day it's gone.'

'Where does it end up?'

'Don't know. I can follow the trail for a bit, but it pings all over the world. Whoever set this up really knew what they were doing.'

Wolfe frowns. 'This is dead dodgy. Why does the Chancellor have an account with a Soweto headmaster who's moving millions around in a way that's untraceable?'

'Got any contacts in Johannesburg?' Butcher asks. 'Someone who can sniff around a bit?'

A man comes to mind. The same man Caroline asked about last night. A man Butcher is deeply suspicious of, and for good reason. Regardless, she has thought about him every day since he left the country four months ago, wondering if he ever made it to South Africa alive. Surveilling Ximba would be a walk in the park for him. Perhaps she could use this as an excuse to get in touch.

Wolfe looks up. Butcher is studying her face, a deep frown on a brow already etched with lines. 'Someone trustworthy,' he adds.

He knows who she's thinking about. She's annoyed with herself for being so transparent. She has one other contact there.

'A South African police officer,' she says. 'Totally trustworthy. I'll give him a call.' Wolfe steps outside and breathes the crisp morning air deeply. She refocuses and dials Mike Thusago.

When she first met 'Bra Mike', as he's known in Soweto where he was born and now works, she was writing a piece on crystal meth, produced in Soweto that ends up on British streets. It was one of her first big stories. Thusago was the only cop prepared to talk to her. They became friends. The last she'd heard, he'd been made sergeant.

'Olivia? It is good to hear from you. How are you?'

In the background she hears the clamour of car horns and the groan of a truck dropping a gear. 'I'm well. Sounds like you're driving. Are you okay to talk?'

Thusago chuckles. 'I am, Olivia. You have good hearing. I'm driving Jacob to school. I heard about the shooting. You were hit. In the head. I tried to phone you, but the hospital asked me to leave a message. Did you get it?'

'I did, Mike, and thank you. Apart from headaches, I'm fine.'

'You are very lucky, Olivia. So, what can I do for you?'

'I need your help. Information on a South African man. Lives in your neck of the woods. Would you have time to look into him for me?'

'For you, I will make time.'

'He's headmaster of a school in Meadowlands West–'

'Mazwi Ximba?'

'Yes, that's him. You know him?'

'Of course. He's well-known in Soweto.'

'Is he a friend?' Olivia holds her breath for the response.

'No, but he is well-liked.'

'Okay. I need you to keep what I'm about to say to yourself.'

'Of course. What is it, Olivia?'

'Ximba may be involved in something criminal. He's moving lots of money through at least two bank accounts.'

'How much?'

'Millions of rand.'

Thusago laughs. 'No way. It can't be the same man.'

'I'm sorry to say it is.'

She can hear Thusago breathing, a truck's brakes screeching. 'If this is true, why is a British journalist like you interested? Soweto is a long way away.'

'There's a connection to somebody in England. It's politically sensitive. Very.'

'Okay. What do you want to know?'

'Any criminal connections, odd behaviour recently, any links to the UK. Is he under investigation in South Africa?'

'He's not. I would know if he was. I will see what I can find out.'

'He mustn't know he's being investigated.'

'I understand.'

'Thank you, Mike. Naturally, I'll pay you for your time.'

'I am happy to help out a friend, Olivia. No payment.'

She can hear his little boy chattering to himself in the background.

'How old is Jacob, now?'

'Six. A big strong boy. Loves cricket. Hates reading, but I hope he will learn. And how is Mozart?'

When Wolfe was last in South Africa, Thusago overheard some heated phone conversations between her and Cohen, who, as usual, wanted a major story at breakneck speed.

'As cantankerous and brilliant as ever. *The Post* will only be available online from next month. Moz is devastated.'

'It is the future, Olivia. The format does not matter, as long as journalists are free to write the truth.'

'I'm not sure how many police officers would agree with you. You're a man after my own heart.'

'Ah, Olivia, my heart is already taken. It belongs to my wife, my son, and South Africa.'

11

Wolfe steps through the revolving doors, hot on the heels of Moz Cohen who strides across *The Post*'s glass-fronted lobby towards the lifts. Cohen is dressed in the same grey tweed jacket, flat cap, and Barbour oilskin coat he's worn to and from work ever since Wolfe has known him.

'Morning, Mr Cohen,' says the security guard who has worked there almost eleven years.

'Morning, Frank. Family doing well?'

'Yes, all fine, thank you.'

'Call me if the world comes to an end.'

'Will do, sir.'

Wolfe has heard this familiar exchange so many times; she finds herself mouthing the words in sync with the two men.

Her phone rings. It's Mike Thusago. Perhaps he's changed his mind. She steps away and lets the lift go without her.

'Mike. How's it going?'

'I have some information.'

'That's quick.'

'I dropped in on an old friend. She's a cleaner at Moeta High School.'

'Ximba's school?'

'Yes. Look, Olivia, I need to know you'll protect my friend's identity.'

'She's an anonymous source. You have my word.'

'All right. A few nights ago, she saw something.'

'Her name?'

'Mama Gcina.'

'Mama?'

'Yes, that is how everybody knows her. Grandmother to twelve kids.'

'Okay, what happened?'

'She was working. Didn't realise Ximba had stayed late. His door was closed. Somebody was shouting. Angry. The man shouting told Ximba to stop whining. Said Ximba was getting well paid and to keep his mouth shut. Then, she says, the headmaster's door opened and out steps Major-General Msiza.'

'Who is?'

'Commander of a cluster of police stations in Soweto. Ximba's school is within his jurisdiction.'

'Is this a problem for you, Mike? Is Msiza your boss?'

'No, I am with the Narcotics Bureau.'

'Okay. What do you think was going on between them?'

'Look, bribery and corruption are rife here. But why Msiza would pay Ximba, I don't know. I've only heard good things about the general.'

'Your informant is certain it was Msiza?'

'Oh yes, she has a particular reason to know him well.'

'Which is?'

'He sent her son to prison.'

Wolfe grimaces. 'This isn't a revenge thing, is it?'

'No. I've known her all my life. She's a God-fearing woman and she wouldn't lie.'

'Did Msiza notice her?'

'Yes and no. She was mopping the floor. Msiza walked past her without a glance. After she left, the headmaster made a phone call.'

'To who?'

'She doesn't know. She heard him say, "I must see you." I guess the person asked why because the next thing Ximba says is, "I want my signature off that account."'

'She's sure that's what Ximba said?' Wolfe asks.

'Positive.'

'Sounds like we've found the weak link. Can you keep an eye on him until I get there?'

'You are coming to Johannesburg?'

'Yes. I'll text you my flight details when I have them.'

Wolfe turns around and heads for *The Post*'s underground car park where she's left her Harley. She needs to get to the airport. But first she must clear it with Cohen. She dials his number.

'It'll have to wait,' Cohen snaps. 'I'm late for a meeting.'

'How about I give you a good reason to be late?'

'Is it front page material?'

'Oh yes.'

'You have thirty seconds.'

Wolfe updates him on Mazwi Ximba, how he moves the money from the Virgin Islands account to a FirstRand account and then on to another.

'School teacher? Fuck me! I must be in the wrong business,' says Cohen.

She adds the details of the Ximba–Msiza conversation.

'That's just hearsay.'

'True, but Mike says his source can be trusted. I need to go to Johannesburg.'

'What am I? A bloody travel agent?'

'Give me a week.'

She hears the rap of Cohen's knuckles on the desk. 'Three days. And try not to get yourself killed, will you?'

12

The chauffeur-driven silver Range Rover pulls over and Casburn steps into a cream leather cocoon. As soon as he's shut the door, the vehicle pulls away and joins the traffic crossing Westminster Bridge.

'Sir?' Casburn hasn't been informed why he's meeting his boss in this manner.

'So, Wolfe is going to Johannesburg. You're certain?' Sutton asks.

'She's booked a flight, leaving tonight. I've been monitoring her credit card transactions.'

'Interfering bitch,' mutters Sutton. He pulls a photo from an A4 Manila envelope, which he hands to Casburn. 'Recognise this man?'

Male, late forties, double-chin wider than his neck, low side-parting, eating caviar.

Casburn thinks he recognises him. 'Is that Yury Sukletin?'

'Correct. What do you know about him?'

'Russian. Billionaire. Casinos in Russia and Las Vegas. Word is he makes his real money from prostitution and people-smuggling. Charming individual, I'm sure.'

'He's close to Putin.'

Casburn nods, but wonders where this is going.

'Take a look at this.'

Another photo. Sukletin and Harold Sackville, seated in white wicker chairs, sharing what looks like Pimm's and lemonade. Sukletin is laughing. They're outdoors. It's clearly hot, as they're both wearing Panama hats, sunglasses, and what look like linen suits.

'When was this taken?' Casburn asks.

'Last year.'

'Where?'

'A wildlife reserve near Johannesburg.'

'So Sackville has poor taste in friends. How does this relate to our investigation?'

'Sackville is going to Jo'burg this weekend. Without his family. And it just so happens that Sukletin is in Jo'burg the exact same time. Remarkable coincidence, wouldn't you say?'

'Where are you going with this, sir?' Casburn asks. 'You think Sackville is peddling his wares to Putin via Sukletin?'

'That's your job to find out. One of your jobs.' Sutton pops the photos back in the envelope. 'The other is to keep Wolfe under control.'

'Sir, I can't–'

'Let's just say if that journalist uncovers the Chancellor's relationship with Sukletin or anything else damaging to this government, it will not be good for your career. Are we clear?'

'Yes, sir.'

'Your boarding pass and itinerary.' Sutton hands him a smaller envelope. 'South African police have assured us of their complete cooperation. Your contact is Major-General Msiza. His details are in there.'

'How much does he know?'

'Just that we're investigating Mazwi Ximba in connection with possible money laundering involving a British citizen. Nothing more. Keep it that way.'

Casburn expects the car to stop, their meeting over, but it seems Sutton has more to say.

'If she won't listen to you, will she listen to Vitaly Yushkov?'

Casburn's grip on the envelope tightens. 'I have no idea where he is, sir.'

'But you know people who do.' Sutton narrows his eyes and gives Casburn a penetrating stare.

Casburn might work for Sutton, but he'd be an idiot to piss off the Secret Intelligence Service. So he avoids the question. 'Yushkov would rather roast in Hell than listen to me.'

'That's your problem. Just get her to stop. Yushkov's number is in the envelope.'

Casburn pockets the envelope, although he'd rather tear it to shreds. In his mind's eye, he sees the abandoned warehouse, the blistering hot lamps pointed at Yushkov whose wrists and ankles are zip-tied to a chair, his body pulverised like steak with a tenderising hammer, out of his mind with the sodium pentothal he's been injected with, begging them to save his sister. He still hears Yuskov's sobs. Still sees the tears seeping from the man's swollen eye. He knows he should have done more to stop the interrogation spiralling out of control and he'll never forget the video he saw later, of Yushkov's sister's brains sprayed over a wall somewhere in Russia.

Casburn suddenly realises the car has stopped and Sutton's driver has opened the door for him. He gets out onto a damp pavement.

'You report to me and me alone on this one,' Sutton calls out.

13

JOHANNESBURG, SOUTH AFRICA

Olivia Wolfe glances up at the domed roof of the arrivals hall at Johannesburg's O.R. Tambo International Airport, then down to the barriers separating arriving travellers from those who await them. She spots Mike Thusago leaning on the rail: shaved head, high forehead, average height, slim and muscular: a marathon runner's build. He straightens at the sight of her and waves enthusiastically.

'Welcome to South Africa.'

'Good to see you, Mike.'

'And you.' He nods at the thirty-litre capacity backpack slung over her shoulder. 'I'm guessing no checked luggage, right?'

'Everything I need is here,' Wolfe pats her go-bag.

It is one of two backpacks she keeps ready to go at a moment's notice. One is packed for colder climates and the other for hotter. As it's autumn in Johannesburg, she's got the cold-climate bag with her, plus a few lighter items of clothing. Hidden in the folds of a shoulder strap, beneath a metal buckle, is a tiny lock-pick, which has so far fooled airport security screening. A metal water bottle is clipped to the exterior and doubles as a club should she need it. In her toiletries bag, is the plastic knife disguised as a comb that Butcher gave her.

She has learnt from past experience that her inquiries can bring on violent retaliations, so it pays to be prepared.

She follows Thusago through the crowded terminal, down an escalator, up another one, and then out into the startlingly bright morning sunshine.

'It's good to get out of that stuffy plane. Thanks for picking me up, by the way. I hope you haven't taken time off work?'

'Not a problem.'

With the sun in her eyes she almost fails to notice Dan Casburn walking briskly towards a marked South African police car. A uniformed officer holds a rear door open for him.

'Would you believe it,' Wolfe mumbles. She halts and grabs Thusago's arm. 'Give me a moment. It's best he doesn't know you're helping me.'

'Who is he?'

'A British detective.'

'I'll wait inside by the escalator.'

Wolfe jogs over to Casburn, calls his name. He turns and shows no surprise at her appearance.

'You knew I was on this flight, didn't you?' Wolfe asks.

'Of course.'

'What are you doing here, Dan?'

'I'm co-operating with the South African police. And you?'

'I'm following a lead. Probably talking to the same people as you. Why don't we work together? We'll get a lot more done that way.'

'You don't listen, Olivia. When I said you should butt out, it was for your own good. The best thing you can do is go on safari, then go home. Tell Moz there is no story. You made a mistake.'

'Why would I do that?'

He flicks a look at her that she could almost mistake for concern. 'It's not worth it, Olivia. Trust me on this.'

Perhaps she's reading him wrong, but Casburn seems edgy. Does he know about the Msiza–Ximba connection? A corrupt senior police officer would make things very difficult for him. On the other hand, if Casburn doesn't know about Msiza's link to Ximba and proceeds to tell him everything, then the person behind the criminal activity funded by the secret account will go to ground, and Wolfe will have made a wasted trip.

'Dan, can I have a word in private?' She glances at the SAPS officer watching her and Casburn.

'Make it quick.'

They step away from the car. She keeps her voice down.

'It's possible a senior SAPS officer is involved.' Wolfe doesn't want to be specific, because Thusago's informant may prove unreliable. 'Like the kind of senior officer you are possibly going to meet.'

Casburn's features harden. 'Oh, of course, there has to be a corrupt cop involved, doesn't there? What is it with you media types? You can't get through the day without some kind of cop-bashing.'

'All I'm saying is–'

'Leave it, will you?'

He walks to the car and gets in the back.

'At least tell me where you're staying,' she calls.

'No chance.'

Wolfe watches the police car drive off. One thing is for certain. She's in the right city.

Thusago's black VW Polo lurches forward a few feet, then stops. A petrol tanker's compression brakes hiss. In the left-hand lane, a battered old pick-up with ten black workers in the open tray at the back spews dark fumes from a broken exhaust pipe. They've been in a traffic jam since they left the airport.

'You want to go home, shower, get something to eat?' Thusago asks. 'We can then work out a plan.'

'I'd rather crack on. I only have three days.' Wolfe had slept most of the thirteen-hour flight so she's buzzing with energy. She fills him in on the British Virgin Islands account, and its two signatories: Harold Sackville and Mazwi Ximba.

Thusago laughs nervously. 'You're telling me a Soweto school teacher has a share of two-hundred-and-seventy-two million rand! You have to be joking!'

'I'm not. Interesting, isn't it? The cleaner at Ximba's school. Mama Gcina? I'd like to talk to her first.'

'She may not want to talk to you.'

'But you'll vouch for me, right?'

'Sure, but I can't change the colour of your skin.'

'I'd still like to try.'

'Okay, I'll take you to Soweto.'

'How much time can you give me?'

'As much as you need.'

Wolfe gives him a quizzical look. 'How come?'

He shrugs.

'So, when are you back on duty?'

'I guess I should come clean.' He pauses. Glances at her.

She waits.

'I'm... on sick leave.'

'Nothing serious, I hope?'

His hands on the steering wheel have a tremor. 'They say it's post-traumatic stress. I can't go back to work until the psychiatrist gives me the all clear.'

'Oh Mike, I'm so sorry. What brought this on?'

An uncomfortable pause.

'We were called out to a home invasion. The parents murdered, two kids still alive. The suspects were holed up inside. They fired at us. So many times.' His voice is shaky. Distant. 'My partner... he was shot. He died.'

'That's not your fault.'

'It is,' he says, snapping his head around. 'I froze. I couldn't fire my weapon.'

'Do you know why?'

'They're saying it's PTSD. Almost every day there's a shooting.' He shakes his head. 'Now I'm going stir crazy, Olivia. I have too much time... to think... about him. His death. I need to keep busy.'

'Are you getting help? Counselling?'

He nods. 'Yes, but it achieves nothing. I have nightmares. Every night I see him lying in a pool of blood.'

Their car comes to a stop and so does their conversation. She feels so very sorry for him. She's known army personnel with PTSD. Some years back in Afghanistan she was imbedded with a British regiment. When their tour was over, three of the squaddies she got to know returned home well and truly fucked up, their behaviour erratic, their mood swings extreme. She has no idea how severe Thusago's PTSD is, but he is her only contact in Johannesburg and she needs his help.

'Shit, Mike. I wish you'd told me this before I hopped on a plane.'

14

They turn off the freeway and head for Soweto, passing a roadhouse and pizzeria offering curry bunny chow. Many of the houses are little more than loosely constructed sheds, whereas others are brick, with watered gardens and security grilles on doors and windows. Children on their way to school walk in the road, chatting and laughing. Beyond an arid patch of empty land a small hill appears to be smoking, but as they draw near she sees the hill is in fact a mound of dumped rubbish that's being burned.

'How does a British cabinet minister even know a Soweto teacher?' Thusago asks. 'Have they met?'

'I don't know. But I intend to find out.'

'This is bad money, Olivia. Ximba won't talk. If he does, he's a dead man.'

'If your informant is right and Ximba really does want out, maybe I can rattle his cage enough to get him to tell us what's going on?'

'He won't talk without guaranteed protection for him and his family.'

'Is there somebody you trust to give him that protection?'

Thusago thinks about this. 'Yes. But we'd need compelling

evidence. A confession, or proof the money is funding criminal activity.'

'What did you find out about Mazwi Ximba?'

'Like me, born in Soweto. He studied hard, one of very few of his generation who made it to university. Still lives here, in a newer area called Diepkloof. But it's no mansion, Olivia. It's the kind of house a black headmaster of a poorly-funded school would have. He drives a two-year-old Toyota Corolla. Nothing flash. No criminal record. Never been overseas.'

'Then he's the perfect cut-out. A respected pillar of the community with no criminal record.'

Deep in thought, she curls her tongue and plays with the stud in it. 'Say it is money laundering, what illegal activity could generate such huge sums?'

'It is *maningi mali*. Big money. Maybe conflict diamonds, drugs, or perhaps poaching. If I were a betting man, I'd say a drug cartel is behind it.'

They drive past a wall with a hand-painted sign announcing a 'Tour Stop'. A minibus has pulled over and a dozen or so tourists are taking photos of the neighbourhood. There's also a red arrow pointing to 'The Museum', but all Wolfe can see is an old woman sitting outside a ramshackle house.

'This is Orlando East. Not far to go,' says Thusago.

For a while, she gazes out of the car window, watching the people of Soweto. Her mind wanders to Christmas Eve, when she'd said goodbye to Yushkov as he boarded a container ship to South Africa. That was four months ago. *He may still be in the country. Perhaps even in Johannesburg?* Her hand moves to her jacket pocket and she traces the bulge of the Nokia phone. He gave it to her when he left England. He warned her to use it only in an emergency. It has just one number programmed into it: his. But there is no emergency, just her desire to see him. Her thoughts turn to their twenty-four hours in a house in west London; to Yushkov humming as he used the espresso machine; to his warm body, holding her close; to the tenderness of his touch; to his raucous laughter at some throwaway comment she'd made. Hidden from the people hunting them, she had imagined the house was theirs and that they were a normal couple living normal lives.

Wolfe takes the Nokia out of her pocket, switches it on and stares at the only number in the contacts list.

Thusago glances at her, then the phone. 'Something troubling you?'

'No,' she says, putting the Nokia away.

'You are unsure if you should call somebody?'

Wolfe smiles. 'Maybe.'

'Can this person help you?'

'It's personal.' How much should she tell Thusago about Yushkov? 'If I contact him, I could put him, and maybe us, in danger.'

'How?'

'There are people who want him dead. His own people.'

Thusago nods slowly. 'Is this Vitaly Yushkov?'

Wolfe shoots him a suspicious look.

'I am not reading your mind,' says Mike, amused. 'Your relationship with him was all over the news.'

'It was mostly lies, and embarrassing photographs.'

'But it cost you dearly?'

She nods. 'I was accused of terrible things. Humiliated. And it doesn't stop.'

'How do you mean?'

'When people look at me, they don't see Olivia Wolfe, journalist. They see the woman who made love to a man many still believe is a Russian spy. Even my colleagues whisper behind my back. The pictures of us making love still circulate.' Wolfe gnaws at a fingernail and rips it off. 'One day, I'll find the son of a bitch who took those photos. One day.'

'There is one rule for men and one for women when it comes to sex. You were condemned unjustly, Olivia.'

'Thank you, Mike. I appreciate you saying that.'

'But you're not going to like what I'm about to say.' He pauses. 'If this man has done so much damage to your reputation, it is not wise to contact him.'

'I know that.'

'Why do you want to phone him now?'

She hesitates.

Thusago gives her a knowing look. 'Ah, I see. He is in South Africa? Yes?'

'Could be.'

They are silent again.

'He was a soldier, wasn't he?'

'A long time ago. More recently, an engineer.'

'How does he work, if he is hiding from people?'

'He'd have to work cash in hand, somewhere that doesn't ask questions.'

'There are many ways a soldier can earn money in South Africa and keep a low profile. Most of them are not good. Enforcer, bodyguard, mercenary, poacher. You may not like what he has become.'

She gives him a wry smile. 'I'm not known for doing the sensible thing, Mike.'

'And you love this man?'

'Jesus, that's getting personal.'

'Olivia, I know this kind of man. He will bring you nothing but trouble. You only have three days to find your story. I think he is a distraction you do not need. But,' he gives her a wide grin, 'your heart must decide.'

'That's my problem, Mike. My heart decides too much.'

Wolfe snatches the Nokia phone from her pocket before she changes her mind, and dials.

Will it even ring? Will he answer?

Wolfe hears an automated voice asking the caller to leave a message. What if someone else picks up her message? She must be careful what she says.

A beep. It's recording her silence. A terrible thought shoots into her head. What if Yushkov doesn't want to see her?

Seconds tick by and the mobile continues to record her silence.

'It's Olivia. There's no emergency. I'm in South Africa. Please call me.' She disconnects.

'Will he call back?' Thusago asks.

'I have no idea.'

15

The skyline is dominated by the brightly painted murals of Orlando Towers, two decommissioned cooling towers now used by tourists for bungee jumping: a soccer player running, a kid racing a go-kart, a string quartet playing, Nelson Mandela smiling, a train swirling like a snake around the tower: their energy and joy lifts Wolfe's spirits. Thusago's revelation about his PTSD had worried her. He's her sole contact in Johannesburg and she has just three days to find out what illegal activity the British Chancellor and a Soweto headmaster are involved in.

They turn a corner. Outside an Engen petrol station, a huddle of women on milk crates wave and beckon. On the ground before them are dresses, shoes, tablecloths and garden pots they are selling. Thusago keeps driving, makes a left turn, then pulls up beside a hand-painted sign saying 'Public Phone', but the phone box is nowhere to be seen. On the other side of the narrow street two teenage boys sit on the kerb next to a pile of corn for sale.

Thusago gets out of the car and calls to the boys by name. Their faces quickly morph from blank stares to bright smiles. The youngest shouts, 'Bra Mike!'

'Howzit my bru?' says the older boy, who crosses the street and gives Thusago a high five. The look he gives Wolfe is less than friendly.

'Watch my car, will you?' Thusago asks, 'I'm visiting Mama Gcina, okay?'

'What you got for me?' asks the boy lifting his chin.

'Five rand now,' he says giving him a coin. 'Five rand later. If you keep my car safe. Got that?'

'Yes, boss.'

'Share it with your brother,' says Thusago, nodding in the direction of the smaller boy guarding the corn cobs.

Wolfe follows Thusago along a sandy path that zigs and zags between a jumble of houses, some corrugated iron shacks, some brick. Above the dishevelled roof lines Wolfe sees a faded Coca Cola sign nailed to a pole announcing the location of the Justice Tuck Shop.

'That's Mama Gcina's shop.'

'She cleans the school and runs a shop?'

'Yes, she needs the money to look after her son. I should warn you. He's very ill. AIDS.'

Four young men pass them talking loudly, but they stop their chatter when they notice Wolfe.

'Outsiders are not welcome here,' says Thusago.

The Justice Tuck Shop is no bigger than a garden shed, leaning almost as though in exhaustion against the side of a small brick home. Its red colour, selected perhaps to match the Vodacom sign hung on the wall, leaps out from the shaded jumble of structures. Rusted security grilles are bolted to the front of the shop, making it seem like a prison cell, with a rectangular gap in the middle to allow for the exchange of money and goods. A bowed sheet of corrugated iron sticks out from the shopfront, creating an awning held up by wooden posts at each corner, which, like the rest of the shop, look close to collapse.

Under this porch an elderly woman with a pink and blue headscarf, in a loose-fitting dress two sizes too big for her, sits on a plastic milk crate, talking to a little girl no more than five years old.

'Is that Bra Mike I see?' the old woman asks the five-year-old, pointing at them.

'Yes,' says the little girl, nodding definitively.

The old lady rises slowly, as though her joints had rusted in places.

'*Sawubona*!' They hug. 'Who is this?' she asks, peering short-sightedly at Wolfe.

'This is the journalist I told you about.'

'I don't like strangers. I told you this.'

'Olivia is a friend. I can vouch for her.'

'I don't want trouble.' The old woman tells the little girl to go home.

'I just want to hear your story,' Wolfe says, stepping forward. 'You will be anonymous.'

'*Izit*?' the woman asks Thusago, seeking his confirmation.

He nods.

'It is quiet today,' Mama Gcina says. 'Time for a cup of tea.'

She hangs a hand-painted *Closed* sign to the outside of the shop door, locks and bolts it. They follow her into an immaculately clean lounge-cum-kitchen. The lino floor is pitted with holes and a small fridge rattles. Next to it is a two-ringed electric hob and a kettle. A faux-leather black two-seater sofa faces a hefty CRT TV. Underneath a sheet, on a single mattress on the floor, somebody is curled up sleeping.

On hearing them enter, the sheet is pushed away, and a man peeks up at them like a shy child. The skin across his cheekbones is so fragile and sunken it resembles parchment, and his arm is little more than bones draped in skin.

'Dumisani,' says the old woman to the invalid. 'You remember Bra Mike? His papa used to live in Phatshwane Street.' Dumisani blinks, his eyes appearing disproportionately large in his gaunt face. 'Mike became a mighty fine police officer. You remember Mike, don't you?'

Dumisani extends his bony arm. 'Hey bru.'

Thusago gently takes his hand. 'How are you, my friend?'

'Not good, brother.'

Thusago gestures for Wolfe to come closer. 'This is my friend, Olivia. She's a journalist. From London.'

'*Izit?*' says Dumisani.

'Hello Dumisani,' Wolfe takes his skeletal hand. 'Nice to meet you.'

Mama Gcina nods with approval. 'I will make us tea. Please, take a seat.' She gestures to the sofa, then opens a glass kitchen cupboard, takes out two china cups and saucers, and uses a towel to dust them off. They're clearly kept aside for guests.

'Can you tell Olivia what you heard last week at the school?' says Thusago.

'That evil man!' Mama Gcina says with surprising venom. 'Look what he did to my poor son!'

'Calm down, Mama,' says Dumisani.

'Do you mean Ximba or Msiza?' Wolfe asks.

'That evil policeman. He framed Dumisani, that's what he did! May he burn in Hell.'

'Will you tell me about it?' Wolfe asks.

'Fifteen years ago, Msiza was a beat officer,' says Dumisani. 'They were on patrol. He left his partner in the car to get coffee. His partner was white. The car was attacked, the cop dragged to the ground. Msiza panicked. Fired. Killed his own partner. The mob ran. I tried to help the officer. Tried to stop the bleeding. Msiza handcuffs me, says I fired the shot, even wrapped my fingers around his gun which he later said I had taken...' Dumisani's voice trails away, exhausted.

Mama Gcina adds, 'It was my son's word against a police officer. He didn't stand a chance.'

Dumisani tries to wipe away some drool from his mouth with a trembling hand. 'That pig, he is now Major-General of police. Me? I was raped in prison. I have AIDS. Where is the justice?'

'I'm so sorry, Dumisani.' Wolfe sits next to him on the mattress. She takes his hand. 'Are you getting treatment?'

Mama Gcina answers. 'There is a very good clinic. They have the drug he needs. It is expensive for us, but my grandson, Owethu, he's a clever boy. He works nights and pays for his father's treatment.'

Gcina hands Wolfe her tea, then Thusago his. 'Rooibos,' she says to Wolfe. 'Hope you like it.'

'Tell them what you saw at the school, Mama,' says Dumisani.

The old woman has her tea in a mug. She sits slowly and grimaces. 'My hips don't work as well as they used to.' She sips the rooibos, seems to study Wolfe, takes her time. 'I think you are a good woman, Olivia. I have made up my mind. I will tell you.'

Mama Gcina's version of events is almost identical to Thusago's, except for one detail.

'I was so afraid that monster recognised me. I had to know. He was parked at the front. Through a classroom window I watched him go to his car. His phone rang. He answered. Then he said...' Mama Gcina clenches her eyes shut, trying to remember. 'I want to get this right,' she says. 'Msiza said, "Yes, she's reported it, but nothing will be done."'

Mama Gcina opens her eyes. 'My memory is poor these days. Wait!' Using the table to help push herself up to standing, she shuffles to the kitchen and picks up a mobile phone that's recharging. 'I recorded it,' she says. 'Just like my grandson showed me.'

16

Mama Gcina's arthritic fingers tap the screen of a new model smartphone with increasing irritation. Wolfe places her cup and saucer carefully on the floor and gets up from the mattress she's been sitting on. If this informant has indeed filmed Major-General Msiza incriminating himself, this could be the leverage she needs to persuade Mazwi Ximba to talk to her.

'Can I help, Mama Gcina?' Wolfe asks.

'Why won't it play?' Gcina mutters. 'Stupid machine.'

'Can I take a look?'

'My lovely grandson gave it to me. He'll know what to do.' She calls out, 'Owethu! Help your poor grandma, will you?'

A boy who looks about fifteen emerges from an adjoining bedroom, an earbud in one ear, the other bud hanging loose over his shoulder. He's in a white T-shirt with an image of the popular South African rapper N'veigh on it, distressed designer jeans, and Nike sneakers. In contrast to his grandmother, his clothes are new and expensive. Owethu looks at Wolfe, his eyes narrowing with suspicion.

'Who are you?'

Gcina answers for her. 'A journalist. All the way from London.'

'What does she want?'

'To know about the pig, Msiza.' She waves her smartphone at him.

'What are you trying to do, Mama?'

'I want to play my video.'

Owethu frowns. 'Don't show them this.'

The old lady slaps his hand playfully. 'It's okay, Owethu. Bra Mike is a friend, and this English lady wants to know the truth. She can help us.'

'We don't want help from *umlungu*.'

'Where are your manners?' admonishes his grandmother. 'Go shake her hand. She is a famous journalist.'

Owethu doesn't budge.

'Do it!'

The teenager begrudgingly does as he's told.

'Play it for them, will you?'

They huddle around the boy so they can all see the small screen. The footage is jumpy, but it clearly shows a SAPS uniformed officer in his late forties leaving the school, heading for a black Mercedes Benz. His mobile rings. He answers.

'Yes, she's reported it, but nothing will be done,' Msiza says, clearly annoyed. 'They have better things to do than look for missing persons.'

Msiza is silent as his caller speaks. He kicks a tyre.

'You said there's no body. So, what's the fucking problem?' he demands.

Msiza waits for the answer, then says, 'Yes.'

The clip ends with the officer driving away.

Wolfe glances at Thusago for confirmation. 'That's Msiza, right?'

'Yes.' he replies. 'But we must be careful not to jump to conclusions.'

This must be difficult for Thusago, a SAPS officer, to process. However, in Wolfe's mind, it's clear Msiza is part of a cover-up, possibly of a missing or dead female. But now is not the time to debate this.

'I told you, Mama,' says Owethu, giving Thusago an angry glare. 'He's a cop. They stick together.'

'Owethu,' says Wolfe, 'I want to get at the truth as much as you do, and Mike is helping me do it. He's right. Msiza could find a way to explain this.'

'I'm telling you, they're evil,' says Owethu. He points at Dumisani lying on the mattress, emaciated and weak. 'Msiza did this. Sent an innocent man to jail. And my headmaster is a filthy pervert.'

'Wait a sec,' says Wolfe. 'Why a pervert?'

'I've seen the website he visits. It's sick.'

'How do you know?'

'He brings his own laptop to school sometimes. It's easy to hack.'

Wolfe's heartbeat has etched up a notch.

Mama Gcina steps between them. 'Owethu! Enough!'

'Let him speak,' Wolfe pleads.

But the old lady is too busy admonishing her grandson. 'We agreed. No more hacking. You want to go to prison like your father?'

'Owethu,' says Wolfe, raising her voice to be heard. 'What website?'

'Women being raped. Then killed. Maybe they were acting, but it didn't look like it.'

Gcina gasps and stumbles. Wolfe grabs her arm to steady her.

'I'm sorry, Mama Gcina, I must see the site.'

The grandmother nods, sits, dazed.

'It's on the dark web,' Owethu says, going to his room and reappearing with a tablet computer. It doesn't take him long to locate the site. Wolfe takes one look and tells him she's seen enough. It's a snuff video site where viewers can share their violent fantasies in a secure chat room. Wolfe swallows down the bile in her throat.

'Are you certain Ximba visits this site?'

'Yes.'

'I'm going to ask a hacker mate in London to monitor his online activity. I'm guessing you have his email and password?'

'I can monitor him for you. I've done it before,' says Owethu.

'Thanks, Owethu, you've already done enough.'

Owethu nods, but the edges of his eyes and mouth droop with disappointment.

Wolfe turns to Thusago. 'It's time we paid Mazwi Ximba a visit.'

17

There is a little wooden sign sticking out of the blue flowers of a plumbago shrub bordering the Moeta High School car park. On it is painted the word *Headmaster* in large black letters. His car is not there.

'He drives a white Toyota Corolla,' Owethu says from the back seat. 'He's usually in early.'

Thusago pulls up across the street. Kids carrying heavy bags on their backs stream through the school gates towards a series of single-level brick buildings with sloping, red corrugated iron roofs. Others loiter outside in groups, talking, laughing.

'What's with the dark glasses and baseball cap?' Owethu asks, leaning through the gap in the front seats. 'Is that because you're undercover?'

'Something like that,' she replies.

'Maybe I should stay. Help you. You know.'

'Your grandma would be furious. And it's best for you if you're not seen with me, okay?'

Wolfe's phone beeps. A message from Ponnappa:

The subject must be jumpy. He's changed password. No problem getting in, will take more time though.

'Who's Jwala Ponnappa?' Owethu asks, reading the message over her shoulder.

Wolfe hastily puts her phone away. 'Time you went in, isn't it?'

'She your London hacker?'

Wolfe doesn't answer.

'How old is she? Got a picture?'

Wolfe can't help smiling. 'Maybe I should put you two in touch. Then you can ask her yourself.'

'I know what she's gonna do to get Ximba's password. Spear-phishing, right? Send him a fake email with a link. It will look like it's from his bank or somewhere he trusts. When he clicks on it, he'll see his bank's login, only it's fake. At the same time, the link is downloading malware that lets her control his machine from anywhere – open his files, read his emails, see his web history, as long as his computer is on. Am I right?' he says, confidently.

'You know your stuff. Have you thought about a job in cyber security? It pays well. And it's legal.'

'I'm doing just fine as I am.'

'Your night job, what is it?'

'Night porter, why?'

'I'm guessing it's not your baggage-carrying skills that's earning the money to buy your nice clothes, or your grandma's phone, or your dad's medication. Be careful. You'll get caught and end up doing time.'

'What are you saying?' His voice has a hard edge.

'Don't waste your talent. I nearly messed up at fourteen. I was lucky I had somebody to help me find my way.' She's thinking of Jerry Butcher. Instead of arresting her when he had the chance, Butcher helped her get her life together. Her boyfriend went down for statutory rape of a minor and dealing in class A drugs. Butcher gave her a chance to make something of her life. 'Take this.' She hands the boy her business card. 'I'll connect you to Jwala.'

Owethu takes her card and pockets it. 'Nail Msiza and Ximba for me, okay?' he says, opening the rear door and getting out. They watch him cross the street and join the throng of kids.

'Speak of the devil,' says Thusago.

A white Corolla turns into the school car park and comes to a halt in the headmaster's spot.

Wolfe opens her door.

'You want me to come with you?' Thusago asks.

'He'll recognise you. Stay here.'

Wolfe jogs across the road and through the gates.

The stocky, silver-haired headmaster is in a grey suit that might have fitted well once, but no longer. As Ximba leans forward to take his briefcase from the back seat, the jacket fabric pinches at the waist and shoulders.

'Mr Ximba?' Olivia asks.

He twists around, a beaming smile on his face, which quickly fades when he sees Wolfe, a white woman in a cap, leather jacket and biker boots. She's clearly neither a parent nor a student.

'Yes?' More of a challenge than an affirmation.

'My name is–'

His phone rings. He checks the caller ID.

'I must take this.'

He faces away from her and listens. Looks out into the street, eyes darting one way, then the other. Wolfe thinks he's searching for Thusago's car. But Ximba stares in the other direction, at a black Toyota Prado. He locks eyes with a white man at the wheel who has a phone to his ear. His sunglasses and the distance make it impossible for Wolfe to see the driver clearly. The four-wheel drive's engine roars to life. Ximba scuttles away from Wolfe, panicking.

'I cannot speak to you,' he barks over his shoulder. 'This school is private property. Please leave.'

'I just want to ask–'

He rounds on her, eyes wide, nostrils flared. 'No! Leave now, or I'll call the police.'

'Okay,' Wolfe says, backing away. 'I'm leaving.'

Given his connection to the Major-General, Wolfe doesn't want to risk spending her three days in South Africa stuck in a police cell.

She heads for the street. The black Prado accelerates away, but she clocks the number plate.

Somebody has warned Ximba not to talk to her. Who?

18

Casburn wanted to meet at Johannesburg's central train station, patrolled by armed police and awash with security cameras. But Yushkov had insisted on Joubert Park after dark – easier to avoid CCTV, lots of tree cover, poorly lit, and closed at night. So no witnesses. Casburn waits for him next to the fountain at the park's centre. The splashing drowns out much of the traffic noise, as it will their conversation should anyone try to eavesdrop. He resists the urge to check his Glock 26 in a holster under his loose-fitting jacket.

He's sitting in the open, dark shadows all around, and no backup. He can't believe he's doing this.

To his right, there's movement. He peers into the semi-darkness. A couple, arm in arm, laughing, their steps wobbly. They shouldn't be here. They head into the trees, fumbling with each other's clothes, so engrossed in each other they don't even notice him. *Don't get distracted.* He turns back to find Vitaly Yushkov standing in front of him. He has forgotten what a big fucker Yushkov is. It takes all of Casburn's training and self-control not to flinch.

'Come with me,' the Russian says, starting to walk away.

'No,' says Casburn. 'We talk here.'

Yushkov turns back to face him. They're five feet apart and

Casburn wants to keep it that way. The floodlit fountain throws flickering dapples of light across the Russian's face and body. He has a raised scar under his eye. Casburn remembers the skin splitting.

'Are you carrying?' Casburn asks.

'*Nyet*. But you are.' Yushkov stares at him. Cold. Unblinking. 'You killed my sister,' he says, so quietly Casburn almost misses it.

'I did not. She died in Russia.'

Yushkov takes a step forward. Casburn watches the big man's hands. Clenched fists. 'I asked you to trade. Her life for mine. You did not do this. You killed her.'

He takes another step. Casburn draws his weapon. Points it at Yushkov's chest. 'Don't come any closer.'

Yushkov stops.

'Step back.'

He does. 'You think I have come here to kill you? You do not know me, Casburn. Remember that.'

Casburn lowers the gun. 'I want to talk about Olivia Wolfe.'

'So, talk.'

'Do you know she is in Johannesburg?'

A brief frown. Momentary confusion in the Russian's eyes. 'What I know doesn't matter. What do you want?'

'She's working on a story that's politically sensitive. Some powerful people will not take kindly to her interfering. I want you to persuade her to drop it.'

Yushkov laughs raucously, head thrown back, as if they are sharing a lewd joke. This is not the reaction Casburn was hoping for.

'Olivia is causing you a problem? I say, "Good!" Why should I give a shit?'

'Because she doesn't know what she's getting herself into.'

'Olivia is a brave woman. She can look after herself. You are wasting my time.'

'I want you to meet her. Warn her. She'll listen to you.'

'You think I am at your... how do you say, beck and call? You are wrong.'

Yushkov stalks off. Casburn catches up with him, puts a hand on his shoulder. 'Wait! One phone call, and the SVR will know where to find you.' Russia's external intelligence service, the SVR, has been hunting Yushkov for a while. 'And you know what that means.'

Yushkov slaps Casburn's hand away as if it were an annoying fly. 'So, this is how it will be. You will never let me be free.'

'All I am asking is that you meet Wolfe. You want to see her, don't you?'

'Of course, I want to see her,' he says, momentarily dropping his guard. 'I cannot.'

Casburn senses he's found Yushkov's vulnerable spot.

'Why can't you? A man like you could find a way.'

Yushkov doesn't answer.

'Why the fuck can't you see her?' Casburn shouts.

Yushkov drops his gaze. 'It is dangerous for her.'

'Don't give me that. You can meet in secret. This is what you're good at.'

There is no response. Just a cold stare.

'Well?'

'I must let her go,' Yushkov says, almost a whisper. 'Give her time to forget. To find someone else.'

For a few seconds Casburn is lost for words. 'Well, I'll be damned. She wasn't just a fuck, was she? You actually care for her?'

Before Casburn knows what is happening Yushkov has grabbed the pistol from Casburn's holster. The muzzle is barely a foot from his face.

'Take it easy, Yushkov.'

'It is *your* job to protect British citizens. Olivia is a British citizen. Now do your job.' Yushkov ejects the magazine and throws it and the Glock into some bushes. 'Do not *ever* contact me again.'

Casburn has one card left to play. He didn't want to use it, but now he has no choice. 'Yury Sukletin. If she keeps going, that's who she's going to piss off.'

'Sukletin?'

'Yes.'

Yushkov takes a deep breath. Nods. 'I will talk to Olivia.'

19

They are at Ntsitsi's street stall in Diepkloof. Wolfe swallows her last mouthful of one of Ntsitsi's famous kotas: a hollowed-out quarter loaf of bread that's filled with potato fries, Russian sausage, cold meat, cheese, and mango atchar.

'Delicious. Just what I needed,' she says, sucking her fingers clean. 'You sure you're up for a stake-out tonight?'

'Sure.'

They'd driven past the headmaster's house earlier.

'Good. Any chance you could run a check on the black Prado's number plate?'

'I don't know, Olivia,' Thusago replies. 'I'm on sick leave. People will ask questions.'

'Maybe someone who owes you?'

'I'll see what I can do. Lerato might do it.'

Thusago makes a call, claiming somebody dinged his car and drove off, and he wants to trace the driver.

'She'll get back to me,' he says, pocketing his phone. 'How did you remember the plate, anyway?'

'Taught myself to spot details like that. It's saved my life more than once.' She wipes her mouth with a napkin. 'Any idea about what's going on? So far, we've got a British Chancellor linked to Mazwi Ximba through an offshore bank account with twenty million dollars in it. The account is registered to what appears to be a shell company, ZIB Trading. And we have a high-ranking police officer, Major-General Msiza, possibly covering up a missing woman's murder.'

'My first thought is drugs. South Africa is a major transit point for heroin trafficking, some of it destined for your country, and, as you know, crystal meth is very big business. Your Chancellor would be able to get the drugs into the UK unnoticed. Ximba may be the money-man, greasing palms, bribing customs officers.'

'And Msiza?'

Thusago grimaces. 'Not so long ago our National Police Commissioner, Jackie Selebi, was convicted of corruption. He was getting paid off by a drug syndicate. So yes, if the commissioner is guilty, then Msiza could be, but I hope he is not. He's made it his mission to stamp out corruption, or so he says. I want to believe our senior officers are serving their people, and not just themselves.'

Wolfe considers this for a moment. 'You mentioned earlier this could be about conflict diamonds. That's not likely, is it? I thought they came from war zones like Sierra Leone?'

'You are right and you are wrong. There is always conflict over diamonds, Olivia. It does not matter if they are from war zones or mined here in South Africa. Do you know Ackerman Mining?'

'Yes, it's second only to De Beers, isn't it?'

'It is. Last year, there was a strike at Ackerman's biggest mine in the Limpopo Province. Police officers fired on the demonstration, killing seventeen men. They said the workers attacked them. Witnesses say this is untrue. It is possible the officers were ordered to shoot. Ackerman is a very powerful man.'

'That's interesting. I've looked into Sackville's background. It turns out he was at school in South Africa with Clive Ackerman and they're still friends.'

Thusago raises an eyebrow. 'That could be a problem. Clive

Ackerman is protected. It will be very difficult to get information on him.'

Wolfe shrugs. 'Maybe Ackerman is irrelevant. I can't imagine him risking everything to sell illegal diamonds when he has more than enough that are legit.'

'There are rumours. Small independent operators near Ackerman's largest mine generally produce average stones, but recently they have apparently been selling diamonds of exceptional quality. What I tell you has not been proved, but the word is these diamonds come from Angola and Ackerman is paying to have them laundered.'

'So, what are conflict diamonds worth?'

'It is said the blood diamonds funding the war in Sierra Leone were worth one hundred and thirty-eight million US dollars per year. And the war went on for eleven years.'

'So much money. So much misery.' Wolfe sighs and stares out of the window, shaking her head slowly. 'And poaching?'

'I know something about this. Before I met Camila, I had a girlfriend who worked for the Department of Environmental Affairs. Wildlife trafficking is the fourth most lucrative illicit trade, after drugs, humans and firearms. And rhino horn is the most lucrative of all.'

'Who drives it? Trophy hunters?'

'No, the real drivers are the Asian syndicates. They fund military-style poaching operations and smuggle the horn into China and Vietnam.'

Wolfe Googles rhino poaching on her iPhone. 'It says here South Africa has the world's largest rhino population, but nearly 7,100 have been poached since 2007. My God, so many. Why? Because some limp-dick wants to have a horn on his desk?'

'You have such a way with words, Olivia.' Thusago laughs. 'But yes, to these Vietnamese businessmen it's a status thing. Or a gift to cement a deal. Sometimes they share a drink of horn powder in water to celebrate a new business relationship.'

'It's also supposed to cure all manner of illnesses, isn't it?'

'Yes. In China and Vietnam they believe it has medicinal qualities.'

'But it's just keratin, isn't it? Like my fingernails.'

'Yes, but it's sold as a cure for almost anything: fever, erection problems, even cancer. And people pay a fortune for it. It is one of *the* most precious commodities on the black market today. When I last checked, horn was selling for $60,000 per kilo, which puts it up there with cocaine and heroin.'

'I had no idea.'

Thusago's phone rings. He answers, pulls out a small notepad and jots down a name and address.

'So, Lerato came though?'

'She did. The black Prado is registered to Terry Blunt at a business address for the KwaZulu Natal Co-operative. Sugar cane.'

'That's interesting. Zoe Blunt is down as the director of ZIB Trading, and I'm guessing they're related. I'll message Jwala and ask her to look into Terry Blunt. Check for a criminal record.' Wolfe Googles the name. Finds a photo of him taken in Zimbabwe in a sugar cane field. 'Let's go take a look at the KwaZulu Natal Co-operative.'

An hour later, they pull up outside a row of brown brick warehouses in Wynberg, on an industrial estate popular with mechanics, second-hand car dealers and importers of electricals. On the other side of a nine-foot-high mesh fence, trucks thunder down the freeway, flinging dust and litter into the air.

'There's warehouse eight,' Wolfe says, pointing. 'Can't see any signage for the co-operative, though. Can you?'

'And no trucks with the company logo either.'

'And no black Prado. I'm guessing he's out. I'll take a closer look. You want to come?'

'What are you going to do?'

'Just going to snoop around. Maybe you should stay here. Warn me if anyone turns up.'

Wolfe switches her phone to vibrate, dons her baseball cap and sunglasses in case there are security cameras operating, and, as always, takes her go-bag with her, strapped to her back.

Hard rock music booms from the auto repair shop next door, competing with the revving of car engines and the clank of spanners. The roller door is padlocked. To its right is a door painted green which has been reinforced with steel plates and is locked. She presses one ear against it and covers the other, trying to drown out the loud music. There's no doorbell. She can't hear anybody on the inside. She looks up. No security cameras either.

'He's not there,' calls out a man in a boiler suit having a smoke outside the next-door unit.

'You mean Terry?' she asks.

'Yeah.'

'Know when he'll be back?'

'No idea,' he says, taking his last puff before stamping the butt under his boot and shuffling back into the repair shop.

Wolfe looks around at Thusago in his car. He won't like what she's about to do, which is why she suggested he stay behind and keep watch. She imagines Jerry Butcher shaking his head, telling her not to do it, reminding her that the tricks her brother taught her helped to land him in jail. But Sandra West was killed because of what she knew. And Msiza is possibly involved in another woman's death. She can't hang around and wait for somebody else to die. There's no point contacting Casburn. He has his own agenda and he doesn't trust her. She reasons that all she is going to do is take a look inside.

She peels her pack's straps off her shoulders, checks there is nobody from the repair shop watching, then slides a lock-pick from its sheath, hidden inside the left-hand strap. Then she slips it into the lock. It takes a bit of jiggling but in less than a minute there's a click and she hurries inside the warehouse.

Blotchy sunlight penetrates the grimy glass-panelled roof, revealing an almost empty space which must be over a thousand square feet. There doesn't appear to be anybody around. At one end are floor-to-ceiling racks designed to support merchandise. At another, a jumble of broken pallets. At the back, a cabin-like office with a window, in darkness. No bagged or raw sugar. No forklifts. The space is dusty and lacks the caramel smell of sugar production. In fact, there is nothing even remotely to suggest a sugar co-op is based here. Wolfe peers through the cabin's office window. Computer, monitor, filing cabinet, ashtray, bar fridge, shabby sofa. She tries the door. Locked. Feels her phone vibrate in her pocket. A warning? Adrenaline rushes through her body.

The sudden clank of the roller door rising startles her. As the gap under the door widens she hears the rumble of a car's diesel engine. She can't escape the way she came in, because she'll be seen. There's nowhere to hide except behind the cabin. She races behind it to find two half-full skip bins. She crawls between them on her hands and knees.

A vehicle is driven into the warehouse, the roller doors shut. Her view is blocked by the cabin. Boots crunch grit. A key rattles in a lock. The cabin floor creaks. A fluorescent light blinks several times and comes on; it's an unhealthy greenish-white light seeping out of the office into the rest of the warehouse interior. A phone rings.

'Everything's on schedule.' Male. Zimbabwean accent. Deep voice. Probably Terry Blunt. 'Yes, everyone is coming.' A pause while he listens to the caller. 'Yes, him too.' Another pause. 'The first one arrives Friday night.' Pause. 'Yes, I'm meeting Ximba tonight.' Pause. 'I will.'

Metal rasps on metal as a filing cabinet opens and closes. Lights go out. The cabin door shuts. A long beep. Wolfe catches a glimpse of the man leaving with a black briefcase. It's Blunt. The roller door opens and he reverses out, then closes it behind him.

Wolfe crawls out of her hiding place to find a light flashing inside the cabin. Blunt has set an alarm. There's nothing more she can discover here, so she leaves, careful to lock the green door behind her.

'Jesus!' says Thusago, almost jumping out of his skin as she gets in the car. 'I thought he'd found you.'

'Blunt didn't know I was there. It was worth the risk. I learned three things. One, that warehouse isn't used to trade sugar cane. Two, he's meeting Ximba tonight, but I don't know where. And three, someone or something arrives here Friday. That's the day I'm due to fly back to England.'

'What will you do?'

She looks him in the eye. 'I'm not leaving until I know what the hell is going on.'

20

Wolfe bowls a tennis ball at six-year-old Jacob Thusago. His orange plastic cricket bat connects for a cover drive that belies his age, and the ball flies towards his father at waist-height. Mike makes a big show of missing the catch. Jacob squeals with delight and makes two runs before his dad throws the ball to Camila, waiting at the stumps.

'Time for dinner,' says Camila, her Chilean accent soft and lilting. She winds her long black hair into a tight sausage-curl on the top of her scalp and secures it with a hair clip. She's a petite, pretty woman with olive skin and eyes that turn down at the edges, which gives the impression she is sad.

'Olivia, will you help me?'

'Sure.'

'No. Pleeeeese,' the little boy begs. 'Don't take Olivia.'

'Papa will keep playing,' Camila says.

Jacob pouts. 'But I want Ol-iv-ia,' he wails.

'After dinner you can show Olivia your Transformer Steeljaw, okay?'

'Okay.' The boy gives an exaggerated sigh and stabs the bat into the parched ground.

'He's adorable,' says Wolfe, stepping onto the back deck and following Camila into their modest bungalow.

Camila takes a casserole dish from the fridge and places it in the pre-heated oven. 'A dish from home. Cazuela de Vacuno. Beef stew with vegetables, garlic, onion, oregano, paprika. I hope you like spicy?'

'The hotter the better. What can I do?' asks Wolfe.

Camila glances out through the kitchen window where her husband and son have resumed their cricket. 'To be honest, I wanted to talk. About Mike.' Camila holds up a bottle of pinotage. 'Like to try some South African wine?'

Wolfe has a stake-out planned for tonight, but she accepts to keep Camila company.

'What's up?' Wolfe asks.

Camila looks down. 'Mike isn't well. He told you, yes?'

'He did.'

'There are days he won't get out of bed. On others he is angry.'

'You think working with me will make him worse?'

'No. I haven't seen him this happy for a long time. No, it's not that.' Camila sips her wine. 'Keep him safe, will you? He's... he's vulnerable right now.'

'I'll do my best.'

'It is good for him to have you here. I think you will prove to be better therapy than his psychiatrist.'

Jacob runs into the kitchen and wraps his arms around Wolfe's legs.

'He wants to be with Olivia,' Thusago says, his eyes roaming from the empty kitchen workbench to the oven where the stew is already cooking. 'That was quick.' He gives Camila a questioning look.

'Team work,' says Camila, raising her glass at Wolfe.

'To team work.' Wolfe touches her glass to Camila's in a toast.

'Olivia,' says Thusago, 'I'd like to show you something.'

'Can I come?' asks Jacob, clinging to Wolfe's jeans.

'Not this time,' he says, prizing Jacob away and leading Wolfe into a small study.

He shuts the door behind them. A collage of family photos in a gold frame hangs on the wall opposite his desk. The picture dominates the small room. Thusago takes it down. Behind it is a wall safe. He opens it with a key. At the bottom are documents and passports. On the only shelf are two pistols, the larger one she recognises as a Beretta PX4. He takes out the other, smaller handgun.

'Do you know how to use a pistol?'

'I've fired both pistols and rifles at targets, but that was a long time ago.'

'This is a CZ 75 Compact. It's light and easy to conceal. It has two safeties: a firing pin safety and de-cocker. As you haven't a lot of experience, you're better off using the de-cocker. I'll show you.' Thusago demonstrates how to use the de-cocker and load the magazine. His hand has a slight tremor. When was the last time he handled a loaded gun? Was it when he froze and his partner got shot? 'The sight is outfitted with a three-dot illuminating system for better aiming in poor visibility. I want you to have it.'

'Thanks, Mike, but I don't need it.'

'You *do* need it. This is South Africa. People here carry guns. Ximba is at the bottom of a criminal food chain. There will be a man he reports to. This man will have enforcers. Thugs. With guns. And so it will go on, all the way up to the man behind it all. It doesn't matter if it's drugs or ivory or rhino horn or conflict diamonds. These people will be heavily armed.'

'I can defend myself in other ways.'

'I know you can. But martial arts aren't enough. Please take it.' He places the pistol on the scratched desk. Next to it, he puts a box of fifty Federal 9mm 147 grain Hydra-Shok cartridges.

Wolfe has never carried a concealed weapon. Never killed anybody.

'Here,' he says, pulling a hip holster from a desk drawer. 'Put this on your belt.' He slaps it down on the desk next to the gun. Wolfe steps way, repulsed.

Thusago turns his attention to the Beretta, loading it. He puts on a shoulder holster under his jacket. When he's finished, he looks up. The CZ 75 hasn't moved.

'Please,' says Thusago. 'Take it.'

Through the door Jacob calls out, 'Can I come in, Daddy? I want to show Olivia something.' The door knob wobbles.

Thusago scoops up the CZ 75 and hides it in a desk drawer, just as the little boy enters. He's holding a small book in his hand.

'Olivia, will you read this to me?'

Wolfe kneels down and takes the book. It's an English collection of traditional Zulu stories with beautiful illustrations. 'Which story?'

The King of the Birds.

21

HELSINKI, FINLAND

As soon as he heard of Helsinki's ghost town he knew where he would end the man's life.

On his iPad is the target's photo. Ailo Lod, twenty-three, works for a human rights charity. The assassin's lip curls. A do-gooder. He detests do-gooders. Long hair like a girl, tortoiseshell glasses, and a sparse goatee. He won't put up much of a fight.

The drive to Kruunuvuori, the site of a small community of abandoned villas deep in a forest, will take him thirty-five minutes. He's already driven the route. Capturing Lod will be a piece of cake. Getting him from the car boot and into the villa he has chosen will be the difficult part. It's a ten-minute walk through the forest. And that's without having to drag an unconscious body. The graffitied and crumbling houses have been left to rot since the seventies, so he's not expecting company. But why drag a dead weight through a dense forest when you don't have to? His reconnoitre solved the problem. Water laps at the villas' shore, so a stolen rowboat will serve as transport.

The hired Skoda Octavia Wagon has plenty of boot space. Two large tarps, ropes and a spade. Who would have thought buying a machete in Finland would be so fucking hard? A large cleaver will have to do.

It's fucking cold, and he's thankful for the heated car seats as he waits for Lod to leave his workplace and unlock his bicycle from a bike rack. The bloody city is littered with bikes. In winter the sun only notches above the horizon at eleven thirty in the morning, and falls again an hour and a half later. Why would anyone want to live in such a miserable place?

Scrolling through photos of the villas he took earlier, he studies the one he's selected. Two levels, a massive hole in the upstairs floor, splintered wood strewn all over the ground floor, broken furniture, graffiti in bright colours on the outside cladding. He visualises his victim waking, groggy, confused. Finding himself chained up. He will slash Lod's spine first, so his victim can't use his legs. He'll unchain his captive and give him ten minutes to crawl to freedom. If Lod's got any guts, he'll try to escape, and end up cutting his hands on the splintered wood and broken glass littering the derelict home.

His fans love it when he makes funny quips. He's got the perfect one for Lod. 'Spineless wimp!' he'll yell. That'll get him some laughs. He'll shoot a video this time, so they hear everything.

When he's not hunting people, he hunts animals. The fun is not in a clean kill. It's in deliberately wounding it so its death is slow and agonising. He'll stalk the wounded beast, then stand over it as it takes its last breath. As he will do with Lod.

His phone rings. Seeing the caller's ID, he answers immediately. An unscheduled call sets his nerves on edge.

'Yes?' he says.

'I need you back in South Africa.'

'Do I deal with Lod first?'

'How long will it take?'

'I can be on a flight tonight and in Johannesburg tomorrow morning.'

'Make sure you're on that flight. No games, you hear? We don't have time for that.'

'You pay me to do a job for you. You don't dictate how I do it.'

'Samuel, I tolerate your dramatics because you never fail me. However, this time above all I need speed. You understand.'

It wasn't a question. It was an order.

'I understand,' Samuel says, but he can't disguise the disappointment in his voice.

His employer continues, 'And another thing. No live streaming. No chat rooms.'

'You've enjoyed my work in the past.'

'I have. But this is different. The South African, Russian, Swazi, and this Finn must disappear without a trace.'

'Nobody will know what happened to Lod except you and me,' Samuel lies.

'Good. I'm sending you your next subject.' Samuel's phone pings – he has a message, no doubt with a photo attached. 'Mazwi Ximba. He is no longer loyal. Make it look like an accident. And no theatrics.'

Samuel's grip on the steering wheel tightens. He wants to tell his employer to get fucked, but he pays well above market and usually doesn't interfere.

'One more thing. A woman. I want her watched.'

'I don't do surveillance.'

'You do whatever I tell you.'

22

Thusago pours coffee from a thermos flask and hands the cup to Wolfe. She takes a sip. Through the lounge room window of the solid mustard-yellow house in Diepkloof they watch Ximba and his wife, Funani. He has changed into a casual shirt and jeans. She is in a purple and blue kaftan and a chunky beaded necklace. He has his arm around her as they watch television. Wolfe yawns, checks her watch. Almost eleven and Terry Blunt is a no-show.

'He definitely said he'd see Ximba tonight,' she says. 'So, where is he?'

'Maybe Ximba's waiting for Funani to go to bed? She may not know what he's involved in and he wants to keep it that way.'

'I'm thinking Blunt is his handler.'

'Could be.'

She glances at Thusago. 'You're happy to stay a little longer then?'

'Guess so.' He zips up his coat. Hugs himself against the cold.

A light goes on upstairs and Funani draws the bedroom curtains. Ximba leaves the lounge room too.

'Maybe he's going to bed?' Wolfe asks.

A few minutes later, Wolfe gets a message from Ponnappa.

Ximba has clicked the link I sent. About time!

She shows Thusago the message.

'So now Ponnappa can see what he's doing on his computer?'

'She can.'

The bedroom light goes out. The house is quiet.

Mike tilts his seat back and closes his eyes. Soon he's snoring. Wolfe's eyelids droop. Her head slowly inclines forward, eyes closed.

Wolfe's burner phone vibrates. Startled, she fumbles to answer it.

'Hello?' Her tone guarded.

'Olivia? Are you okay?'

She recognises the Russian accent, his unhurried speech, the way he pronounces her name.

'Yes. I'm fine.'

The scrape of an ill-fitting door distracts her. Ximba appears through a side passage gate and gets in his car. She shakes Thusago awake.

'Mike, he's leaving.' She points through the windscreen.

'Shit!' Thusago hurriedly turns the ignition, and they head off after the receding tail lights.

'Are you in danger?' Yushkov's voice is tinged with anxiety.

'No,' says Wolfe. 'I'm working a story. Tailing someone. But that's not why I called. I'm in South Africa.'

His breathing is slow and regular. She holds hers.

'Who is with you?' Yushkov asks.

Unsure how he will react if he knows she is with a cop, she says, 'A friend. He's helping me. He can be trusted.'

'His name?' There is an insistence in Yushkov's voice that sets her on edge.

'I trust him. That should be enough, Vitaly.'

He is silent again. Down the line she hears men's voices, but they are too distant to make out what they say.

When Yushkov speaks again, it is in his native tongue. He knows she has some basic Russian. He asks, again, if she is in danger. He tells her to keep the line open if she needs help, so he can trace her. Wolfe replies in Russian, telling him she is safe and in Johannesburg.

One final test.

'What is the shape of the scar on my left shoulder?'

'A star. I have traced its outline with my tongue,' she says in Russian.

Yushkov laughs. 'I am sorry, Olivia.' He reverts to English, his tone softened, intimate. 'I had to be sure.'

'And you, are you okay?' she asks.

'Yes, I am okay.' The silence drags out, neither of them sure how to fill it. 'It is good to hear your voice. I have missed you.'

'And I you. Are you still in Durban?'

'*Nyet*.' Someone shouts at Yushkov, *Let's go*. 'I cannot talk now. I will call you soon. I want to see you.'

The line goes dead.

Thusago looks askance at her. 'Looks like Ximba's going to Douglasdale. Must be meeting Blunt there.'

She stares out of the window.

'That was Yushkov?' Thusago asks.

'It was.'

'And?'

'I don't know. He's calling back.'

They lapse into silence. Thusago keeps on Ximba's tail.

'This is strange,' says Thusago. 'Fourways is for tourists and party-goers. Young people. What's he doing here?'

23

The venue is drenched in red light and as the crowd of 150 people jumps and writhes to the band, it seems to Wolfe as if the whole room is pulsing, spinning, flailing. The upper level is all seating, arranged like a theatre's upper circle, with bar staff constantly tending to the patrons. Wolfe squeezes through the throng searching for Ximba.

She'd tailed Ximba out of a multi-story car park and into a shopping centre, up the escalator and into Tanz Café, although why such a huge music venue should be given that name she can't imagine. Thusago, who has met Ximba before and therefore might be recognised, has followed at a distance. He was meant to join her inside the venue, but so far he's a no-show.

Where are you? she texts him.

It doesn't take long for Wolfe to pinpoint Ximba, seated at one of the semi-circular booths at the rear. The man next to him is white. She inches closer. Using the crowd to hide her, she surreptitiously snaps photos of both men.

Terry Blunt is middle aged and heavily built, with a receding hairline, and moustache. He leans back, arms out wide on the top of the red leather banquette, seemingly relaxed and confident. In contrast,

Ximba leans forward, using his hands for emphasis, shaking his head, visibly distressed. In the next booth, two couples in their twenties have amassed a collection of empty wine and beer glasses. One pair heads for the dance floor. Wolfe sees an opportunity. Switching on her video record button, she holds her phone low against her thigh, then pushes through the throng towards one of the vacated seats.

'Mind if I sit here for a minute?' Wolfe asks the man and woman seated arm in arm.

'It's taken,' says the attractive blonde woman.

'Please? Just while your friends are dancing. There's nowhere else, and my feet are killing me.'

Wolfe swivels her phone towards Ximba, keeping it hip height, as if she's simply holding it.

Ximba says to Blunt, 'I don't care. I can't do this anymore.'

'They'll be back soon–' the pretty blonde begins, but the boyfriend jumps in. 'Come on, Mel, just a few minutes.' Then he asks Wolfe. 'Is that a British accent?'

Blunt takes one arm from the back of the banquette and lays it over Ximba's shoulders. Ximba flinches. 'Grow a spine, will you?' says Blunt.

Wolfe tunes out of the Blunt–Ximba conversation long enough to answer the young guy's question, knowing the whole thing is being recorded. 'Yes, I'm English,' Wolfe says. 'On holiday. And you? Scottish?'

'Inverness.' He puts his hand out. 'I'm Cameron. This is Mel.'

In the next booth, Ximba raises his voice. 'I could lose everything. He's police, for God's sake!'

Is Ximba referring to Casburn or Thusago, or even Msiza?

'I'm Beth,' Wolfe says, shaking Cameron's hand. Mel looks none too happy. 'I'm loving the band.'

'They're local. Good, aren't they?'

Blunt says, 'Don't be stupid, man. He won't let you go.'

The dancing couple leave the dance floor and look at Wolfe expectantly.

'I'm off.' Wolfe stands up. 'Lovely to meet you.'

Wolfe has run out of excuses to hover near Ximba. So she mingles with the crowd, but stays near enough to watch both men.

Where is Thusago?

Blunt abruptly gets up and heads for the exit. Ximba stays put and stares at his beer. Does Wolfe stick with Ximba or follow Blunt? Perhaps the Zimbabwean will lead her to someone higher up the chain of command? She checks her phone again. Nothing from Thusago.

Ximba still inside club. I'm tailing Blunt just leaving. Can you stick with Ximba? she messages.

Wolfe heads out of the venue, blinking at the sudden brightness of the shopping centre. Looking down the mall's central void, she locates the white Zimbabwean striding down the escalator. She can see him clearly now: tanned skin, hair the colour of wheat and a thick coppery moustache. His short-sleeved shirt reveals strong arms.

Wolfe runs to keep up. He exits and turns right. The street is bustling with people partying. She makes sure to keep a few people between her and her quarry so as not to get noticed. He enters a twenty-four-hour mini supermarket and buys a pack of cigarettes. Wolfe hovers outside. Checks her phone. Still nothing from Thusago. She dials his number. It goes to voicemail.

Blunt pays for his cigarettes, leaves the shop and lights one. He's no more than a few feet from her, but he doesn't look her way. He walks further down the street and turns right, leaving a trail of smoke behind. As Wolfe turns the corner, she is headlocked by a muscular arm, her back pulled hard against someone's chest. She immediately drops her chin, just as Butcher taught her, so her assailant finds it harder to crush her windpipe. He smells of cigarettes and cheap aftershave. She feels the cold of a gun barrel pressed against her temple.

'Who are you?' Blunt says.

She has underestimated him. His movements are swift and skilled – probably ex-army. With a gun at her head, there's a limit to what she can do to escape. But he's not using a suppressor. So, she reasons, he won't pull the trigger. Too many people are still about who will hear the gun fire. The last thing he probably wants is the police asking questions. And Thusago is nearby. He must be. And he's armed.

'Ow! You're hurting me.'

His mouth is so close to her ear she can feel his hot breath. 'I said, who are you?'

'Beth. Beth Summers. Let me go!'

'That burnt-out cop sent you, didn't he?'

He knows about Thusago? How?

'What cop?' Wolfe says.

'He was parked outside the warehouse earlier.'

'No, I don't know any cop. I'm on holiday here.'

'Oh yeah? You tell that loser to keep his Kaffir nose out of my business, you got that?'

Behind her, a bottle shatters. Her captor swings around, dragging her with him and points what she now recognises is a Colt M1911. But there's no one there. Just a cat scrounging for food from bins. Now is her chance. His gun points forward, not at her. She steps to one side, which forces him to tilt. Now she puts her left leg behind his right, using her leverage to force him to lean forward as if he's bowing. Twisting her head, she squeezes it out of his now loosened hold. She yanks his arm back behind him sharply, and knees him as hard as she can in the groin. He collapses, moaning. She rips the Colt from his fingers.

'*Fok jou*, bitch!'

He hits out with his elbow. It connects with her stomach. Stunned by the blow, she drops the gun. He seizes it, then staggers down the narrow street. Wolfe is too winded to give chase. He tumbles into his vehicle and speeds away.

Wolfe dry retches. Her whole body trembles.

It's a while before she notices a man kneeling between two parked cars, a Beretta pointing straight at her.

24

In a lonely side street Wolfe freezes, a gun trained on her. Only a few feet away on the main drag of the Fourways entertainment district, revellers chatter and laugh, a car horn honks, the pounding beat of jazz pulses. Competing aromas of cooked food, some pungently spicy, some doughy, some fatty, others sweet like pancakes, carry on the chilled night air, but Wolfe is only aware of the sour smell of her fear.

'Don't shoot. I'm unarmed.'

The gunman crouched between two parked cars, a silhouette in the shadows, makes a strange sobbing sound. He stands, takes a step forward.

'I couldn't do it,' he mumbles.

'Mike? Is that you?'

'I couldn't fucking do it!'

Thusago waves the pistol around. His finger on the trigger. Does he even have the safety on?

'Mike, it's me, Olivia. Just put the gun down. Please.'

Thusago stares at the pistol as if he has only just noticed it.

'Mike, listen to me. Put the gun away. Nice and slowly.'

'He had a gun to your head and I froze. I froze!'

His gun-hand hangs at his side.

'Please give me the gun. Everything's fine now,' says Wolfe, getting off her knees.

She inches closer, her movements smooth, despite the pain in her gut.

Wolfe lays her hand on his and loosens his grip, one finger at a time, then flicks the safety catch and shoves it into her waistband.

'Come on, Mike, let's get you home.' She loops her arm through his.

He stumbles like a drunk. 'I was in the club. Saw you. Saw your text. I was afraid, so afraid. I ran from the club, saw you walking down the street. Pulled myself together enough to follow.'

'Everything's okay, Mike. Stop giving yourself such a hard time.'

It takes an age to get Thusago back to the car park and into his car. She finds his car keys and drives away, tyres screeching.

'He saw you outside the warehouse. He knows who you are.'

Thusago screws up his face as if about to bawl. 'He'll come after my family. What have I done?'

'We'll make sure they're safe.'

'I can't do this anymore. You see that, don't you?'

'I do. I'll find a motel in the morning. I won't involve you anymore; I don't want to put your family in danger.'

She's on her own now, in a country she knows little about.

'If the offer still stands,' she says, 'I'll take the CZ 75.'

25

The black and silver BMW R1200 GS Adventure motorcycle Wolfe hired first thing in the morning is a dream to ride.

Without Thusago to guide her, and unsure where her investigation will lead, she hired a bike that is comfortable in both the city and off-road. The satnav directs her to Mazwi Ximba's house. Reference to 'circles' and 'robots' had her initially confused until she worked out they were roundabouts and traffic lights. Hoping the headmaster hasn't yet left for school, she dismounts, hastily padlocks the bike and helmet to a lamp post, then rings the doorbell.

Funani, in a pink dressing gown, twitches a floral curtain away from a window by the door.

'Mrs Ximba? I'm a journalist,' Wolfe calls out. 'Can I speak to your husband, please?'

The curtain drops back across the window and Funani disappears.

'Mr Ximba?' calls Wolfe. 'Please can we talk? I'm Olivia Wolfe from *The Post* in London. We met yesterday.'

Inside the house, there's an angry exchange.

'The neighbours!' says Funani. 'Shut her up.'

A scowling Ximba opens the door as far as the security chain will allow. He's dressed for work in a suit.

'What is the meaning of this?' says Ximba. 'I'll call the police.'

'I don't think you will,' says Wolfe.

She holds up her phone and presses play. The video she shot last night at Tanz Café runs. The loud music in the background is distracting, but Ximba can clearly be heard to say, *I don't care. I can't do this anymore.* His companion, Terry Blunt, replies, *Grow a spine, will you.* Wolfe fast forwards. Blunt says, *Don't be stupid, man. He won't let you go.*

'How did you...? Dear God!'

'I was there last night. Watching you with Terry Blunt.'

Ximba squeezes his eyes shut, takes a deep breath, and then reopens them.

'He promised me,' Ximba whines.

'Promised you what?'

'Nobody would know. Nobody would get hurt. We'd retire rich. The mayor would finally show me some respect.'

Wolfe wonders which mayor and why his or her respect was so important, but she doesn't want to get distracted from her mission. She wants to know how the millions of dollars are generated and who is in charge.

'I'm not interested in embarrassing you, Mr Ximba. I imagine you've been pressured, maybe threatened? Talk to me now, and you won't see me again.'

He whispers, 'Please, my wife doesn't know. Come to the school later. Please?'

'What time?'

'Midday,' he whispers. 'To my office. And tell the British policeman to stay away.'

Casburn.

'You've spoken to him?'

'No, I have not,' Ximba hisses. 'I cannot. He'll get me killed.' Then he raises his voice, 'Now go away!'

26

The motel room is clean and basic, and the rattling hum of the air conditioning drowns out most of the traffic noise. It overlooks the car park and street, which enables her to keep an eye out for unwanted visitors. An exterior walkway runs past her first-floor room, with steps at either end leading down to the car park. This gives her options if she needs to run for it.

Wolfe is seated on the sagging double bed when her phone rings.

'What's up?' she asks Casburn. He only contacts her when he wants something.

'Mazwi Ximba is dead.'

Wolfe inhales sharply. 'What? No! I saw him only an hour ago, alive and well.'

'Well, he's very dead now. Car accident. Why did you see him?'

She's too shocked to answer. 'Poor man. How did it happen?'

'Hit side-on by a lorry. Smashed into a wall. Didn't stand a chance.'

'And the other driver?'

'Hit and run.'

Wolfe puts a hand on the bed to steady herself. 'It was deliberate. It has to be.'

'How would you know that?' There's weary condescension in his voice.

'We'd arranged to meet at midday. Somebody didn't want us to talk.'

'I told you to leave well alone.'

'Blunt. It has to be,' she says to herself.

'What?'

'Blunt knew Ximba was going to talk.'

'Who the hell is Blunt?'

Wolfe picks up her helmet. 'Tell me where the accident happened. I'll meet you there. Then I'll explain.'

After hovering around the crash site for an hour, getting only scraps from the local cops and the cold-shoulder from Casburn, Wolfe decides to move on.

An accident, they say. The lorry was stolen. No leads on the driver. No CCTV camera. As Wolfe sees it, this is the work of a pro. No skid marks, so the driver made no attempt to stop. *And* he chose this section of road because there were no security cameras.

Wolfe straddles her BMW motorcycle. She can't help thinking she is responsible for what happened to Ximba. She's angry. She wants to confront Blunt, but what would be the point? She has no proof Ximba's death was suspicious, let alone that he was involved. And, if he was, confronting him would only serve to alert him that she's suspicious. Her best option is to talk to Funani, his widow.

'Hey!' Casburn calls. He jogs over. 'Leave Terry Blunt to me.'

Earlier she'd filled him in on her two encounters with Blunt and played the video footage of Blunt and Ximba at Tanz Café.

'And you tread carefully with Msiza,' Wolfe replies. She nods at the cops near the shattered vehicles. 'It's murder. You know that, right?'

'Possibly.'

Wolfe rides away, glad to leave the wreckage behind. Whatever Ximba may have done, he didn't deserve to die.

When Wolfe pulls into Ximba's street she is surprised to find a crowd of TV reporters and camera crews camped outside the deceased man's house. Wolfe zeros in on the youngest, a black woman chatting to a photographer.

'What's happening?' Wolfe asks.

'You don't know?' says the reporter. She looks Wolfe up and down. 'I guess you're not from around here. His wife is sister to the mayor.'

Now Ximba saying how much he craved the mayor's respect makes sense.

'Well connected then, huh?' observes Wolfe.

'Very. We're waiting for a comment from her, and for the mayor to arrive. I'm Busisiwe, *Soweto Times*. Trainee. Mr Ximba was my headmaster.'

'So, you asked to cover this story?'

'Yeah. Could be my big break.' She tilts her head. 'Is that an English accent?'

'Yes. From *The Post*.'

Busisiwe's eyes open wide in recognition. '*The Post*? What are you doing here?'

Perceptive woman.

'Working a different story. In the neighbourhood. Have the police come and gone?' Wolfe asks.

'Just left.'

'Anyone special turn up?'

Busisiwe grins. 'You know something, don't you?' Before Wolfe can respond, the reporter mouths a big, 'Oh! I get it. It's not an accident, is it?'

Wolfe is guarded in her response. 'Police say it is. Recognise any of the officers who came here?'

'You want something, you got to give me something in return.' Busisiwe folds her arms.

'How about an exclusive with the widow?'

'You could do that?'

'Yup.'

'Okay. It's a deal. The top guy, Major-General Msiza, turned up an hour ago. Probably paying his respects to the mayor's sister. And…' The young reporter pauses, frowning.

'And?'

'And then four officers went inside. No idea what they were doing because all the curtains and blinds were drawn.'

With a sinking feeling, Wolfe guesses they were searching for Ximba's laptop. Msiza is tying up loose ends.

'Did they leave with anything?'

'Maybe three, four boxes.'

'Wait here. I'll talk to Funani. And if anyone asks, you don't know who I am.'

27

Wolfe jumps the back fence. Through the kitchen window she catches a glimpse of movement. Funani is on the phone, emphasising her point with jerky hand movements. Wolfe waits. As Funani's call finishes, she looks up, sees Wolfe, and flings open the back door.

'You! You were here this morning. You upset my Mazwi.'

'I'm so sorry for your loss–'

'It's your fault. You threatened him. He wasn't paying attention.'

'Mrs Ximba, please, can I come in. It wasn't me he was afraid of.'

'What are you talking about?'

Funani's eyes are red and puffy from crying, but she is otherwise immaculate: white dress with pale green leaves on it, chunky white necklace and earrings, her straightened hair in a perfect bob.

'The crash wasn't an accident. I think he was murdered.'

'You people will say anything for a story.'

'My name is Olivia Wolfe, from *The Post* in London. I've been to the scene of the accident. There were no skid marks and it happened at a spot with no CCTV. He was about to tell me something important, and now he can't. I think your husband was murdered.'

'No, no, the police said it was an accident.'

'I think they're wrong. Please, Funani, let me explain.'

'Why would anybody want my poor Mazwi dead?'

'If I'm right, your life may be in danger too.'

'Me?' Funani steps aside to let Wolfe enter. 'Five minutes. That's all.'

The house may have a tired exterior, but the kitchen is brand new with a gleaming stainless-steel refrigerator, polished stone countertops and even a Nespresso machine. Perhaps Ximba was spending some of his hidden fortune after all.

'They left such a mess. Why?' Funani shakes her head.

Cupboard doors hang open, drawers removed, and their contents scattered over the floor. The hallway is equally littered with possessions cast onto the carpet.

'Did the police do this?' Wolfe asks.

Funani raises a tissue to her eyes. 'They took things. They wouldn't tell me why. When my brother finds out, he will be furious. Msiza will answer for it. My brother's the mayor, you know.'

'What were they looking for?'

'I don't know. Mazwi's study looks like a bomb's hit it.' Tears roll down her cheeks.

'Do you have family?' Wolfe asks. 'Someone who can be with you?'

'My sister is on her way.'

'Shall I make some tea?' Wolfe asks.

'You British! Will tea bring back my husband?'

Wolfe looks down, unsure what to say. 'I'm sorry.'

When Wolfe looks up, Funani is studying her face. 'Why do you think it wasn't an accident?'

'There's no easy way to say this, I'm afraid. I think your husband was involved in something illegal. He probably had no idea how dangerous it was. And when he tried to get out of it, he was killed.'

'Illegal? No, no. He's a law-abiding man. That can't be right.'

Wolfe doesn't want to hurt her needlessly, but she has to ask the next question. 'I saw your husband meet a man called Terry Blunt at Tanz Café at eleven thirty last night. Do you know this man?'

'No, no, you are wrong. Mazwi was working in his study. He was here.'

'You were with him?'

'No, I was asleep. He was catching up on paperwork.'

'I'm sorry to say he left the house at eleven.'

Funani frowns. 'You were watching him? Why?'

'Because I want to find out who is behind this.'

Funani raises her hand to her heart. This is clearly very hard for her to take in. 'I don't know this Terry Blunt.'

'Did Mazwi have any connection to England?'

Funani laughs. It's a bitter, sad laugh. 'We have never left this country.'

'Any friends in England?'

'No. Why?'

'Just dotting the i's and crossing the t's.' *God, I sound like Casburn*, she thinks. 'Did the police take his laptop?'

'Yes.'

And the Major-General will wipe it clean.

The doorbell rings. 'That will be my sister.'

'Funani, can you go stay with her? It would be safer.'

'You're frightening me.'

'Please, stay with your sister. At least until the funeral.'

'What did he do? You must tell me.'

'He was getting paid by some dangerous people. I don't know why. But I'm going to find out.'

'It's me!' calls the visitor from the other side of the front door. 'Let me in.'

'Here,' says Funani, jotting down her mobile number and handing it to Wolfe. 'I have to know. Call me as soon as you know anything. And leave the back way.

'One more thing. There's a young reporter from the *Soweto Times* outside. Name of Busisiwe. She went to your husband's school. She wants to write a feature on him. She's a lovely girl. Will you give her the chance?'

'Funani!' The sister bangs on the door. 'Who's there with you? Let me in!'

'She will say nice things about Mazwi?' Funani asks.

'I will ask her to.'

Funani nods. 'Mazwi would want me to encourage his students. I will see her.'

Wolfe leaves by the rear door and joins Busisiwe at the front, just as Funani's sister enters the house.

'Funani will do the interview,' says Wolfe. 'Make him shine, for her sake. She needs something good in her life right now.'

28

Samuel watches a small but athletic young woman with short, dark hair talk briefly to a reporter, then head for her motorcycle. She walks past his pick-up, unaware of his presence on the other side of tinted windows. If he were to unwind the window he could reach out and touch her leather jacket. He senses her strength. Her resilience. She will be a challenge when the time comes. Why else would his client want her watched?

He usually receives a detailed brief on each target. This time it was just a blurred photo of an unidentified white woman in a black baseball cap and sunglasses, shot outside Moeta High School on a cheap phone. No name, no address. Only that she was in Johannesburg and working with a screwed-up Soweto cop named Mike Thusago.

As soon as Samuel landed in Johannesburg, he'd dealt with Ximba. Crushing his car had been an adrenaline rush, but over too fast. The police fell for it, of course. He later returned to the crash site and waited. If the woman was a reporter as he suspected, she'd turn up. Sure enough, there she was. Then he followed her here, to the dead man's house.

He taps the name of his client on his phone. It only rings once before it's picked up.

'I have her in my sight,' he says. 'You want me to take her?'

'Not yet. There's a British detective sniffing around too. Asking questions about Ximba. I don't want him getting suspicious. Have you worked out who she is yet?'

Samuel scratches the dark stubble on his cheek, irritated. He doesn't like being played with. 'You pay me to kill, not write bloody CVs.'

'She's Olivia Wolfe, a London journalist. Some might say infamous journalist. Ximba's grieving widow gave us the heads up.'

Samuel smirks. *Clearly, not so grieving.* He'd lay money on Funani taking Ximba's role as the syndicate's banker. He leans forward, the steering wheel pressing into his chest, as Wolfe straddles the motorcycle. She handles the bike's size and weight well. There's something feline about the suppleness of her limbs and the smoothness of her movements. He smiles. She's not like any journalist he's dealt with before.

29

Wolfe takes one more look through the motel room's only window, pulls the faded orange curtain back into position, then connects to Butcher Investigations through Skype. Butcher greets her. Ponnappa is in the background, seated at her monitor.

'Found some interesting stuff on Ximba's computer,' Ponnappa says. 'I've copied the good bits. Give me a sec and I'll be with you.'

In the meantime, Wolfe updates Butcher on Ximba's sudden death and what she saw and heard at Terry Blunt's warehouse.

'Done a background check on Blunt,' says Butcher. 'Born in Zimbabwe. Military for three years. Then a farmer. Grew sugar cane, so he knows the industry. But here's where it gets interesting. In 2000 Blunt was accused of smuggling elephant tusks inside containers of sugar cane. Never stood trial. He fled to South Africa, claiming his farm had been seized and his life threatened under Mugabe's ethnic cleansing. He was given asylum.'

'So, he has a connection to poaching?'

'Yes. There's more. A cold case involving a sugar cane farmer. Blunt's KwaZulu Natal Co-op wanted to buy him out. But the farmer didn't want to sell. Anyway, the guy turns up dead. Blunt was questioned, but no one was ever prosecuted.'

'I'm getting a bad feeling about him.'

'Agree. We'll see what we can do to track his business activities. Imports and exports. This could be how they move illegal goods around,' says Butcher.

Ponnappa walks her wheeled chair over to Butcher's monitor and waves at Wolfe. 'This is what I've got so far on the headmaster. First up, his online banking shows he's been moving money to and from ZIB Trading for at least twelve months. But following the money trail is tough. It'll take time.'

'Great work,' Wolfe says. 'I'd love to know where all this money is going.'

'There's more,' Ponnappa says. 'Owethu was right about Ximba. He was one sick puppy. Liked to visit snuff sites. Really horrible stuff. Most of his emails are mundane, but there's one that's got an encrypted file attached and the subject is: *You'll enjoy this*.'

'Can you open it?' Wolfe asks.

'Almost there. I'll ping you a message when it's done.'

Wolfe's burner phone vibrates. 'Give me a moment,' she says, and steps out of the webcam's view.

'Olivia are you alone?' Yushkov asks.

Wolfe eyes her laptop screen. Sees Butcher waiting patiently. 'No.'

'Can you be alone?'

'Yes.'

Wolfe calls out. 'I've got to take this. Give me two ticks.'

Putting on her baseball cap and sunglasses, she looks through the door's spyhole, sees nobody, and unlocks it. Outside the room, the air is heavy with diesel exhaust. She goes to the far end of the walkway and sits on the top step.

'We can talk now.'

'There is a place we can meet. Tonight,' Yushkov says.

'Tonight? But... You're in Johannesburg?'

'I will be.'

'For how long?'

'One night.'

'Really? Just one?'

'I must be somewhere tomorrow.'

That evasiveness again. Is this to protect her, or is he keeping something from her?

He continues, 'Olivia, I am sorry it must be like this.'

'Give me the address,' Wolfe says. Her heart beats as if she's just done a workout.

'Do not put it in your phone or write it down.' He tells her. She repeats it back to him.

'I'll be there from midnight until dawn,' he says.

'Why can't you stay longer?'

'I have commitments.'

'What kind of commitments?'

'Work. Listen to me, Olivia. You must be certain you are not followed.'

'I am always careful.'

'Be extra careful.'

'Are you being watched?'

'No. You are.'

Her stomach feels as if it's flipped over. 'Who by?'

'A professional. That's all I know. I will try to find out.'

It's a good job Wolfe is sitting down. People have threatened her before, but a professional killer is something else altogether. However, what's freaking her out the most is that Yushkov knows about it. How?

Before she can say another word, he is gone.

30

Wolfe slips back into the motel room and sits in front of her webcam, just as Ponnappa, thousands of miles away in London and clearly visible through their Skype video connection, punches the air. 'Ha! You can't shut me out!' she shouts at the screen.

'You're in?' Wolfe asks.

'I'm in!'

'Liv?' says Butcher, leaning forward to scrutinise her face. 'You look very pale. Is everything all right?'

Wolfe waves away his concern. He would be profoundly disappointed if he knew she had contacted Yushkov. And if he even suspected there was an assassin watching her, he would be on the next plane to Johannesburg. The last thing she wants to do is place him in danger.

'Jet-lagged, that's all,' she says.

Butcher raises a disbelieving eyebrow, but lets it pass.

Wolfe continues. 'What have you got?'

'Let's see,' says Ponnappa, opening the folder.

Inside are numbered photographs. They appear as thumbnails, too small to see the full detail but big enough to know there's a lot of blood.

Ponnappa clicks on the first photo.

Amateur shot. Probably taken on a phone using a flash. Heavily vignetted, the edges of the image are too dark, while the centre is over-exposed. There's a lot of red that glistens like silk. Amongst the red, a closeup of a face, taken in side profile. African origin. Young, not much older than Owethu. It takes a second or two for Wolfe to realise there is something missing. Where the victim's nose had been, there is only severed cartilage and bone.

'What the fu... That's barbaric. Why would anyone do that?' says Ponnappa.

'I have no idea,' Wolfe's voice is thin, her stomach churning. She can't quite believe what she's seeing.

'The blade would have been very sharp and strong,' says Butcher. 'Maybe a sword or machete?'

Ponnappa covers her mouth. 'Please tell me he was dead when they did this.'

'God, I hope so,' says Wolfe.

Her stomach heaves as the second photo opens. The same victim. A man. A full body shot. What remains of him. He's lying on cracked concrete, limbs splayed. His ears have been cut off, then neatly placed on the ground either side of his head. His right hand has been severed, just above the wrist, and shoved into his mouth.

This is too much for Ponnappa who springs from her chair, gagging. A door bangs as she leaves the office.

'He's showing off,' says Butcher, 'hence the subject line, *You'll enjoy this.*'

'It also tells us the murderer is connected to Ximba and that Ximba liked to see people being hacked to death. And to think he was a school teacher. Jeez.'

'I hate to say it,' Butcher says, 'but I think the victim was alive through this torture.'

Wolfe swallows back the bile creeping up her throat. 'Why do you say that?'

'If he was dead, there wouldn't be anywhere near this much blood.'

'Dear God.'

31

There are twelve photos in the encrypted file. The first two images had Ponnappa running to the bathroom. Wolfe, too, can barely hold on to the contents of her stomach. She is shaking, her skin cold and clammy. She's seen death before. But she's never seen a body so mutilated. Body parts deliberately severed. The third photo of the young man she suspects is Somali is a graphic close-up of his open jaw from which his severed hand is protruding.

'It's like the sicko is having fun. Mocking his victim,' Wolfe says to Butcher who is at the other end of the Skype video call.

'I've seen some terrible things in my time,' says Butcher, seated in his office in London, 'but this has to be one of the worst. A sadistic psychopath. I suspect the other images are not going to be pleasant. Do you want to continue? Probably best not to wait for Jwala.'

'I'm ready,' Wolfe replies.

The fourth photo is of a Caucasian woman. Brown hair. Blue eyes. Maybe mid-twenties.

'Another victim,' Wolfe says.

The woman is vertical, wrists bound with plastic ties, one end of a meat hook supports her bindings and the other end hangs over a horizontal ceiling rail, forcing the victim's arms straight up.

'What's that in the background?' Wolfe asks.

'Cattle carcasses,' says Butcher. 'Looks like a meat locker or slaughterhouse.'

The woman's face is a blur of movement, her mouth open.

'She was alive,' breathes Wolfe, barely able to speak.

Butcher runs a finger over dry lips and nods.

In the fifth photo, her nose has been sliced off, leaving a gory, gaping hole. Both ears have gone too. There is the briefest of moments when Wolfe has a vain hope the torturer stopped there. But when Butcher opens the sixth photo, Wolfe cannot stop a sob escaping her mouth, or the tears that sting her eyes.

The woman's belly is sliced open from top to bottom, her intestines trailing to the ground. And more.

'No, no, no, please tell me that's not... not a foetus.'

Butcher doesn't answer. There's no need. At the woman's feet lies an unborn child.

'I am going to find you,' says Wolfe. 'You sick fuck.'

She wants to punch something. Anything. She's up and pounding her fists into the mattress. What monster could rip an unborn child from a mother's womb and watch it die?

Even the hardened ex-detective has turned away. There's a wailing sound behind him. Ponnappa has both hands over her mouth, tears streaming down her cheeks.

'Can you cope with more?' Butcher asks.

Wolfe knows these barbaric images will be gouged into her memory for always. 'Yes.'

The next three shots are of a platinum blond man, a little older, perhaps in his thirties. His nose and ears are cut away like the previous victims, but this time the ears rest on his eyes and the nose protrudes from his mouth. He's lying on rotting wooden planks.

'Different location, different sex and age. The only thing they all have in common is the removal of the nose and ears,' says Butcher.

Images ten, eleven and twelve are of a Caucasian man in his late sixties or early seventies, weathered skin, bound around the chest by thick rope to the trunk of a tree, his mouth gagged. The ground is sandy. His nose and ears have been cut away but are not in any of the pictures. Instead, two of his fingers have been shoved into what were once his nasal cavity and maxillary sinus.

Butcher and Wolfe stay silent for a while. So overpowered with emotion, she can't think. She takes some deep breaths.

'A male killer?' Wolfe asks.

'I think so,' says Butcher. 'Women are more prone to commit crimes of passion, to kill in the moment. These murders are planned and meticulously executed. He'd study his victims. Watch them. Plan where he's going to take them. Three of the victims are male. He'd need the strength to immobilise them and possibly drag them to where he tortures them. And don't underestimate the strength it takes to hack through bone. So, yes, the killer's a man. He's probably killed before. Knows what he's doing. Likes to brag. And the arrangements he makes with the body parts, they've got to mean something to him. I'm sure there is a pattern here. We just can't see it yet.'

32

It's as if Butcher has been switched to mute. She sees his lips moving, but the last words she hears are *He'd study his victims. Watch them.*

Wolfe's eyes dart from the door to the window. She moves the curtain a fraction. Peers out. No sign of Blunt's Prado, or anyone suspicious in the motel car park.

'Where did you go?' asks Butcher. She's out of the webcam's range. 'What's wrong?'

'I think someone's watching me,' Wolfe says, not taking her eyes off the street.

One car has arrived in the car park since she last looked. A blue Suzuki Celerio with a child's seat in the back.

'Who?' Butcher asks.

'Don't know.'

The setting sun rests just above the rooftops and shines directly into her eye. She squints. It's hard to see detail. A white utility truck, known locally as a bakkie, pulls out of a second-hand car sales yard. She watches it drive away, then sits back on the bed so Butcher can see her through the webcam again. 'Maybe he turned on Ximba. Killed him. And now he's after me.'

'What makes you think that?' asks Butcher, his voice a pitch higher.

'A tip-off.'

'From who?' asks Butcher.

'It doesn't matter.'

'Of course it bloody matters!' snaps Butcher. 'It's your life we're talking about.'

Wolfe is taken aback. Butcher is normally preternaturally calm. That's one reason why he excelled as a detective. However much pressure he was under, however abhorrent the crime, he rarely let it affect him.

'A source.'

'We've always been frank with one another, Liv. Why shut me out now?' Butcher's eyes narrow and lips tighten. 'It's Yushkov, isn't it?'

A pause. 'Yes.'

'Jesus.' He looks down, shaking his head. She can see his jaw muscles tighten. 'He's in Johannesburg, isn't he?'

'Yes. He warned me there's an assassin watching me.'

Butcher inhales deeply, looks up. 'Did he give you anything else? Like a name?'

'No.'

Ponnappa, her face leached of its natural colour, looks over Butcher's shoulder. 'What about Casburn? He could be tailing you,' she says.

'Yushkov knows Casburn. It's not him.'

'Terry Blunt?' Butcher suggests.

'I don't think so. Blunt is heavy-handed. Loud. He's too clumsy to be an assassin.'

'How does Yushkov know?' Ponnappa asks.

A question Wolfe hasn't dared contemplate. 'He didn't tell me.'

'Olivia, think! What kind of people is Yushkov involved with to know this stuff?'

The wrong kind of people.

'We gave him little choice.'

'*We?*' Butcher's freckled face flushes with anger. 'This country gave him a pardon, which is more than he deserved. He was a Russian bloody spy.'

'No, he wasn't, and he saved my life more than once.'

'And you saved him from a life sentence, more's the pity. Can't you see he'll destroy you? Stay away from him!' Butcher's chair hits the floor as he suddenly stands and walks away.

Ponnappa grimaces, her eyes following Butcher who is now off-screen. 'Yushkov can help keep Olivia safe, right?' she tentatively suggests. 'Maybe it's a good thing Yushkov is around?'

'He's going to find out who it is,' Wolfe says.

Butcher comes back into view. 'Sorry, Liv. I shouldn't have lost it. Look, I detest the man. And I hate to say it, but if a professional killer is after you, Yushkov is handy to have around.'

'I don't need saving.'

'Christ!' Butcher slaps his palm on the table. 'Then come home. You're no match for a psychopath.'

33

Wolfe feels the residual heat of Butcher's fury long after their Skype connection is cut. She hastily warns Owethu and Mama Gcina. The assassin may have seen her with them, so they should be wary. Next, she tries to reach Thusago, but he doesn't pick up, neither his mobile nor landline. She tries not to let it bother her, but she's worried. She emails Cohen an update, with twelve photos of the victims attached, then tries phoning Casburn, leaving a voicemail message.

Dan. It's Olivia. I have evidence of four murders, connected to Ximba. Please call me. It's urgent.

She has no idea where the murders took place. Which country, even. So who does she contact? With Major-General Msiza potentially involved in a cover-up, Wolfe doesn't want to contact SAPS.

As darkness blankets the motel, Wolfe feels increasingly nervous. She double checks her go-bag. Checks the knife-comb is easy to grab. Checks the CZ 75 Thusago gave her. She chambers a round, then decocks the hammer. All she then has to do is give a squeeze on the double action trigger – this way if she has to react, she won't have to remember to flick the safety off. For the first time in her life she wears a gun holster on her belt. It feels awkward, weighty on her hip.

Unable to forget the photographs, she steels herself to look at them again. This time at the location. As she scrutinises the three images of the woman in the slaughterhouse, she notices a gold cross on a chain around her neck. Wolfe zooms in, then dials Butcher on FaceTime.

'I think the female in the slaughterhouse is Russian,' says Wolfe. 'She's wearing a Russian Orthodox cross around her neck.'

'Well spotted.' She waits for him to bring up the photo on his screen. 'But that doesn't mean she was killed in Russia. She might be Russian Orthodox and living in, say, South Africa.'

'I don't think so. Check the first photo of her. Bottom right. The cranberry juice bottle.'

She waits for Butcher to comment. 'Chudo-Yagoda?' he says.

'Exactly. I'd put money on it that's only available in Russia.'

'Then we can rule out Blunt as the killer. He's never left Africa. I checked.'

'Okay. But I think one of the victims was murdered in Africa, possibly South Africa.'

'How so?'

'Look at the old man. See the tree?' She pauses while Butcher finds the right image. 'That tree bugged me. I'd seen one like it before. Now I remember where. Outside Ximba's school. Give me a sec and I'll google it.' She searches, using the tree's identifying features: long thorns and large ear-shaped seeds. She finds what she's looking for. 'Got it. It's a camel thorn. Found mainly in Southern Africa.'

Butcher considers this for a moment. 'Have you talked to Casburn? You should brief him as soon as possible.'

'Tried to. Left him a message.'

Butcher taps a finger on the cleft of his chin, thinking. 'There's something else. Not related to this investigation.' He looks at her sheepishly. 'I've got someone keeping an eye on Davy.' Her brother.

Wolfe frowns. 'Why would you do that?'

'I'd have thought that was obvious, Liv. He blames you and me for his jail time.'

'He's harmless, Jerry.'

'Maybe not. He was seen talking to a PI. This guy is the scum of the earth. An ex-crim. He passed Davy an envelope. Looked like cash.'

The tip of Wolfe's tongue plays with the stud in it. 'Okay. That's weird.'

'Yes, I thought so too. Maybe Davy's being paid for information?'

Her phone rings. Thusago is trying to reach her. 'Jerry, gotta go. It's Mike. We'll talk soon.'

Wolfe connects to her incoming call.

'What's so urgent?' says Thusago, abruptly.

Wolfe tells him about the gruesome images and the news she is being watched.

'I think you should leave town,' she says. 'Take your family away. Somewhere unexpected.'

Thusago is silent.

'I'm so sorry, Mike. I wish I'd never involved you,' she says.

'You think he killed Ximba, don't you?'

'It makes sense.'

'I will not run.'

'Your wife and son need you. Stay with a friend. Take a holiday.'

'I will think about it.'

The line goes dead.

34

Samuel looks straight at Wolfe as she peers out of her motel room window. But she can't see him, parked down the road, the setting sun in her eyes. He thought she'd noticed him when he was in the second-hand car lot, which is why he'd driven away, nice and casual. Then double-backed later.

Stake-outs drive him crazy. And boredom stresses him. And when he's stressed the grafted skin on his neck gets itchy, like a healing scab.

He undoes the top button of his collared polo shirt and scratches the raised, square-shaped patch of skin on his neck. It has never felt like it belongs to him, like a large Band-Aid forever stuck to him. The transplanted skin came from his thigh, which, like the rest of him, is hirsute, but for some reason the graft has always been hairless. So it stands out. Draws people's stares. Which is why he's stuck with wearing collared shirts.

As he thinks about Msiza, his nails dig deeper into his skin. That parading peacock couldn't even manage to find Ximba's laptop. Nobody seems to know where it is. Not even Funani. Does Olivia Wolfe have it?

His client wants it to protect the syndicate. Samuel wants it because of the photos he emailed Ximba. If the boss knew he'd been sharing pictures of his kills, he's pretty sure he'd find himself hunted by another assassin. At the very least, it's bad for business.

He reckons the black kid helped Wolfe steal Ximba's laptop. It will take her a while to bypass the encryption, and even if she does, she won't be able to trace the file back to him. He's used a VPN. And the victims' bodies will never be found. Except for the local guy maybe. Samuel left something behind. It was a joke. He couldn't resist doing it. Now he wishes he hadn't. Were the accolades he got worth it? His followers in various dark web chat rooms said he was a genius. A magnificent statement. So yes, it was worth it. At the time.

Now he has to clear up his mess.

His phone rings. The boss. Samuel shifts in his seat, uneasy. The call is unexpected.

'Yes?' Samuel answers.

'The journalist. Olivia Wolfe. I want her dead.'

Relieved this is not about the photos, Samuel asks, 'How?'

'I want her to disappear. No body.'

Samuel smiles. 'Thank you,' and he means it.

Wolfe leaves her room, crash helmet in hand, and scampers down the steps to the car park. She's changed her clothes. Looks like she has lipstick on.

'Got to go, boss. She's on the move.'

Wolfe gets on her motorbike. She has a bag on her back. Could the laptop be in it? The bike's engine growls into life. Samuel is torn. Follow her or search the room? Follow.

He'll come back and search the motel later. Samuel turns the bakkie's raspy ignition. She takes a left. He's facing the other direction, parked on the right-hand side of the road. The evening traffic is heavy. Slow-moving. Wolfe accelerates, weaving through the traffic jam. Samuel forces his way out into the traffic, but he can't make the U-turn. A tanker truck blocks him. He cranes his neck around, watching his target disappear.

'Fuck! Fuck! Fuck!'

35

The overweight, white-haired Sergeant Donaldson leans back in his chair. It's patently obvious to Dan Casburn that Donaldson is on the home stretch to retirement and has no intention of letting an outsider rock the boat.

'As I've already explained,' Donaldson sighs, 'there's nothing to investigate. It was a traffic accident, man.'

'With the greatest of respect, there's plenty to investigate,' says Casburn. 'Mazwi Ximba was under investigation. He was linked to a UK national. Possible money laundering. The morning he died he was going to meet a journalist. Perhaps he was going to tell all. We'll never know, because he was conveniently killed in a road accident. The truck driver doesn't brake. Flees the scene. The accident happens at a CCTV blind spot. What does all this say to you?' Casburn asks, the derision in his voice barely disguised.

'Says he was having a run of bad luck.' The officer grins, then possibly realises he's gone too far. He clears his throat. 'Sir, you haven't shown us a shred of evidence. You won't even give us the name of this British person he was allegedly working with.' Donaldson leans forward. 'Ximba was a model citizen. Liked and respected.' He checks his watch; he wants to go home.

Casburn blinks once and his jaw sets tight, slicing in half the Nicorette gum he's been chewing.

'At least get forensics to fingerprint the truck cabin,' Casburn says.

'Ach, sorry. No can do. Gone to the scrapyard.'

Casburn looks at the wall behind Donaldson, at a photo taken when he was a young officer. A graduation ceremony. Every face is white. Casburn isn't really interested in the photo. He's buying himself thinking time. The message is loud and clear: Ximba's death is not going to be investigated and South Africa's police force is not going to co-operate, contrary to Msiza's warm promises of support.

What a waste of time.

Casburn's mobile rings. He grabs it, sees the caller ID is Olivia Wolfe, the last person he wants to talk to. He declines the call, switches the ringer off and pockets it. Donaldson uses the break in their conversation to walk to the door and open it.

'Sergeant, I have a few more questions, and in the spirit of co-operation between our two forces I hope you can spare me a few more minutes of your precious time.'

This time the sarcasm is not lost on the sergeant.

'My pleasure,' he replies, with equal sarcasm. He closes the door and slumps down into his desk chair.

Casburn goes for the jugular. He's got nothing to lose.

'Can you explain why Major-General Msiza is involved in this case if we are just dealing with an accident?'

'You are mistaken. He is not.'

'I'm confused. Why then would he visit Funani Ximba a few hours after the accident?'

'Ah, he was simply paying his respects to the mayor's sister.'

'I see.' Casburn sees very clearly. 'Your officers removed items from Ximba's home. I'd like to see them.'

'Of course.'

Casburn stands.

'If you find the truck driver, I'd like to question him. Here is my card. Call me on that number.' He places his business card on Donaldson's desk. 'Thank you for your time.' *You arsehole*, he thinks.

Casburn holds his cool until he reaches his hire car, then he kicks a tyre. His first investigation as leader of SO24 is going nowhere and he looks like a complete twat. Everywhere he turns he's blocked. He hates feeling powerless. And he detests lazy coppers. His phone vibrates, and he checks the screen. It's his boss, Sutton. *Perfect!*

'Sir?'

'The Chancellor has cancelled his African trip.'

Casburn wants to swear, but he holds his tongue.

'Do you know why?'

'No, but I think it would be fair to surmise that somebody informed him that you were asking awkward questions about his co-signatory.'

'So, Sackville is going to try to distance himself,' says Casburn. 'Is Sukletin still coming?'

'Yes, but he changed his plans. Dropped his visit to Jo'burg. Flies into Zimbabwe Saturday morning. And out Sunday evening.'

'Landing at Harare?'

'No, Buffalo Range Airport in the south.'

'Never heard of it.'

'I suspect that's the point.'

'Then where?'

'We don't know. You need to be at Buffalo Range Airport before Sukletin lands. Your visa has been arranged.'

'Thank you, sir.'

'How are you finding the local police?'

'Unhelpful. Obstructive. I'm beginning to doubt Msiza, sir.'

'Then work solo. You haven't much time before Sukletin arrives. Find out what's going on. I'm relying on you, Casburn.'

'Yes, sir.'

Casburn sits in his car for a while, grappling with his next move. He didn't get any sleep last night. Not that it would normally bother him. But he knows when he's been outmanoeuvred, and it galls him. Maybe Wolfe knows something helpful? Should he return her call? His mouth is parched. He really could do with a drink. A strong drink.

Fuck that. Wolfe will just pump him for information. He's had enough.

He drives to the nearest bar. He plans to stay there until they kick him out.

36

The dog fight has started. He can hear the savage snarls, the yelps of pain, the men surrounding the pit yelling, 'Kill, kill, kill!'

Samuel is parked outside the abandoned JMT building in Newtown. The whole decrepit warehouse is covered in graffiti, like scars on the fighting dogs. The punks who do it call it 'street art' and say their inspiration is Roger Ballen. Do they think the pit bulls give a shit? Or that the punters even notice? Or that the bums who huddle here at night feel better about their fucked-up lives because of it? He snorts a derisory laugh.

Samuel knows what true art is.

He started with animals. As a kid, it was cats. Drowning, strangling, smashing. But after the initial thrill, there was nothing to keep the memories alive. So, he started borrowing his father's camera and photographing the bodies, arranging them in patterns, secretly developing the film.

His family's tobacco farm in Vaalwater in South Africa's Limpopo province was beset by black thieves who would climb the fence to steal the maize, their secondary crop. At twelve, Samuel's daddy taught him to use a rifle. They'd shoot to kill. At first, Samuel didn't know what happened to the bodies, then one day he discovered severed human feet in the freezer, buried deep beneath the meat. 'My trophies,' his daddy explained. 'Don't you go messing with them, you hear me?' Three years later Samuel found a naked thirteen-year-old white girl in the maize. Dead. Bloody, it looked like she'd been raped too. She looked so pretty, but he could make her look better. Samuel took the severed black feet from the freezer and carefully placed them along the dead girl's spine. It said everything he had to say about his country. He took photos, shared them in chat rooms visited by like-minded people. It was beautiful, they said. Expressive. They wanted more.

Startled back to the present by a Mercedes crawling along the dark street, Samuel watches the lone driver go past. Probably searching for prostitutes or drugs or both. No threat.

Samuel likes coming to this derelict neighbourhood. No CCTVs. Nobody will question him. Here, he fits right in. But tonight, he can't relax. Olivia Wolfe has seen to that. Unable to follow her, he doubled back to her motel, opened every drawer, turned the bed upside down, cut open the mattress, prodded every loose tile, checked every possibly hiding place. But no laptop. Not even hers.

He knew she was a cut above the rest. He's researched her. She's survived war zones. Witnessed genocide. She's brave. Maybe a bit reckless. She pursues her goal, no matter what. He knows what it's like to be driven. And, he thinks, running a tongue over his upper lip, she's a dirty bitch. There are photos of her on the Net, taken some months ago, fucking a Russian spy. She nearly lost her job because of it. He's fascinated by her body piercings: tongue, nipples, belly button. He wonders if she enjoys the pain when the skin is first punctured. He imagines ripping the piercings out. He's going to make her do things she never imagined.

He's getting hard just thinking about it.

37

Samuel gets out of his pick-up. The freeway traffic reverberates above, punctuated by the staccato beats of tyres crossing joins in the concrete. From inside the derelict building, a dog squeals. It knows it's going to die. Those who bet on the weaker dog yell at it to fight. Those who bet on the stronger dog scream at it to finish the job.

Distracted, Samuel doesn't hear the soft tread of somebody behind him until almost too late. He darts to his left just as the knife is jabbed upwards into the right-hand side of his back, just below the rib cage. It misses the obvious target – his liver – penetrating the fleshy part of his waist, puncturing skin and muscle. Samuel inhales. The pain is intense. Exhilarating. Certainly not debilitating. The blade is ripped out, the assailant intent on striking again. His moves are powerful and unflinching.

Samuel bends his knees, and leaning back against his assailant, pushes the soles of his feet up onto the side of his bakkie. He pushes back hard, forcing the attacker backwards, staggering. Samuel may be short, but he's wiry and fast. He already has a hand inside his jacket and grips a M9A3 Beretta with a suppressor and night sights. Samuel turns fast, the pistol drawn. The man he faces wears a ski mask, the blade he carries is a hunting knife with serrated edge.

His opponent is a tall, muscular man, but this doesn't mean he's slow. The attacker throws himself to the ground and rolls. Samuel fires. There's an unmistakable grunt as the bullet hits its mark. He still somehow manages to roll behind one of the freeway's pillars. Samuel fires again, too late.

He's at a disadvantage now, out in the open. This is a battle he knows he'll lose. Samuel thrives on surprising his enemy, disabling them before they can put up a fight.

Samuel runs for his bakkie, yanks open the driver's door, has one leg in the footwell when he is literally dragged from the cabin by his jacket. A muscular arm closes around his throat in a chokehold. He tries to point his pistol behind him, but his hand is slammed down onto the bonnet so hard, he expects broken bones. The gun tumbles to the asphalt from his now useless hand. He's hurled to the ground, the back of his head smashing into the roadway. Samuel almost passes out. When he opens his eyes, the man straddles his chest, his knees crushing each arm, his own M9A3 aimed at his forehead.

'Move one millimetre and you die,' says the man.

'What do you want?' asks Samuel.

Sirens blare. Red and blue lights flash. Two police cars head for them. Samuel's assailant glances over his shoulder then down at his target. Why doesn't he pull the trigger?

The man leans so close Samuel can feel his breath on his face through the slit of his mask. He presses a forearm down hard on Samuel's throat, the gun muzzle boring into his temple.

'Go near Olivia Wolfe, you die. You tell the man you work for she knows nothing.' He pushes down harder on Samuel's throat. Puce in the face, Samuel is close to passing out. 'Tell him Msiza has the laptop. He's double-crossed you. You understand?'

Samuel's vison is blurred. He chokes, trying to respond. Tyres skid. The headlights are blinding.

'Police! Drop your weapon!'

Samuel doesn't see the fist coming. A sudden burst of agony and he's out cold.

38

Wolfe flies along the M1 on her motorcycle heading northeast. Normally vigilant, she now borders on paranoia, constantly watching for vehicles following her. When she's about halfway to the destination Yushkov gave her, she leaves the freeway and heads for a multi-storey car park. She knows it has two exits. She's done her homework. Killing the engine in a dark corner on the first level, she waits. Her hand rests on her holster. From her vantage point she has a clear view of the entry boom gates. In ten minutes, only four vehicles enter, none of them suspicious. Perhaps Yushkov is wrong. Where is the assassin he claims is watching her?

She leaves via the rear exit, which takes her to a different street from the one she used to enter.

Accelerating, she weaves in and out of traffic, watchful for speed cameras and police cars but determined to flush out anyone following her. She checks her mirrors every few seconds. As far as she can tell, no one manoeuvres to keep up with her.

Her next stop has also been carefully researched: a biker's bar. She leaves her motorcycle in the midst of twenty or so others parked out front and enters The Workshop. Inside, a band plays heavy metal. The air is hot and thick with the smells of leather, cigarettes, beer and chips. She orders a Castle Lager and a beefburger, then takes a seat on a high stool facing the front window so she can watch both her bike and new arrivals. She doesn't touch the beer: she has to keep her wits about her. But she bolts the burger. Then checks the time: 11.37pm.

Two middle-aged bikers with shaved heads and tattooed arms, pull up outside and join a group on the front deck smoking joints. They talk and laugh, posing her no threat. A young guy gets out of a car and has a smoke. Wolfe watches as one of the middle-aged men buys some pills off the dealer.

'You haven't touched your beer.'

Standing near her, a man who looks to be in his thirties, with a long but well-groomed auburn beard and buzzcut hair, grins at her. His pupils are too wide, his manner a little too intense. He moves from foot to foot repeatedly. She wonders what he's on.

'Here,' she replies. 'You have it.' She pushes it along the narrow table towards him. 'I've got to go, anyway.'

'But you just arrived. What's the rush? I'll get you something else. What would you like?'

Perhaps he's just chatting her up? Or is he a killer?

Wolfe flicks a look out of the window. Another bike pulls up. No new cars. No sign of Blunt's Prado. No apparent interest in her. Except for this guy.

'You a regular here?' she asks.

'Yah.' He sits on the stool next to her, his feet twitching up and down repeatedly.

Wolfe leans in. 'Do you know the barman?'

'Yah. Why?'

She drops her voice, forcing him to lean close. 'Just heard the cops are about to raid this place. Tonight.' She slides off the stool. 'I'm outta here.'

He jerks his chin up. 'How do you know?'

'Scanner. Police radio.'

'You serious?'

Wolfe nods and heads for the door, then looks back.

He's talking to the barman. Word spreads fast, as she had hoped. Wolfe pulls on her helmet, straddles her motorcycle and waits. It's not long before half a dozen others get on their bikes. Like a motorcade, with identical cars switching places to disguise which car the VIP is in, Wolfe leaves the car park amidst six other bikers, secure in the knowledge it would be virtually impossible in the darkness to work out which bike is hers.

39

Wolfe switches off her motorcycle's engine, dismounts, and padlocks it to a young jacaranda tree, three houses down from the address Yushkov gave her. It's two minutes to midnight and leafy Norwood Avenue is noiseless. The large houses are in darkness behind their security gates, the affluent residents sound asleep. The go-bag on her back with its ESAPI bulletproof plates and the gun in her holster are comforting, but she can't help asking herself, yet again, if this meeting is madness.

The house she is looking for is hidden behind a dense twelve-foot-high cypress hedge, but the electronic gates are wide open. Yushkov hasn't said who owns the property, or if they'll be there. The windows are dark. The only light comes from a bell-shaped porch light over the front door.

The drive is narrow, lined on both sides by cypress trees. The pale light of the almost full moon helps Wolfe find her way. The drive opens out into a paved turning circle with an ornamental fountain at its centre. She's reluctant to ring the doorbell and she can't look into the front windows either: azaleas and hydrangeas crowd too thickly under the windows to clamber through. Feeling increasingly on edge, Wolfe sends Yushkov a message on her burner phone:

Arrived. Where are you?

The phone is switched to vibrate: the last thing she wants to do is wake the neighbours and have the police banging on the door. A bird's high-pitched shriek shatters the quiet. She's heard it before. A nightjar. But it has her spinning around, searching the shadows for Yushkov.

He assured her this place was safe. It feels far from it. She hasn't told anyone where she is, not even Butcher. Especially not Butcher. For the umpteenth time Wolfe checks the time: 12.03am. He said he would be here at midnight. So where is he?

There's a clank. Wolfe jumps. Then an electronic whir. The wrought iron gates at the end of the drive are closing. Somebody is operating them. If it's Yushkov, why hasn't he shown himself? Is this a trap? She stares at the burner, frowning. Still no message.

A crack of twigs behind her. Wolfe spins, the pistol drawn. A tabby cat freezes, then scuttles into the bush.

40

Wolfe's burner phone vibrates. A message at last:
Go to back of house.

With pistol raised, Wolfe follows the flagstone path, ducking under low-hanging branches. She uses her phone's torch. Wolfe navigates past a rectangular table in glass and metal with six chairs. Beyond, a slice of lawn and a kidney-shaped fishpond, with a wall of cypresses.

A light suddenly blazes through two narrow stained-glass windows, either side of a stable-style back door. Wolfe almost has a heart attack. She retreats into the shadows and holds the CZ 75 steady, aiming at the middle of the door. It opens, the wood warped with age, scraping on the flagstones. She cannot see much more than a silhouette of a tall man with wide, muscular shoulders who almost fills the doorway, but she instinctively knows it's Vitaly Yushkov.

'Why is it when we meet, you always try to kill me?' he asks.

She doesn't have to see his face properly to know he is smiling. Wolfe lowers the gun to a forty-five-degree angle and relaxes her finger on the trigger. 'Maybe because you have a knack of freaking me out.' She glances up at the rear bedroom windows, lights out, curtains drawn.

'What is this place?' Wolfe asks.

'The owners are away. The dogs are with them.'

'So, we're breaking and entering?'

'I have permission.'

'Cameras?'

'None. If you saw the dogs, you would understand.'

'You are alone?'

'I am always alone.' It is a matter-of-fact statement. His life is, by necessity, a lonely one.

'Are you going to invite me in?' she asks.

Yushkov steps out of the way. She holsters the pistol and enters the house.

To the left is the living room, the sofa in bold floral fabric. Ahead is a kitchen, the floor tiles are terracotta, the ceiling, exposed honey-coloured beams. Shaker-style wooden chairs, solid table, Aga cooker, blue and white china plates on a wooden wall rack. The back door clicks shut behind her. She swivels round. Yushkov turns the key in the lock, bolts it, then leans with his back against the door. He is still. His pale blue eyes study her face.

She takes a good look at him. Same lop-sided smile. The semi-circular scar under his left eye has faded, but is still raised, the result of an interrogation that almost killed him. His beard is new, the colour of pale driftwood. Befitting of a man forced to drift by forces beyond his control. Until this moment she had no idea his fair hair was wavy. The last time she saw him he had a buzzcut. He now looks younger, leaner, fitter. Perhaps life in South Africa suits him.

'It is good to see you,' he says.

Feeling self-conscious, Wolfe tucks a strand of hair behind an ear and opens her mouth to speak, then closes it. She'd imagined throwing herself into his arms, but now she's here, she feels an odd sense of despair. Here is the man she wants more than anything, and yet she can only have him for a few hours.

His smile fades. 'What is wrong?'

He takes a step towards her. Instinctively she puts out her hand to stop him. He freezes.

Wolfe cannot look at him. Instead, she stares at a tiny beetle scuttling past the skirting board. She fears he will see her need. How much she has missed him.

'I hoped you would call,' Yushkov says.

Another step closer. He could touch her, but he doesn't. He removes his leather gloves and pockets them. His smell is familiar and comforting: soap and sun-baked skin, and the faintest hint of cigarettes. In black T-shirt, jeans and heavy boots, his gear is the mirror image of hers.

'Guess you didn't get the memo,' Wolfe says, tugging at her black T-shirt, her voice flaky, the joke lame.

'I guess not.' Yushkov tilts his head to one side. 'What is wrong, Olivia? Were you followed?'

'No, it's not that.' She tries to find the right words. 'Seeing you again is... difficult... bittersweet.'

Yushkov wraps his arms around her, his touch as light as a sheet on her skin. Almost a foot taller than her, she is lost within his embrace. For the first time since she arrived in South Africa, she feels safe. The irony is not lost on her. After all, most people believe him a killer.

He says in her ear, 'Every day I think of you. I have missed you, Olivia Wolfe.'

41

Wolfe is the first to pull away from their embrace. She needs to get used to seeing him again and to the weirdness of their situation. She dumps her bag under the kitchen table and drapes her jacket over the back of a chair. Her holstered pistol is now visible.

'Nice piece.' Yushkov nods at the CZ 75 in her holster. 'Where did you get it?'

'A friend.'

'It is good you are armed.'

On the table are two shot glasses and a bottle of Zubrówka Zu Bison Grass vodka. The drink has a greenish hue.

Yushkov pours them both a drink, then takes her hand. It envelops hers, the skin rough, but the grip is light. He leads her into a lounge room of chintz floral sofas and armchairs, and bookshelves overstuffed with paperbacks and travel books. The matching chintz curtains are drawn. Neither turns on a light. Wolfe sits on the sofa crossed-legged facing him.

'At least some things never change,' she says, raising the glass. She remembers celebrating the successful outcome of a scientific expedition in Antarctica with Yushkov, drinking way too much of his vodka. That was probably the last time she saw him really happy. Laughing and joking. After that, their brief moments of pleasure were tinged with fear.

'What shall we toast?' Wolfe asks.

'To this moment.'

'To this moment, and others,' Wolfe says pointedly.

He says nothing. The glasses chime as they touch. Wolfe watches as Vitaly downs his vodka immediately, then she finishes hers.

'Why are you in Johannesburg?' Yushkov asks.

A few months ago she trusted this man with her life. But his reluctance to talk about his work makes her reticent to talk about hers.

'Following some leads. Possible money laundering by a British national with ties to South Africa.'

Yushkov pours more vodka. 'Who is the Englishman?'

Wolfe tenses. It dawns on her that they can never have a normal conversation. 'I'm not sure yet. And you? You have a job?'

He tilts his head. A silent apology.

'This isn't going to work, is it?' she says. 'You can't tell me what you're doing here, and I can't tell you either.'

Wolfe has an odd sensation that he is far away, as if looking at him through binoculars.

'We don't have to talk,' Yushkov says. 'Let me hold you. Please.' He kicks off his boots, lays his head on one armrest of the sofa and drapes his long legs over the other. Perhaps he's right. Perhaps they shouldn't talk. Wolfe removes her boots and lies next to him on the soft cushions, her head in the crook of his arm. He strokes her hair, then kisses her nose.

'I have dreams about your nose.'

Wolfe laughs.

'Why do you laugh?'

'Because of all the bits of me you could dream about, you choose my nose.'

'I have dreamt about your skin, too.'

He strokes her cheek with the back of his fingers. The barest touch. Her heartbeat quickens. She knows her desire blinds her.

Makes her vulnerable. She should push his hand away. Ask him how he knows about this hitman. Then leave. No good will come of prolonging their fractured and dangerous relationship. Except that their connection is nothing like she has ever experienced before.

Instead of stopping him, she brings his palm to her lips and kisses it, then cups it against the side of her face.

'And your lips,' Yushkov says. 'I dream about your lips. And that stud in your tongue.'

He lifts her chin and kisses her mouth. Just a peck, over in a second.

'I cannot change the situation, Olivia. I wish I could. I wish we could be like normal people. Go out to dinner, drink, make love. Live together. I would want this very much.'

'With me?'

'Of course with you. But my life is mapped out. By others. It is not the life I want, but it is the one I have. It is not possible for me to have a relationship. You know this, don't you?'

'I know you think this. But give it time. We can work something out.'

Yushkov hugs her tight. 'Do not hope for this.'

He sounds defeated. This is not the Yushkov she knows.

'What's going on, Vitaly? Something's wrong.'

He places a finger on her lips. 'We only have a few hours.'

'Then let's make the most of them,' Wolfe says. *And sod the consequences*, she thinks.

42

Yushkov switches off the only light in the house and leads her up the stairs and into a bedroom where he opens the drawn curtains enough to allow moonlight to penetrate the darkness. He takes off his belt. Attached to it is a hunting knife which he places on the bedside table.

'You won't need that,' he says, looking at the pistol on her hip.

He unholsters her pistol and places it next to his knife. His arms close tight around her. He whispers, 'You want this?'

'I want this.'

He lifts her T-shirt over her head, dropping it to the floor, and unclasps her black bra. He gazes at her body for a long moment, then caresses her breast and runs his finger over her nipple ring. Wolfe is conscious she's not as trim as when he last saw her. Her head wound, and the resulting migraines, scuppered her gym routine.

As if reading her mind Yushkov says, 'You are as beautiful as I remember.'

His fingers slide down her stomach to the pearl in her belly button piercing.

'You still wear this. Good.'

Wolfe grips the bottom of his T-shirt and lifts it. He helps her. As he pulls it over his head, he winces. There's a large and livid purple bruise on his lower right ribcage. At the centre is a blackened circular wound. Her touch causes his muscles to spasm.

'What happened?' she asks, knowing the answer already.

As a foreign correspondent for *The Post*, she had been embedded with the British SAS in Iraq as part of the effort to reclaim Mosul from Isil. A soldier removed his damaged body armour. It had stopped the bullet, but his skin was an angry confusion of red, purple and yellow, in much the same way Yuskov's is.

'If I say it was an accident, will you believe me?' he asks.

'You know I won't.'

'I was shot. The vest saved me. I am not hurt.' He places a finger softly on her lips. 'Forget it. It is not important. This is important.'

He kisses her on the lips, the tip of her nose, and runs his tongue down her neck. He sucks on her skin, it briefly smarts. She laughs.

'I haven't had a love bite since I was a teenager.'

'I don't want you to forget me.'

'No chance of that'

Still in her jeans, Wolfe lies on the bed and beckons him to her.

Yushkov lies next to her and runs his tongue over her breasts, then takes a swollen nipple between his lips, and squeezes. He plays with the silver ring through her areola.

'It must be painful. To pierce something so sensitive.'

'It was kind of erotic.'

Yushkov raises an eyebrow. 'This is true?'

'I have a high pain tolerance. It felt more like a sting. As a kid, I fell and broke two bones in my fingers. I didn't even notice until I saw them bent back the wrong way.'

'You are lucky. Less pain is good.'

Yushkov runs his tongue down her stomach to her belt line. He undoes her jeans and pulls them down slowly, kissing her mound, her inner thighs, her ankles. He pauses to gaze at her body before he peels off her black knickers. His stare is so intense, it's as if he sees her very soul.

His tongue migrates up her inner thigh and touches her most

sensitive spot. She inhales sharply. Already aroused, it will not take long for her to orgasm.

'I want you inside me,' she says.

He lets go of her hips and sits up. 'It is too fast. We should take our time.'

'I can't wait. From behind,' she says, nodding at the mirrored wardrobe.

'You will always surprise me,' Yushkov says.

She lies face down on the bed, with her feet on the floor. She turns her head to one side, so she can watch him in the mirror. He runs his fingers down her spine and parts her thighs. She feels the tip of his cock brush her clit, then push into her. Wolfe cries out.

'This way, I will not be able to hold back. Are you sure?' he asks.

'I'm sure.'

He takes a measured breath then moves slowly within her. She watches him in the mirror. His eyes follow the contours of her body. His muscles tense.

Wolfe lowers her hand to her already stimulated clit. She keeps her touch feather-light. Their need is intense. The heat within her grows. There's an unbearable ache. Almost unaware of what she is doing, she pushes back onto his cock, forcing him deeper into her. His grip on her tightens. His rhythm speeds up. She turns her head again to see him in the mirror, his every muscle taut. Wolfe brings herself close to the edge. She spasms. He feels it and loses control, plunging into her. The burning heat of her orgasm ripples through her belly again and again.

43

Wrapped in each other's arms, tangled in the sheets, their heartbeats slowing, their bodies begin to cool. Yushkov turns on his side and props his head up in one hand. Not for the first time he winces, his ribcage's bruise clearly painful.

'There isn't a day goes by without me wondering where you are and what you're doing,' she says. 'I need you in my life, Vitaly.'

Yushkov pulls away from her and sits up.

'Vitaly?'

'Do not fall in love with me, Olivia.'

His words hit her like a slap. Wolfe struggles to catch her breath. Waves of competing emotion battle inside her: embarrassment, grief, anger.

'I must go,' she says, throwing back the sheets and heading for the bathroom.

In one fluid movement, Yushkov is up and barring her way.

'My words came out wrong. English is not my first language. Please.' Wolfe won't look at him. Her eyes are watery. 'You are very special to me, Olivia. If my life had not taken this course, I would be with you. But I cannot be the man you deserve.'

'Why? In time, things will calm down. We can be together. There has to be a way.' She hears the pleading in her voice and knows she probably sounds pathetic.

His silence crushes her.

Wolfe pulls away, grabs her pistol and holster, picks up her discarded clothes, runs down the stairs and hastily puts them on.

Yushkov appears, dressed. 'Stay a while. Please.'

'No.' Wolfe takes her leather jacket off the back of the chair.

'It was selfish of me to ask you here. I know this. But I had to see you one more time.'

It takes a few seconds for the words to sink in.

'One more time?'

'There are things I cannot tell you,' he begins.

'You're in trouble?'

He nods.

'Let me help you,' she says.

'You cannot.'

'For God's sake, Vitaly, whatever you've done, just tell me.'

He shakes his head.

Wolfe picks up her backpack and helmet.

'This is *not* the end, Vitaly. I won't let it be.'

'You will hear things that will make you doubt me.'

'Like what?'

'Let me say what must be said.' Yushkov stands so close she feels his breath on her face. 'Leave South Africa. Today. Go to the airport. Do it now. You have everything you need in that bag. Do not go back to your motel.'

'Why?'

'I can do no more to protect you. The man watching you is brutal. He goes by the name of Samuel.'

Wolfe struggles to find her voice. 'What else can you tell me?'

'He has a skin graft on his neck. A raised square patch. Rumour has it the surgeon did a bad job. Samuel killed him for it.'

'Jesus Christ.' Wolfe shudders. 'What nationality is this Samuel?'

'Nobody knows.'

'What else?'

'He is in Johannesburg and drives a white Mitsubishi Colt pick-up. Old model.'

Wolfe opens her eyes wide. 'How could you possibly know that, unless...'

'I am trying to protect you.'

'Tell me how you know Samuel.'

'Casburn found me. We talked.'

'*What*? You hate Casburn.'

'Casburn fears you are in danger,' says Yushkov. 'I know this to be true.'

'Wait a second. You talked about me? With Casburn?' She cannot keep the bewilderment from her voice.

'Yes.' Yushkov takes her hand. 'I hate him for what he did. But he tells the truth when he says you must leave South Africa.'

Wolfe rips her hand away. 'I will not be told what to do by either of you.'

'Then there is nothing more to say.'

Yushkov unlocks the back door, switches off the light and steps outside. Wolfe follows. He hastens down the side path. The night sky has turned indigo. Dawn is approaching. Wolfe catches up with him at the front of the house and grabs his arm.

'I will leave South Africa. Right now. But only with you.'

'I can't.'

He speeds up, heads down the drive. The electronic gates open. In the distance, a police siren wails. It barely registers with Wolfe. Her feet won't move. Is this how it ends?

When Yushkov reaches the street, he looks back at her. Stock-still.

'Я люблю тебя!' he calls out.

Then he is gone.

The police siren grows louder. Closer. The gates begin to close. She runs through them and along empty streets to her bike, kicks it into life and tears off, the scream of the engine competing with the siren to upend the pre-dawn quiet. She takes the first turn off

Norwood Avenue, narrowly missing a police car, no doubt heading for the house they've just vacated. A house that's covered in their DNA. She doesn't care. All she can think of is Yushkov's last words.

At the very moment she has lost him, he tells her that he loves her.

44

Ever since Wolfe was a child, puzzles have fascinated her. Perhaps that's why she's drawn to Yushkov, a man with more secrets than she's had birthdays. In the past, he had confided in her. Now, Yushkov has built a barrier that she can't get through. He's hiding something and she suspects it isn't good.

Riding through the night, she resolves to heed Yushkov's warning to be extra vigilant. But she is absolutely not leaving South Africa until the Sackville-Ximba-Blunt mystery is solved.

Wolfe arrives at her motel and, with engine running, looks up at her room. She immediately knows there's been an intruder. She had carefully drawn the curtains last night and now there is a slight gap. The window is shut so it can't have been moved by the breeze. Wolfe has all her belongings in her backpack so there is no need to go in. She takes off.

She hurtles down side roads, turning left and right randomly, watching for a tail. She leaves her bike in a motorbike parking zone amidst four others, and heads across the street to a café for breakfast. It's packed with construction workers and tradesmen. She orders a long black and a bacon and egg roll, then checks her phone. It's

7.18am. Nothing from Casburn, but there's a message from Thusago. She listens to it:

Call me. I have something for you.

Wolfe dials Thusago's mobile. It goes straight to voicemail. Perhaps he's asleep. It's still early. She leaves him a voicemail, then texts Casburn:

Dan, I have information for you. It's urgent. Call me as soon as you can.

Wolfe checks her emails. Two from Cohen. Short and to the point.

These photos are explosive. Call me!

Followed by:

Fucking call me will you!

It's 6.23am in London. Cohen will be at work already. She phones him.

'About time,' Cohen grumbles. No hello, how are you. 'And where the hell are you? I can hardly bloody well hear you with that racket in the background.'

'Stop your grouching, Moz. You've seen the photos.'

'I have. Who else has them?'

'Apart from Ponnappa and Butcher who broke the encryption, I don't think anyone else knows about them, except the killer, of course, and whoever has Ximba's laptop. I've tried to get hold of Casburn, but he won't return my calls.'

'Tell me everything,' says Moz.

Wolfe explains why she thinks one victim may be South African, the other Russian. 'Jerry thinks they were alive during their mutilation.'

'I've seen some terrible things in my time. But this... this is hideous. Barbaric. That poor woman and her...' He clears his throat. 'Stick close to Casburn. He'll have the right contacts. Interpol. Russian police.'

'Not going to happen, Moz. He wants me gone from this country.'

'Then we run the story.'

'That'll send the killer to ground. Give me a day to see what more I can find out, then we'll make a decision.'

'Call me in twelve hours without fail.'

Wolfe skims her other emails. Nothing new from Ponnappa or Butcher. She tries phoning Casburn again. No answer. Frustrated, she eats her bacon and egg roll and downs her coffee. She tries Thusago's mobile again. Then his landline. Gets voicemail. Why isn't he answering?

What did he want to tell her?

45

Neighbours walk their kids to school. Car doors slam. A radio blares from the house next door. A teenager argues with his mum at the bus stop. The street is abuzz with morning activity.

Thusago's house is quiet. Too quiet.

His car is parked out front, which tells Wolfe he didn't heed her warning. Unless they took a rental car? There's no sign of movement through the windows. Wolfe rings the bell. No answer. She tries opening the door. Locked.

Wolfe knocks, hard. 'Mike,' she calls, 'are you there?'

A mum and three kids from the house next door race to their car.

'We're going to be late. Hurry!' says the mother.

'Excuse me!' Wolfe calls. 'Have you seen Mike or Camila this morning?'

'Not this morning,' shouts the woman as she herds the kids into the car.

Wolfe walks around to the rear deck. She peers through the glass sliding doors. On the kitchen table, a plate. One, not three. The chair left as if somebody has pushed it back to get up. Perhaps Camila and Jacob have gone away and Mike stayed behind?

Don't jump to conclusions.

Wolfe tries the sliding door. It opens. Fear flutters in her stomach. She draws her pistol.

'Mike?' she calls.

Silence.

In the kitchen, everything is neat and tidy. She touches the plate. It's cold, the macaroni cheese with bacon congealed and half eaten, a used fork on the table next to it.

'Mike? Are you there?'

Up the hall to Thusago's study. She pauses in the doorway. The safe door is open. Books and files scattered on the floor. The desk chair is overturned. Burglary? Are the thieves still here?

Her breath comes in short, urgent bursts. Should she call the police? She hears something. A whimper? Her grip on the CZ 75 tightens. If she wastes time calling for help, she could be too late.

Her overloaded brain clicks into gear. The spots on the wall begin to make sense. An arc of blood spatter. *No, it can't be*. Wolfe takes a step into the room, her finger on the trigger. Then another. Behind the desk lies a man she hardly recognises. Mike Thusago. A gory mess, his face and chest sliced open in long, deep strokes, the carpet around him a pool of congealed blood. She knows she shouldn't touch him. It will contaminate the scene. It would be a miracle if he survived such an attack, but she thought she heard a whimper.

'Mike? It's Olivia.'

She holsters the pistol, kneels close to his head, the blood seeping through her jeans. She tries to find a pulse. His skin is cold. She leans close to what remains of his face, hoping to hear or feel his breath. Nothing. When she sits up, she has his blood on her cheek. Up close, she realises the cut to the top of his skull is so deep she can see the grey of his brain.

'Oh Mike. I'm so sorry. So sorry.'

Wolfe backs out of the study, leaving bloody footprints on the floor and runs from the house. She heaves up her breakfast onto the back porch. With trembling hands, she dials the only person in Johannesburg who might help her. Casburn.

'I'm kinda busy, Olivia,' Casburn says, his voice rough, as if he's had a big night out.

'He's dead,' she babbles. 'They killed him, Dan. Oh God. They...'

'Slow down.' His tone changes instantly. Attentive, calm, alert. 'Who's dead?'

'Mike... Mike Thusago. And it looks like I did it.'

46

Casburn finds Wolfe kneeling on Thusago's front porch, staring at her bloody hands. Mike's blood. Her friend. Because of her he's dead. Camila, a widow. Jacob, without a father. She prays to God they are unharmed.

I should never have got him into this.

Wolfe only notices Casburn when the porch step creaks. He leans over her. He reeks of beer. His shirt is creased.

'Dan?' Wolfe says, still staring at her hands.

'Yes,' Casburn says, crouching down.

He glances at the pistol on her belt. 'I need you to hand me the weapon. Nice and slow. Keep your finger off the trigger.'

Wolfe looks down at the holster as if she didn't know she was wearing it. 'Of course.'

She hands it to him.

Casburn's bloodshot eyes flick to the red boot prints that lead from her into the house. At the vomit next to her. At the blood on her cheek.

'Is Thusago alive?'

'No. I checked.'

'Where is he?'

'The study.'

Casburn stands up, then glances inside. 'Stay here.'

Wolfe waits. In the distance, there's the wail of police sirens. Of course. Casburn had to call it in.

He reappears beside her.

'I didn't do it, Dan. You've got to believe me.'

'Who is he?'

'A friend. Helping me out. A cop.'

Casburn clenches his eyes shut. 'Fuck.'

'It's bad, isn't it?'

'It's bad any way you look at it. But a cop...' He studies her face. 'Anyone else in the house?'

'No. I don't know where his wife and son are. I told Camila and Jacob to leave town.' Her hand shoots up to her mouth. 'What if he's got them?'

'Who?'

Wolfe rocks back and forth.

Casburn squints at her, shakes his head. He thinks she's lost it.

'What were you doing here?'

Wolfe frowns. What was she doing here? 'I... I was worried. He didn't answer his phone. Somebody's been watching me. Watching us. He butchered those people–'

'Hold on. What people?'

The sirens grow louder and her panic rises. Once she's in custody, she'll be at Msiza's mercy.

'My messages. Didn't you get them?'

His voice is distant. Her brain moves so slowly she can only think of one thing. She starts to wriggle out of her backpack.

'What are you doing?' Casburn asks.

Her arm is out of one strap, then the other. Wolfe pulls her pack around so it rests on her thighs.

'Stop what you're doing, Olivia.'

'You must have this.'

When she looks up, she is staring down the muzzle of his gun. 'Dan? You know me. Come on, what are you doing?'

If Casburn doesn't believe her, then who will? She's a foreign national in a country where she has no allies. Her only friend lies dead. Yushkov has deserted her. She has to find a way to convince Casburn she's telling the truth. The killer's macabre photographs are her only chance.

'In the front pocket,' she directs, 'take the memory stick. Please.' A police car skids around the corner. 'Photos of four murders. They were sent to Ximba. By the murderer. Take it,' she pleads.

Casburn glances behind him, then down at the pack. He holsters his gun, leans forward, unzips the front pocket, grabs the memory stick and pockets it.

'I tried to tell you, Dan. Ximba, this killer, Sackville. Somehow, they're all linked. You've got to believe me. Thusago was murdered because he was helping me investigate. You know I didn't do this, don't you?'

A patrol car screeches to a halt. Two officers train their guns on them.

Casburn shouts out, 'I'm a British police officer.'

He raises his hands above his head and kneels. He looks into Wolfe's eyes, and she swears she sees them soften.

'I'm sorry, Olivia. This is not my jurisdiction. I can't help you.'

47

Samuel let his frustration get the better of him.

If only he'd managed to tail Wolfe. If only he'd found Ximba's laptop. If only he hadn't been made to look like a pathetic amateur by the man who assaulted him. Then he wouldn't have been so angry. He wouldn't have hacked into Thusago the way he did. He lost control. Broke his golden rule.

The boss won't be happy.

Samuel tilts the bakkie's rear-view mirror. His right eye is swollen half-shut, the skin a shade of aubergine. The bridge of his nose is bruised, but not broken. The swelling makes breathing difficult. Another dark bruise is forming across his throat. Talking is uncomfortable. He suspects the last two fingers on his left hand are broken.

The pain doesn't bother him. It energises him. He learned this from his father. The beatings made him weep like a girl at first. Then he grew angry. Then strong. He learnt to hold on to the emotion, to turn it against his enemy.

Who attacked him? Almost killed him? He has to be a professional. And how did the man know he was watching Wolfe? Samuel has only seen Wolfe with two men: Thusago and the British cop,

Casburn. Neither have the assailant's big build or his weird accent. Samuel doesn't like unknowns.

He knocks the rear-view mirror away, disgusted by his appearance, then makes a phone call, leaving a coded message. He isn't looking forward to the conversation. The callback comes almost immediately.

'Is it done?' the boss asks.

'We have a small problem.'

Samuel confesses to taking photos of his kills and then sharing them with Ximba. He doesn't mention the chat room where he also shared them. Samuel waits for the reaction.

'Go on,' the boss says quietly.

Samuel shifts in his seat. He's sweating profusely.

'Wolfe's been sniffing around Ximba's home and school. She may have his laptop and so she could have seen the email.' No comment, no expletives, so he continues. 'The file's heavily encrypted. She'll never get it open.'

Samuel waits. Why doesn't he say anything?

'Then she will know that four missing persons are not missing at all,' the boss finally says. 'She will know they've been murdered. And because of your...' he clears his throat, 'distinctive handiwork, she'll know they were killed by the same person. And she will want to know why. Which is a problem. Will she share them with the British detective?'

'She won't get the chance. She'll be dead by nightfall.'

'Not by your hand.'

'What?'

'Where is Wolfe now?'

Samuel fudges it. 'I'm outside her motel. When she gets back, I'll eliminate her.'

The boss sighs. 'So, you have compromised my business *and* lost sight of your target.'

'Wolfe is elusive.'

'You're losing your touch. Wolfe was arrested for Thusago's murder. Msiza is dealing with her.'

'No. Wolfe is mine.'

'You have failed me. I will call in the debt when I'm ready. For now, keep your head down and leave Wolfe to Msiza.'

48

Casburn's phone rings. It's a Pretoria area code.

'Am I speaking to Detective Superintendent Casburn?'

British accent. From the Midlands probably.

'Who is this?'

'Arthur Scott-Lewis. British Deputy High Commissioner to South Africa.'

Casburn has a bad feeling about this call.

'How can I help you, sir?'

'This conversation will go no further. Do I have your assurance, detective?'

'Yes, sir.'

'You have an exemplary record, both military and as a police officer. A smart man. Ambitious too.'

'Thank you, sir.'

Scott-Lewis clears his throat. 'It would be a pity if you were to blot your copy book, which is the reason for my call.'

Casburn hates being handled.

'Let us imagine a scenario,' Scott-Lewis continues. 'Say I had received a phone call from someone high ranking at the Foreign

Office, which, of course, I haven't. This is just hypothetical, you understand?'

'I understand perfectly, sir.' He knows there's nothing 'hypothetical' about it.

'And say, during this hypothetical phone call, I was informed you are making waves with the South African police.'

'I don't believe that's true, sir. I am working with them.'

'That's good to hear, but suppose in this imaginary scenario there is an agenda you are unaware of. Perhaps there's a – let's call it a difference of opinion, shall we? – between the Home Secretary and the Chancellor. In this little scene, your boss, Sutton, would obey the orders of the Home Secretary, and off you toddle to meddle in something you really should stay well clear of. In this hypothetical situation, it would be wise to secure any information you have developed, return to England and inform your boss there was nothing to be found, therein ensuring SO24 keeps its funding and you, your job. Wouldn't you agree?'

Clearly Sutton knows nothing about this call. Sackville is using the Foreign Office to put pressure on him. Which is a problem in many ways, not the least of which is the Chancellor is demonstrating that he will do everything he can to cover his tracks, including directing powerful people to obstruct Casburn's every move.

Casburn is hung-over and fed-up with being fed bullshit. And now this diplomat has the nerve to think he can manipulate him.

'Hypothetically, if there was a case, I wouldn't be in a position to discuss it with you, sir,' Casburn says. 'But I very much appreciate your guidance. I'll remember it, should the need arise.' He doesn't do a very good job of disguising his disgust. He's never been much of a conciliator.

'I see. It's clear you have no idea what you're messing with. That's a great shame. For you.'

'Will there be anything else, sir? I'm late for a meeting.'

'Promising careers can be snuffed out quite easily, don't you know. Think about this carefully, Casburn.'

'I will, sir.'

Casburn ends the call just in time. A few more seconds and he would have been unable to stop himself from telling the deputy high commissioner to go fuck himself.

49

Wolfe had made her permitted phone call two hours ago. Moz Cohen promised to get the British High Commission in Pretoria involved and hire a bloody good lawyer. But the lawyer hasn't shown and if the commission has interceded on her behalf, she's seen no evidence of it. Her clothes, boots and backpack had been taken away and the jumpsuit she's wearing is several sizes too big.

The interrogation room is painted a drab mushroom shade. It has no windows, just a rectangular table and two chairs. There are scuff marks on the door and scratch marks on the table. It smells of unwashed bodies. High up in one corner, a video camera, its red light blinking, observes relentlessly. Opposite where she is seated, a mirror covers the upper half of the wall, allowing whoever is on the other side to watch the interview. The air conditioning has been turned up to high heat – deliberately. They are literally making her sweat.

'Can I have some water?' Wolfe asks, for the third time.

Seated opposite Wolfe is Detective Superintendent Coetzee. 'Later.'

Next to Coetzee is Detective Inspector Naidoo. So far, he has said very little. He watches her reaction to their questions, arms folded across his chest.

'Where is my lawyer? I have the right to a lawyer.'

'On her way.'

Wolfe sighs, shifting her hands so the handcuffs dig a little less into her wrists. She glances at the female officer standing by the door, who glares back. They think she killed their colleague and friend.

'Detective, I've co-operated. Told you everything I saw and did this morning.' Omitting where she spent the night. 'Mike was a friend. A good man. I want to help you find his killer. But we're going around in circles.'

'Tell me again why you were there.'

Wolfe stares at the mirror, wondering who is on the other side. She can see where this is going. With her out of the way, Msiza just has to stall Casburn long enough so he is forced to return to London empty-handed.

There's a knock on the door and a uniformed female officer enters clutching an A4 Manila envelope. Coetzee nods at the officer, who leaves the room, then he pulls out the photos and lays them on the table, one print at a time, as if laying out the cards in a game of solitaire.

Wolfe was dreading this moment.

'Tell me about these,' says Coetzee.

She looks away, their goriness reminding her of Thusago's harrowing death.

She's in trouble. She has Thusago's blood on her. Her prints are all over his house. On her laptop, photos of four similarly brutal murders. They know she's researching a feature for *The Post*, but she won't divulge the detail or the names of her sources. So far, she's avoided mentioning the Chancellor, but she's running out of time and options.

'Look at them!' shouts Coetzee.

Wolfe opens her eyes and looks down. Her stomach heaves.

'Tell me about them.'

Wolfe glances at the two-way mirror, finding it hard to disguise her desperation. Is Casburn behind the glass? She hasn't seen him since her arrest.

'I found them in Mazwi Ximba's inbox. The man who butchered those people almost certainly killed Mike Thusago and Mazwi Ximba.'

'Mr Ximba died in a car accident.'

'It was made to look like an accident.'

'Horse shit!' says Coetzee. 'Who are these people?'

Wolfe can't stall any longer.

'Mazwi Ximba is signatory on an offshore bank account registered to a shell company, ZIB Trading. The last time I looked, it had twenty million US dollars in it.' Naidoo raises an eyebrow and unfolds his arms. 'A British MP is the second signatory, hence my interest.' If Casburn is watching, she imagines him bristling. 'I suspected money laundering; the funds either proceeds of, or used to bank roll, criminal activity here in your country. Mike was the only cop I knew here. He was helping me–'

'Why would he do that?' Naidoo interrupts. There's a non-too-disguised fury about the man. Coetzee gives Naidoo an irritated glance.

'Because he was on sick leave and bored. And I asked him.' She pauses. 'I guess he wanted to prove to himself that he was over his PTSD. Ready to go back to work.' The words catch in her throat.

'Go on,' Coetzee says.

'When Ximba died, we both suspected murder. Ximba was going to talk to me. We'd arranged to meet. Whoever is behind those millions had Ximba silenced. After that, Mike backed out. To protect his family. I kept going. A friend in London helped me access Ximba's personal emails. One was encrypted. She broke the encryption, and this is what we found.'

'Who is your hacker?'

'I can't tell you that.'

'Think again. All I see is a woman who has photos of four mutilated people in her possession. There's no evidence they came from the headmaster.'

'Please, listen,' Wolfe says, clasping her hands together on the table, 'the man who killed Mike shared these photos with Ximba.

He's out there. In your city. He must have seen Mike with me. He wants me dead too.'

Naidoo snorts in disbelief.

'Why didn't you bring these to us?' Coetzee asks.

Because Major-General Msiza is involved. Wolfe chooses her words carefully.

'I tried to get hold of DS Casburn. To show him these images. He wasn't answering.'

'I ask again, why didn't you bring them to us?'

Wolfe stares at the mirror. *Stop this interview, Dan. You're leaving me no choice.*

'You should talk to Detective Superintendent Casburn.'

'I'm talking to you. Answer the question.'

The door opens, Casburn strides in. 'Detectives, can I have a word?'

50

Tan Nguyen tilts his office chair back, casting his view upwards to the arched ceiling, as he listens to the pretty voice on loudspeaker. His eyes come to rest on the glass panels at the arch's apex far above him, which is the only source of natural light in the cavernous room. There are no windows behind the sixteen sets of sealed shutters, just brick wall. His office is a replica of the lavish Central Post Office building in Ho Chi Minh City, right down to the cream, gold and forest green paint and the ornate encaustic floor tiles. The temperature is kept within a tight range of a couple of degrees by an air conditioning system used in museums to preserve ancient and fragile exhibits.

'It really is very generous,' says the CEO of Vietnam's largest children's charity. Recently divorced, a ferocious networker, big breasts, even if they are implants. She might make him a good second wife. 'We couldn't continue our work without your support.'

'It's my pleasure,' says Nguyen, who picks up one of three rhino horns displayed on his desk and strokes it. 'I will be at the fundraising dinner.'

'And your wife?'

'Sadly, she passed away three months ago.'

'Oh, I am so sorry.'

He reads voices well. She isn't sorry. She's calculating her chances. He politely finishes the call, then gets up, placing the giant horn carefully back on his desk.

The soles of his bespoke Oxfords tap on the tiled floor. He thinks best on the move.

He halts in front of the wall-mounted head of what was once a fourteen-foot-tall bull elephant, the magnificent tusks, yellowed and battle-scarred, eight metres long and weighing ninety pounds. He'd watched it fight off younger pretenders, mortally wounding challengers. He was the king of his domain. It took four carefully placed bullets to bring it down without damaging the head and tusks. The rest of the herd's tusks had brought in a tidy sum.

He walks on.

Next, mounted on a marble plinth, a leopard, baring her teeth, tail curling up behind it like a scimitar. The taxidermist was a wizard. Only the stillness betrays its lifelessness. He recalls her bravery, defending her two cubs, despite the tranquilliser dart. And the cubs had fetched a good price from zoos in China and Pakistan, too.

Further along, the head of a Western Black rhinoceros. He reaches out and strokes the grey leathery skin criss-crossed with a myriad of lines and runs his fingers up and down the two magnificent horns. His most prized piece. There were few specimens like this in private hands, and there would be no more coming onto the market. He chuckled to himself. Extinction did wonders for secondary market prices.

He bypasses his other trophies and stops outside two cherrywood doors, twice his height. They are French polished, finished to such a shine he can see his reflection.

He sees Tan Nguyen, respected businessman, philanthropist, pillar of the community, a champion of wildlife protection and children everywhere. He checks his Rolex GMT-Master II. Sadly, he doesn't have time to enjoy the very special collection behind the door.

'Later,' he says, his lips almost touching the wood, his breath leaving a hint of condensation behind.

Back at his desk, he dials Major-General Msiza. The line is encrypted, the call untraceable.

'Here's what I want you to do with Wolfe and Casburn.'

51

The female officer ignores Wolfe's attempts at conversation, although she has at least brought her a cup of water. Since Casburn intervened, she hasn't seen Coetzee or Naidoo. She folds her arms on the table, rests her head, and waits. They have her watch, but she guesses an hour has passed. What is Casburn telling them?

From the day she first met Casburn, she has never doubted his dedication. Dogged. Ambitious. Unswerving. To all intents and purposes, he seems a by-the-book detective. But Wolfe knows Casburn's book has a whole section in it that goes way beyond standard operating procedures. His superiors are not the kind of people who get squeamish. He gets results.

Doubt erodes her initial relief at seeing him, like water drip, drip, dripping on soft stone.

Would such a man as Casburn leave her here to rot? Has she finally become too inconvenient? Their relationship is mainly adversarial, but is she naïve to think there is also a mutual respect? If nothing else, he owes her. She warned him Msiza may be corrupt. She gave him proof of four barbaric murders he would otherwise have known nothing about.

The door opens. She looks up and suddenly feels very cold. The officer is six two, maybe taller, two hundred and something pounds of muscle turned to fat. The insignia on his blue uniform shirt and cap tell her he's a SAPS Major-General.

'Leave us,' he snaps at the female officer, who stands to attention. 'We are not to be disturbed.'

'I'd like her to stay,' says Wolfe.

'Go!' he orders. She scampers from the room.

Wolfe looks at the two-way mirror, then the video camera on the wall. The red light is off. Nobody is witnessing this. There will be no recording. Wolfe straightens her back and keeps her hands still. He must not see she is afraid.

Major-General Msiza's greying hair and round face gives him an affable, fatherly look. But the unhurried, deliberate way he places his hat on the table, then sits, and the scowl he gives her, leaves her in little doubt that this is anything but a friendly chat.

'Major-General Msiza, we both know a male officer cannot be in here alone with a female,' says Wolfe.

'You're in my country now, Ms Wolfe. You do things my way.'

'And what is your way, Major-General?' She holds up her handcuffed wrists. 'Handcuffed, denied a lawyer, I haven't been charged. You have no right to hold me.'

'You've murdered one of our finest officers–'

'I did not kill Mike, but I bet you know who did. The same man who murdered Mazwi Ximba. Goes by the name of Samuel.'

Despite this carefully orchestrated meeting, Msiza flicks a look at the wall camera, perhaps checking it is switched off.

'You need to understand how things work here, Ms Wolfe. How we do business.' He pauses, lowering his voice. 'How we choose who to convict. Do you follow me?'

'I follow. You betray those who need protection and let killers go free. How am I doing?'

'You have upset powerful people. People whose support I intend to keep.'

'Who exactly?'

'We have compelling evidence that you murdered a police officer.

A witness will testify to hearing you argue with Thusago moments before he died–'

'What witness?'

The Major-General raises a hand and continues, 'And we have found the murder weapon. It has your blood and prints on it.'

'This is bullshit!'

Msiza leans forward. 'You will leave South Africa. Immediately. You will drop this fantasy you call a story. There is no shell account, no money laundering, no vast conspiracy as you seem to suspect.'

Msiza pauses to let his words sink in. Then he continues.

'Or you will be convicted of murder. Judges have a very poor view of cop killers. And, sadly, people like you don't last long inside.'

Wolfe has no doubt he will not only ensure her conviction, he will also set up her murder in prison.

'Mike Thusago was one of your own, for Christ's sake, and you're prepared to let his killer go? How can you live with yourself?'

Msiza's fist slams down onto the table. Wolfe flinches.

'Decide now and decide fast, but let me make it clear. There is no story here. You will be crushed like an ant underfoot if you persist.'

'I will not help you cover up these murders. And Casburn won't let you either.'

'The British detective? Ah, sadly he has been called back to England. Urgently.'

'No, he wouldn't do that. I don't believe you.'

Msiza checks his watch. 'He boards his flight in three hours.'

'I want to see DS Casburn.'

'He's already left.'

Wolfe can't believe it. Six people, possibly more, are dead, and their deaths are linked to the British Chancellor. Why would he leave?

'I need to talk to my lawyer,' she says, stalling.

Msiza picks up his cap and stands. 'Decide. Now. I leave this room, the offer goes with me. You know, you may not even make it to court. Killing a cop? My men may have trouble controlling their anger. You understand?'

'Casburn will keep investigating. The truth will out.'

Msiza shrugs. 'What truth? It is already too late.'

Wolfe blinks twice. 'Too late?'

'Choose! Leave here a free woman or stay a murderer. Which is it to be?'

Wolfe closes her eyes. If she can get back to England safely, she can continue her investigations. Msiza can't reach her there.

'I need an answer.'

'Tell me one thing. Are Camila and Jacob safe?'

'They are.'

Relief floods through her. 'All right, I'll leave.'

Msiza nods. 'And one last thing, Ms Wolfe. Do not think you can return to your country and continue to interfere in the affairs of others. You think you cannot be reached in England? You are wrong.'

52

People point and stare. Wolfe can't blame them, handcuffed as she is to a plain-clothes officer and escorted by a uniformed one. They frogmarch her to the front of the British Airways check-in queue, the passengers next in line grumbling at the delay. The plain-clothes officer, Sergeant Erik Johansson, shows his warrant card and presents two tickets and their passports.

'You're not serious,' Wolf says to Johansson, 'you're escorting me all the way to London?'

Johansson ignores her. The ground crew makes a phone call, then checks them in as quickly as possible, clearly keen to get rid of her. They are swept through passport control and security.

'Can I have my phone?' she asks Johansson who carries her day-pack over one shoulder.

'No calls.'

Wolfe wants to phone Camila to say... what? How sorry she is? How she blames herself? Promise Camila she'll find his killer? But it will have to wait. Standing a few feet away behind them is the uniformed cop, his hand resting on his holster. Johansson cannot take his Vektor Z88 service pistol on board.

Boarding commences. Passengers with young children and those needing assistance go first.

'We're last on,' says her travel buddy.

'Great,' she says, 'so everyone gets to look at the woman in handcuffs.'

Johansson yanks her cuffed hand his way, the metal cutting into her skin. She grits her teeth.

'If I had my way, you'd be dead in your cell.'

Ignoring him, Wolfe watches the queue of people boarding, willing them to get a move on. As long as she's on South African soil, Msiza can change his mind.

'You try anything on the flight, I'll break your arm.'

She's planning on sleeping, if he'll let her.

The last stragglers race to the gate. The departure lounge is almost empty, save for a backpacker who dashes past them, late for the flight.

'Move,' orders Johansson, walking forward and handing both their boarding passes to the gate staff.

'Sergeant?' somebody says behind them. 'I'll take her.'

53

Casburn holds up his warrant card. 'Detective Superintendent Casburn, Metropolitan Police. I'm escorting this woman back to London.'

'Sir, I have my orders. I'm being met at Heathrow by one of your lot.'

'The orders have changed,' replies Casburn.

Casburn notices Johansson's uniformed colleague closing in.

'Don't embarrass yourself, son,' says Casburn. The officer stares at his senior for direction.

'It's okay,' says Johansson, 'everyone stay calm.'

The flight attendant glances nervously between Casburn and Johansson. 'Umm, we have to close the flight,' she says.

Casburn looks at Wolfe. 'Trust me.'

Wolfe nods. She'd rather take her chances with Casburn.

Johansson makes a call. He scowls, undoes the handcuffs, and drops Wolfe's day-pack at her feet.

'My passport?' she says, hand out.

Johansson slaps it into her hand.

'She's all yours. But I stay until that plane leaves.'

'That would be a waste of your time.' Casburn cuffs Wolfe to his left wrist. 'I have a charter flight waiting.'

'What?'

'You heard me.'

'For fuck's sake,' mutters Johansson, who gets his mobile out of his pocket.

Casburn takes Wolfe's arm. 'Come with me. We're late.'

He leads her away from the gate. 'Come with us if you want,' Casburn calls over his shoulder.

The force of Casburn's rank and authority drags the SAPS officers along without further argument.

'This feels familiar,' he says, leaning close.

Not so long ago, Wolfe was handcuffed to Casburn on a flight to the USA.

'It's not necessary,' Wolfe says.

Casburn flicks a quick look at her. He smiles. 'I know.'

He leads her through the arrivals hall. In the waiting zone, a hire car idles, the driver wearing a black suit, pristine white shirt and a thin black tie. *SO24 clearly has a decent travel budget*, Wolfe thinks.

'Wait!' calls out Johansson, jogging up to them.

Casburn doesn't stop. 'You want to see her leave the country? Get in,' he says, gesturing to the black Audi A8. 'You get in, the Major-General pays, though.'

The officers stop short, indecision and anger fighting for control of their expressions. The driver opens a rear door. Wolfe doesn't hesitate. She dives in and sits behind the driver's seat.

'Which charter company?' Johansson asks.

'Private Air.'

Casburn shuts his passenger door and orders the driver to get moving. Through the tinted window, Wolfe watches the two officers run off, presumably to their car, with the intention of meeting them at the Private Air hangar.

'Can we have music?' asks Casburn. The radio is switched on. 'Louder.' He doesn't want to be overheard.

'I thought you'd left me in the shit.'

'Tempting.' Casburn's normally deadpan face cracks into a

genuine smile. 'To think I could have been rid of you forever. I must be off my head.'

She nudges him in the ribs.

'Thanks, Dan. Really. There was a moment there when I thought Msiza might go through with his threats.'

'I know.'

'How?'

'I was watching.'

'You were behind the mirror?'

Casburn nods.

'He didn't know you were there, did he?' she asks.

'Nope.'

'He said you were leaving. He was lying, right?'

'I've been given a good reason to.'

'Are you crazy? We're making headway.'

'I can't talk about it, Olivia.' His voice is weary.

'What's happened? Something's changed?'

'I'm hardly going to tell you, am I? You're a journalist.'

'Forget what I am. This isn't about *The Post* anymore. I'm going to find Mike's killer. It's the least I can do for his widow and son. So level with me, and I'll do everything I can to help you.'

'Have you levelled with me, Olivia?' His look is penetrating. For a fleeting second, she wonders if he knows about her meeting with his old adversary, Yushkov.

'Everything I said during my interview was true. The man behind these murders is a professional killer. Goes by the name of Samuel.'

'We're looking into him.'

'We find Samuel, we find who's giving the orders,' Wolfe says.

'As long as he doesn't find us first.'

54

Seated next to Casburn in a chauffeur-driven car, Wolfe has a moment to observe his puffy eyes, his stubble and his open shirt collar, yellowed with sweat and grime – Wolfe guesses he hasn't changed it for a while. The Casburn she knows is obsessively neat, his immaculate appearance an outward display of his self-control and eye for detail. None of this applies to the man next to her.

'Level with me,' Wolfe says, trying to ignore the yeasty sourness of last night's beer on his breath. 'Are you jacking this in?'

Casburn rubs a finger across dry lips. His hand has a tremor. 'I'm stuck in the middle. Sackville's mob wants me to stop. My commander wants me to keep going.'

'What happens to you if you keep going?'

'Not sure. SO24 could lose its funding and I lose my job.'

'I'm sorry it's turned out like this.'

Casburn rummages in his pocket. 'You even think about publishing any of this and I'll make you wish you had taken your chances with Msiza.' He finds his Nicorette gum and starts chewing aggressively.

'Of course I won't,' she says. 'What are you going to do?'

'I've warned my commander. He wants me to keep going, but he'll still have a job if the shit hits the fan. And I won't.'

'Can't he protect you?'

'You know how it goes, Olivia. He'll protect himself first.'

'Sackville is behind all this. Whether directly or indirectly. We can't let him get away with it.'

'You don't get it, do you? I'm not like you, Olivia. My life has been the army, the SAS, the Met. We get orders. We follow them. But I'm out on a limb here. And whatever I do, I'm going to piss off somebody who can seriously fuck up my life.'

'I get it, Dan. Believe me. Moz wants to publish the 'four murders' story. I won't give it to him. At least not until I've found Samuel. Moz will go off his rocker. He'll find some way to punish me. Maybe even fire me.'

Casburn leans forward and asks the driver, 'Got any water, mate?'

'Yes, sir, in the seat pocket,' the driver replies.

Casburn drinks in great gulps.

'Big night?' Wolfe asks.

'Butt out, Olivia.'

'Okay, then how about this? You find an excuse to stay here a day or two. Tying up loose ends, that sort of thing. We team up. If we get nowhere, you fly home.'

Casburn looks away, then back to her.

'I can't believe I'm saying this.' He finishes the last of the water and pops the empty bottle back into the seat pocket. 'If we do this, I have to know that nothing I say, nothing we learn, gets published without my say so. And I mean nothing.'

Wolfe plays with her tongue stud, thinking. *Moz will hate this.*

'Moz already has the murder victim photos. He could publish them, but without me the story will be weak.'

'You've got to make sure he doesn't, Olivia.'

'I'll do my best.'

Casburn makes a phone call. Tells the woman from Private Air there's been a change in plan.

55

The driver pulls up at a guarded gate. Beyond the wire mesh fence are small planes and helicopters, and a sign on one of three Portakabins announcing Private Air. No SAPS car. No Sergeant Johansson or his side-kick.

Casburn unlocks her handcuffs, gets out of the parked limo, takes her arm and leads her into the Private Air reception.

He signs some papers. The lady behind the counter is wearing a pale blue suit and a name badge with Amelia on it. She points at a four-seater Robinson R44 helicopter in the same shade as her suit. Wolfe notes that next to it is the Gulfstream G650 that Casburn was due to take to London. It seems the powers-that-be are *very* keen to get him back to London, no matter what the cost.

'Keep your head down when you get in,' says Amelia. 'You said you needed to leave immediately. The pilot is waiting.'

'Where are we going?' Wolfe asks Casburn, following Casburn out of the Portakabin.

'Nokuthula Reserve.'

'Where's that?'

'Eighty miles from here. Pieter Venter's wildlife park.'

'Who is Pieter Venter?'

'One of the four photographed victims.'

'He's South African? I knew it!'

'You were right,' Casburn says. 'Pieter Venter, sixty-three, reported missing a week ago by his daughter, Hannah.'

A marked police car pulls up outside. Sergeant Johansson gets out, watches them. They both pick up the pace. The pilot gives them a wave from inside the chopper. The two-bladed main rotor and tail rotors start moving. They duck low and climb in, Casburn at the front, Wolfe in the back. They are told to buckle up and wear headphones. Outside, Johansson races to the fence, grabs hold of the links, and shakes it, yelling at them. The rotor noise drowns him out.

'So, you do listen to me?' Wolfe shouts at Casburn.

'Sometimes.'

Casburn turns around and gives her a wink, then puts his headphones on.

56

Even though Wolfe's headphones protect her ears from the pounding beat of the helicopter's rotors, she still feels the sound waves reverberating in her chest. She tunes in and out of the conversation as she thinks through Casburn's decision to stay in South Africa. He's taking a huge risk. As she is. Cohen wants a story. He won't wait forever. The pressure is on both of them to prove Sackville's guilt and find Thusago's killer.

Her thoughts move to the killer. Are Ximba and Thusago his fifth and sixth kills? Even though the MO is different, she's convinced it's him. Perhaps Hannah Venter, the deceased's daughter, knows something useful.

'Does Hannah know I'm coming?'

The pilot, Henry Clarke, replies, '*Ja*. I let her know.' He points out the town of Rustenburg far below. 'Not far now.'

'Henry,' says Casburn. 'I have to be in Zimbabwe some time tomorrow. Can you take me?'

'Zimbabwe? That'll take a bit of organising. Got a visa?'

'Yes.'

'I should be able to. Let me see what I can do.'

Why Zimbabwe? Wolfe wonders.

'There's Nokuthula,' Clarke says.

Wolfe looks down and sees an expansive, parched landscape and a road scored across it, partially obscured by wind-blown rust-coloured sand. Running parallel to the road is a high mesh fence – at least twelve feet, if not taller – topped with several horizontal rows of wire.

'Is that an electric fence?' Wolfe asks.

'*Ja*. Not that it does any good,' says Clarke.

'How do you mean?' Wolfe asks.

'Poachers get in anyway.'

They fly low.

Just inside the padlocked main gate, a man sits on a milk crate, smoking, his rifle leaning against the trunk of an African wattle. Clarke loosely follows a dusty unsurfaced road that meanders through the savannah. A tower of giraffes strip the leaves from the upper branches of a stand of acacias, their lithe pinky-grey tongues unperturbed by the three-inch-long thorns. A herd of impala scatter ahead of the chopper, fleeing from the rotor's noise. Wolfe spots four rhinos grazing serenely a few feet from the perimeter fence, ignoring the aircraft passing over them.

'Hannah won't be happy,' says Clarke.

'Why?' Wolfe asks.

'They're too near the fence. Easily shot. I'll tell her so they can shoo them away.'

'You know Hannah well?'

'Grew up round here. We went to the same school. Her father is a legend. His murder is a tragedy.'

Casburn looks at Clarke. 'What makes you say it's murder, Henry?'

'Pieter would never just disappear. This place is in his blood. And Hannah is his only child.' The pilot shakes his head. 'Somebody killed him, for sure.'

'Who do you think did it?' asks Casburn.

'Poachers. And not the local villagers. I mean mercenaries. Ex-soldiers mostly, from Mozambique. Pieter stood up to them, patrolled day and night. Even shot one of them on his property. It was self-defence, but he had one hell of a time proving it.'

'What about the police?' Wolfe asks.

'They don't give a shit.'

'Who runs the reserve with Pieter gone?' Wolfe asks.

'Hannah. With Tumi, the reserve manager. They've got four guys from Zimbabwe who help with night patrols, and some rangers who work during the day. Then there's the overseas volunteers and university students who come and go, but they're doing research or projects and don't have anything to do with the day-to-day running of the place. Oh, and Rudy and Ben.'

'Rudy and Ben?'

'Rudy's the night-time guard dog and Ben is the handler.'

'One guard dog for all this?'

'They can't afford more.'

'Hannah's not married?' Wolfe asks.

'Widow.'

'How big is the reserve?'

'Thirty thousand hectares.'

'That's a lot of ground to cover.'

'Too much. They're fighting a losing battle, what with poachers and the drought.'

Nokuthula isn't what Wolfe imagined a game reserve to be. It's not thick with trees or lush vegetation. It's not open grassland with endless thousands of wildebeest. It's an undulating series of low hills and shallow valleys, with sparse clumps of tough grass and thorny trees puncturing the iron oxide-stained sandy soil. The main watercourse through the reserve is virtually exhausted, as though suffocated by the dry season. A series of man-made waterholes serve to support the reserve's inhabitants.

'When we get rain,' says Clarke, 'this place is lush and green and brimming with wildlife. You're not seeing it at its best.'

Clarke flies over a couple of large wooden huts that remind her of community halls with expansive deck areas, and half a dozen khaki canvas tents that look to be permanent fixtures.

'Visitors' camp,' says Clarke. 'Where students and volunteers stay. Empty at the moment.'

The banks of the adjacent waterhole are scarred with wide cracks and have baked in the sun like clay, the water level half what it clearly should be. A black-backed jackal and some warthogs drink the murky water.

'The drought looks bad,' she says.

'*Ja*. Worst in fifty years. Our farmers are going bankrupt. Food prices are through the roof. Reserves like this struggle to keep their animals alive. And without the animals, they have no visitors and therefore no income. Problem is Nokuthula has to spend almost all its funds on protecting the rhinos. When their water pumps break, they can't afford to replace them.'

'How do big reserves like Kruger cope with poachers?'

'They're run by South African National Parks. They get government funding. Have an army of well-trained people patrolling fences and they're doing a good job protecting their animals. But poaching isn't their only problem. Border jumpers from Zimbabwe and Mozambique get into South Africa through the park.'

Clarke points at a flat, rocky ridge below them. 'We'll land there. Near Hannah's house.'

A dazzle of zebras bolt, leaving dust clouds in their wake, as the chopper approaches the flat ridge. To their right is a single-storey house, surrounded by a chain wire fence topped with barbed wire. Two Jack Russells, their front paws on the gate, stare up at them, jaws opening and closing in rapid barks that Wolfe can't hear. Behind the dogs, an ostrich parades up and down the small compound.

Clarke skilfully touches down, the rotors whipping up a dust haze. They wait until the blades have slowed before getting out, keeping their heads low. The compound gate is padlocked.

'Hannah?' Clarke calls.

Apart from the dogs and the ostrich, there's no sign of life. No vehicle either. Clarke dials her number on his phone.

'Not enough signal,' he complains. 'You have to find just the right spot. You got more than one bar?' he asks.

Wolfe checks her mobile. 'Nothing.'

'Me neither,' says Casburn.

'Does she know we're coming?' Wolfe asks Clarke.

'*Ja*. She said she'd meet us here.'

57

NOKUTHULA, SOUTH AFRICA

Isolated. Lonely. The house exterior looks tired, much like the dogs panting at the gate. What must it be like here alone at night?

A swirl of red dust follows a white vehicle heading their way. It sways from side to side, bouncing over the deeply potholed dirt track. The pick-up truck has tiered seating in the open tray at the back. It skids to a halt. The Jack Russells bark, stumpy tails wagging. Hannah Venter gets out of the vehicle; her expression is grim. She's a tall woman in her thirties in head-to-toe khaki. Her walk, fast and urgent. Her tanned face bears the telltale lines of someone living an outdoor life.

'Hannah? Has something happened?' Clarke asks.

Hannah shakes her head. 'It's too much, Henry. I can't...'

On her hands are brown stains. Blood stains. 'Is somebody hurt?' Wolfe asks.

'How rude of me,' Hannah says, giving Wolfe a pinched smile. 'You must be Olivia Wolfe. Henry tells me you're a journalist. Welcome.' She shakes Wolfe's hand. Her palms are calloused, her grip firm.

'Thank you.'

'Detective Superintendent Casburn,' Hannah shakes his hand. 'I can't tell you how relieved I am that somebody, finally, wants to find Dad.'

Wolfe doesn't envy Casburn the task of informing Hannah her father is dead.

'Can we go inside?' asks Casburn.

'Of course,' Hannah says, 'but I can't talk now. I have to deal with something urgent. I'll show you around, then I may be gone a few hours. I'm sorry.' Her voice is shaky.

'Poachers?' Clarke asks.

Hannah nods. 'Last night. They killed Lottie, and Mad Max...' her voice cracks.

'Oh no,' says Clarke. 'Who's with them?'

'Tumi and two rangers. He's called the police, but they haven't shown. We've been waiting all day.'

'All day?' asks Wolfe. 'Poaching is a crime, isn't it?'

'Legally, yes. But poaching isn't taken seriously. It's going to be a battle to even get them here.'

'I'd like to help. I'll go with you,' says Wolfe.

'I'll stay here.' Casburn checks his phone. He has no signal. 'I need to make some calls. Where can I get a signal?'

'You have to find the right spot. The back porch is usually the best place. And I have internet access. Follow me.'

Unlocking the compound's padlock, she leads them through the dusty yard and into her house, the Jack Russells jumping up excitedly.

'Don't worry about the ostrich,' says Hannah, as the six-foot-high bird comes up to Wolfe. 'She's just curious.'

The small house is clean and simply furnished. Clearly running a wildlife reserve isn't making Hannah rich, but the view from the back porch is spectacular. Raised up above the savannah, there are miles and miles of open plain and an uninterrupted view of South African wildlife. Wolfe spots giraffe, impala and zebra in the short time it takes Hannah to jot down some details on a writing pad and hand the note to Casburn.

'My internet name and password, and my mobile number,' Hannah says.

'I'm heading to Rustenburg to refuel,' says Clarke. 'I'll come back later.'

'Stay the night, Henry. We can catch up on old times,' Hannah says. 'It's rare I have company these days.' She looks at Casburn and Wolfe. 'Please, be my guests tonight.'

Wolfe has no intention of leaving the reserve until she has answers, so the offer of a bed is most welcome. She gratefully accepts.

Casburn wastes no time getting down to business. His laptop is out and switched on as he dials London on his phone. Wolfe guesses he's hoping his team has information about Samuel. And also the identities of the other victims.

Wolfe really should contact Cohen. But what is she going to tell him? That she's given Casburn her word everything they discover is off the record until he says otherwise? That will *really* make Cohen's day.

To avoid his wrath, she shoots him a quick text message letting him know she is safe, that she is meeting with victim number four's daughter, and she will call him soon.

A few seconds later, Cohen replies.

What are you playing at? We need to talk. Stop bloody texting me.

Wolfe climbs into Hannah's vehicle, her leg pressing against a South African R1 Battle Rifle lying against her seat, the muzzle facing up. 'Is this safe?' Wolfe asks.

'*Ja*, safety's on.'

A male voice crackles over the two-way radio.

Hannah responds, 'Tumi, what's happening? Over.'

'We have a problem,' Tumi replies.

58

When Wolfe was *The Post*'s Foreign Correspondent in Syria, she was embedded with a British Army unit. She vividly recalls sharing a joke with a soldier, moments before he was catapulted into the air by an IED, both legs blown off. Thrown to the ground and concussed, it took what seemed like an eternity for the ringing in her ears to subside. She will never forget the first thing she heard: the soldier's screams.

During the siege of Homs, she tried to rescue a mother and two children trapped beneath rubble. She found the youngest first, the little boy's body crushed. None survived. In each case, Wolfe had reported what she saw, so the world would know how the innocent victims of war – the women and children – suffered. Over time she found a way to cope with seeing so much suffering, to distance herself so she could do her job. She had increasingly relied on alcohol to forget, on pills to control her tremors. The Yemeni Civil War was the last straw, with thousands of civilians bombed. After three years in war zones, she told Cohen enough was enough.

Wolfe thought she'd seen the last of such slaughter.

She was wrong.

Tumi, a tall man in khaki, and a younger ranger next to him, have rifles raised and pointed at a cackle of hyenas, drawn by the scent of the carcasses.

'I don't want to shoot them,' Tumi says, 'but we can't keep them away much longer.'

'Call the police again,' Hannah says, her R1 Battle Rifle slung over her shoulder by its strap. 'They're more likely to listen to you than me.' Tumi flicks a questioning look at Wolfe. Hannah introduces her. 'Tumi led an anti-poaching team in the Kruger for four years. Thank God, he's with us now, although I wish we were as well-resourced. If we were, maybe this wouldn't have happened.'

'They will always find a way in, Hannah,' says Tumi, who lowers his rifle and uses his phone.

Hannah leads Wolfe to a nine-foot-long female rhino lying on her side, her legs rigid.

'This is Lottie. Twelve years old,' says Hannah. 'Her mother died soon after she was born. A poacher's bullet. So I hand-reared Lottie. She was very special to me.'

The rhinoceros's grey hide is a myriad of crossing lines like chain mail, except nothing could protect her from the ferocity of the attack. Wolfe is at the rear of the animal. There's a deep gash across her lower back. Blood has dried almost black on her skin, flies buzzing frantically in and around the wound.

'They macheted her spine,' says Hannah. 'Severed the spinal cord so she couldn't use her back legs. She was helpless.' Hannah points to scuff marks in the dirt behind the animal. 'Look there. She would have been terrified. Screaming in pain. She'd have no understanding as to why she was attacked. She tried to drag herself away, using her front legs, the back ones trailing behind her. The poachers would be shouting, dogs attacking her face, legs, biting, snarling.'

Is it the needless brutality, or that the animal could never win against such odds that fires up Wolfe's anger? She tries to put a lid on it, keeping her questions practical.

'How did they find her?' Wolfe asks.

'They pay someone to watch the fence. If they see rhino, they tell the poachers. Sometimes they use helicopters to track them, sometimes drones.'

'Drones?'

'There's big money behind poaching. Rhinos are easy targets. Especially white rhinos. They're gentle, slow-moving grazers. You point a *geweer* at them,' she shakes her head, 'I mean gun, and they'll just look at you.'

Hannah leads Wolfe around to where Lottie's head rests in a pool of blood. She swats away the flies.

'They did this to her when she was conscious. She'd have felt every cut.'

Wolfe winces at the sight of her. Part of Lottie's face has been hacked away. Muscle, bone and brain had spilled into the dirt. Only her lower jaw, one ear, brow and eyes remain.

'They used an axe, cutting into her skull, gouging out the base of each horn, first the big one at the front, then the smaller one. They wanted the whole horn, even what's buried in her skull. The bigger the horn, the more money they get. Can you imagine the agony?' Hannah asks, her voice breaking.

Wolfe cannot even begin to imagine. Bile rises up her throat. She swallows.

'Why take one ear?'

'Proof to the buyer in Vietnam the horn was taken from a living animal.'

'Isn't the horn enough?'

'Vietnamese men who want to show off their wealth and status pay for a rhino to be slaughtered. They want to brag that the animal was killed for them.'

'And the feet?' Wolfe asks.

She points to where the rhino's front feet have been chopped off, leaving bloody stumps, the bone protruding from jagged flesh.

'Sold as paper weights.'

'Tell me about the poachers.'

'Gone are the days when poachers were villagers, just wanting to feed their family. These days, poachers are well-equipped, well-trained mercenaries. Armed with AK-47s, they have dogs, night-vision goggles, sometimes drones. They get paid well, but the real money is made by the criminal syndicates in Vietnam and China. They fund the poaching. They drive the illegal trade in horn. Middle Eastern countries such as Yemen and Oman buy intact horns for ceremonial daggers and jewellery, but it's a much smaller market.'

'Why didn't they simply shoot her?' Wolfe avoids looking at the mutilated rhino. 'Put her out of her misery?'

'Gunshots make too much noise, draw unwanted attention. So the animal suffers a slow death.' Hannah kneels and points to shoe marks and paw prints in the sandy dirt. 'You see these? Looks like there were four of them, plus maybe six or eight dogs. Probably Mozambique ex-soldiers. The border's not far from here.' Hannah points out tyre tracks. 'Not made by our vehicles.' Hannah looks in the direction of the perimeter fence. 'Lottie has been dead for about twelve hours. The horn would have been in Mozambique within a few hours and then hidden inside a shipping container headed for Asia.'

'Hidden inside what?'

'Sugar cane, most likely. It's easy to hide horn and tusks that way. Very difficult to search. Sharp and heavy.'

'Does the name Terry Blunt mean anything, or the KwaZulu Natal Co-operative?'

'No. Why?' Hannah says.

Tumi's angry voice interrupts.

'It's been six hours, for God's sake, man,' Tumi says into his phone. 'How much longer...?'

Hannah shakes her head. 'If they turn up at all, it'll be a miracle.'

She leads Wolfe to a second dead rhino. 'Mad Max, female, she was two weeks to giving birth.'

The same hacked head, the top of her face carved out like a new moon. One ear removed. But what causes Wolfe's stomach to churn is what the poachers did to her next. Spilling out from Mad Max's belly, her womb and intestines, pale and limp in the red dirt. Wolfe retches. Lying next to his mother is the body of a fully formed rhino calf.

'When they tore him from his mother's womb, he was alive.'

Wolfe runs for some bushes and heaves up her guts, then wipes her mouth with a tissue. When she looks up, Hannah sits with her back to Lottie's wide shoulders, the giant animal and the young woman connected for the last time. Hannah lowers her head so it rests on her arms. She's talking to herself, or perhaps even to the dead rhino.

'I will be your voice,' Hannah says, 'I won't give up.'

As Wolfe watches Hannah, she has a light-bulb moment. She can't believe she hasn't made the connection before.

The four murder victims were mutilated in the same way as these rhinos: noses sliced off, ears removed. And the female victim, the woman Wolfe believes to be Russian, had her unborn child ripped from her belly, just as Mad Max's calf was ripped from her womb.

The serial killer is imitating rhino poachers. He collects macabre trophies. Not horns and animal feet, but human noses and hands. Why?

59

'Finally,' says Tumi, pointing at the south-east gate.

A white boxy van marked with yellow and blue chevrons is ushered in through the reserve's main gate by a security guard. It moves slowly, veering off the dirt road at one point, then swerving back. The riot vehicle has seen better days. Even the bull bar at the front is dented and rusting, and the steel grilles over the windscreen look as if they've taken a hammering. The faint sound of dance music gets louder the closer the vehicle gets.

Tumi shifts position so he stands next to Hannah. 'Try not to get angry,' he says to Hannah. 'It won't do any good.'

Hannah nods.

Three uniformed male officers. One white, two black. The driver slams on the brakes at the last minute, barely stopping in time, throwing grit and dust into the air. The doors are thrown open and the white officer waves at them, as if joining them for a picnic. He shakes Hannah's hand. 'Sergeant Du Preez,' says Hannah. The officer's eyes are bloodshot, and he reeks of beer.

'Thank you for coming. Poachers got in last night, killed two of my...'

The other officers head straight for the two dead rhinos, taking no care to avoid the footprints or tyre tracks in the dirt. Hannah explodes.

'What do you think you're doing?' she shouts, running to block their path. 'You're contaminating a crime scene.'

'They're just animals,' says one of the black officers, who introduces himself as Constable Commey. He tries to step around her.

Tumi blocks Commey's path. 'Poaching is a crime, my friend. Be careful where you step, man. There are footprints, dog prints, cartridges. You see?' He points.

Commey moves his hand across his face as if swatting a fly. 'They're long gone.'

Hannah directs her attention on the sergeant. 'Is this a joke to you?'

'Of course not. Now step aside. Let us do our job.'

Du Preez orders his men to watch where they walk. 'Those horns would be worth a bit, huh?' Hannah bites her lip. 'When did this happen?'

'Twelve, thirteen hours ago.'

'Nothing we can do. They're in Mozambique by now.'

'Can't you identify them or something? Maybe they stopped for petrol. There must be a way.'

Commey gives Lottie a kick in her rump. 'We'll start a fire.'

Wolfe assumes he means to keep the men warm while they cordon off the scene.

'You're not eating my rhino,' Hannah says. 'Jesus Christ! You don't give a shit, do you? *And* you're bloody drunk.'

Hannah yanks open the police vehicle's passenger door. An empty beer can rolls out and lands in the dirt. The foot well is littered with them. There's also an unopened six-pack waiting to be drunk. 'This isn't a bloody party!' She's close to tears.

Commey sniggers.

Wolfe takes photos of the beer cans and the officers with her iPhone. 'Drunk on duty. Rustenburg police officers a disgrace. Find rhino poaching a joke. That'll make a great news headline.'

'Who the hell are you?' Du Preez asks.

Wolfe introduces herself then adds, 'I know journalists with the *South African Herald*, too.'

'Now wait a minute,' says Du Preez, 'there's no need for that.'

'Are you going to take this crime seriously?' Wolfe asks him.

Du Preez gives her a venomous look, then directs his men to cordon off the area. They move with sullen slowness.

'I'll stay here,' Tumi says to Hannah. 'You go home.'

Hannah takes a long look at her dead rhinos. 'Make sure they are gentle with them,' she says to Tumi. 'No fire. No meat. No drinking. When they're done, I want them off my land.'

60

From Hannah's back porch, the dusk sky is blood-orange. On the horizon, silhouetted spindly trees, the branches almost devoid of leaves, look like skeletons dancing a crazy dance. Hannah sits in a wicker swing chair, her Jack Russells lying either side of her. She leans forward, her body tense. She'd barely eaten the meal she'd prepared for them earlier.

'Can we talk about your father?' Casburn begins.

Clarke, returned from refuelling the chopper, moves his chair close to Hannah as if trying to shield her from what's coming.

'What do you want to know?'

'As I mentioned on the phone, I'm from a specialist unit known as SO24. We investigate potential overseas threats to London, but my remit covers threats to the whole of the UK as well.'

'I don't understand,' says Hannah. 'What has this got to do with my dad? He's not a threat to anybody.'

Good question, Wolfe thinks.

'I'm investigating a series of murders, committed in different countries–'

Hannah's breath catches in her throat, like a hiccup.

Casburn continues, '–by a serial killer.'

'What are you saying? Is Dad... is he one of...?'

'We haven't found his body. But I have a photograph of a man we believe may be your father and I'd like you to take a look at it.'

'Photograph?' Hannah repeats.

Casburn produces an A5 sized envelope. 'I need to know if this is Pieter Venter. But I have to warn you, you'll find it distressing. The man in the photo has been... disfigured.'

'God *in Hemel*,' Hannah whispers.

Both dogs sense her anguish and jump down from the back of the sofa and onto her lap.

'Wait,' Clarke says. 'I know Pieter. I can identify him. Don't make Hannah do it.'

'No,' says Hannah. 'I must.'

Casburn lays a print on the table.

Hannah leans closer and blinks, a puzzled expression on her face. 'What am I looking at?'

She picks up the photo, her hands and the photograph trembling. A sharp intake of breath and the colour drains from her face. 'Dad?'

'What in God's name have they done to him?' Clarke says.

Wolfe is seated opposite Hannah, so the image is upside down for her, but every detail is etched on her mind. A man tied to a camel thorn tree, his nasal cavity a gaping wound, into which his two severed fingers have been inserted in what Wolfe now realises is a mockery of a rhino's two horns.

'What... what did they... do to him?' Hannah asks, her voice barely audible.

'Hannah, I need you to be clear. Is this Pieter Venter?'

She nods.

61

Hannah Venter drops the photo of her murdered father as if it's burnt her fingers.

'I knew. Just knew. But not like this.' Clarke tries to put his arm around her, but she pushes it away. 'No, Henry.' She picks up the photo from the wicker table and waves it at Casburn. 'Why did you lie, Detective? Why tell me you didn't know? Of course he's bloody dead. Look!'

'Hannah, we have photos. No body,' Casburn says. 'And we needed verification.'

'Where is he?'

'I was hoping you would recognise the location in the picture. Can you take another look?'

'I've already searched everywhere. Phoned everyone we know. Put up posters in town.'

'Do you recognise that tree?' Wolfe asks, drawing Hannah's attention back to the photograph.

'The camel thorn? So what? They're everywhere.'

'Where did you last see your father?'

'Here. He has a house down by the campsite's watering hole, but he usually eats with me here. We had breakfast as usual, then he headed for Rustenberg. He needed a new part for a water pump.'

'Can anyone confirm he left the reserve?'

'Yes, the guard said he did.'

'I'd like to see his cabin and talk to that guard.'

'Of course.'

'Did Pieter get any death threats?' Casburn asks.

'Plenty. Dad frequently got anonymous phone calls, threatening to cut his throat, kill me, that sort of thing.'

'Anyone in particular?'

'There's a poaching gang in the village, half a mile from our northern perimeter. A man called Fezile leads it. He poaches smaller mammals. Antelope, impala. But it's not him. Fezile doesn't have enough guts to follow through, or to... mutilate like that.'

Casburn jots down the name on a small notepad. 'Anyone else?'

'Let me explain what we're up against. There's a war going on. A war we're losing. We're fighting a faceless enemy, thousands of miles away in Vietnam and China. They drive the trade in horn. Fund it. They supply weapons, vehicles, helicopters. They bribe officials, the police, our government, their government. My father dedicated his life to this reserve. It's been a haven for endangered rhino for twenty-two years. I'll tell you who killed Dad. A poaching syndicate.'

Hannah stands suddenly, dropping the photo, the dogs tumbling off her lap. She races into the house.

'Let me talk to her,' Wolfe says, picking up the print.

Wolfe finds Hannah sitting on the edge of her bed, a box of tissues beside her. 'How will I tell Nathan?'

'Nathan?'

'My son. At university.'

'Perhaps wait until we know more?'

'Oh God. This is so terrible.'

'It must be such a shock,' Wolfe says. 'I can't imagine what you're going through.'

Hannah dabs her eyes with a tissue. She nods. 'I'm sorry, I didn't mean to react like that. I...'

Wolfe sits on the bed next to her. 'Casburn wants to find whoever did this. He can't do it without you.'

Hannah blows her nose. Dabs her wet face. Tries to compose herself. 'I think I know where... he died,' Hannah says.

'Where?'

'The tree. I know it. That particular one was hit by lightning. It split the trunk.'

Wolfe holds up the photo.

'You see the way its trunk divides in two,' Hannah says, 'and the wide, low-hanging canopy? We used to have a tented hide there. To watch wildlife drink at the waterhole. Last year we built a proper hide – wooden, with reed roof and benches to sit on. It's more comfortable than a tent.'

'This tree is on your reserve?' Wolfe asks.

'It is.'

62

Wolfe sits in Hannah's Land Rover. It's parked in the front yard. Beyond the wire mesh fence the reserve is pitch black. Wolfe needs privacy, and this is the only place she can talk without being overheard. Hannah has left the windows down and the cool night air makes her shiver.

Inside the house, Hannah argues with Casburn. Hannah wants to find the split camel thorn tonight, but Casburn insists they go at first light. Stumbling around in the dark is a great way to compromise a crime scene.

Wolfe's mobile phone rests on the dashboard. Through their FaceTime connection she sees Moz Cohen's long face. Her editor has his phone lying at a forty-five-degree angle which gives her an unflattering view of his scraggy neck and hairy nostrils. Behind him, there's a glimpse of blond wood panelling on the wall and a large framed sepia photo taken around 1900 of King's Cross and the Regent's Canal. In it, horse-drawn carts carrying goods to market clog up the narrow streets. Wolfe knows the picture well. Cohen is in *The Post*'s executive boardroom.

'How kind of you to finally make contact,' Cohen says, sarcastically. 'I get you a damn good lawyer, she turns up at the cop shop, and you've buggered off!' he gripes.

'I never saw her.'

'Where are you?'

'A wildlife reserve near Rustenburg owned by the South African victim, Pieter Venter. Casburn is with me. He's risked his career to keep me in the country.'

'I hope he's also paying your expenses.'

Why is Cohen in the boardroom? He hates the boardroom. Hates kowtowing to the directors. So why is he there?

'Is somebody with you?' she asks.

Cohen waves a hand about as if signalling to people in the room. 'I thought the directors might like to say hi.' He leans close to his phone. 'Of course there's nobody with me. Sheesh!'

'So why the boardroom?'

'My office is bugged.'

'What about your mobile phone?'

Cohen rolls his eyes in exasperation. 'I'm not using my mobile. It's a burner phone.'

'Who's bugging you?'

'Take a guess.'

'SO24?'

'Nope.'

'Somebody high up in government?'

Cohen gives her a nod. 'Got it in one. Had a visit from the Men in Black today, doing their best to look intimidating with their gelled, pansy hair and their clichéd stern faces. Flashed badges like they were the keys to the Holy Grail. Wanted to search my office. Told them to go fuck themselves.'

'I'm guessing you're not using your laptop either?'

'Nope. Using a brand spanking new one.'

'Did they get a warrant?'

'Yup. Came back. Did the search.' Wolfe feels her stomach squirm. 'But as you've given me half of fuck all, they left with very little intel. Apart from–'

'The photos of the four murder victims?'

Cohen nods.

'Shit!'

'I got the feeling they didn't know about the murders, which is odd. I guess Casburn isn't sharing?'

This is awkward. Wolfe hates holding out on Cohen, but she must keep her word to Casburn.

The larger of the Jack Russells has followed Wolfe and whimpers to be let into the vehicle. She opens the door and he jumps in, then onto her lap. The dog attempts to lick her phone. Cohen gets a close-up of the dog's tongue.

'I see you're taking your assignment seriously.' Cohen's upper lip is curling into a sneer. He isn't exactly known for his love of animals. Or of people, for that matter. Wolfe picks up the Jack Russell and puts him gently on the seat next to her. Cohen taps his skeletal fingers on the polished tabletop. 'Bored now. Are you going to tell me why my office has been trashed by MI5's Batman and Robin, or do I have to ask Casburn?'

Keeping her voice low, Wolfe explains her theory that the Chancellor is linked to an Asian crime syndicate operating in South Africa, involved in the illegal trade of rhino horn. Her theory is that Ximba was the money launderer and that Major-General Msiza ensures law enforcement turns a blind eye.

'From what I know of Pieter Venter,' she says, 'I think he and the three other victims were a problem for the syndicate and were killed because of it. I don't know why yet.'

Wolfe explains the similarity between the mutilated murder victims and the butchered carcasses of the rhinos she's seen.

Cohen interjects. 'Perhaps the killer was making a point. Sending a message – oppose rhino poaching and I'll butcher you?'

'Possibly, but I don't think so. So far, there are no bodies. The photos were in a highly-encrypted email. I don't believe they were meant to be seen by anybody, apart from the killer and Ximba. If their deaths were a warning, their bodies would have been easily found and the photos widely distributed.'

'And Mike Thusago?' Cohen asks.

'Made to look like a robbery gone wrong.' Wolfe winces, the memory of his bloody body hits her like a migraine. 'I got Mike killed, Moz. I shouldn't have involved him.'

'Rubbish. You didn't force him to work with you.'

'I know, but–'

'But nothing. He chose to do it. Just like he chose to ignore your warning. Stop blaming yourself.'

'But his wife and son…'

'Will be well taken care of, I've made sure of that.'

Wolfe falls silent. Her boss is a bad-tempered slave driver most of the time, but occasionally he surprises her. 'Thank you, Moz.'

'I don't want thanks. Those photos are bound to leak. I want *The Post* to break the story. No mention of the Chancellor. For now. Keep that powder dry until we know more about his involvement.'

Wolfe clears her throat. Cohen isn't going to like this. 'I can't do that. Not yet.'

Cohen's wiry eyebrows meet in the middle. 'And why the hell not?'

'Because we made a deal,' says Casburn, his interruption making Wolfe jump. Casburn leans in through the vehicle's open window. She turns the phone so Cohen can see Casburn, who continues, 'Olivia is helping me with my investigation. Nothing will be published till I say so.'

The last time Cohen and Casburn crossed paths was when Casburn's team raided *The Post*'s offices.

'With the greatest of respect, Dan–' Cohen begins.

Casburn talks over him. 'I need to ask you to sit on the photos, Moz. Don't publish. It's a matter of national security.'

'National security, my arse,' says Cohen. 'Why don't you add a terrorist threat while you're about it? That's the one you lot usually use to keep the media from publishing, isn't it?'

'Olivia has given me her word.'

'Total bollocks, she wouldn't do that. Olivia?' says Cohen.

'It's true,' Wolfe replies.

She has seldom seen Cohen so livid. He loves play-acting the tyrant. He gets a kick out of scaring his green reporters. His favourite trick is to storm up to someone's desk, slam down a rival journalist's printed story and yell so everybody can hear, *Why didn't we get this scoop?*

Now, Cohen's deep-set eyes are glassy with fury, his lips pursed into a tight line.

'Olivia, what the hell have you done?'

'This is more important than a story,' she says.

'You're a journalist. Not a cop. Do your job.'

Her heart races. Her job is everything. She has no husband or boyfriend, no family. *The Post* is her family. Her promise to Casburn means she's crossed a line and she may not be able to cross back. But she owes Thusago's family. And she can't find his killer alone. Like it or not, she needs to work with Casburn.

'I can't do that, Moz. Not until we find Mike's killer.'

63

Clarke has offered to sleep on the sofa, which leaves Casburn and Wolfe sharing a room. Fortunately, there are two beds. Wolfe chucks her backpack on the bed nearest the window, turns her phone to silent, plugs in the recharger, then sits on the edge of the bed. Her boots connect with an old pair of man-sized running shoes. On shelving opposite, various trophies and a framed photo of a teenager, perhaps eighteen, playing rugby. Tall and dark, like his mother. On a lower shelf, textbooks on civil engineering. It's Hannah's son's room.

Wolfe is desperate to sleep, but her mind is buzzing. *Pieter Venter's body could be on this very reserve. He is the key to solving the mystery: what connects the four victims?*

Wolfe pulls out her laptop and does a search on Hannah's father. Pieter Venter came to wildlife conservation late in life. Born in Zimbabwe, he ran a successful garden centre until one night it was torched, and his family home attacked. That same night, he fled his homeland with his wife and children. His bank account was frozen. He arrived in South Africa with just US$5,000. He took the first job he could get – insurance sales. Not surprisingly, he hated it. Four months later he saw an ad for a security role on thirty thousand hectares of land near Rustenburg upon which were several factories that were being closed down. He took the role and negotiated with the landowner a lease which allowed him to set up a wildlife reserve on that land. Wolfe found herself admiring Pieter's intrepid spirit and his determination.

Pieter became a champion of rhino conservation and a regular speaker at the Global Regulation of Wildlife Trade convention, better known as the GROWT convention, in which representatives from countries all over the world vote on the status of endangered species and agree on measures to ensure their survival.

Was Venter killed because he was outspoken about the need to save the rhino?

Wolfe is distracted from her thoughts when Casburn's hushed phone conversation outside the bedroom window gets louder.

'So, she *is* Russian,' Casburn says. 'Do we have a name?' He jots down some details. 'That makes it more complicated.' *Certainly does*, Wolfe says to herself. The Russian police are not known for being co-operative.

He is quiet for a while.

'Under investigation? What in God's name for?' A pause as he listens to the response. 'That's ridiculous.'

Wolfe keeps reading up on GROWT. The next meeting of member nations is in Johannesburg on Sunday – in three days' time. Venter was due to speak.

Casburn again. Louder. 'No, sir, I won't. Not yet. This poses a very real threat, and not just to London.'

Wolfe closes the laptop, then slides her comb-knife under the pillow. She undresses down to her T-shirt and panties and gets into bed. There's a knock on the door: three knocks in fact, firm and evenly spaced.

'Come in.'

Casburn drops a black duffel bag on the floor. She watches him place his pistol under his pillow.

'So, she's Russian?' Wolfe asks.

He shakes his head. 'You were listening. Why aren't I surprised.'

'You were going to tell me anyway, right? What else do you know?'

'Marta Ramazanova, Russian, twenty-eight, reported missing four days ago by her boyfriend.'

'Is she connected to rhino poaching?'

'Not that we can see.'

'That's my theory blown then.'

'I'm under investigation,' Casburn says.

'For what?'

'Looks like Msiza has made a formal complaint. Intimidating and reckless behaviour, jeopardising a SAPS investigation.'

'So, Sutton has caved in to pressure?'

'Looks like it.'

'I'm sorry, Dan. What are you going to do?'

'Nail Msiza. Nail Samuel. Nail the syndicate. You?'

'The same.'

'Are you going to Zimbabwe tomorrow?' she asks.

'That depends on what we find tomorrow morning.'

Wolfe pulls the bedspread over her and curls up on her side, her back to Casburn.

'Goodnight,' she says.

There's a rustle of clothing, followed by a creak as Casburn gets into the wood-framed bed.

'Cohen will forgive you,' he says.

'Doesn't matter.' It's bravado. 'Finding Mike's killer does.'

Wolfe waits for him to turn out the light, but he doesn't.

'Why?' he asks.

Wolfe turns to face him. He is propped up against the pine headboard shirtless, his SAS-badge tattoo on his arm visible. Wolfe had always thought it depicted a winged dagger, but she recently learned it is King Arthur's sword, Excalibur, surrounded by flames.

'Why what?' she asks.

'Why are you doing this? Risking your career?'

'Same reason you are, I guess.'

He cracks a smile.

She continues. 'And I gave you my word.'

'Maybe I've underestimated you.'

'Maybe. We're in this together, Dan. I've got your back. I hope you've got mine?'

'You have.'

'Hey, do you snore?'

'And what if I do?' he asks. 'Are you going to suffocate me?'

Wolfe smiles. 'Maybe.'

64

The rising sun is split horizontally, half cerise and half orange. In the distance, silhouetted giraffes move gracefully, their long necks rocking forward and back as they walk. Wolfe wishes she had time to enjoy the reserve's magnificent animals. But the clock is ticking, and she and Casburn are running out of time. She finishes her black coffee, then puts her day-pack on her back. Casburn looks less haggard this morning. He grabs a bottle of water and heads for the door. Waiting in a patrol vehicle out front is Tumi and four men from the poaching patrol. Clarke leans against Hannah's pick-up. He's joining the search party.

'Do you have a firearm?' Hannah asks Wolfe.

'No.' The South African police kept Thusago's pistol.

'You need one,' Hannah says. She goes into her bedroom.

'I don't think that's a good idea,' says Casburn, pausing on the doorstep.

Hannah reappears with two rifles. One of them Wolfe recognises as the R1 Battle Rifle with wooden handle that was in Hannah's vehicle yesterday, but not the other.

'Have this. Swedish Mauser. Perfect for bushveld. It will take down a kudu or a person. Not good for bigger animals.' Wolfe takes it.

'Can you fire a rifle?'

'Yes. I learnt in Syria.'

Casburn raises a cynical eyebrow.

'Do you want me to run through loading and firing?' Hannah asks.

'No need. Straight bolt action; it's a cock on close.' She puts out her hand. Hannah passes her a box of 6.5mm cartridges, and Wolfe slips a round into the chamber and flips up the safety towards the scope.

'Impressive,' says Casburn. 'Let's go. Hannah, I'd like to ride in the cabin with you. I have some questions.'

'Fine, I'm sure Henry won't mind sitting in the back.'

Wolfe joins Tumi in the cabin of a Nissan Patrol pick-up, with the four other rangers in the back tray. They set off. The mood is sombre.

'Does your wife live on the reserve with you?' she asks him. He wears a wedding ring.

'No, she is in my village, with our children. My people are Ndebele, from the Northern Province.'

'How often do you see your family?'

'Once a month.'

'That must be very difficult for you. Why do you do this?'

Tumi glances at Wolfe. 'It's money for my family. My kids can go to school. But it is more than this. These animals need protection. If we do not protect them, they will be eradicated.'

'How can the poachers be stopped?'

'Ah, that is a very big question. Everyone has a different opinion and they cannot agree. This is the real problem.'

'I'd like to hear your personal opinion.'

'Kruger is one of Africa's biggest game reserves. It has excellent anti-poaching patrols. But when we arrest poachers, they do not go to prison. Many are freed, and they keep poaching. We need poachers convicted. They must know they will go to jail for a long time.'

'There's a ban on the trade in rhino horn, correct?'

'Since 1977 there has been a ban on the international trade, yes. I believe this is the right thing to do, but Hannah thinks it is wrong. As I said, people who care for the rhino cannot agree on a way to save it.'

'What do you think would happen if the trade ban was lifted?'

'I think a legal trade would expand demand for horn and lead to even more poaching. And I think a legal trade is very difficult to regulate, because there is so much corruption.'

'What does Hannah believe?'

'Rhino horn can be harvested without hurting the rhino. They are anaesthetised, and the horn is removed by vets. Hannah could then sell it on the open market and use the money to pay for more resources to protect her rhinos from poachers. I understand why she thinks this. Private reserves like this one do not get government support. If Hannah can sell horn in a regulated market she will have the money she needs to stop poachers.' Tumi glances at Wolfe. 'Hannah struggles to pay us. She cannot repair the fence. I do not think she can keep going much longer.'

Half an hour later, the vehicles halt a short distance from a kidney-shaped waterhole and a wooden box of a hide with a ramp leading up to it. On the other side of the waterhole is a camel thorn tree, the trunk split halfway up causing the branches to hang outwards, like the letter M. It's the tree in the photograph.

They all get out of their vehicles. Hannah has gone white.

'Hannah, stay here,' says Casburn. 'You shouldn't see–'

Hannah interrupts. 'I have to do this.'

'It's been a week,' says Wolfe. 'This isn't how you want to remember him. I promise you. Someone I loved... died. Alone. When I found her, she'd been dead two weeks. I barely recognised her. You know the saddest thing?' Wolfe takes Hannah's hands. 'I can't remember her as she used to look, only as I found her. Don't do this to yourself. Hang on to those happy memories.'

'No, I...'

'Please,' says Wolfe. 'Wait here. If we find him, we'll tell you, okay?'

'Okay.'

Casburn stares at Wolfe so intently she feels uncomfortable. She can't read his expression. Curiosity? Sympathy?

Casburn asks everyone to gather round. 'This may be a crime scene and we should treat it that way. If we find something, anything that could relate to Pieter's disappearance, you do not touch it. You step back and call me over. Is everyone clear?' Everyone nods. 'And put these on your shoes.' He hands out blue slip-on booties. 'I want to avoid our footprints getting mixed up with the perpetrator's.'

Once they have slipped on the booties, Casburn heads for the camel thorn, and everyone follows except Hannah, who leans against her dusty bakkie, arms folded.

The tree is bigger than Wolfe imagined – the top would force an adult giraffe to stretch its neck.

'Boot marks,' Casburn says, pointing at the sandy ground beneath the tree.

'We had students here three weeks ago,' Tumi says.

'Still. One print could belong to the man we're looking for. I don't want anybody coming near this.'

'I can't see any rope,' Wolfe remarks.

In the photo, Pieter is tied to the trunk with rope. Casburn leans close to the flaky bark and inspects it.

'There are marks. Something's dug into the trunk, possibly rope.'

There are dark stains beneath the cuts in the bark.

'Hyena,' Tumi says pointing to paw prints.

Casburn organises everyone so they form a wide circle around the tree. Clarke joins the circle. 'Walk outwards slowly, eyes on the ground. Shout if you find anything unusual. Okay?'

They nod.

'The hide?' Casburn continues. 'Locked?'

'It should be,' Hannah answers, appearing at their side. 'I can't stay away. I have to know.' She holds up a chunky set of keys.

Casburn doesn't try to change her mind. 'Who else has a key?'

'I do,' Tumi says.

Tumi, his crew and Clarke set off searching the ground around the tree. Casburn hands Wolfe and Hannah a pair of latex gloves.

They take the ramp to the hide's door. It's shut. There's a padlock – unlocked.

'Padlocks are easy to pick,' Wolfe says.

Through the door she hears buzzing. She swallows down a gag reflex. 'You hear that?'

Casburn nods. 'Hannah, please. You don't want to see this.'

'I must.'

Casburn opens the door. The smell is foul, but not as hideous as to be expected from a week-old dead body. Enough light penetrates the dark hide through the open door and the long rectangular slit of a window to know there is no corpse inside. Just a wooden bench.

Wolfe follows the sound of the buzzing, using her iPhone's torch to search the space. She kneels and studies the rust-brown floorboards.

'I think it's blood.'

Flies whisk past Wolfe's face. Her torch beam follows them to a dark corner. Something black and writhing is nailed to the wall. She moves closer. The stench is rancid. She gags and covers her nose and mouth. The black moving mass on the wall is hundreds of flies. Casburn swipes the insects away, but within seconds they cover every millimetre of the bloated zip-lock plastic bag. It's full of gas and decomposing goo. Casburn takes photos, then carefully unpins the bag and takes it outside. The angry swarm follows him.

'I'm calling this in.'

'What is that?' asks Hannah, her voice high-pitched. 'For God's sake, tell me.'

65

From a safe distance, Samuel watches the group through binoculars. It's like watching reality TV, except he has a vested interest in the outcome. After all, Venter was his kill.

The pittance he paid the guard at the main gate was worth it. He'd alerted Samuel to Wolfe's arrival yesterday. This time, he's a step ahead of her, and two steps ahead of Nguyen. Because Wolfe hasn't left the country as Nguyen believes, and neither has Casburn. Msiza has fucked up. Samuel smirks. They've outsmarted the boss, and that doesn't happen often.

Samuel is parked inside Nokuthula, hidden behind a couple of moepel trees. He adjusts the sight on the binoculars and homes in on Wolfe. She has an arm around Hannah, consoling her. Samuel shifts his view to the detective. Casburn places the fly-blown bag containing the only remaining piece of Pieter Venter inside a cooler box.

'You made the mess, sonny Jim,' as his father used to say. 'So clear it up.'

That's what happens when it's a rush job. Mistakes are made. Samuel scratches his neck's scar. He knew he shouldn't have done it. But he just couldn't resist. His fan club goaded him. This time, they said they wanted it to be funny. So, after he dragged Venter's body into the hide to chop it up, Samuel had bagged Venter's nose and hung it on the wall. He wanted Hannah to find it, and he can't help feeling irritated with Casburn and Wolfe for spoiling his carefully prepared nasty surprise. He glances at the video camera on a tripod next to him, recording the activities around the hide. At least he gets to share this with his followers. Satisfied he has enough footage, he uploads it to his favourite chat room, via a proxy server. Comments are posted almost immediately.

'Is that what I think it is? Cool, man.'

'Nothing like a bag of decomposing gloop at breakfast time!'

Feeling cocky, Samuel dials Nguyen, then waits for the callback – their usual routine.

His phone vibrates. On the sixth ring, he answers, deliberately taking his time.

'I thought you should know Wolfe hasn't left South Africa,' Samuel imagines a drum roll in his head, 'and the British detective hasn't either.'

'How do you know?'

'Because I'm watching them. At Nokuthula Reserve. They flew in last night.'

'Flew?'

'Chopper. Some tour guide by the name of Henry Clarke. He's still here.'

'How much do they know?'

Samuel explains about the bagged body part they've found.

His boss says something in a language he doesn't understand. It doesn't take an Einstein to realise he's furious.

'You told me their deaths were untraceable. No bodies.'

'And *you* told me they'd left South Africa,' Samuel snarls.

'Your vanity has jeopardised my operation.'

Samuel imagines slicing Nguyen. 'Hey! I'm about to save your operation. Msiza messed up, not me. I'm the only one who knows where they are.'

Nguyen is quiet. 'Have they contacted the police?'

'They were here yesterday. Poachers killed some rhinos. They kicked the dirt for a bit then left. Haven't been back.'

'I need to contain this. I can't have my guests worried.' He pauses. Samuel hates his silences. His shirt collar chafes his skin. He scratches. 'Tell your man on the gate to contact Rustenburg police anonymously.'

'Why?'

'He'll plant evidence proving local poachers killed Venter.'

'Consider it done. And?'

'Sabotage the chopper so it can't fly.'

'Then?'

'Disappear.'

66

Casburn paces up and down outside the crime scene tape set up by local police. He's on the phone talking to Clarke. Beyond the yellow tape, surrounding the hide and the area leading to the camel thorn tree, a crime scene manager and a forensic team are busy photographing and collecting evidence.

'Can it be fixed?' Casburn asks Clarke.

Earlier, Clarke had gone back to Hannah's house, getting a lift with Tumi and the poaching patrol guys. He'd wanted to do pre-flight checks for their trip to Zimbabwe. Wolfe still doesn't know why he has to go there. He's keeping her in the dark and it makes her uneasy.

Casburn listens to Clarke's response and clearly doesn't like it. 'I can't wait that long, Henry. I'm sorry. Can you do me a favour? Can you find another chopper pilot who'll take me?' A pause, as he listens. 'If not, I'll drive.'

'What's up?' Wolfe asks, his phone conversation over.

'His chopper's out of action. Something to do with the rotors.'

'Why the urgency, Dan?'

'I have to be somewhere tonight or latest first thing tomorrow.'

Wolfe rolls her eyes in exasperation. 'When are you going to trust me?'

An officer named Jackson calls the crime scene manager away. 'We've got something.'

Wolfe and Casburn can't cross the tape, but they can follow the men as long as they stay outside the perimeter.

Jackson bends his knees and points at the gap beneath the hide. The structure is raised up on bricks at each corner, leaving a space beneath large enough for a man to crawl through. A much younger officer lies underneath on his belly. His torch illuminates a machete, lying in the dirt.

'The murder weapon,' Jackson says, smugly.

Wolfe leans close to Casburn. 'I searched there earlier. There was nothing.'

The younger officer wriggles out from the gap, the machete gripped by a gloved hand. The blade is clean.

'If it's the weapon, it's been wiped,' says Casburn.

Hannah squints at the blade. 'This is pointless.' She walks away.

'Do you recognise it?' Wolfe asks catching up with her.

Hannah keeps walking. Wolfe grabs her arm. 'Well, do you?'

'Yes,' she snaps.

'Whose machete is it?'

'It belongs to Mpande Khoza. He carves a snake onto the handle. It's his way of claiming it.'

'And who is Khoza?'

'Local poacher. Small time stuff. Gazelle and zebra. Sells it to butchers.' Hannah shakes her head. 'He didn't do it. Not Dad.'

'How do you know?'

'All this,' she gestures to the hide. 'Too calculated. Too detailed. Khoza wouldn't bother leaving trophies. Anyway, he doesn't kill people.'

'Is it possible he travelled overseas recently?'

'You've got to be kidding! He can barely afford to feed his family. I doubt he even has a passport.'

Wolfe doubles back and pulls Casburn aside. 'Hannah thinks it's a set-up.'

Casburn's mobile rings. He answers with a brusque, 'Yes?' Then he turns his back on Wolfe and walks away, his tone softer. 'Oh, you know, had a bad morning. What have you got for me? ... Good work. Email me everything.' He ends the call.

'I could do with some good news,' Wolfe says.

Casburn keeps his voice down. 'Not here. Look, I can't stay. I've got things to sort out.'

'I'll go with you,' says Hannah. 'I can't bear to watch this anymore.'

'I'll come too,' says Wolfe, keen to keep close to Casburn. 'I need to clear my head. I'll get in the back.'

She climbs into the vehicle's tray of tiered seats and takes a back seat. It's a crisp, sunny April morning and the cool air is energising.

Wolfe's phone rings. The caller ID is blocked. She answers.

'I believe you are a woman who values her privacy.'

The voice is male, educated, the hint of an accent.

'Who is this?' she says, instinctively looking around the savannah for the assassin.

'Someone who also values their privacy. And you are threatening it.'

67

Wolfe doesn't hear the rusty chassis squeak or feel the jolt as the pick-up sways in and out of potholes. The vast expanse of bushveld has disappeared. She doesn't even notice the giraffe's ungainly lurch as it canters across their path. She sees nothing, hears nothing, but the handrail she grips and the voice on the other end of the line.

Wolfe tries to sound chilled, even though fear clings to her skin like a spider's web. 'Come on, tell me who you are.'

The bakkie sways into a pothole. Wolfe slides along the slippery seat and has to grab the safety bar with her free hand, almost dropping her phone.

'I'm more interested in you, Olivia Wolfe. You have a brother, Davy, recently released from prison. You're the daughter of Edward and Catherine, from Dulwich Hill, London. You broke your leg at five, jumping off a garage roof, convinced you could fly. Davy taught you to box at ten. You were a school boxing champion at twelve.'

How does he know this? He must have her medical records. And more. Only two people know she was convinced she could fly as a kid – Davy and her dad. Nobody knows where her dad is. Her brother, however, would happily share such details if he thought it would hurt her.

'Am I talking to Samuel?'

He ignores her question. 'Your dad disappeared when you were fourteen. Your world imploded, didn't it? You were daddy's little girl.'

He is stirring up painful memories, memories she has fought so hard to suppress.

'You went off the rails then. You lived in a squat with your drug-dealer boyfriend until the police raid. That's when detective Jerry Butcher came into your life. You owe him a lot, don't you?'

He's demonstrating his power. His web of contacts. His ability to reach people she cares about. She knows she mustn't let it get to her, but it has. The caller is intelligent, authoritative. No, this isn't Samuel. This has to be the man Samuel reports to.

Think, Olivia. Think. The best form of defence is attack.

'You're the head of the poaching syndicate,' she says, 'I want to meet you. Tell me where and when.'

'There is no poaching syndicate, Ms Wolfe. It only exists in your imagination.'

'Then who are you?' Wolfe activates her incoming-call recording app, silently cursing herself for not doing so earlier.

It's as if she hasn't spoken. 'Butcher never charged you, did he? Because of him you went back to school. He's always looked out for you, hasn't he?'

A hot flush creeps up from her chest to her face. He's pressing all the right buttons: she will always protect Butcher.

'This is boring me. Let's talk about four mutilated bodies. Why did Samuel kill them?'

'I'd prefer to talk about the gym in Tooting where Butcher and Ponnappa run their PI business. They're snooping around my business, just as you are, and it has to stop.'

She is shaking with fury. 'What do you want?'

'You know what I want. Leave well alone, Olivia.'

'I don't give in to threats.'

'Then dear old Butcher and sweet little Ponnappa are not long for this world.'

She forces a laugh. 'You're no match for them.'

'Are you sure? And what about Butcher's wife and kids, and Ponnappa's family?'

She sucks in her breath. Holds it. She cannot risk their lives.

'I'm listening,' she says.

68

'What's got into you?' Casburn asks, sitting on the wooden steps leading up to Hannah's kitchen door. He bounces his right leg in irritation. He talks to her. Something about new intel. She isn't listening.

An hour earlier, Wolfe's blackmailer had made her an offer. Return to the UK. Drop the story. Never interfere with his business again. In return, Butcher and Ponnappa will be left alone.

'You're booked on an afternoon flight tomorrow. Take it,' the caller had said. 'And don't tell Casburn about this conversation.'

Back inside Hannah's compound, Wolfe paces the front yard like a caged animal, trying to think of a way out of her predicament.

'Did you hear me?' says Casburn. 'I said, we've identified the last two victims.'

Wolfe hears his voice, but his words wash over her. She threads her fingers through the wire mesh of the fence, her back to him, a momentary break in her pacing. She kicks the fence. And again. She doesn't know what to do.

'Hey! Are you listening?' Casburn shouts.

'What? Sorry, say it again.'

'Can't you sit still for one bloody minute?'

His words finally reach her.

'This is how I think best. When I pace,' Wolfe says, whirling around to face him.

'Do it somewhere else. You're pissing me off,' Casburn barks.

'If you don't like it, *you* go somewhere else!'

'Fuck you!' says Casburn.

Wolfe feels a rush of fury. People she loves are in danger. Everyone is telling her what to do: Yushkov, Cohen, Casburn, her blackmailer. She can't think. She just wants to hit back.

'Stand up!' she yells.

'You're losing it, Wolfe. Get a grip.'

'I'm going to kick the shit out of you.'

Casburn sniggers, 'Yeah, right.' But as Wolfe rushes him, Casburn jumps up only just in time. 'What the fuck's going-?'

Before he can finish, Wolfe lays a right hook into his jaw. His head jerks to one side, he stumbles, but he's fit and strong and he instinctively defends himself. He hits back. Wolfe has her hands up to protect her face, so he punches her in the stomach. She doubles over, winded, stumbling backwards.

'Don't think I won't hit you again,' Casburn shouts, his spittle bloody. 'You want more, I'll give you more.'

Wolfe is gasping for breath. 'Stop!' she says, peering up at him, hand outstretched to placate him.

But she's received harder punches before. When she trains with Butcher, he doesn't hold back.

The tension in Casburn's body relaxes. He mirrors her. That's when she charges, headbutting him in the stomach. The force of it throws him backwards on to the ground. She loses her balance and lands on top, her head pounding from the impact.

Casburn blinks a few times, his face screwed up in pain. 'Fuck that was devious,' he pants. 'You... gonna... stop... now?'

'Yes... are you?' she says between gasps.

'Yes.'

Wolfe slides off his torso and sits in the dirt next to him. 'Bloody hell, that hurts,' she says rubbing her forehead.

'Hard stomach,' says Casburn. 'Too hard for your head.' He bursts out laughing.

It's infectious. She laughs. She can't stop. She's crying with laughter.

Hannah stands in the doorway watching them. 'What's going on?'

'Just letting off steam,' Wolfe replies. 'We didn't mean to be disrespectful or anything.'

'Not at all. It's good to hear laughter for a change.' Hannah vanishes into the house.

Casburn wipes away a trickle of blood from his mouth. 'You know, you fight well, if a little crazily.'

Wolfe's laughter fades away. It has to be one of the nicest things he's said to her. Perhaps the only nice thing. 'Thanks.' She picks up some dirt and lets it trickle through her fingers. 'I'm fucked, Dan. Whichever way I turn, I'm fucked.'

'What's happened? Moz gone and fired you or something?'

'Not exactly.'

She falls quiet. She doesn't know what to do.

If she tells Casburn about her blackmailer, how will he react? She can't risk doing anything that jeopardises Butcher's and Ponnappa's safety, but it's possible Casburn could help keep them alive.

'I got a call. From the man himself. The syndicate leader.' She looks up at Casburn. His expression has changed. Hard. Attentive. Detective-mode.

'You *what*?'

69

Under President Robert Mugabe's rule, you could buy almost anything in Zimbabwe. Which is how Nguyen, a Vietnamese national, became the owner of a 162,000-hectare private reserve and hunting lodge on the eastern bank of the Shashe River.

The land was once four separate privately-owned game reserves. The white owners were removed, their land designated for Zimbabwe's war veterans. But Nguyen offered Mugabe's son, Robert Junior, double what the land was worth, and the war veterans were allocated land somewhere else. Patrolled day and night, the guards have orders to shoot to kill. Nguyen has spent a small fortune on restocking the park with lions, leopards, elephants and rhinos bred in captivity for the sole purpose of being hunted. His guests are guaranteed a kill. His guides make sure of that.

Nguyen does not fear for his life in Zimbabwe as many foreigners do, because he has the protection of Robert Mugabe Junior. More than that, Mugabe often utilises the lodge for his most private business meetings. As do others whose relationships Nguyen wishes to cultivate. Far from prying eyes, arms dealers come to Nguyen's property to meet with regime leaders condemned by the pitifully weak United Nations. Russian oligarchs can satiate their appetites for pretty young girls or boys, knowing their secrets are safe.

Best of all, he is praised by conservationists worldwide for his magnificent contribution to the conservation of African endangered species. Staged photos of him at the reserve have appeared in publications as diverse as the *National Geographic*, *Time* magazine, and *The New York Times*.

From the lodge's semi-circular lounge room, he looks beyond the waterhole where elephants wallow in muddy water, to the private runway and aircraft hangar where his Learjet glints in the sun. Any moment, his first guest will land. Yury Sukletin, a key member of the syndicate. What Sukletin sees in the weak-chinned, wimpy British Chancellor he really can't imagine. Perhaps it's the attraction of opposites? Or perhaps it's the secrets Sackville whispers to his lover at night? What was that eighties British comedy show called? *Little and Large*?

'Harold, will you let me speak?' Nguyen says into the phone, finding it hard to disguise his exasperation.

If Sackville wasn't essential to his business, he'd have the twat eliminated. The man hasn't stopped whining for two minutes and fourteen seconds and Nguyen is running out of patience.

'Of course,' Sackville mutters. 'But you must understand, it's my neck on the line here. It's not your name on that bloody bank account.'

'It is under control, Harold–'

'No, it isn't! I've pulled every string possible to stop Casburn. It's getting awkward. I've already involved the Foreign Office. And the police commissioner. If I push any harder, someone will smell a rat.'

'He's been ordered back to London, am I correct?'

'Yes. But–'

'And he's under investigation?'

'Yes.'

'Good. Make sure he's taken off this case.'

'Yes, yes,' Sackville mumbles irritably. 'And Wolfe?'

'I have made her an offer she can't refuse.'

'What if she does refuse?'

'Journalists like her have an unfortunate knack of disappearing.'

'Oh God!' Sackville whimpers.

'Harold, there was no need to cancel your flight. We need you here this weekend.'

'Of course it was necessary. I can't come anywhere near you. In fact, I shouldn't be bloody talking to you.'

'Yury will be disappointed.' *Lovers are so easy to manipulate*, he thinks.

Sackville sighs. 'As am I. I just can't risk it.'

'Harold, let me be clear. I expect you here on Saturday. Some big decisions need to be made. Two members are jittery. Nervous of the increasing media attention poaching is getting these days. I want you to smooth troubled waters. It's one of your many strengths.'

'I really can't come.'

Nguyen makes a mental note to ask Sukletin to speak to Sackville. After all, it was Sukletin who introduced the British Chancellor to the syndicate, and it was Sukletin who persuaded him to control the money, together with Ximba.

'Do I have to remind you about the flat in Swiss Cottage your wife knows nothing about? My gift to you.'

'All right, all right. Just keep your voice down, will you.'

'In your absence, decisions that affect your future will be made. And you may not like them.'

'Are you threatening me?' Sackville's bluster hardly hides his cowardice.

'No, Harold. But I expect to see you tomorrow.'

70

Wolfe and Casburn sit side by side with their backs against the compound's mesh fence. Wolfe's phone is balanced on her knee. He listens intently as she plays the recorded conversation she had with her blackmailer. She studies Casburn's side-profile for a reaction. But he has his poker face on. The recording ends.

'I have to do what he says. I can't let anything happen to them.'

'Have you told them about this?' Casburn asks.

'Not yet. I know how Jerry will react. He won't give in to a blackmailer. He'll continue investigating the syndicate, no matter what I say.'

Casburn pulls a packet of Nicorette from his jeans' pocket. Throws two pieces into his mouth and chews. Hard.

'If you do what this guy says and give up, he'll always have a hold over you.' He gives her a hard stare. 'Butcher and Ponnappa will never be safe and nor will you, as long as he's out there.'

'I know that. But if I don't get on that plane he'll send someone to kill them.'

'I can organise for them to disappear. There's a witness protection house in Wales I know is empty. They could go there until we've caught the son of a bitch.'

Wolfe considers the offer. 'But what about their families, Dan? He threatened them too.'

'That's harder to sort out. Their immediate family could go with them. I could find a second house. But the more people we have to move, the more likely it is that the syndicate will catch on to what we're doing.' He pauses. 'We're so close to finding him, Olivia. Don't give up now.'

She makes a WhatsApp call to Butcher and Ponnappa. It's lunchtime in London. She explains everything. As she expected, Butcher digs his heels in. Ponnappa is nervous and doesn't want her family to be hurt.

'My mum and dad and sister have to come too. And the dog,' Ponnappa says.

Casburn makes the necessary arrangements for SO24 to pick up Butcher and Ponnappa, and their immediate families, and take them to Wales. He expects them to be in their protected houses by nightfall.

That done, Casburn checks his watch. 'I've got to get to Rustenberg airport.' He gets up and brushes dirt off his jeans. 'Henry's found somebody to fly me to Zimbabwe.'

'Fly *us*, you mean.'

'You don't have a visa.'

'Come on, Dan. You want my help, so tell me why you're going there?'

'Okay.' Casburn sits back down next to her. Chews his gum. 'Yury Sukletin.'

Wolfe's eyes bulge. 'Russian billionaire and criminal? What's he got to do with this?'

'Long story. I'll start at the beginning.' He clears his throat. 'The Home Secretary became aware Harold Sackville was meeting Yury Sukletin regularly. He feared Sackville was sharing highly sensitive information with the Russian, who, by the way, is a close friend of Putin's.'

'Why the suspicion? There could be many legitimate reasons why they would bump into each other.'

'Because every year for the past three years Sackville takes a long weekend to South Africa. Each time he meets with Sukletin. They dine together.' He looks at Wolfe. 'They sleep together.'

'Okay, I didn't see that one coming.' Wolfe mulls it over. 'And if word gets out that Sackville has a sexual relationship with a Russian criminal with close ties to Putin, *and* has millions stashed in a dodgy bank account, it could rock the foundations of our government. Undermine confidence in our leaders.'

'It also just so happens that the man funding London's new casino in Shepherd's Bush is Sukletin. We suspect our Chancellor had something to do with Sukletin's successful bid.'

'A scandal like this could force an election.'

'The economy could take a nose dive.'

They both go quiet.

'When did you learn about the offshore account?' Wolfe asks.

'Shortly before you did. We suspected Sukletin had somehow persuaded the Chancellor to join his syndicate. To manage the money side of things.'

'So, all those questions you asked me in Kensington Gardens were about finding out how much I knew?'

'It was.'

'I'm still not clear why we're going to Zimbabwe.'

'We?' He shakes his head. 'Because Sukletin is flying into Buffalo Range Airport in Zimbabwe tomorrow at eight in the morning and I for one want to know where he's going and who he's meeting.'

'You think he's meeting Sackville?'

'Last I heard Sackville cancelled his flight. He must have got wind I was asking questions about him. But Sukletin is still going to Zimbabwe, so there has to be somebody else he wants to meet. Could be the syndicate leader with any luck.'

Wolfe stands up. 'I'll get a visa. I'm coming with you.'

71

Tumi drops them off at Rustenburg Airfield and they head straight for the cream-coloured bungalow where they are to meet their pilot. A bald man behind the counter, sporting a name badge with Jacobus on it, welcomes them with a warm smile that fades fast when Casburn introduces himself.

'Ah,' Jacobus says, looking sheepish. 'There seems to be a problem. The flight plan's been rejected.'

'Rejected?'

'*Ja*. And no visa.'

Casburn shakes his head. 'My visa was organised. I was told to pick it up here.'

'I'm sorry, sir, there is no visa. It's been cancelled.'

'Why didn't you call me?'

'I tried. Your number rang out.'

'What number do you have?'

Jacobus reads it aloud. One digit is incorrect.

Wolfe looks at Casburn. They both know that political strings have been pulled to prevent Casburn entering Zimbabwe.

'Try changing the booking into my name, Olivia Wolfe,' she suggests.

'Olivia, you can't do this alone.'

'Just bear with me, Dan. I want to see if I'm blocked too.'

'Can you give me a few minutes?' Jacobus disappears into a back room.

'I'll get Tumi to come back.' Casburn makes the call.

Wolfe goes outside to a small courtyard with benches under thatched cover. She sits in the shade and uses WhatsApp again to contact Butcher. She wants to know he's all right. He tells her they're on their way to Wales.

'Want to hear some good news?' Butcher says. 'We've been monitoring Blunt's sugar cane company. Jwala set up some alerts. One came up. A shipment of uncut sugar cane left the Port of Maputo, Mozambique, this morning, on container ship, *Thanh Dat 01*, headed for Saigon Port.'

'Vietnam? Is Blunt's name on the paperwork?'

'It is. Here's where it gets interesting. One extra container was loaded onto the ship that's not recorded in the documents.'

'This could be how they get the horn into Vietnam. Any idea when the shipment reaches Saigon?'

'In six weeks.'

'I'll talk to Dan,' Wolfe says. 'See if there's a way to get those containers searched.'

Through the window she sees Casburn beckoning her.

'I have to go now, Jerry. And thank you for everything.'

'Stay safe.'

Back inside the helicopter company's reception area, Casburn does not look happy.

'You're blocked from entering Zimbabwe too,' he says. 'Looks like we're going to have to take the overland route. And that'll take a bit of planning.'

'At least I have some good news,' Wolfe says.

72

Hannah points at a map on her computer screen. Almost the entire length of South Africa's Kruger National Park, running north to south, borders Mozambique. Only the park's northern end borders Zimbabwe.

It's early evening. Wolfe and Casburn are back at Nokuthula. Dirty plates are piled up in the kitchen sink. The hearty meal of boerewors – thick South African sausages – bread rolls and salad, has rejuvenated everyone.

Tumi shakes his head. 'That section of the Kruger is well patrolled. And it's dangerous. Last week a border jumper was killed by a lion. The park is full of wild animals that hunt at night. You will be easy prey.'

Hannah looks at Wolfe. 'I don't think this is a good idea, Olivia. Even if you do manage to cross into Zimbabwe on foot, the border patrol tends to shoot first and ask questions later.'

'A key player in the syndicate is arriving in Zimbabwe tomorrow morning, so we have to try,' Wolfe says. 'It might be the only way to find out who's behind Pieter's murder.'

Hannah takes a deep breath. 'Then your best bet is the Beitbridge border crossing. Tens of thousands use it legally, but it's also used for illegal crossings. Our poaching patrol guys all come from Zimbabwe. Legally. Dad organised their visas. But they all know people who've got into South Africa illegally at Beitbridge.'

Hannah zooms in on the map and traces a route which bypasses the official border post. 'You're best off crossing in the small hours of the morning, when the patrols are tired and bored. Your difficulty will be the road that runs parallel to the fence because it's patrolled. Take a look at this.'

She opens up a recent article in the online newspaper *The Citizen*, and points at a photo of border jumpers at the Beitbridge border. It shows a woman and two men trying to squeeze through a gap in a fence of thick wooden planks which must be seven or eight feet tall. 'Somebody sawed a hole through the wood, so they can avoid the electric fence at the top.'

'*Impisi* cut the hole,' says Tumi. 'They make border jumpers pay them to use it. They're thieves, man. Can't be trusted.'

Casburn shakes his head. 'I'd rather take my chances through the Kruger.'

'I will take you,' says Tumi. 'I worked in Kruger Park. I will guide you.'

'Tumi, no,' says Hannah. 'It's too risky. And I need you here. I can't run this place without you.'

So focused have they all been on the monitor, they haven't noticed Henry Clarke walk into the house, until he runs the tap to wash the grease off his hands.

'No need, I'll fly you,' Clarke says, lathering up his hands. 'Finally got the chopper working. Somebody cut the fuel line.'

'Are you sure?' Hannah asks, clearly shocked.

'*Ja*. The cut is clean. Somebody wants my chopper disabled.'

Hannah shakes her head. 'The people here are loyal. They love this reserve as much as I do. They would never do that.'

'I know what I saw, Hannah,' says Clarke, drying his hands. 'But it's all fixed now. I'll sleep in the chopper tonight. I'm not going to let some bastard sabotage it again.'

'You'd really fly us to Zimbabwe?' Wolfe asks. 'We don't have visas. It's illegal.'

'And what they are doing to Hannah's rhinos is illegal. I can get you in and out without raising alarm bells.'

'I'm in,' Wolfe says. She looks at Casburn. 'You?'

'Yes, I'm in,' says Casburn.

'When can we leave?' Wolfe asks Clarke.

'Dawn. It's a difficult flight. I need some daylight.'

73

It's one in the morning. Despite the cold night and her light nightwear, Wolfe has kicked off the heavy blankets. She can't sleep. Next door, Hannah is also restless, the floorboards creaking as she moves about. The poor woman may never sleep soundly again, given what she now knows about her father's death. In the bed next to her, Casburn is dead to the world. He lies on his stomach, his head facing away from her, his right hand under the pillow where his pistol lies.

A floorboard in Hannah's bedroom creaks. She's pacing again.

An exterior security light flicks on. Wolfe sits up and grabs the rifle lying against the bedside table. Moments later, through the thin curtains, she sees the silhouette of an ostrich's broomstick neck and head. She breathes a sigh of relief. She glances at Casburn, who hasn't moved. Asleep, his angular features are softened. He, too, has kicked off the bedclothes, exposing his bare upper body.

Bored with her insomnia, Wolfe gets up and feels her way to the bedroom door. She'll make herself some tea and catch up on emails. She creeps past Casburn's bed, then stops. A tattoo on his right shoulder blade. It looks like a woman's face, neck and shoulders.

Wolfe moves closer. Shoulder length hair. Looking over one shoulder, smiling. Alluring. No name. No inscription. Who is she?

The exterior security light goes off and the room is plunged into blackness. She turns away from Casburn and manages to find the door.

'She was my wife.'

Wolfe blanches. Casburn was asleep, wasn't he? She turns back and can just make out the dark outline of him in bed. He hasn't moved so much as an inch.

'She was beautiful,' says Wolfe.

'Still is. Now get some sleep.'

'I can't sleep.' She opens the door.

'Your blackmailer,' says Casburn. 'I've heard his accent before.'

'Where?'

'Vietnam. But educated in England.'

'What were you doing in Vietnam?'

'Never you mind.'

74

Seated at Hannah's dining table, Wolfe is avoiding reading Cohen's email. The subject isn't exactly inviting: *You've gone too far this time.*

Instead, she's supergluing the comb-knife Butcher gave her to the inside of one of her fourteen-inch-high lace-up boots. The handle sits just below the top of the right boot and the sheath, above her outer ankle. Well-hidden but easy to get at. The sheath, disguised as a comb, won't be very comfortable against her leg, so she'll wear an extra pair of socks. The three-inch blade is enough to cause some serious pain and, if it hits the right organ, could take an attacker down. Their imminent trip through the Kruger and into Zimbabwe is fraught with danger. But this extra precaution has more to do with a feeling she can't shake – a feeling she's being watched. Is Samuel close by?

Satisfied with her handiwork, Wolfe can't put it off any longer. She opens Cohen's email.

Olivia,

Far be it from me to jeopardise a police investigation, but your job is not to solve crime. That is Casburn's. This paper can barely afford to fund your trip let alone for you to play detective. Times are tough, and budgets are tight. If you continue to work for Casburn, he can pay for your time.

I have contacted a friend on South Africa's Herald *and brokered a joint exclusive re the four butchered victims, with a focus on Pieter Venter. He is poised to take over the story. I need to know whether you work for me or the Met by return email. If I haven't heard from you by tomorrow 9am London time, I will publish.*

Yours, Moz Cohen

Wolfe leans back in her chair. Cohen's actions are understandable. The story is dynamite. *Her* story. But she's given Casburn her word. And she has to get justice for Mike's family. If *The Post* and the *Herald* publish, the syndicate could go to ground. She just needs more time. Will he listen to her?

Moz, please. This is about more than four murders. It's about exposing a criminal syndicate and its leader. We're almost there. Just a few more days?

She sends her email.

A door opens and Hannah walks in, fully dressed, her dogs close at heel. She carries a rifle.

'I didn't mean to disturb you,' Wolfe says.

'You didn't. I can't stop thinking about Dad. It's driving me insane. I'm going out,' Hannah says.

'That's a bad idea, Hannah. We don't know where your dad's killer is. It's safer to stay here.'

'Can't,' Hannah replies. 'Night patrol. I'm on the one to four shift. Tumi will clock off soon.'

'Can't somebody else do it? Someone from poaching patrol?'

'They can only cover so much in one night. No, I have to do it.'

Hannah tells the dogs to stay and heads for the door. They sit and look up at her with disappointed eyes.

'I'll come with you,' says Wolfe. 'Give me a minute to dress.'

'Bring your rifle. I'll lend you a warm coat. Your jacket won't be enough.'

As Wolfe dresses in her warmest clothes, she considers waking Casburn to tell him where she's going, then thinks better of it. She has never seen him so strung out. Let him sleep. They'll be back by four and he'll be none the wiser.

75

The Land Rover's headlights are on high beam. Beyond the reach of the beam is pitch black. Wolfe is glad for the quilted coat Hannah lent her, as the dashboard tells her it's seven degrees Celsius. Hannah wears a khaki, padded coat with leather collar. The rifles sit in the footwell next to Wolfe, safety catches on.

'Why bring the backpack?' Hannah asks, flicking a look at the bag forcing Wolfe forward a few inches in her seat.

'Comes with me everywhere. Saved my life many a times.'

'How?'

'It has an ESAPI ballistic plate down the back. Protection from bullets and knives. And I've got a few useful gadgets to help me stay safe.'

'I've often wondered about journalists. Is it dangerous work?'

'Can be. If you're doing it right,' Wolfe raises a corner of her mouth in a half smile.

Hannah hands her a small white remote control. She nods at it. 'It controls the searchlight on the roof. Scan from side to side. A foot or two off the ground. We're looking for eyes reflected in the beam.'

Wolfe fiddles with the remote and quickly gets the hang of it. She swings it to the left and it lights up the grassy bushveld.

'Animal eyes?'

'Dogs. Poachers use starved dogs. Their eyes reflect the light and show up like white discs in the darkness. If we see them, we have to move fast. If the poachers hear us coming, they cover the dogs' eyes and hide until we pass by.'

'Where are we heading?'

'Section three,' says Hannah. 'Tumi reported a gunshot, near four of our rhinos. I want to check on them,'

Wolfe swings the searchlight to the right.

Hannah continues. 'It's almost a full moon tonight. That's bad for us. Poachers don't even need torches to see.'

'You normally do these patrols alone?'

'Ja.'

'And if we find poachers?'

'I radio in, get backup. Fire some warning shots.'

'And do they run?'

'These days? No. The horn is too valuable.'

'Do you fire at them?'

'It's illegal, even if they're killing our animals. We can only fire in self-defence, and the problem is that it's their word against ours.'

'I thought you said these guys have AK-47s? They're not likely to miss.'

'That's why so many rangers die doing this job.'

Wolfe swings the searchlight back across the front of the bakkie and over to the left.

'What's that?' Numerous small lights.

'Tilt it lower.' Hannah halts the vehicle and Wolfe adjusts the searchlight's angle.

At first Wolfe thinks she's looking at large dogs.

'Hyenas,' Hannah says.

Despite the engine's rumble and the bright light, the animals amble away calmly.

Hannah accelerates. 'The rhinos should be just over this ridge.'

'If nothing changes,' Wolfe asks, 'how long before rhinos are extinct in South Africa?'

'Ten years.'

'Ten?'

'In the last ten years this country's lost seven thousand one hundred rhinos to poachers. In another ten they'll be gone, except for the ones in captivity or under armed guard. That's no life for an animal that likes to roam and forage.'

'So, what's the answer?' Wolfe asks. 'Find a way to reduce demand?'

'Ah. That's hard to answer. Everyone has a different view. Conservation charities argue we need to change attitudes in the countries that import horn. But that means changing centuries-old beliefs in places like Vietnam and China.'

'You mean believing rhino horn cures anything from headaches to erectile disfunction?'

'Exactly. These myths persist because it's cut with drugs like paracetamol or Viagra. The biggest problem is we're up against a ticking clock. Even if we could convince ninety-nine per cent of people in Asia that rhino horn has no medicinal properties, demand from the one per cent left will still lead to the rhino's extinction.'

'I've heard that cutting the horn off or staining it a bright colour reduces the likelihood of poaching?'

'It can. We're going to have to de-horn our remaining rhinos. But it's dangerous, for the rhinos as well as the vets. And costly. And even then, poachers sometimes still kill them for the part of the horn left inside their skull.'

'And staining the horn?'

'Makes it harder to sell as a complete horn, but it can still be sold for powder. So, I'm not convinced staining the horn is the answer. I wish it were, believe me.'

'Can the South African Government do more?'

'Yes, they should, because tourism is one of our biggest income earners, and tourists come to see the wildlife. But education and health desperately need funding too. And the syndicates spread a lot of money around.' Hannah takes her eyes off the bumpy road for a few seconds, glancing at Wolfe. 'Private reserves like ours don't get funding. And unless something changes soon, we may have to close down.'

'What will happen to your rhinos if you do?'

'I don't want to think about it. Nobody wants to take them. The cost of protecting them is too high.'

'There has to be a solution, surely?'

'In my mind, there is. But it's not popular.'

Hannah changes down a gear as the old vehicle struggles up the steepening ridge.

'You think the international trade in rhino horn should be legalised?' Wolfe guesses.

'I do and not because I want to get rich, but because I want to save my rhinos. The ban was put in place forty-three years ago. Over that period poaching has sky-rocketed, and horn has become *the* most valuable commodity in the world. It was supposed to make it harder for poachers to find buyers. It has failed miserably. All it has done is driven the trade underground, and the only people benefiting are the criminals driving the illegal trade.'

'That's a controversial stance, Hannah. I imagine your view isn't popular with conservation charities.'

'No, it isn't. But it's the same argument for legalising the drugs trade. Legalise the trade in horn and we take the control away from criminals. With a legal market, the money made from their sale can be ploughed back into protecting rhinos. Then conservation will become an attractive job, because people can make a living out of it.'

'Is that what your father believed?'

'Yes. He was going to speak at the next GROWT convention and argue for lifting the ban.'

They reach the top of the ridge, gears grinding. Wolfe swings the searchlight round.

The windscreen shatters. Hannah shrieks. Glass explodes inward. In shock, Hannah takes her foot off the accelerator. The old Land Rover slows.

'Drive!' Wolfe yells. 'Go!'

76

Hannah's door is wrenched open. She is grabbed by her coat. Clinging to the steering wheel she tries to kick her assailant. The man has no face, just two eyes and a mouth, the black balaclava a blur against the night.

Wolfe grabs her rifle. The Swedish Mauser is long and unwieldy in the confined cabin, and precious seconds are lost. She clicks off the safety and aims. He has Hannah by her ankles and drags her from the cabin. She lands with a back-breaking thud. He leans over her. Wolfe fires, the recoil smashing into her shoulder, the sound battering her eardrums.

Wolfe can't see either of them from the cabin. Hannah screams. Wolfe has missed her mark.

Throwing open the passenger door, she scrambles out. Hands shaking, she reloads, then creeps around the rear of the now stationary vehicle, to avoid being blinded by the headlights. She peers around the corner. The man straddles Hannah. She fights him off, clawing at his mask. He raises the butt of his rifle and smashes it down into the woman's face.

'No!' Wolfe yells.

He throws himself to one side of the unconscious woman. Wolfe fires. His left arm jolts. He rolls, jumps up, and charges. She has no time to reload. Instead she swings it at his head. He ducks. Grabs her rifle. Yanks it from her grasp. Chucks it away. She unclips her metal water bottle from its carabiner and, gripping the plastic ringed stopper, swings it like a club at the man's head. He blocks her with his arm, but stumbles backwards, his heel catching on a root or stone. He grabs her jacket and they both fall sideways into a dry ditch. She loses her grip on the water bottle. It rolls away. Too dark to see where. Wolfe scrambles out of the ditch. Her boot smacks into his discarded rifle. She recognises the H&K G28 semi-automatic from her time embedded with US Marines in Afghanistan. She scoops it up. Swivels and aims it at the ditch where her assailant was mere seconds ago. But he's gone. She swings the rifle around, searching. No sign of him.

With sickening clarity, she realises it can only be one person. He's followed her here. He has a marksman's rifle. He's brutally attacked Hannah. And now he wants her.

Samuel.

Wolfe races to Hannah's side. Her face is covered in blood. Wolfe checks for a pulse. Finds one and feels Hannah's breath on her face.

'Hannah, wake up,' Wolfe whispers. Then peers around into the night. Where is he? Increasingly desperate, Wolfe shakes the injured woman. 'Hannah! We have to go.'

Hannah opens her eyes, but is unable to keep them open for more than a few seconds. Wolfe has to get her into the Land Rover. It's their only chance. She grabs her under her arms. Wolfe is strong for her size, but Hannah is a dead weight. Wolfe struggles to lift her high enough to get the semi-conscious woman half onto the seat. There is a startling ding. The front bonnet. Shit! He has another rifle. But there was no report, so he must be using a suppressor. Wolfe ducks and shelters Hannah with her body, using her backpack with its bulletproof plate to shield the injured woman. Another bullet punctures a tyre and the vehicle lists to one side like a ship taking on water. He's disabling their means of escape.

Two more shots and the headlights go out.

77

Fear is paralysing. Freezes the mind and body. Wolfe can't let her fear take over.

Think methodically, that's what Butcher would say. Wolfe takes stock of the situation. Apart from the moonlight, they have been plunged into darkness. Her go-bag is still on her back. She has a semi-automatic. If she drags Hannah into the bush, perhaps they can hide out long enough to be rescued? If Hannah lives that long. Wolfe doesn't know how bad the woman's injuries are. But she knows that Samuel will find them. He's a professional.

Wolfe spots the two-way radio inside the cabin. She lunges for the handset. With no idea which frequency to use, she presses the talk button.

'Emergency. Help us. Gunfire. Hannah is injured. Section three, near the fence.'

A bullet zings past her hand and smashes into the dashboard.

Wolfe drops the handset. Ducks down. That was close. But he missed the radio.

Wolfe pants. Picks up the handset again.

'This is Olivia Wolfe, over. Emergency. Section three. Can anybody hear us? Hannah is badly injured. We're being shot at…'

The rapid thud of boots on hard ground, closing in on her. She sees him, the silhouette of a man running, rifle in hand. His legs and arms are skinny, but he's bulky across the chest. Of course, he's wearing a bulletproof vest.

Wolfe's hands are empty. The semi-automatic lies on the ground next to Hannah. A mistake. She scrambles out of the vehicle and dives for the G28. Her hands are soaked with sweat. She picks it up, hopes to God the magazine has bullets left, aims and fires. Samuel ducks behind some trees.

Wolfe can't leave Hannah behind. But she can't save her if they are both taken. She's a fast runner. Calculates the distance to Hannah's house at a steady jog. Twenty minutes maybe. Too long.

A new plan. She will lead Samuel away from Hannah.

Wolfe jumps up and bolts towards a thicket. She is fit and agile. But she doesn't know the terrain. She suspects he does. If she trips and falls, he'll catch her. It isn't long before she hears the snap of twigs and the thud of boots behind her. Good. If she can keep this up long enough, perhaps Hannah will come around and call for help? Wolfe almost topples over a clump of tall grass. She keeps going.

Follow me, she thinks. *Leave Hannah alone.* Out of nowhere, she collides with a tree branch. Thorns cut her face and snag her hair. She protects her face with her arms and keeps going. But the low, spikey branches are treacherous and slow her down. Her only comfort is that it will also slow the man hunting her. Not far away, a dog barks. Poachers? She'd rather take her chance with them than the psycho hunting her. Wolfe veers right and follows the sound of barking.

Peering into the blackness behind her, she sees only camel thorn trees. Twigs underfoot crack. He's out there somewhere. Or is it a wild animal? The clump of trees comes to an unexpected end. She's in open plain and tall grass. A sitting duck. She catches her foot on a termite mound and stifles a cry as her ankle twists at an awkward angle. She keeps running. The dog, if it was a dog, is now silent. To her left, something large moves slowly out of tree cover. Wide and three metres long, its head down, grazing. It snorts and looks up. The moonlight illuminates the female rhino's two horns, one large, the other smaller. Then another rhino follows, and another. Despite Wolfe's terror, she is momentarily in awe of their gentle majesty.

An idea comes to her. It's risky.

Wolfe slows her pace. She doesn't want to spook them. First the leader, then the other rhinos, lift their heads and look her way. Their eyesight is poor, but they rely on scent and hearing. Their ears twitch back and forth like elliptical satellite dishes searching for a signal. She tries to quieten her ragged breath. She wonders if they sense her fear. If they panic and run, she might be trampled. Wolfe creeps closer. A baby rhino grows skittish. It rushes forward, then seems to change its mind and hides behind its mother. Wolfe stops and waits, even though she desperately wants to keep moving.

The rhinos shuffle forward in a tight group, then lower their heads and graze. The leader has a huge belly: could she be pregnant? She lifts her head and sniffs the breeze, then moves in Wolfe's direction. The others do the same. Wolfe can't believe her luck. Then she remembers she's wearing Hannah's coat. It carries Hannah's scent. Hannah has looked after these rhinos since she took over the day-to-day management of the reserve twelve years ago. They feel safe with her. Wolfe stays still, hoping her own smell won't cause them to turn and run. The leading rhino sniffs her and snorts, so close, she can feel the animal's warm breath. Wolfe shifts into the middle of the group, their massive bulk hiding her from the assassin.

78

Samuel observes her through night-vision goggles from the seclusion of a clump of camel thorns. The goggles' long-range infrared and thermal-sourcing capabilities means he can track not just Wolfe's warm body, but even her hand and foot prints, normally invisible to the naked eye at night. Using them, he has navigated his way through the thorny trees without a scratch. Wolfe is fit, there's no doubt, and, unlike other female victims, can control her fear. Fascinating. Her decision to hide amongst the rhinos is both daring and clever. He has no idea why the dumb creatures haven't run away or even charged her. Perhaps because she isn't afraid?

Luck is on his side tonight. The crash of rhinos shifts in his direction, and Wolfe with them, ducking low in their midst.

He considers Venter's daughter lying unconscious where he beat her. He should have tied her up and gagged her. But there had been no time. When Wolfe bolted, he chose to pursue her. She is the ultimate prize. He wonders how long she will endure what he has planned for her? Minutes? An hour? Two at most. A soldier he once tortured screamed like a baby after fifty minutes, begging for death. That was a record. Most last a minute or two. Perhaps Wolfe will break that record?

The rhinos are very close to Samuel now. Will Wolfe bolt when they reach the trees? Samuel raises his rifle, ready to shoot her in the legs if she does – just enough to incapacitate. The lead rhino stops, lifts its head, ears twitching. It turns away. What is the fucking thing doing? The other rhinos follow, upping the pace. Can they smell him? He has no choice but to wait. If he moves now, the beasts will hear him.

Wolfe has her back to him. The wind has picked up, blowing across the arid open space, hitting her square in the face. He is downwind, so the rhinos won't pick up his scent. If he creeps up behind her, she won't see him approach. He looks down, planting each foot carefully, the shuffling of the animals' giant hoofs masking any sound he makes. Perhaps the smallest rhino senses him? It moves away from the back of the group towards its mother, exposing Wolfe in the middle.

His rifle is slung over Wolfe's shoulder. Silly girl. She should have it in her hand. He is so close that if he stretches out his arm, he might just touch her. She has a fruity shampoo smell, mixed with deodorant and warm skin. No rancid stench of fear. Unable to resist, Samuel brushes his fingers across the very tip of the hair above her neck. Then retracts his hand fast.

Wolfe brushes the back of her head with a hand, as if checking for an insect caught in her hair. Samuel smiles. Enough foreplay.

Samuel draws his knife and bends down. He intends to cut the tendons in the back of her legs.

She'll collapse like a rag doll.

Wolfe shudders, as if somebody has blown on the back of her neck.

The baby rhino is skittish and runs from the back of the group to be closer to its mother. Why is it nervous when the others are calm? Wolfe snaps her head round and out of the corner of her eye, sees a human shape right behind her. Something dark and lumpy protrudes from his face, like he's a robot. Has to be night-vision goggles. In his hand, a knife. He bends, aiming low. Wolfe spins round and kicks, smashing her boot into his goggles, knocking them off-centre. Samuel grunts as the solid equipment gouges his cheekbones. The force of the kick propels him to the ground. The rhinos scatter, leaving Wolfe alone. He recovers fast, throws the goggles to the ground and lunges at her legs with the knife, holding the weapon low.

Wound, but don't kill, Wolfe thinks. *Samuel wants me alive.*

Wolfe jumps sideways, then tries to grip his knife hand, pushing it away from her. With his other hand he punches her stomach. Winded, gasping, she collapses to the ground. He grabs her hair and holds a hunting knife against her cheek.

I will not die like this.

Wolfe bites into his knife hand with every bit of strength she has. He yelps.

So focused is she on the blade, she fails to see his fist swinging into the side of her face. A moment's agony, then nothing.

79

Hide in plain sight. That's one of Samuel's tricks.

Some years ago, after a particularly difficult kill, he hid in his victim's home for two days while the police swarmed through it gathering evidence. When they'd packed up and left, he came out of his hiding place and simply walked away.

He plans to hide Wolfe in plain sight. He's selected the hut Hannah uses as a classroom for students and volunteers. The camp is empty. It's miles from any habitation. Nobody will hear her cries. By the time anyone realises she's missing, she will be dead, and he'll be long gone.

Samuel looks askance at Wolfe lying on the passenger seat next to him, blood dribbling from her mouth. On her forehead, several cuts from thorns. Red blood on white skin and black hair. He has his very own Snow White. That would make a good theme of his next artistic creation. Snow White in seven pieces. It has a certain ring to it.

This is the first time since he began working for Nguyen that he's taken a prisoner because he wants to. Not because he's paid to. Which makes it all the more exhilarating.

He drives past the largest hut where students and volunteers eat and socialise. It has a viewing deck which overlooks one end of the semi-circular watering hole. He keeps going. Past the rain water tank on stilts. Past the toilet block. He pulls up between two tents, hoping to keep his pick-up hidden. Somewhere in the distance a black-backed jackal whines, its call plaintive. The lecture hut is ahead. It overlooks the farthest end of the watering hole. At the water's edge, some zebras are drinking, the white of their stripes seemingly reflecting the moonlight. When he opens his door, the screech startles them and they bolt.

Samuel carries Wolfe into the classroom, kicking the unlocked door open. Chairs and benches are arranged in rows. At the front of the room are two whiteboards and a chunky, rectangular farmhouse table on heavy wrought iron legs in the shape of an X. One cross at each end. Placing Wolfe on the floor, her back to one of the X-shaped legs, he checks she's still unconscious, then he uses handcuffs to secure her to the table. He smiles at the irony that she's wearing Thusago's handcuffs. He knew they'd come in handy.

Confident she's going nowhere, Samuel takes his time collecting his tools from the truck. He calls the duffel bag his surgeon's bag, given most of the items inside are designed for surgical use. A second bag, hard-cased like a toolbox, contains syringes and drugs, chosen for their pain-inducing and hallucinogenic qualities. He particularly likes combining the mind-altering drugs with one that sends the body into agonising cramps, the victim's limbs spasming uncontrollably.

80

Wolfe opens her eyes. Everything is monotone, dark, blurry. Something tickles her cheek. She imagines she hears the beat of wings. She moves her head to one side. Her jaw throbs but whatever was tickling her face has gone. The ground is dusty, smells of warm, old wood. She blinks. Where is she?

Wooden panels above her. Too low to be a ceiling. Something cold and hard against her hands. Her hands? Above her head. She tries pulling them down. Muscles ache. The clank of metal on metal. Something sharp and cold cuts into her wrists. She tries again. Clink. Looking up, she waits for the rocking motion to pass. Focuses hard. Sees handcuffs encircling her wrists.

Adrenaline rushes through her body.

What does she remember? Gunshots. Hannah screaming.

Samuel.

She tries opening her mouth to scream. The stab of pain is intense. Is her jaw broken? The room rocks back and forth. The room? What room?

She is his prisoner.

She shifts her legs. No chains, she can move them freely. Where is Samuel? Is he in the shadows watching her? Why doesn't he say something? Instead of pulling her arms down she stretches them out. Touches the wooden surface above her. Is it a table?

In the distance, a car door creaks. Rusty hinges. His vehicle. He is nearby.

She knows what he does to his victims. She's seen the photos. She breaks out in a sweat, her heart pounding.

I'm not his victim. I won't be his victim.

Wolfe tries to slow her rapid breathing. *Think! You can get out of cuffs. You know how to do this.*

Wolfe pushes against the iron table legs. Something cushions her back. Lumpy. She still wears her backpack. Thank God. Her fingers pick at the strap over her right shoulder. It has what appears to be an overlap of fabric with a machine-sewn seam. She digs a fingernail under the flap and finds what she's looking for. A lock-pick. Teases it from its hiding place. Breaks the single stitch that holds it in place. *Don't drop it.*

She can't see the tiny keyholes in each cuff. She must do it by touch alone. She only needs to unlock one cuff, then she's free. After several stabs, the pick finally slides into a hole in the left cuff. She struggles to grip the tiny pick between her slick fingers. Struggles to turn it. Finally, a click. She pulls her left hand free.

A car door slams shut and she almost yelps. *He's coming.*

Wolfe clambers up, using the table to steady herself. Fumbling in the semi-dark, she feels for a window latch, finds it, opens it wide, sees dirt on the other side. Head first, she wriggles through the narrow gap, landing in the dirt.

She tries to get her bearings.

At first Wolfe thinks she sees little cabins with pitched roofs, but these roofs sag and the walls flap in the breeze. Tents. To her right, ripples of moonlight dance on a waterhole. She knows this place. She flew over it two days ago. The volunteers' camp. And it's empty. She runs.

81

A smile stretches Samuel's thin lips and a rush of anticipation warms him like a shot of whisky on a cold night. Wolfe is a worthy opponent. She must have had a lock-pick on her. Clever minx.

Samuel does not have feelings in the way he understands others do. Anger and hatred he can do. Sexual arousal? Of course. Love? Compassion? Empathy? Never. They are weaknesses. Weaknesses that can be exploited. Admiration? He's come close to it a few times. Samuel's pretty sure he admired his father, although he's never quite sure where fear ends and admiration begins.

His victims always disappoint him. Not one has earned his admiration. But Wolfe shows potential.

He leaves his two bags on the table and peers out of the open window. If she runs straight ahead, as they usually do, she'll pass some tents and end up at the kitchen-dining hut. Beyond that, there's very little. Open terrain. Nowhere to hide. From his toolbox he takes a filled syringe and pops it in a coat pocket. Checks his hunting knife is on the back of his belt. No more shooting. Too much risk the noise will carry and somebody will hear it.

And he wants Wolfe alive.

Ignoring the tenderness of his bruised eye sockets, Samuel puts on his night-vision goggles and jogs around the outside of the hut to the open window. The sandy ground is riddled with fresh boot marks.

He follows her trail. As he expected, she's heading through the tents. Good. A game of hide and seek.

The camp is ten miles from the nearest habitation, thirty miles from the nearest road. He took Wolfe's phone so she can't call for help. She has no gun. She's totally isolated.

The thrill of the chase.

'O-liv-ia! Ready or not, here I come,' he calls.

He wants her freaked, so she makes a mistake.

Her footprints lead him down a sandy incline. To his left, a circular steel water tank with side ladder. Next a paved driveway that leads to the large hut with steps leading up to it. There's a confusion of partial footprints, some large sized, some smaller, left behind by whoever was here last. It doesn't matter. He's certain she's in the hut.

Samuel takes the syringe from his jacket and removes the cap. The step up to the entrance creaks. If she's inside, she'll know he's coming. If he was her, he'd wait just inside the door and smash him with a pot or something heavy.

Changing his mind, he walks around the hut to the viewing platform. There are wooden benches and a circular open fireplace of charred logs and ash. Glass double doors lead to the dining room, the tables set up in a rectangular shape. He heads for the double doors, turns the door handle. It's either jammed or locked. He pushes. It scrapes across the floorboards. He curses to himself. Methodically, Samuel checks under the tables, then heads for the kitchen, swivelling his head one way and then the next, looking for her heat signature.

A fridge hums. He sniffs. Cooking fat and the faint smell of lemon. What else? Is the sweat hers or part of the building?

Suddenly he is blinded, as if a laser points straight at his eyeballs. He rips off the goggles, his eyes burning. The fucking bitch turned on the lights! He's smacked from behind. Dazed, he opens his eyes, sees beyond the dancing white blobs. Wolfe swings a frying pan at his head again. He dives for her legs and rips them from under her.

Wolfe hits the ground hard.

82

Butcher trained Wolfe to react fast when under attack. Samuel stands over her. She's winded from the fall. The hut lights dazzle. She squints up at the assassin. It's imperative she gets up. While she's prostrate, she's at his mercy.

Except for them, the camp is deserted, and nobody knows where she is. Samuel leans in. She blinks. What's in his hand? A syringe. Wolfe reacts. Turns on one side, props herself up on one arm, and kicks fast and hard at his hand, over and over, pounding him with thick-soled biker boots. She mustn't let him use the syringe. As she kicks, she claws at the floor, dragging herself away from the killer. But he keeps coming. A powerful kick to the stomach has Samuel reeling back. Wolfe jumps up, then hurtles down the steps to the exterior deck, jumps the deck's barrier, drops into blackness, landing four feet below. Wolfe sprints for the waterhole. She prays it's deep enough to hide in.

The water is shockingly cold. The mud sucks at her boots. She wades in further, heading for the dense reeds, her clothes heavy, dragging her down. Warthogs snort in panic and scatter, tails high. Samuel gives chase. Leaves the hut lights on. Good. Surely somebody will see them? Or is everybody asleep?

Shoving reeds out of her way, she heads for deeper water. *Stay still and duck low, or keep moving?* She peers behind her. Can't see him. Wolfe kneels behind dense reeds, the muddy water up to her shoulders. Is there something in the water Samuel fears? Snakes? Hippos? Wolfe dare not move.

A snap as a reed breaks. The water ripples. Something or someone is very near.

Samuel sees her, the glow of her body a vivid green through the night-vision goggles. Wolfe's ingenuity excites him. The chase thrills. But he's never liked water and he's now up to his hips in it. He just has to get near enough to stab her neck with the paralysis drug. He moves as quietly as possible.

Wolfe is straight ahead. Her head turns in his direction. Then she disappears. Where did she go? The water ripples. Ah, the clever bitch has swum away.

In the distance, a beam of light cuts through the darkness. *Fuck!* Somebody has seen the hut's lights. The single beam bounces up and down and then forms two beams. Headlights. Samuel wades out of the muddy water. He'll need his guns.

They will not take her from him.

Wolfe has seen the vehicle's lights too. Hope energises her. She stumbles and falls face down in the water, her legs numb with cold, the waterhole's bed, slick. She's up again, legs pumping, shoving the reeds aside.

The vehicle screeches to a halt. Doors swing open. Two people get out. The headlights are blinding. She can't identify them.

'Olivia!' Her name is called over and over. Two voices. One familiar. Casburn's.

'Over here!' Wolfe tries shouting between gasping breaths, her muscles screaming, the water like glue. 'Help me!'

Faster!

Casburn doesn't hear. Doesn't see her emerge from the waterhole. He and the other man head for the hut with lights on. She reaches solid ground, her sodden boots, heavy, her feet sliding inside them. She heads for the light and the rumble of the truck's engine.

'He's got a rifle!' she calls.

An ear-splitting gunshot booms. Bats screech and fly from the trees. Wolfe throws herself to the ground, grazing her hands. She looks up. Forty or so feet away, a man lies splayed on the ground outside the big hut.

'Dan?' she calls. 'Are you okay?'

'Yes,' replies Casburn from behind the vehicle's open door, pistol raised and ready to fire. 'Tumi's been shot.'

Tumi moans, calling to God for mercy. She has to help him. This is all because of her. Samuel followed her to this reserve. He's already taken Hannah's father. She can't let him take Tumi too.

If Casburn breaks cover, he will die. She's about to bet her life that Samuel wants her alive. He easily could have killed her many times before now. He hasn't. He drugged and handcuffed her. Probably intends to torture her, like Pieter Venter. It appears that everyone else in the killer's mind is expendable: Hannah, Tumi, Casburn. Samuel might shoot to injure her, but it's a risk she's willing to take.

She bolts towards Tumi.

'Dan! Stay where you are,' she yells. 'He'll shoot you.'

Casburn shouts back. 'Get down.'

Wolfe keeps running.

Casburn moves his pistol, searching for a sign of the assassin's location. But even with her minimal knowledge of firearms, she knows a pistol won't be much use. Samuel is too far away. Seems to have a clear line of sight. Has a long-distance rifle.

Tumi clutches his stomach. He's shaking. Moaning he's cold.

Ten feet to go. A shot rings out and sends dirt flying just ahead of her. Wolfe looks up. It came from the direction of the water tank. It has a ladder and a narrow platform around it. A perfect vantage point. That was a warning shot. Samuel wants her to stop.

I'm not stopping. No way.

'Get down, Olivia!' Casburn shouts.

'He won't kill me. Wants me alive.'

'Where is he?'

'Water tank,' she says.

Another shot only just misses her boot. By design, not accident. She's right: Samuel wants her alive. It also tells her he's a very good shot. Wolfe throws herself to the ground next to Tumi.

'Tumi?'

His eyes are glazed, his jaw locked into a grimace, his shirt is soaked in blood. 'Oliv... help–'

Tumi's head flops to one side. She checks his pulse. Nothing. 'Tumi?' She presses her ear against his chest. No heartbeat. She closes his eyes. 'I'm so sorry.'

Anger builds inside her. Tumi was a good man. And now he's dead. Killed trying to save her. And she could put an end to this. With one shot. Wolfe has never taken aim at someone with intent to kill. But all she can think about is stopping the monster from killing again.

Wolfe looks up at the water tank. 'You bastard!' she screams. 'I'm coming for you! You hear me!'

Wolfe grabs the RI Battle Rifle, the same brand as Hannah's. It's surprisingly heavy.

'Throw it to me,' Casburn shouts.

Casburn is former SAS. He will hit his target. But Wolfe hesitates, overcome by an aching need for revenge. It's as if her brain is in lock down and the only message getting through is *kill Samuel*.

'Olivia, don't! You're completely exposed.' From where Casburn shelters behind the car door, he frantically gestures at her to join him.

A bullet thuds into the ground next to her. The shock snaps her out of her crazy thoughts. She scuttles over to Casburn. Hands him the rifle.

'What the hell were you–' Casburn begins.

'Tumi's dead, Dan. It's Samuel.'

'You sure it's Samuel?'

'I'm sure.'

'Call Hannah. Number's in my phone. We need backup and fast. Phone's in my jeans pocket.'

Wolfe shoves a hand into the pocket. 'I swear, this is the only time I'll ever rummage in your pants.'

The truck jolts, and tilts to the left. He's taken out a tyre, the same trick he used earlier on Hannah's vehicle. Another bullet shatters the windscreen. Wolfe stares at Casburn's mobile phone. 'Shit! No signal. Two-way radio?'

'Too risky. We're sitting ducks. Okay, let's nail this son of a bitch,' Casburn says. 'Water tank?'

'Yes.'

Casburn takes the rifle, unfolds the bipod which takes the weight of the mid-section and stabilises the muzzle, and also makes it easier to move up and down, left to right. He checks the twenty-round detachable box magazine, then lies in the dirt on his stomach with the vehicle's door above his head. 'It's an oldie. Let's hope she's still accurate.'

He peers through the rear scope. 'I can't see him.'

'He was there a few seconds ago.' She crawls closer to Casburn. 'Did you find Hannah?'

'She found us. Tough lady. Drove on bald tyres. Woke us up.' He moves the muzzle slightly. 'Where did you go?' he says to himself, trying to spot the assassin.

'Police coming?'

'Yes, but they'll take too long.'

Casburn moves the rifle a fraction to the left. 'Ah, there you are,' says Casburn, aiming for a tent. 'You sneaky bastard.'

'He's wearing a bulletproof vest,' Wolfe says.

'Fine. I'll take off his head.'

Casburn's finger gently squeezes the trigger. The crack and following boom stuns her. An empty cartridge flies through the air and lands on the ground. Samuel returns fire. A bullet clanks into the pick-up truck. The next hits its mark. Casburn cries out and rolls back under the door, dragging the rifle with him. His eyes are clenched. He clutches his chest.

'I'm hit.'

83

Blood wells through Casburn's splayed fingers. 'Jesus!' Wolfe tears off her quilted coat, rolls it into a ball and stuffs it inside Casburn's jacket to stem the blood flow.

'You're going to have to do this,' says Casburn, voice ragged.

'I'm a crap shot.'

'Kill him before he kills us,' Casburn gasps through gritted teeth. 'He's behind the nearest tent. Left side.'

Wolfe takes the R1 and gets into position, belly on the floor, searching for Samuel through the scope. Her hands tremble. *Can I kill in cold-blood?*

There's a blur of movement between two tents. Samuel is out in the open, about to dive behind another tent. Wolfe holds her breath and squeezes the trigger. The rifle butt kicks back into her shoulder painfully. The noise is deafening. Then, nothing.

'I missed. Can't see him.'

The rifle is suddenly blown out of her grasp, the shockwave reverberating up her arm. Wood splinters. She screams. The rifle lies three feet away, the stock splintered, the sight shattered. Wolfe watches in horror as Samuel sprints at them.

Casburn sees him too. 'Go! Now! Get help.'

'I'm not leaving you.'

'Stop arguing. Key's in the ignition.'

'You're coming with me.' She takes an arm. 'Get up!'

Casburn clings to her, teeth clenched. Struggles up, then collapses back to the ground.

'No time,' Casburn mutters, grimacing.

Samuel is almost upon them. She has only a few seconds to make a decision. She'll do what she did when Hannah was wounded. She'll get Samuel to chase her. Lead him away from Casburn.

She bolts. Not towards the cover of the reeds, or into the dark bushveld, or through the jumble of tents. She heads for the camp's kitchen-dining hut.

Follow me, you son of a bitch.

Wolfe takes the hut's steps two at a time, throws the door open, her eyes overwhelmed by the sudden bright light. Slamming the door behind her, she curses. No lock. Looks around. Tables and chairs. Wildlife pictures pinned to the walls. A tea urn and mugs. But no landline. She kills the lights. On all fours, she feels her way through the darkness to the kitchen, following the fatty food smells.

'O-liv-ia!' Samuel calls, his voice taunting. 'I have something you might want to see. Why don't you come out?'

Wolfe has reached the kitchen sink. Above it, moonlight spills through the window and reflects off the taps. On both sides of the sink are countertops in wood.

Does anybody know where they are? Did Tumi call it in before he was shot? Wolfe raises her head above the sink, just far enough to see outside. Bathed in the pick-up's headlights, Samuel holds a pistol to Casburn's head. Rifle slung over his shoulder. Casburn's arms are behind him – probably handcuffed.

Casburn calls out. 'Run!'

Samuel responds by wrenching his arms back further. Casburn groans.

'Let him go. It's me you want,' she shouts.

'Come out. Or he dies.'

For the first time, Wolfe can see some of Samuel's features.

Receding hairline, five foot eight, wiry and muscular. Bulletproof vest over his shirt. Rifle slung over his shoulder. Nothing remarkable about him.

'Undo his cuffs,' she shouts. 'Let him walk away. Then I come out.'

'No!' Casburn shouts.

Samuel smirks. 'So he can get help and spoil my fun? I don't think so. Surrender and you have my word I'll let the filth live.'

'I've got a better idea. You and I leave this place. Leave Casburn behind. He lives. I go with you voluntarily. That's the deal.'

'You're in no position to make deals. I kill him now, then you.'

'But that's not your style, is it, Samuel? Sure, you can kill us. But where's the satisfaction in that?' Wolfe pauses. Samuel is silent. He's listening. 'I've seen the care you take with your victims. The precision. The... creativity.' Wolfe almost chokes. Her flesh crawls. But she must be convincing. 'You have followers, don't you? People who appreciate your work?'

Samuel tilts his head to one side, listening.

'Olivia, don't,' Casburn pleads.

Wolfe ignores him.

'I can be your greatest work. But nothing comes for free. My price is his freedom.'

'Olivia, for God's sake!' Casburn says.

Samuel digs the muzzle of his pistol into Casburn's face. 'I'll shoot him right now!'

'No, you won't. If you do, you'll never have me. I swear to you. I'll kill myself before that happens.'

'Ballsy bitch, aren't you?' Samuel peers down at Casburn for a moment, then up again at her. 'You have a deal.'

'This is a contract, Samuel,' Wolfe says. 'I need to know you're going to honour it.'

Samuel lowers the pistol. Unlocks Casburn's handcuffs. 'I will.'

84

Hands above her head, Wolfe leaves the hut. Her legs threaten to give way. A voice screams in her head to stop. She lifts her chin, stiffens her back, trying to disguise her terror. Casburn is on his knees, slumped forward.

'No,' he says. 'Go back.'

She hears him, but if she listens they're both lost. Her eyes are locked on to Samuel.

When she is about halfway between him and the hut, Samuel raises his hand. 'That's far enough. Take off your pack. Drop it.'

Wolfe is loath to lose it, but she won't make the same mistake twice. He must have worked out the lock-pick was in her pack. Reluctantly she slides the straps off her shoulders and drops the bag to the ground.

'Good. Keep coming.'

All too soon, she has closed the gap between them.

'Here I am, Samuel. Now Casburn leaves, unharmed.'

Samuel raises his pistol and aims it at the back of the detective's head.

'We have a deal.'

Samuel smiles. 'He wanted you,' he says, 'in perfect condition.

Delivered to his door. But he broke our contract. So now you're all mine.'

In perfect condition for what? And who? Her blackmailer?

'Samuel, please,' Casburn says. 'If the contract's cancelled, let us go. You don't have to do this.'

'Ah, now I have a new contract. With Olivia. She must keep her promise.'

'Okay, Samuel. You have me. Casburn gets in the bakkie and drives away, okay?'

Samuel laughs. A childish giggle. How can a man who tortures and murders laugh like a child in a playground?

'What's so funny?' Wolfe asks.

'You.' The smile is gone.

'Where's he going? Huh? Bleeding like a stuck pig. Can't walk. Truck's busted. And, besides, I like an audience.'

Wolfe suddenly feels very cold. Her saturated clothes and the frigid night air are nothing to the harrowing realisation her gamble has failed.

And now they are both screwed.

'Help him inside,' Samuel orders.

Wolfe places an arm around Casburn's back. 'I'm sorry,' she says to him. He puts an arm around her shoulders.

'Move!' Samuel waves the pistol at them.

Casburn sways, his face contorting with pain. He leans on her. The blood stain on his shirt is spreading. He's growing weak.

'If you get the chance, run,' Casburn whispers.

'We're both getting out of here. Or not at all.'

Plastic ties bind her wrists at shoulder height to a thick bar on the door of an industrial-sized oven.

Wolfe has made a terrible mistake. A mistake that will cost them both their lives.

She'd hoped to give Casburn a chance. To live. Instead, they are both Samuel's prisoner. Casburn lies on the kitchen floor, face white and slick with sweat, panting heavily from the exertion. Samuel hasn't cuffed him. It's obvious he's too weak to cause trouble.

Samuel undoes the Velcro straps of his bulletproof vest and pulls it up and over his head, then rubs his ribs.

'Not a bad shot,' he says, kneeling next to her. His breath stinks of biltong, a dried meat.

'You're a tricky one. Anything else concealed?' he asks, patting her down, a hand lingering on her inner thighs.

'Leave her alone,' Casburn says between ragged breaths.

'Shut up, filth. One more noise from you and I'll cut your tongue out.'

Samuel touches her breast, his fingers tighten, pinching a nipple through her T-shirt. She fights the inclination to cry out.

He smiles. 'Ah. So it is true. You have piercings.'

Wolfe looks into the coldest pair of eyes she's ever seen. Like two black marbles. His hand moves to the other breast. She pulls her head back and then thrusts it forward, aiming for his nose. She misses and hits his forehead. Samuel barely flinches. Casburn lunges for the pistol holstered on Samuel's belt. He's too slow. Samuel kicks Casburn's face, hard. The detective's eyes roll back into unconsciousness.

'Leave him alone!' Wolfe yells.

The slap he gives her stings. 'Shut the fuck up.'

Making him angry only makes things worse. Wolfe struggles to calm herself. After two or three deep, shaky breaths, she softens her voice. 'Let him go, Samuel. Please.'

'I told him to behave. Now he has to be punished.'

Samuel draws his pistol and shoots Casburn in the foot. 'Now he can't run.'

Casburn jerks, his eyes fly open, screaming.

Samuel drags him towards the kitchen island bench and uses a plastic tie to secure him. Then he rummages in a cupboard under the sink, pulls out a torch. He switches it on and the beam lights up the underside of his chin. 'Reminds me of when I was a kid, making creepy shadows on the wall,' he says, swinging the beam playfully from her to Casburn.

Suddenly Samuel is in her face.

'Open your mouth.'

'What?'

'You do as I say, remember?'

'If you let him leave.'

'Nuh-uh.' He shakes his head. 'I have plans for him. Open your mouth or I'll necklace him. Got the tyres just outside. And petrol.'

A sob escapes her throat and she hates herself for showing fear. She opens her mouth.

85

Samuel peers into her mouth as if he were a dentist doing a tooth extraction.

'Ah there it is.'

Filthy fingers fill her mouth, his fingernails scratch at her tongue. Wolfe gags. She can't breathe.

'Don't bite me. He'll die if you do.'

Samuel forces her jaw wider. It feels like he's going to dislocate it. She retches. A tug. She jolts, eyes wide with panic. He's got hold of her tongue stud.

'I could rip it out, you know. Split your tongue in two. Like a snake.'

She chokes, mouth full of fingers and saliva, her eyes plead with him. He lets go of the stud and wipes them on his jeans.

'Not yet,' he says.

Wolfe coughs. Then spits away the grit and sweaty residue from his fingers. Before she can take a proper breath, a tea towel is shoved between her teeth and tied behind her head.

'As for you,' Samuel says to Casburn. 'You can watch. Admire my precision.'

Samuel leaves the hut, taking the torch. Wolfe tries to speak, shouting through the towel, but it's just muffled noise. She lifts up her boot and rests it on Casburn's hip. She nods at it.

'Mhhhhhhhhhh.'

Inside the boot's padded tongue is a three-inch blade. She wants Casburn to pull it out and give it to her.

Casburn shuffles closer, but each movement is clearly agony. He reaches out and touches the toe of her boot. Wolfe gestures upwards with her head. Casburn follows her direction. His hand slides up to the boot's tongue. She nods enthusiastically. He squeezes the tongue, clearly feels something. Tries digging his fingers underneath. Fails. Undoes the laces.

Samuel clomps up the outside steps. No time to tie her laces, Casburn tucks them into her boot. Wolfe scrambles back to where she was when Samuel left. Casburn lies on his side, panting.

A large black duffel bag lands heavily on the kitchen table. Samuel sets the torch up on a chair, the beam on her, then props his phone up against the side of the duffel bag, the screen facing her. Kneeling next to Wolfe, he tugs down the tea towel.

'Say hi,' he says. 'Shame you can't wave. They'd like that.'

She glances at his phone. He's opened up a live link. 'Who's watching?'

'Artists like me.'

Artists? Christ! Psychopaths more like.

'How do you know them?'

'Chat room. My chat room. Invitation only.'

'So those photos? The four victims with their noses sliced off. They were shared in your chat room?'

'No, no, not victims. I made them more beautiful in death than they were in life.'

Samuel opens the bag and takes out what looks like a drill with a long rotating blade. She stifles a scream. She has to find a way to connect with him. Keep him talking. But God knows how to connect with a psychopath who gets off on other people's pain.

'This is used in knee replacement surgery. Very effective at removing kneecaps, too.'

He places it carefully on the kitchen table. Next a metal hammer, plyers, forceps, scissors, sutures, then a machete. 'Good for hacking, but can be inaccurate and messy.' Next, a scalpel. 'Excellent at peeling back skin.'

Wolfe stares at the phone. Who is watching? Are they all as sick as Samuel? He sees her look.

'If you think they'll help you, you're wrong.'

'Why cut off the noses, hands and feet? What were you trying to say?'

He walks over to her, scalpel in hand. 'I'd have thought you'd have worked that out. A bright girl like you.' He holds the scalpel up to her face. Wolfe flinches. 'Look around you.'

Wolfe peers around the wooden hut.

'Not here,' says Samuel, irritated. 'Out there.'

'Poachers.' Wolfe says after a few seconds. 'Slicing off noses instead of horn. And the ears are proof of the kill.'

'And the fingers in Pieter's skull?'

She wants to scream, *You sick fuck*! She counts to three. Just keep him talking. 'His horns,' she answers. 'Like a rhino.'

'Top of the class.'

'Why?' she asks.

'It's a theme. But I'm bored with it now.' He runs the scalpel down her neck, pausing over her carotid artery. 'Tonight, I'm going to explore a new theme.'

The blade is millimetres away from ending her life. She stares at Casburn. He's not moving, eyes closed, breathing shallow. He's lost a lot of blood.

'Dan! Talk to me!'

'Looks like he isn't going to make it,' Samuel says. 'Shame.'

'Please, help him. You have me. He doesn't need to die.'

'Everyone dies. You will die here, so will he.'

No! I will not die.

She racks her brain for a way to distract him. 'Why those specific people?' Wolfe asks. 'Russia, Finland, Oxford. Why travel all over when you could do your work here?'

'Simple. I do the hit, create my art, then make sure the bodies are never found.'

Keep him talking.

'Why the Russian woman with the unborn baby?'

Samuel slides the scalpel under the neck of her T-shirt, then jerks the blade outwards, slicing open the T-shirt top to bottom, revealing her bra. Wolfe glances at the phone on the table, with its live feed, people getting a kick out of her terror.

Well they can't have it. They won't see her screaming, begging for mercy.

Samuel tuts at her. 'I know what you're doing. Keep him talking. Blah, blah. Like we're old buddies. Get me to say things I shouldn't. Reveal secrets. Then you run.' He leans close. 'Only thing is, you can't run.'

'Humour me.'

Samuel runs fingertips over her upper arm. 'So smooth. This is the first piece.'

He presses the scalpel blade into her skin and begins cutting.

86

It's like a blowtorch to her skin, setting her every nerve on fire. Jaw clenched, fists balled, Wolfe stares at the pattern on a tea towel draped over the back of a chair so as to not give him the satisfaction of screaming. It has South African birds on it, each one named, but the wording is the wrong way up. This gives her something to think about. The blade slices across her arm. Tears escape her eyes. She's furious with herself.

Don't show your pain. Focus on the birds.

There's one with a red head and back, and black belly. She deciphers the upside-down lettering. *A red bishop.* A brown bird with black and white wings and a crazy hair-do like a punk with feathers. *Hoopoe bird.* She grinds her teeth, trying to imagine the sound it makes. *Fish eagle clutching a fish. Huge talons. Magnificent bird of prey.* She pants with the exertion and the bright, burning pain.

'Beautiful,' says Samuel. 'A perfect crimson smile. Look!'

Wolfe doesn't want to see it.

'Look!' he yells.

She drags her eyes away from the sanctuary of the birds. He holds up a crescent-shaped piece of skin ten centimetres long. Her skin. Her vision blurs. She can't help peering down at her arm. Raw and bloody, an open wound a few millimetres deep. She starts to hyperventilate. How much more of this can she take? *Birds. Think of the birds, flying free in the sky.* Wolfe closes her eyes again. What was that Zulu story she read to Jacob? That's it: *The King of the Birds*. How did it go? *The animals had appointed their leader. Bhubesi, a mighty lion. But the birds wanted their own leader. The fish eagle, Nkwazi, assumed he would be king. But the kori bustard and the eagle owl challenged him. What were their names?*

Something wet touches the skin beneath the wound. Dear God, he's licking the blood running down her arm. She does her best to block him out.

What were the challengers called? Never mind. There was a tiny bird, Southern African warbler, who said he wanted to be king. All the birds laughed at him. So, they set a test to see who would be most worthy: they must fly up into the sky and the bird that flew the highest would be the king.

'Open your eyes,' Samuel says, his fingers pushing up her lids. 'Look at me!'

His mouth is bloody. Her blood. His hand is on his crotch. There's no mistaking his erection. He's getting off on her suffering. Her stomach heaves. And again. She can't stop it, and throws up, turning her head to one side. Samuel leaps back, narrowly avoiding being hit.

'Filthy bitch!'

He seizes the tea towel, wets it in the sink, wipes her face and the gelatinous vomit on the floor, then chucks it in the bin.

Her birds are gone.

Samuel has put the severed patch of her skin on what looks like kitchen greaseproof paper. A long strip of paper. Plenty of space for more pieces of skin. Casburn hasn't moved, eyes closed as though comatose. Beneath his wounded foot, blood has pooled. There is no point calling to him. He cannot save her. He cannot even save himself.

Her chin is grabbed. 'You're not putting on much of a show.' Samuel flicks a look at the phone, the live feed running. 'You're an interesting one, though, I'll give you that. I cut you. You don't scream.

I wank off. You puke. What's that about?' He scratches at a square patch of scarred skin on his neck.

Wolfe doesn't answer.

As before, she tries to distract herself. She goes back to the story of the contest to be *King of the Birds*. The three big birds and the tiny warbler flew up into the sky. Whoever flew the highest was the winner.

'Tell me!' Samuel yells in her face.

But the warbler was clever. He hid under the fish eagle's wing and hitched a ride. The owl, then the bustard, gave up and the exhausted eagle thought he had won. But the little warbler came out from under his giant wing and flew higher than the eagle. The bird of prey could not keep going and so the little bird, that everyone had underestimated, won the competition. Can I be that little bird? she thinks.

'You're used to pain, aren't you?' he says. 'Who did it to you? Father? Brother? Boyfriend?'

She doesn't answer.

Suddenly his eyes widen. 'Ah, I get it,' he continues. 'A self-harmer.'

'Did you cut yourself too?' Wolfe asks, holding his gaze.

'I knew it,' he says triumphantly. 'You're used to this. Was it razor blades?'

'Sometimes,' she replies. 'You?'

If she can connect with him, perhaps he won't kill her.

'I enjoyed it,' Samuel says. 'It felt good. Like I could conquer the world. And you?'

Wolfe looks away.

'Answer me!'

'I...' This is taking her to a place she vowed never to return. She looks at him again. 'Self-loathing. Blamed myself for Dad leaving. Mum said it was my fault.'

For a split second she thinks she sees something close to sympathy in the softening of his stare. Then his eyes narrow. He looks at the arm he has cut into.

'You fucking liar! No marks.'

'Wrong arm,' she says. 'I'm right-handed. So, I cut the left.'

Samuel steps over her, pulls up the sleeve, peers at the pale underside of her left arm. It's covered in thin, pale scars, thirty or more.

'I'm not lying,' she says.

He strokes her hair, like you would a dog. 'I see that.' Then goes to the table and opens a hard plastic suitcase she hasn't seen before. 'You know what this means?'

'What?'

'It means we're going to have to try harder. I see that now. Can't disappoint my audience.'

She's failed to bond with her captor.

Samuel opens the case. Inside are syringes and vials of liquid. She almost wets herself. What horror is he about to inflict on her next? She can't keep this up. The talking, the pain. Pretending to be brave. Casburn is bleeding out. Dying. This has to stop.

'Hey!' she says, addressing the voyeurs watching her torture live, looking straight at the phone's screen, 'Poaching syndicate! Yes, you. The Metropolitan Police are onto you. All you sickos are going to jail for life. Harold Sackville! Your career's over. Yury Sukletin! Putin can't protect you anymore. Terry Blunt, your shipment won't reach...'

The smack in the mouth slams her head back into the oven door.

'Shut the fuck up!' Samuel yells.

Wolfe shouts, louder this time. 'You kill me, all hell breaks loose. They will hunt you down–'

He smacks her across the mouth again. 'I said, shut it!'

Samuel's phone rings, terminating the live feed. On the screen is a phone number. She recognises the country dialling code: Zimbabwe. She memorises the number, repeating it over and over in her head.

87

Samuel's phone conversation is brief.

'You think I do this for money...? I don't give a fuck!' Samuel yells. The person calling shouts back. Samuel is puce in the face. 'Okay, okay, no more audience.'

The phone is shoved into his jeans' back pocket. 'Arsehole!'

'Boss not happy?' A glimmer of hope. Perhaps he'll stop torturing her?

'You stupid bitch!' he screams into her face. 'Because of you, I'll have to hurry.'

Samuel no longer moves with languid ease. There is an efficient urgency about him. Selecting a syringe, he injects her left forearm, forcing whatever it contains into her body.

'That should do it,' he says.

It runs cold through her veins. 'What did you give me?'

'It magnifies pain.'

God help me.

'You're afraid,' he says, guessing her thoughts. 'Good. You should be.'

Keep him talking.

'Promise me one thing, Samuel. Whatever you do, make it beautiful.' *He thinks it's art, for Christ's sake. Play along.* 'And take photos. If this is the last of me, then make it magnificent.'

'The more pain you feel, the more beautiful you'll be.'

Wolfe can't keep up the façade any longer. She can hardly breathe. Claustrophobic panic. She tugs at her bindings, the plastic ties cut into her wrists. The pain from such a simple movement catches her by surprise. She gasps. The drug is working.

Samuel watches. 'It's time. The stomach, near the pubic bone, is particularly sensitive.'

The scalpel digs into her flesh just below a hip bone. This pain hits her with the force of a gale, unlike anything she's ever known before. Her ear-splitting scream even causes Samuel to pause. It no doubt carries out across the campsite.

'At last,' he says. 'You make me happy.'

Wolfe can take pain better than most. But this is unbearable. She pants, eyes clenched. *How can I stop him? How? Anything. I'll do anything.* Wolfe forces herself to look at her torturer. His head is a few centimetres from hers, his focus on his scalpel.

'Samuel?'

He looks up. She kisses his lips. He tastes of sour milk, spicy meat and unbrushed teeth. She forces herself to ignore the stench.

Samuel pulls his head back. Confused. Shocked. Wary. He withdraws the scalpel. 'What are you doing?'

'I want you,' she says.

'What?'

'I want you. Fuck me as you cut me,' she says.

Samuel sits back on his haunches, frowning. Exactly what she had intended.

'What is this?'

'Cut me again.'

'Where?'

'Thigh, but not too deep. You want me alive, don't you?'

'You like this?' Part incredulous, part hopeful.

'I feel everything. It's terrifying and amazing,' she replies. 'Take off my jeans and fuck me as you do it.'

'I... don't...'

'I don't care. Do it.'

Wolfe sees the tremor in his hands as he lays the scalpel on the floor and fumbles with her jeans' button, then the zip. He slides them down her thighs and leaves them bunched above her boots. He uses the scalpel to cut her panties away. It takes all her willpower not to cringe.

'We're not so different, Samuel. Do you see that?' she says. 'Let me hold you.' Samuel hesitates. But she senses the balance of power shifting. 'At least one arm. Let me touch you.'

Samuel severs the plastic tie around her right wrist, then, leaving the scalpel on the table out of reach, he tugs off his jeans and underwear, kicking them aside. Then he pulls her down so she's flat on the floor, her left arm still tied above her to the now open oven door.

'I knew you were special,' he murmurs.

She kisses him again. It's all she can do to stop herself vomiting in his mouth. She bends her knees, so her boots are close to her bottom. She doesn't have long. Her free hand finds the tongue of her boot.

Samuel lies on top of her, crushing her. Her stomach wound is agony and her blood is slippery between them. He fumbles with his dick.

Wolfe plunges the blade into his back, aiming for his kidney.

88

Wolfe rips the blade from Samuel's back and stabs again. His body jerks and he grunts. She's missed her mark. If she'd hit a kidney, he'd be dead. Wolfe pulls her legs into her chest, stomach muscles screaming, then kicks out at his chest with every ounce of her remaining strength. Her kick propels Samuel backwards and onto the floor. He roars, yanks the knife – still embedded in his back – out, and flings it away.

Samuel battles to get up. Staggers towards the table. Grabs a machete. Limps towards her.

She has nothing to defend herself with, and one arm is still cuffed.

Samuel collapses to his knees. But he has the strength to raise the machete above his head. She throws a punch up and into his throat with every ounce of panic, terror and rage she has. Samuel falls to the side, making sucking, gasping sounds. She's crushed his throat.

Wolfe rips the machete from his hand, uses it to cut the plastic tie holding her, and stands up on unsteady feet.

Samuel's face is puce, swollen. He's suffocating. His end is near.

All Wolfe feels is incandescent, destructive hatred.

It tightens her muscles. It empowers her. Like an ice addict, she feels unstoppable. She wants to tear him limb from limb. She wants him to feel the pain he's inflicted on her. And on others.

'You evil piece of shit,' she shrieks, raising the machete above her head.

Out of the corner of her eye she sees Casburn's hand move. His eyes flutter. He's watching. She hesitates, then slams the machete down, slicing clean through Samuel's wrist, just a few seconds before he finally dies.

89

Casburn drifts in and out of consciousness, his skin grey and clammy. Wolfe searches for a First Aid kit. Finds one. Finds clean tea towels. Uses a couple against Casburn's chest. Bandages them in place. She daren't take the boot off his injured foot so she uses a tablecloth wound around and around the boot to compress the wound. Every move is agony for her.

Wolfe covers the open wound on her arm with a large sticking plaster and then uses a couple on her stomach where he cut her. She swallows some painkillers. Her torturer is dead, his face bloated, his body twisted, his eyes bulging. Even in death, they seem to watch her.

In his jeans, she finds his mobile phone. It's switched on. She doesn't know Hannah's number or anyone's on the reserve. She dials emergency services, asks for an air ambulance, explains as best she can their location.

'Two gunshot wounds. Chest and foot. He's lost a lot of blood. Semi-conscious. He's hardly breathing. Please hurry.'

They tell her it could take thirty minutes to reach her and to use car headlights to illuminate a flat and open area for the chopper to land. She thanks them. But thirty minutes is too long.

She needs more immediate assistance. Racing from the hut, she dives into the pick-up's cabin. Grabs the two-way radio and calls for help, trying every frequency. Just when she is about to give up, a man named Kwende answers.

'I am Poaching Patrol. Who is this?'

Wolfe explains who and where she is.

'Hannah tell us to search for you,' Kwende says. 'I will be with you very soon.'

'Thank God.'

'We will bring torches and guide the helicopter. Soon it will be sunrise. It will be okay, Miss Wolfe.'

'Wait! Can you contact Henry Clarke?'

'Yes. He is searching for you.'

'Tell him we need his helicopter. The air ambulance will take too long. We need him to fly Casburn to hospital.'

'I will tell him this. But he went to sector three. Far away.'

'Ask him anyway, please.'

'I will do this.'

All Wolfe can do now is wait and try to keep Casburn conscious. Maybe Clarke can reach them quicker than the air ambulance?

'Never thought I'd be doing this,' Wolfe mutters. She sits cross-legged next to Casburn and gently holds his hand. 'Dan, can you hear me? It's Olivia. Medics are on their way. You'll be fine. Just stay with me.'

He gives her hand a squeeze. 'I won't... make it.'

'You listen to me, Dan Casburn. You're a soldier. A survivor. You are not going to die. Dan?' Casburn opens his eyes.

'I didn't think...' his voice fades, '...it would be like this.'

'You're not going to die. You're going to be around for years, annoying the fuck out of me.'

The edges of his mouth crease into a weak smile. 'I'm cold. So cold.'

Wolfe lies on her side next to him, her body touching his. She gently lifts his head, so it lies in the crook of her shoulder. She holds him close, her limbs wrapped around him.

'He's gone, Dan. He won't hurt anyone ever again.' No response.

Wolfe lifts her head. Puts her hand against his lips. She feels no breath.

'Dan?'

90

MATABELELAND SOUTH, ZIMBABWE

Henry Clarke's flight plan says he is taking a tourist named Kate Parks from Rustenburg to Hwange National Park in Zimbabwe for a day's safari, returning that night. He's taking a big risk.

'How long before the authorities realise we're not at Hwange?' Wolfe says into her headphones' mouthpiece.

'Not sure. By this afternoon they'll know something's wrong.'

'Thank you for doing this, Henry.'

Clarke flicks her a worried look. 'Are you sure you're up to it?'

Wolfe touches the bruise on her swollen cheekbone. 'I have to be.'

The cuts to her arm and her lower abdomen have been cleaned, stitched, and dressed.

'It's only temporary,' the paramedic who treated her had said. 'We need to get you to hospital.'

Instead, she had talked him into injecting a local anaesthetic into her arm and abdomen. 'Just a few hours, then I'll take myself off to hospital. I have to find who's responsible for this.'

'They were right,' Clarke says. 'You should have gone to hospital. Your wounds could get infected.'

She doesn't know whether it's exhaustion, shock or the local anaesthetic, but Wolfe shakes her head, struggling to think clearly. At least the pain is being kept at bay. Her mind turns to Casburn.

Clarke looks her way, sees the worry on her face. 'He's at the best hospital. They'll look after him.'

She nods. Wolfe is in fresh clothes, has repacked her go-bag, added binoculars, and carries Casburn's pistol.

'Are you sure about the location?' Clarke asks.

Far beneath them is the bridge spanning the Limpopo River, which marks the border between South Africa and Zimbabwe.

'Yes. Ponnappa doesn't make mistakes.'

'Ponnappa?' Clarke asks.

'A British cybercrime expert. Just before he died, Samuel received a call from a Zimbabwean number. Turns out it's a 162,000-hectare private reserve about halfway between Thuli and Bulawayo in Matabeleland South. It was bought four years ago by a company registered in the Cayman Islands.' Wolfe looks at her watch. 'Let's hope he's still there.'

'And you think whoever made that call runs the poaching syndicate?'

'I do.'

'Then he'll be heavily guarded. And Matabeleland South is a poor district. The people are starving and angry. It's very dangerous for a white woman.' He glances at her.

'I know about the atrocities under Mugabe, Henry. But I have to do this.'

Wolfe lies flat on her belly in the tall grass as Clarke's chopper flies away. She is on the outside of a tall, electrified fence, five miles from the property's main homestead – a twelve-bedroom mansion – and four miles from the private runway and aircraft hangar. From where she lies she can't see any security cameras on the fence.

She sets off at a good pace, following the fence line. She wants to reach the house. Inside the fence, the land is flat and parched savannah. Nowhere to hide. She won't enter until she has some cover: she hopes the numerous buildings surrounding the mansion will give her that. The terrain gets increasingly rocky, the grass and low scrub punctuated by boulders which slows her progress. Every now and again she passes a sign, 'Private Property. Armed Patrols.'

Wolfe stops to take a drink and checks Google Maps. She wipes the perspiration from her forehead. On the other side of the fence are a wind-operated water pump and a man-made reservoir with concrete edges. A pride of lions lies listlessly in the shade nearby. The reservoir allows her to confirm her location. She's around half a mile from the hangar.

Wolfe ups the pace. Inside the compound, a wooden bridge spans a dried-up riverbed. It's the first road she's seen. The land rises. Through the metal mesh she can see the end of a runway and, shimmering in the distance, a collection of buildings hovers into view. She keeps going until she can see the hangar clearly.

Wolfe crouches down between boulders in the shade of a baobab. She retrieves a pair of binoculars and a small digital video camera from her pack. A Cessna approaches, the buzz like an angry hornet. She records its arrival and zooms in on the ID number painted on its fuselage. It lands with a slight hop and then taxis to the hangar. A door opens, steps unfurl. A man descends in a cream suit and pale blue shirt: the mayor of Johannesburg. He's followed by his wife, in a blue and white floral pattern dress. It's the third and final passenger who causes Wolfe to blanch. Dressed in black, it is none other than the grieving widow, Funani Ximba.

Why didn't I see that coming?

Wolfe guesses the mayor makes sure the authorities don't look too closely at the syndicate's activities, and Funani is no doubt just as involved as her late husband in laundering the proceeds. The trio head for a waiting Jeep. They are welcomed by a stocky man in khaki with a protruding belly, straw-coloured receding hair and a darker moustache – Terry Blunt.

A second, larger plane approaches soon after. A glistening G650 Gulfstream. It glides to a landing on the runway, the tyres producing a passing puff of blue smoke as they first touch the runway. The Gulfstream's door gracefully rotates out and down, the stairs folding toward the tarmac. After a few moments, a man in dark grey suit steps out and looks around – probably the protection detail. He's followed by a tall, grey-haired man in a navy-blue suit. Wolfe almost drops the camera. Harold Sackville, Chancellor of the Exchequer.

Something dark and cold slides against her temple.

'Do not move.'

Wolfe freezes. The camera is pulled from her hand, her arms dragged behind her and cuffed. She winces.

'Please, I'm wounded,' Wolfe says.

Some distance away, men are shouting. Her captor leans over her, his mouth close to her ear.

'Do not say my name, Olivia. You do not know me. Do as I say, and I will help you escape.'

91

He hauls Wolfe up to standing and holds her close.

'I don't understand,' she begins. 'What's going on?'

'Over here!' her captor shouts. Two men in khaki uniforms zigzag through the boulders towards them.

'What are you doing?' Wolfe says. 'Let me go.'

'Dmitry!' calls one of the men.

'Dmitry?' she echoes.

Vitaly Yushkov is dressed in the same khaki uniform as the soldiers. *He works for the criminal syndicate? The very syndicate that sent Samuel after her and butchered Thusago?*

'I warned you,' his voice is hushed. 'You should have left.'

'You work for *him*?' Her lip curls in contempt.

The soldiers are almost upon them. Her survival instinct kicks in. Wolfe lifts her boot and slams it down hard on Yushkov's foot. He takes her in a bear-hug she cannot break.

'Say nothing,' he whispers.

All the fight drains out of her. Has he been lying all this time? Is he Vitaly or Dmitry?

Wolfe instantly recognises the man she stands before. His sugar business, which started in Vietnam and is now the largest producer, refiner and wholesaler in all of Asia, is worth billions. But he is much better known as the Bill Gates of Asia, giving millions to charitable causes all over the world. His photos have appeared on the front cover of *Fortune* magazine. Wolfe remembers the article well; it hailed him as a 'mega-philanthropist', but included images from an ostentatious apartment on the Upper East Side facing Central Park. The juxtaposition had jarred. Wolfe has no doubt his substantial net worth is not all derived from sugar. Maybe not even mostly. The illegal trade in rhino horn is extremely lucrative.

Tan Nguyen, aged forty-two, is seated at a desk in a sand-coloured linen suit and white shirt, open at the neck. She can't help but notice two huge rhino horns next to his iPad Pro. Nguyen watches her arrival through round, heavy-lidded, hazel eyes. His dark hair is cut short, which emphasises his pronounced widow's peak.

Yushkov stands behind Wolfe, her arms still bound. He hasn't said a word since they got in the Jeep.

'It's good to meet the famous Tan Nguyen,' Wolfe says. 'I must admit, I had no idea you were the syndicate leader.'

Nguyen nods once. 'Olivia Wolfe, it is an honour to meet you, although your timing is a little inconvenient.' His eyes move from hers to Yushkov's. 'Dmitry, leave us. Wait outside the door. I will need you again.'

Yushkov goes. The heavy door clicks shut. She looks up at the arched ceiling, at the dark green shutters and the cream, gold and green paintwork.

'This reminds me of the Central Post Office in Ho Chi Minh City.'

'You've been there?'

'Many years ago.'

'My sources tell me you killed Samuel. A knife in the back?'

'It was him or me.'

'I congratulate you. Many have tried before you. You truly are a remarkable woman.'

'May I sit?' Wolfe asks.

'In a moment.' Nguyen gets up, his movements graceful as if he were practising Tai Chi. 'Walk with me. I have something to show you.' They begin walking the length of the room. 'Samuel disobeyed me. I wanted you brought to me unharmed.' He glances at her face. 'That bruise will take several days to heal. He cut you too, didn't he?'

'You know he did. You were watching the live feed.'

He inclines his head in assent. 'I will have Anna look after you. My doctor.'

'I'm fine.'

'I insist.' He points to a bull elephant head with enormous tusks mounted on the wall. 'Magnificent, isn't he?'

'More so when he was alive,' she says.

'I disagree.' He gestures to the animal heads stuck on the walls. 'I killed every one of these myself.'

To her left is a whole leopard, stuffed, teeth bared. Further along, a West African black rhino. A Sumatran tiger's head and hide decorates the floor, and a whole cheetah, its limbs outstretched as if in mid run, seems to guard a door at the end of the long room.

'So, this is where you run your poaching operations?' she asks.

'I have people who run my African business.'

'Terry Blunt?'

He inclines his head in such a way that it is neither a confirmation nor a denial.

'And Harold Sackville?' she asks.

'You've made things difficult for Harold. He's here, in fact. Sadly, this will be his last meeting. Harold will resign from the cabinet this week. Family reasons. Someone will take his place.'

They have reached the end of the long room. Before them are huge cherrywood doors with ornate bronze handles. On the wall to their right is a keypad and an eye scanner.

Nguyen continues, 'Your attempt to turn Samuel's followers against us will fail. We're seeing to that even as we speak.'

The matter-of-factness of the statement is chilling.

'Why poach rhinos? Your sugar business is booming. You're rich, respected, famous. So why butcher these endangered animals?'

'Respect. Influence. Power. Not just businessmen. Rival syndicates. Politicians. Governments. I can buy anyone, anywhere. Even you, Miss Wolfe.'

She shakes her head. 'You're wrong. You can't buy me, or detective Casburn. SO24 knows about Sackville and your syndicate.' She lies. 'It doesn't matter what you do with me. Casburn will hunt you down. He won't rest until you're behind bars.'

'Oh, haven't you heard? He died on the operating table.'

92

A beam of light crosses Tan Nguyen's iris. The biometric scanner beeps an all clear.

'I don't believe you,' Wolfe says.

'Two gunshot wounds, collapsed lung, internal bleeding. He didn't make it.'

Nguyen presses his thumb onto a small screen. The wooden doors open electronically, their ornate beauty concealing thick steel. For a few seconds, the room is pitch black and the air conditioning feels arctic after the oppressive heat outside. Nguyen steps inside the vault of a room. His movement triggering sensors. The room lights up. No windows.

'Temperature and oxygen levels are carefully controlled. Come.' He beckons her inside.

'I have no desire to see more dead animals,' she says.

'Perhaps not. But you want to know why Pieter and the others had to die, don't you?'

Wolfe holds back. 'Just tell me. I don't need to go in.'

'If you want to know, you must come with me.'

He walks on. 'Nobody is allowed here except me. You are my first ever guest.'

The doors automatically shut behind them. The room is close and airtight. There is no sound but the tap of their shoes and the soft whisper of the air conditioning. In the centre of the room, much like the best art galleries, there is a cushioned bench, covered in black velvet. He sits and pats the seat next to him. Wolfe hesitates. Sits. Around her are various lifelike waxworks.

'My favourite piece.' He nods straight ahead.

A young woman, naked, reclining on a chaise lounge, much like Manet's painting of *Olympia*. Pale skin, black hair, dark brown, almost black eyes that seem to stare directly at Wolfe. She's in a rectangular perspex box.

'My first wife, Hoa. She shamed me. Looked at other men. We were married less than a year. Now she will only ever look at me.'

'She's not... she can't be real?'

'Superb, isn't she? Preserved perfectly.'

Wolfe cannot speak. She thought the horror show was over now that Samuel was dead. She was wrong. 'You killed your... you had her...?'

'Taxidermy. Very few can manage human skin. I employ the very best.'

'Over there,' Nguyen points to a wall-mounted head, 'Vu Van Tien. Leader of a rival syndicate. He's there to remind me never to be complacent.'

The man's mouth is open, lips peeled back, exposing two gold teeth, his eyes wide. Most disturbing of all is the gaping, frayed hole where his Adam's apple should be.

'What did you do to him?' Wolfe asks.

'He swallowed a Malayan pit viper. The venom is not only deadly, it causes tissue around the bite to die, hence the hole in his throat. Photos were circulated. It sends a message, you see. He tried to swallow my business. I made him swallow the snake, as did his three sons.'

Wolfe stands shakily. 'I want to leave.'

'Not yet,' Nguyen says, pointing to a Caucasian man's head mounted on the wall. 'A prosecutor. He tried to convict me of murder.

Died watching his fiancé being raped then stabbed to death. I find that look of despair on his face quite... moving.'

'This doesn't tell me why you sent Samuel to kill four people. It simply confirms you're a narcissistic psychopath.'

He smiles condescendingly. 'Come now, Miss Wolfe. These people got what they deserved. They brought this upon themselves. Just as you have.'

'How can you say that?'

'Look around you,' he says. 'What do they all have in common?'

Nguyen gets up and points to a man's head mounted on the wall.

'I was grooming him to be my successor. Then the traitorous cockroach stole from me.' Nguyen points to another head. 'This one, a police officer who tried to blackmail me. Can you believe it? Very foolish... this one, a Vietnamese customs officer who thought he could stop me importing horn... what do they and the four you speak of have in common, Miss Wolfe?'

'They betrayed you or stood in your way.'

'Correct.'

'I don't understand,' says Wolfe. 'How did Pieter Venter get in your way, apart from trying to protect his rhinos?'

'You're missing the bigger picture.'

'Tell me.'

Nguyen waves his hand in the air, dismissing her request. 'I have one more thing to show you.'

He points to a vacant space on the wall. 'That's for you.'

93

The hessian hood and gag are stifling. Curled up on her side on the vehicle's back seat, wrists cable-tied, she listens to Yushkov giving orders. She doesn't recognise his harsh monotone. 'Room twelve,' he says. 'Is it ready?' The vehicle jolts. Wolfe's head bangs against the car door. Does Yushkov know about his employer's macabre collection? Will he help her? What would Butcher do? She hears his gravelly voice. *Wait for the right moment.*

'Dmitry! Wait up!' The clipped accent, the barking tone, she knows that voice. Terry Blunt.

Brakes creak, tyres crunch on gravel. The vehicle stops. The diesel engine rumbles, ticking over. Footsteps, Heavy boots.

'Have our guests seen her?' Blunt asks.

'No, sir,' Yushkov replies.

'I don't want to hear a peep out of her. You got that?'

'Yes, sir,' Yushkov says.

'Be careful with her. No more cuts or bruises. You understand?'

'Yes, sir.'

'When you're done, come find me. You're going to Jo'burg. I have a job for you. Meet me at seven sharp.'

The vehicle sets off again, but not for long. Wolfe hears a woman singing in Shona, water splashing. Then men's voices and laughter. Unfiltered cigarette smoke reaches her through the roughly woven fabric of the hood. In the distance, the hum of a light aircraft. Yet another syndicate member landing. Who this time? Perhaps Sukletin? The vehicle stops, doors open, Yushkov's hand on the top of her head, guiding her out of the vehicle.

'Two steps up,' he says.

They are wooden. One, two. Yushkov greets a man she guesses is her guard. Through the coarse weave of the hood she can tell the room she's led into is dark. She freezes, refusing to move.

'Don't fight me,' Yushkov says.

Who is he now? The Yushkov she knows, or Dmitry, the mercenary?

'You'll be safe in there. I will take off the hood,' he encourages.

What choice does she have? At least with the hood off she has more chance of escape. A few steps, then she sits on something soft with springs. A bed. Her unhurt arm is cuffed to what she can only guess is the bedhead. Panic seizes her. A light is switched on, the hood removed. Wolfe squints, sees Yushkov's face close to hers, a man in khaki behind him. Yushkov orders the man outside. The guard smirks at Yushkov, mutters something crude. He leaves, shutting the door.

It's a brick box on a concrete slab. Meticulously clean. Nothing in it but a bed, a ceiling fan and a bucket. The bed has been made, the bedding neatly pressed, probably from the house. The only window is boarded up. A sliver of light sneaks into the room between two boards.

'Keep your voice down. He must not hear,' Yushkov whispers, removing the gag.

Wolfe flexes her aching jaw.

'Drink this.' He offers her a bottle of water which she drinks greedily.

'Nguyen is going to kill me,' Wolfe says. 'He wants to stick my head on the wall in that sealed room of his. You've got to get me out of here.'

Something small and metal is pressed into her palm. She looks down. A skeleton key: the serrated edge has been filed down so it will fit almost any lock. 'For the door,' he says. He hands her a small folding knife with a sprung blade. 'For this.' He points at the plastic tie. 'Do not cut them until sunset.'

Wolfe hides them under the pillow.

Yushkov continues. 'Do not try to leave in daylight. You will be seen. Wait until sunset. The fence behind us has its own power board. Turn off the power and climb the fence. Be quick. It will only be a few minutes, then they will turn on the power again.'

'The guard?'

'I will distract him. At sunset.'

'Aren't you going to Johannesburg tonight?'

'At seven. Sunset is at six. Watch the light disappear under the door and through the window boards.'

Yushkov hands her a burner phone, identical to the one he gave her four months ago. She takes it. Their fingers touch. Neither pulls their hand away.

'Do not use this until you are far from here,' Yushkov says. 'Phone signals are monitored. And do not contact the police. They work for Nguyen.'

She nods.

'The pilot who brought you here. Can he be trusted?'

'You know about...? Yes, I trust him.'

'Phone him when you are far away.'

'Who are you? Vitaly or Dmitry?'

'They know me as Dmitry Lazarev. It is a cover.'

'Why do you need a cover?'

Yushkov withdraws his fingers from hers. 'I am sorry.'

'This is crazy. Come with me.'

'There is something I must do in Johannesburg.'

'So this is goodbye?' she asks.

'It has to be.'

'What is so important in Jo'burg?'

'Keep your voice down. I cannot help you if you betray us.'

'You've already done that,' she says.

Yushkov swears under his breath. 'You do not make this easy, Olivia.'

'What is going on?'

'There is talk about important people. They arrive in Johannesburg. Today. From many countries. Nguyen, he makes a speech tomorrow. I do not know why I must be there.'

The GROWT convention?

Why would the leader of a poaching syndicate speak at a convention on endangered species?

94

Time crawls inside the cell. Wolfe tries to use it wisely, to plan her escape, but the memory of Casburn's limp body, his unresponsiveness when paramedics arrived, weighs heavily. Is Nguyen telling the truth? Did he die on the operating table?

Curled up on the bed, one wrist handcuffed to the bedhead, eyes closed, she sees every detail of her last moments with Casburn. He was close to death when airlifted, his blood loss critical. Perhaps he didn't survive. These last few days, Wolfe has seen a new side to the abrasive detective she hadn't known before. He was willing to risk his life and career to save others. She now knows he once had a wife, whom he clearly loved. She has come to respect and, perhaps, even like him. And she wasn't there to say goodbye. She feels bad about that.

Her thoughts move to Vitaly Yushkov: the one who drove a painful wedge between her and Casburn. She cared for Yushkov, possibly even loved him, believed him to be a good man forced to do terrible things to survive. Casburn always believed Yushkov to be a cold-blooded killer who had pulled the wool over her eyes. Was Dan right after all?

How much of what Yushkov had told her about his torture by

Casburn was true? Was Casburn really instrumental in Yushkov's sister's death? Doubt attacks her memories like termites, making them fragile, tottering things. As the seconds, hours, minutes of her captivity drag on, her faith in Yushkov ebbs and flows. Perhaps Nguyen has some kind of hold over him? Or is this new identity simply about staying alive? The Russian SVR still hunt him. Was this job really Yushkov's only option? The Yushkov she knew would never willingly work for a psychopath like Nguyen. No, there has to be something keeping Yushkov in Nguyen's employment.

Her thoughts turn to Samuel. Until today, Wolfe wasn't aware of what she was capable of. What she was prepared to do to stay alive.

Wolfe sits up suddenly. She feels contaminated. She wants to shower. To scrub away every part of her body Samuel touched. Her pretence to be on his wavelength has taken her to dark places she didn't know she could reach. But most of all, Wolfe is afraid of what she could become. Afraid of the violent hatred Samuel ignited in her. It was wrong to use the machete. She knows that. She has no idea how she'll come to terms with what she did.

Outside her cell's door are footsteps. A woman's voice she hasn't heard before. Wolfe checks the lock-pick, knife and phone are well-hidden under her pillow. The door is unlocked. A blonde woman in her twenties in shorts, trainers and running vest smiles at her.

'I'm here to take you to the shower block. Then I'll see to your wounds.' She is upbeat and jaunty, as if finding a woman handcuffed to a bed in a locked room was a normal occurrence.

'You must be Anna?'

'I'm whoever you want me to be.'

Wolfe goes quietly. Anna, or whatever her name is, hovers over her like a hummingbird at a flower, even watching her in the shower, then dresses her wounds, and gently rubs cream over the bruise on her face.

'That should reduce the swelling and discolouration.'

Wolfe tries to engage with her in conversation, but Anna smiles and says little.

Back in her locked cell, Wolfe lies on the bed, checks everything is under the pillow as she left it. She tries to sleep. But she still has question after unanswered question.

With Samuel dead, is Yushkov taking his place? Is that why he's going to Jo'burg tonight? Wolfe shakes her head. No, he would never do that.

Wolfe thinks back to her conversations with Casburn about Samuel's victims. Four initial kills, four different countries. Nguyen wanted them dead. Why? She knows Pieter Venter was planning to speak at the GROWT convention tomorrow. Were his three other victims linked to that convention? Were their disappearances a warning? *Vote our way, or you will be next.* If she's right, is another delegate to die tonight at the hands of Yushkov and Blunt?

Wolfe clings to the conviction that Yushkov wouldn't help her to escape if he was loyal to Nguyen and Blunt.

She watches the thin ribbon of light beneath the door turn orange. Soon she will know who Yushkov is loyal to. A man's heavy boots thump up the steps. Yushkov is early? The door opens, Blunt stands there, carrying a food tray. The surprise visit unsettles her, but she won't let him see her fear. She sits patiently, watching Blunt enter the room and lay the tray at the other end of the bed. On the tray are three small paper plates and a plastic knife and fork; on one plate is a meat patty, on another something that looks like porridge, and on the last, vegetable stew.

'Springbok burger, vegetables and *sadza* for our guest,' Blunt says. 'Your last supper.'

He's trying to spook her. Her facial bruise will take a few days to heal. Nguyen won't want her killed until it's faded.

Wolfe picks up the burger and takes a bite. She wants information so she's going to make out that she knows more than she does.

'Not sure why you're looking so smug, Terry. The vote isn't quite fixed, is it? Tomorrow may not turn out quite how you'd like.'

Wolfe watches for a reaction.

'And what the fuck would you know?' he says.

'You're short of a vote, aren't you? That's why you're sending that

Russian thug to Jo'burg. That one vote could well and truly mess up your dreams of early retirement.'

'You're all talk. Nothing you say will change the outcome.'

'Who is it this time? Another delegate?'

'Shut up and eat your food.'

'Why bring me my meal? What do you want, Terry?'

'How do you know Dmitry Lazarev?'

'I don't.' She takes another bite of the burger. Chews.

Blunt frowns. 'There was something... can't place my finger on it.'

'I don't make a habit of befriending mercenaries.'

He turns his back on her.

'The delegates are protected. You won't get near them,' she taunts.

Blunt is about to close the door. 'I hear she's pregnant. I guess you might say there'll be two tragic accidents tonight.'

All the blood drains from Wolfe's face. She knows the identity of the intended victim.

95

Wolfe's long-time friend, Caroline Bloom. British Minister for the Environment. Three months pregnant.

The target.

Caroline is voting at the GROWT convention tomorrow, and Nguyen intends to stop her. Adrenaline zings through her body. She has to stop them.

Through the door of her cell, she hears Yushkov's voice over the guard's two-way radio. He orders the man to go to the hangar immediately. A chair scrapes on the deck, boots patter on the wooden steps, then it's quiet. The guard has gone.

Wolfe flicks open the folding knife and cuts the plastic tie around her wrist. She re-folds the knife and pockets it. At the door, she listens. Nothing but the sounds of the bush at night. She tries the lock-pick. It doesn't engage. She inserts it deeper, wiggles it around. She has to get out. Warn Caroline. This time there is a click. Wolfe cracks the door open and peers outside.

Darkness.

The stool where the guard sat is empty. Her holding cell is isolated from other buildings, the communal bathrooms the closest. Garages to her right are lit by security lights. To her left is a row of ten or so single-room bungalows with thatched roofs and wooden deck. Staff quarters. Some are occupied, with yellow-white light spilling out through the doorways and windows. Outside one bungalow, two men talk in Shona. Inside another, a television blares and blue light jumps and flickers across the curtains. A woman hums as she cooks over a little gas camping stove. Far away, Wolfe hears laughter and the clink of glasses. A drinks party. Everyone will be focused on the guests. This is her best chance.

Wolfe slips around the back of her cell. As Yushkov described, she finds a power box fixed to a pole just inside the perimeter. She risks switching on the mobile phone so she can use its torch, and studies a power board. Above each switch, written in marker pen, are letters and numbers: Fen S1, Fen S2, Fen S3 and Fen S4. She doesn't know which one to turn off, so she'll throw them all.

From the house, a burst of laughter. She hears a few words in English. Wolfe studies the phone. It may be a burner, but it can shoot video and take photos. The entire syndicate is gathered in Nguyen's house. If she could get them on video, she'd finally have the evidence she needs. But it's a huge risk. On the other hand, all she has to do is cut the power to the fence, climb over it, and she's free.

Wolfe shuts the power box, checks the phone's battery and signal are good, and sends the same text message to Moz Cohen and Jerry Butcher, their phone numbers etched on her brain:

There will be an assassination attempt on MP Caroline Bloom in Johannesburg tonight. Warn her. Alert SO1.

There's a lump in her throat as she taps in the next few words.

Vitaly Yushkov and Terry Blunt may be the assassins. Tan Nguyen has ordered the hit. From Olivia Wolfe.

Wolfe sends the message, then immediately switches off the phone. She hopes Nguyen's security team hasn't picked up its signal.

Keeping close to the fence she heads for the house. She follows the voices. The gathering is on a raised deck and viewing platform at the rear of the house, surrounded on three sides by frameless glass balustrading, in daylight affording them magnificent views across the waterhole and the bushveld beyond. The ground falls away steeply from the house to the waterhole. Wolfe hides in the dark beneath the platform. From between the deck floor and the bottom of the glass balustrading, she can watch and hear Nguyen's guests.

Nguyen stands at the far end, a hand on the balustrade, talking to Harold Sackville, who is putting on a good show of being jovial and relaxed, but he repeatedly rubs his thumb and first finger together, a nervous twitch Wolfe has seen before in his TV interviews. With them, and seated in a wicker armchair, is the US Senate Majority Leader, Sebastian Lewis. In the armchair next to the senator is the unmistakable Yury Sukletin, who dabs his sweaty face with a handkerchief.

Funani Ximba and the mayor of Johannesburg laugh at a story an Indian woman is telling them, her expansive hand gestures adding a Marcel Marceau quality to the conversation. Wolfe recognises her as Prisha Chawla, known as the Queen of Bollywood, an extremely wealthy movie producer. In another group, seated near an open fire, is George Mokweka, the recently elected President of Mozambique and South Africa's Police Commissioner. They are joined by a smartly dressed Asian man she doesn't recognise, but from the cut of his silk suit, pristine white shirt, mirror shine Oxfords and immaculate grooming, she's guessing he's some ultra high net worth businessman or financier. Waiters move between the guests, offering drinks and canapés. Blunt joins the group and raises his beer bottle in a toast. A chef cooks a springbok on a spit. If Wolfe didn't know better, she could imagine them as wealthy tourists relaxing after a day on safari. But that's not why they are Nguyen's guests.

Wolfe must hurry. It won't take long for her guard to realise he wasn't needed at the hangar. Wolfe turns on the phone and sets it to video record, then positions the camera lens in the gap between the stone floor and the glass balustrade. She swivels it from side to side, hoping to get all of the guests.

Nguyen taps a spoon against his champagne glass for quiet.

'Ladies and gentlemen,' Nguyen begins, 'thank you all for coming. I have called the syndicate together because, as you all know, the GROWT convention is tomorrow. Top of the agenda is the vote on whether or not the international trade in rhino horn should be legalised.'

Murmurs of concern ripples through the group.

'Bloody bunny huggers,' Sackville says, loud enough for Wolfe to hear.

'Do not worry, my friends,' Nguyen continues. 'I have everything under control. Do not forget that I am secretary general of this year's convention and will make the opening address. I'll urge the delegates to continue the ban.' He pauses, gives them a mischievous grin and continues with obvious sarcasm, 'So we can do everything possible to protect these magnificent creatures.'

Sukletin bursts out laughing. Others snigger.

The American calls out, 'As long as they're dead, stuffed and on your wall, huh?' His comment earns him enthusiastic applause.

'As you know, the vote is anonymous. There are countries who want the ban lifted so the money from the sale of horn can go into protecting rhinos from evil poaching syndicates.'

Loud laughter.

'It will be a close call. Or it was going to be a close call. And we all know that if the ban is lifted, the market will be flooded with horn that's been stockpiled for years and it will jeopardise our enterprise. We cannot let this happen.'

His audience is quiet. Worried.

'But do not fear, my friends. I can assure you the ban will *not* be lifted tomorrow.'

'When last I checked,' Sackville pipes up, 'the odds were in favour of ratification. One hundred and forty-three countries. Seventeen will abstain. Seventy in favour of legalisation. That includes South Africa, Russia, Finland, Swaziland, Namibia, and Mozambique.'

'And Britain too,' chips in Chawla. 'I hear your environment minister is voting to lift the ban, despite British public opinion to the contrary.'

Sackville shakes his head. 'I've done all I can to persuade her. Bloody stubborn woman.'

Nguyen says, 'I can assure you matters are in hand. Key delegates will vote "No" tomorrow.' He turns to Sackville. 'Including the UK. It just takes the right kind of persuasion.

'But we cannot be complacent. The next convention is in three years time, when we may not get the outcome we desire. And as South African rhinos become scarcer, we are going to need to expand operations to other countries. We have some difficult decisions to make. This is why I invited you here this weekend, so we can make those decisions. Thank you.'

The senator raises his champagne glass. 'I propose a toast. Tan Nguyen!'

As they raise their glasses, Wolfe creeps away.

96

Wolfe throws all four switches on the power board and looks up at the electric fence. There's nothing to indicate the power is out. She takes off her shirt and balls it around one hand. Touches a wire. Nothing. She starts to climb. The thin wire is tough on her unprotected hand and pain stabs at her stitches.

A shock of bright light and she misses her footing. The compound is lit up like a football stadium. She hears shouting. It won't be long before she has company.

At the top, she straddles the fence, and starts down the other side. More shouting, this time closer. Taking a gamble, she jumps, landing five feet below on cleared ground. Beyond the fence, she can see nothing but night. She has no torch; her mobile phone has very little battery left, and she'll need to use it later to contact Clarke. She wants to run, but it's too risky. One wrong step and she could twist an ankle or plough into a tree or a boulder. So she walks, hands out in front.

Wolfe tries to remember the map she studied in the helicopter. Nguyen's mansion faces north, which means her holding cell faces west. She climbed the fence at the back of her cell, so she is heading east.

Each step takes her further away from Nguyen and closer to freedom. Close by, she hears a rustle. She fears it may be a snake, or a larger predator. A small warthog bolts past her, tail pointed at the sky. Wolfe keeps going. Her brow collides with a low-hanging branch and she starts. She rubs her forehead and looks back at Nguyen's property. The compound is a bright blur in the distance, probably half a mile away. By now they will have no doubt discovered she is missing and sent out a search party. She speeds up. Ahead, two red dots recede into the distance. Then another pair of red dots. Tail lights. It must be a road. Her heart lifts.

She's now better able to see the terrain ahead and starts to run. She hears the grumble of a truck. Closer now, Wolfe realises she's approaching a crossroad, but only one road has continuous street lighting. Three street vendors loiter at the junction – a young man in a yellow and green singlet and baggy red shorts, a teenage girl in a dirty mustard-coloured cotton dress, and a small boy in a brown T-shirt and blue shorts. A car slows at the junction. All three rush over to the passenger window. The man carries a cooler box of canned drinks. The girl has some bananas.

Wolfe has no idea where she is. No landmarks. No buildings. No street signs.

The car accelerates away. The three vendors shuffle back to some plastic milk crates and sit.

Wolfe runs up to them. The man views her with suspicion, his eyes lingering on her bruised face.

'What do you want?' his tone aggressive.

'What is this road?'

'You are lost?' He smiles, revealing a chipped front tooth.

'I'm meeting someone What is this junction called?'

'Why should I help you?' he says with a sneer.

'Let's trade.' Wolfe has little with which to trade. She cannot give up the phone, but she can trade the flick knife. 'Here.' She holds it up. 'It's yours, if you tell me where I am.'

'Maybe I will just take it.'

He lunges at her, but Wolfe kicks out at his chest, sending the man onto his backside. She opens the flick knife.

'Please,' says the girl. 'Don't hurt my brother. This is the A6 road,' she says pointing, 'that is Cecil Avenue.'

'Thank you.'

Wolfe steps away and keeps the knife where all three can see it. She switches her phone on, dials Clarke, gives him her location, tells him the phone is almost out of battery. He says twenty minutes.

'We gave you information. Give me the knife,' demands the young man.

'Not till I'm ready, and it belongs to your sister. I did the trade with her.'

'You should not be here. Who are you with your British accent, huh?'

'It doesn't matter. What matters is what you do now. You never saw me. You do this for me and I will buy all your drinks and bananas.'

'All of them?' he asks, disbelieving.

'Whatever you haven't sold in twenty minutes' time, I will buy them all.' She will have to borrow the money from Clarke. 'Do we have a deal?'

The young man gives her a genuine smile. 'Deal.'

97

Seated next to Henry Clarke in his helicopter, Wolfe's eyelids droop. She can't remember the last time she had a decent night's sleep. Clarke checks his instruments repeatedly and fidgets in his seat. He's understandably nervous.

'The sooner we're in South African airspace the better.'

'How long to Sandton?' she asks through the headphones.

The GROWT conference is being held at the Sandton Convention Centre in Johannesburg.

'An hour, all going well. No telling what'll happen when we cross the border, though.'

Wolfe's burner phone has recharged enough for her to know she has some missed calls. She ignores them for now. Instead, she sends copies of her video of Nguyen and his syndicate to Cohen, Butcher and Ponnappa. Whatever happens in the next few hours, she has to know the footage is in safe hands.

Video of Tan Nguyen, Vietnamese businessman and poacher. Some familiar faces like Harold Sackville. Urgently pass to SO24. Where is Caroline Bloom? Has she been warned? Olivia Wolfe.

In a few seconds, she has three responses.

From Cohen:

If you really are Wolfe, fucking call me. I've alerted SO1 and SO24, so you better be legit.

From Butcher: *Thank God you're alive. I'll forward to SO24 and SO1. They will have people undercover in SA who can evacuate Bloom. She's at Sandton Towers. Call me.*

From Ponnappa:

Mate, be careful. I can track Caroline if I have her mobile and it's on. What's the number?

Wolfe replies to Cohen first:

In helicopter so can't talk. This is Olivia. Proof? You've brokered a joint exclusive of my story with SA Herald, *you bastard. OK? I need Caroline's mobile. Don't have my phone, this is borrowed. Pls try her principal private secretary.*

Cohen has an enviable list of private phone numbers for the rich, the famous and the infamous. Within seconds he sends Caroline's mobile number and also the number for Jamie Osbourne, her principal private secretary, who Cohen confirms is with her in Johannesburg. Wolfe shares these details with Ponnappa and Butcher.

Need floor plans for Sandton Convention Centre, details of security and a day-pass for me? Was told Casburn died in hospital. Can you find out?

Wolfe sends messages to both Caroline and her private secretary, warning them of the planned assassination tonight. No response. She didn't expect Caroline to reply immediately, she is a minister after all, but the more time goes by, the more worried Wolfe becomes. By the time Clarke lands at Rand Airport in Germiston, a privately-owned civil airport used mainly by charter companies and flight schools, Ponnappa has uploaded everything Wolfe asked for into her Dropbox and texted a link to a one-day pass for the GROWT convention.

'I'm not coming with you,' Clarke says, the chopper's rotors still turning. 'I need to be with Hannah. You can catch a ride into town with a mate who runs the flight school here. I'll introduce you.'

98

Wolfe crosses the regal foyer of the InterContinental Johannesburg Sandton Towers, glancing up through the triangular-shaped void to the sixteenth floor. Caroline is in room 1603, but there was no answer when the reception desk called. Wolfe heads straight for the lifts. Her arm is lightly touched by a man with scruffy hair, wearing glasses and a shabby denim jacket, covered in animal charity badges.

'Olivia Wolfe, I'm DC Stone,' he says quietly, his accent Lancastrian. 'Please come with me.'

Wolfe pulls her arm away. 'Who do you work for?'

'SO24.'

'Show me your warrant card.'

'Let's not draw attention to ourselves. Please take a seat,' Stone says, gesturing to one of the numerous leather armchairs positioned around marble-topped coffee tables.

'I don't have time for this, Agent Stone. A friend is in terrible danger.'

She presses the lifts' call button. Stone takes her arm more forcibly and pulls her aside. He holds out his warrant card. Christopher Stone. Metropolitan Police.

'How did you get here so fast?' she asks.

'I'm investigating matters relating to DS Casburn.'

'Where is he? Did he survive?'

'Yes. Critical, but stable.'

'Thank God. They told me he was dead.'

'Who told you?' Wolfe brushes the question aside with one hand. Stone continues. 'I need to know everything. Let's start with who is trying to kill Caroline Bloom?'

'Hang on,' she says. 'I don't know you from a bar of soap.'

'And you're a reporter. You need to give me a good reason to trust you.'

'Fair enough. Caroline Bloom is a friend.' Wolfe is as brief as possible. She tells him how she discovered where Nguyen and his syndicate were meeting, what Yushkov and Blunt told her, and shows the video footage she shot. She explains how Yushkov, who now goes by the name of Dmitry Lazarev, helped her escape, and that he is in Johannesburg. Stone's back stiffens at the mention of Yushkov. 'It's all about the convention's vote tomorrow. Caroline's vote. If they eliminate her, they get the outcome they want.'

'You think Yushkov is the assassin?'

'Maybe. No. I don't know. He left for Jo'burg at seven, which means he'll be here by now.' She feels like a traitor. 'He may just be Nguyen's bodyguard.' Wolfe has had enough of talking. 'Is Caroline safe?'

'Can I call you Olivia?'

'Call me whatever you like. Where is she?'

'I don't know,' says Stone.

'You've searched her room?'

'Yes.'

'Signs of a struggle?'

'No.'

'Is her mobile on?'

'No.'

'Her private secretary?'

'Can't be located.'

Prey

'Her protection detail?'

'Can't be located.'

'Oh shit.'

Stone suddenly looks very young. He's a junior officer sent to South Africa to bring Casburn home. He's out of his depth. 'Additional SO1 officers are on their way, but they won't get here till morning. I was ordered not to alert local police so, right now, you're all I've got.' There are tiny beads of sweat in the cleft of his upper lip. 'I need to make a call. Stay here.'

He moves a few feet away, talks with his back to her. The call is short. He looks more agitated than before.

'You have to leave,' he says to Wolfe.

'What?'

'Your relationship with Yushkov is a problem.'

Wolfe stares at Stone in disbelief.

'No way.' Wolfe gets up and strides over to the lifts and stabs at the call button. 'Caroline's my friend and I'm going to find her.'

'You must leave this hotel.'

'Try and make me.' She glares at him. 'That'll draw some unnecessary attention, won't it?'

'You're going nowhere without one of these.' He holds up a shiny, rectangular pass which gives guests access to their floor and the shared amenities like the restaurant, pool and gym.

'Thanks,' she says, ripping it from his hand. A lift door opens.

'Wait a...' says Stone, following her into the lift.

He snatches the card back. 'Get out.'

'Nope. You need me. I've known Caroline for years. Let me look at her room. I'll know if something's wrong.'

'The boss said you were stubborn. He wasn't wrong.'

'Takes one to know one.'

Stone uses the security card.

'Sixteen oh three,' Wolfe says.

'How do you...? Never mind.'

The doors open on the sixteenth floor. Caroline's room is to the right, and right again. Stone is about to knock.

'Allow me,' says Wolfe. 'Maybe you scared her.'

'Go ahead.'

'Charlie?' she calls through the door. 'It's Liv. Please open the door.' She knocks again. 'Charlie?'

They enter the room. It's dark. Stone slides the card into a slot on the wall and the lights come on. An en suite room in greys and creams, with a king-size bed, desk, and two armchairs facing the window, from which Wolfe can see the city's glimmering lights. The bed hasn't been slept in, and the curtains haven't been drawn. The room looks as though it has just been serviced. Neat. Clean. No sign of a struggle.

Stone checks the bathroom, then unlocks the adjoining door. He yells out a warning and enters the SO1 officer's room.

'Empty. We're wasting time here,' Stone says, joining Wolfe.

Wolfe wanders around the room. Under the desk is Caroline's Furla bucket handbag in tan. Wolfe rifles through it. Purse, make-up bag, breath mints, glasses case and glasses, sunglasses, house keys, mobile phone.

'Where would you go without a handbag and phone at this time of night?' Wolfe asks, frowning at the digital clock. It's 23.37pm.

Inside the mirrored wardrobe is a hotel laundry bag with clothes in it.

'Do you know what she wore today?' Wolfe asks.

Stone checks a spiral bound notebook. 'Navy suit, pale blue blouse, court shoes.'

'The shoes are here. There's the suit. The shirt is in the laundry bag. So she's changed. Did she have a function tonight?' Wolfe checks the hangers. Two evening dresses. One has been worn. The deodorant has left a white mark on the inside of the fabric.

'She was at an official dinner until eleven oh five,' Stone says. 'She was escorted by her SO1 officer through the lobby and into the lift at eleven oh eight. CCTV shows him walking Caroline to her room, then he enters his room next door.'

'Then what?'

'Nothing. Nobody arrived. Nobody left.'

'They can't have disappeared into thin air.'

'CCTV doesn't lie.'

There is an open plastic bag with the hotel logo on it. Wolfe picks it up. 'She's wearing hotel slippers. Where would you go in hotel slippers?'

Wolfe opens the drawers. One running top. One pair of leggings.

'This conference lasts three days, right?'

'Yes.'

'That's odd,' Wolfe says. 'Charlie's a fitness freak. Goes jogging every night. So why only one set of running gear?'

'Why does it matter?'

99

How does a woman just disappear from a hotel with CCTV on every floor?

Stone's mobile rings. He takes the call. 'You sure?' Stone gets his answer. 'I'll be right down.'

'Hotel security,' Stone says to Wolfe. 'They may have a lead. You're coming with me.'

'I'll check the gym.'

'Forget the gym. You're coming with me.'

'Why?'

'I need you to identify someone.'

'Please tell me it's not a body?'

'It's not a body. Come on.'

As the lift opens at basement level, they are met by a security guard named Lwazi. Beneath the hotel and away from the air conditioning, the tunnel-like corridor is oppressive.

'What happened to Fezile?' Stone asks, as they follow Lwazi past the laundry, the huge dryers humming endlessly, full of towels and bed linen.

'Fezile had to go. Family emergency. He tells me you want to find Caroline Bloom. So, I look at the CCTV.'

The corridor opens up to a loading dock. The night air is cooler here but the stench from the rubbish bins is intense. A truck is parked in one of the bays and steam-pressed tablecloths are unloaded and stacked on a trolley by two women in black and white housekeeping uniforms. In the next bay, is a plumber's van.

Lwazi leads them across the loading dock and into another equally sultry, meandering corridor.

'In here,' says Lwazi.

Inside the cubby-hole of a room is a wall-mounted screen, displaying twelve live images from CCTV cameras around the hotel. On a computer monitor, each camera and its location are listed.

'How many cameras does the hotel have?' Wolfe asks.

'One hundred and thirty.' Lwazi sits. 'I want to show you this.' He brings up a frozen image of the loading dock. The time-stamp says 22:50:13. Two men leave a plumber's van, their backs to the camera.

'We did not call in a plumber. I checked,' Lwazi says.

Wolfe and Stone exchange glances.

'Replay it from the moment the van arrives,' Stone asks.

They watch the van arriving at the loading dock. Two men get out. One carries a bag.

'How the hell did they get past security?' Stone asks.

Lwazi rubs his fingers together. 'Money.'

'And where did they go?'

'I do not know. I called you as soon as I saw this,' he said pointing at the screen. 'I must call the police.'

He reaches for a phone on the table. Stone places a hand on his.

'The lives of three British citizens are at stake. Give us a chance to find them.'

'But I must. It is my job.'

'Management will want to know why security failed. How they got in. There's no need for you to lose your job if we find the missing guests first,' says Stone.

'Me? No, no. Fezile was on duty. He must have let them in. I don't know anything about this.'

'Help me find them and nobody need know this ever happened.'

Lwazi's shoulders slump. 'What do you want me to do?'

Wolfe answers, 'Run the footage again.'

The images are grainy, and both men wear baseball caps.

'Is that Yushkov?' asks Stone pointing to the taller, broader man. 'Olivia?'

She feels sick. She had clung to the hope Yushkov would not turn up at Caroline's hotel. But one of the so-called plumbers has Yushkov's build. 'It's possible.'

'And the other one?'

'Could be Terry Blunt. He's got Blunt's belly. But I can't see his face.'

'Where do they go next?' Stone asks Lwazi.

The guard switches to another camera. It covers the corridor immediately outside the basement lift. 'See, they use the elevator.'

'Which floor?'

'I don't know. I must check the cameras on every floor. It will take time.'

'Check floor sixteen and hurry,' says Stone.

Wolfe says, 'They'd need a pass for the lift. How'd they get one?'

Again, Lwazi rubs his fingers together.

Wolfe sighs, nodding.

Lwazi searches for the footage for floor sixteen at the time of the plumbers' arrival.

'If Yushkov were the assassin, how would he do it?' Stone asks.

Wolfe feels light-headed. Perhaps it's the stifling, airless room.

'I can't be sure it's him. I may be completely wrong.'

'Doesn't matter. How would he do it?'

'He's best hand-to-hand. He'd want to get close. Logically they'd go to Caroline's room and pretend there's a problem. Once she opened the door, they'd easily overpower her. But there's no sign of a struggle.'

'I have it.' Lwazi finds the correct time and presses play. No sign of the two men. If they didn't go to Caroline's room, then where did they go?

Something catches her eye. 'Run that again.'

A waiter carries a tray, the plate covered by a chrome cloche. He calls the lift. Then he simply disappears.

'Something's been deleted,' says Wolfe.

'You're right. Probably of Caroline leaving her room.'

'And wherever she went to.'

'I've got it!'

Given Caroline's miscarriages, she might avoid her favourite activity, running. She's staying at a hotel with a pool, which explains where she's gone wearing hotel slippers.

'Bring up the camera over the pool. I want to see it live,' Wolfe says.

'Not working,' says Lwazi. The screen is white noise.

'Was it working earlier?' Wolfe asks.

'Yes.'

Wolfe dives past Stone and sprints along the corridor.

100

Stone swipes his security pass and presses the button for the gym and pool on level seventeen.

Wolfe presses button sixteen.

'We've already been there,' Stone says.

'I checked the plans before I got here,' says Wolfe. 'The lift opens straight onto the pool. We'll have no cover. But if we take the fire stairs, we've got a chance of arriving unseen. The fire door opens onto the changing rooms.'

Stone nods, checks his Glock is fully loaded.

'I can talk Yushkov down,' she says.

'You're an unarmed civilian. Stay out of it.'

Level sixteen. They take the fire stairs. Through a vertical rectangle of fireproof glass, they can see doors to male and female changing rooms. To their right, a floodlit, elliptical swimming pool is surrounded by sunbeds. There's a white bathrobe draped across the back of one. The shimmering turquoise water sends ripples of light onto the walls. Someone is swimming laps. They can't see who.

'Stay here,' Stone whispers, then slips through the door, Glock at the ready.

Wolfe follows. Gets glared at by Stone. The water splashes to a regular rhythm. Wolfe recognises Caroline's wet head of dark curls and releases a breath she wasn't aware she was holding. Around the corner is the lift, and beyond that, the gym, in darkness.

Wolfe freezes when the lift chimes and the door opens. A tall man in plumber's coveralls and a baseball cap heads for the pool. Caroline pauses at one end of the pool, watching. Wolfe mouths, 'Oh no.' She takes a step forward. Stone yanks her back. He raises his pistol. The new arrival kneels at the pool's edge and says something to Caroline, his back to them.

'Who are you?' Caroline says, loud enough for them to hear. She moves away from the man towards the middle of the pool.

Stone steps out from his hiding place. 'Police! Hands on your head, or I'll shoot.'

Yushkov raises his arms slowly and stands.

'Charlie!' calls Wolfe. 'It's Olivia. Get out of there. Get away from him!'

Caroline wades through the water, claws at the steps, slips.

'No!' shouts Yushkov, taking a step in her direction.

Stone fires at his back. Yushkov jolts as if touched by a live wire. His legs buckle. He lands heavily on his knees, then collapses face down on the tiles.

Caroline screams, scrambling to get out of the pool. Wolfe sprints towards her, takes Caroline's hand, pulls her up the steps. 'With me,' says Wolfe, steering Caroline towards the fire exit.

Stone stands over Yushkov, pistol pointed at his body, checking his face for signs of life. Yushkov grabs his ankle, tugs so fast Stone's leather-soled shoes slip from under him. He lands hard and the Glock is jolted free. Yushkov, whose bulletproof vest has saved him, throws himself at Stone, seizing the pistol.

Wolfe sees Yushkov out of the corner of her eye. She can't comprehend what he is doing. He turns one hundred and eighty degrees and points the gun at Caroline.

Wolfe doesn't recognise her own voice. Or her fury. '*You will not!*'

She stands between Caroline and the gun.

Yushkov fires.

The deafening report is like a physical assault. A thought leaps to her mind that there's no way the bullet will miss at this distance. Her pulse is hammering in her ears. It takes a few seconds to register the thud behind them. A metal chair leg screeches over tile. A gurgling sound. Wolfe can't move. Stares at Yushkov. Realises she isn't hit. Caroline shrieks. Wolfe turns and sees Terry Blunt. Dark blood wells from a gaping hole in his throat. He gasps in ragged, wet jerks, like a fish suffocating on the jetty. His fingers are loosely curled around a Colt M1911. Olivia can't believe what has just happened – Yushkov has shot Blunt.

Stone staggers towards Blunt. Takes the Colt. Watches him take his last, futile breath.

Wolfe turns again, but Yushkov is nowhere to be seen.

101

Flags of every nation attending the seventeenth Global Regulation of Wildlife Trade convention adorn the walls of the great hall, soon to be brimming with four hundred and ninety delegates. Three giant audio-visual screens display this convention's symbol – a western black rhino. On the podium, is a long table for the members of the secretariat. To one side of the podium stands a lectern with microphone.

The audience is seated at tables, arranged in rows, covered in white tablecloths. Most have laptops or tablets in front of them.

Wolfe sits in the first row, next to Caroline Bloom. On Caroline's other side is her principal private secretary, Jamie Osbourne, who keeps his head down and looks very sheepish, probably wondering if he'll have a job at the end of the day. Osbourne had stumbled back to the hotel in the small hours of the morning, so inebriated he could barely stand up. His phone was on silent all night and he hadn't noticed the missed calls and messages.

Next to Wolfe is one of two recently arrived SO1 officers. The other is positioned directly behind Caroline. The hall fills up rapidly, but the usual bubbly chatter at events like these is unusually subdued. Security at the convention has been tightened to uncomfortable levels after the assassination attempt. Armed SAPS police officers guard entrances and exits. Metal detectors have checked for firearms, knives and other weapons. Wolfe shakes her head at the memory of last night. Something about horses and gates springs to mind. Still, Nguyen is not easily thwarted. He might try a second time. Wolfe won't leave Caroline's side until the vote is cast and she's on a plane heading for London.

Caroline shakily lifts a glass of water to her lips, spilling a little on the starched tablecloth.

'It's not too late to leave,' Wolfe whispers. 'There's no shame in it.'

'I'm going to vote, Liv. I won't give in to threats.'

Wolfe nods. She would do the same.

Wolfe shifts in her seat. Her wounds throb and the thick dressing covering them makes it impossible to feel comfortable. Caffeine and adrenaline keep her going, but her limbs feel weighed down by exhaustion. She has been questioned by the South African police and SO1 all night and has barely had time to change her clothes before eating breakfast.

The doors at the back of the hall close and armed police stand guard. The first of the secretariat members walks onto the podium, a woman from Kenya. The delegates clap enthusiastically. She's followed by seven other members of the secretariat: South Africa, USA, Brazil, Germany, Nigeria, Japan, India. They wait for the secretary general who will make the opening speech.

'Will Nguyen still come?' Caroline asks.

'I think so,' says Wolfe. 'He thinks he's untouchable.'

'Dad cried with relief when I phoned him,' Caroline whispers in Wolfe's ear. 'I don't think I've ever known him do that.'

Wolfe squeezes her hand.

The secretary general walks onto the podium, waving at the delegates, smiling broadly. Tan Nguyen is the star of the show. His hair is slicked back, his charcoal suit perfectly cut. He looks completely unfazed by Blunt's failure to kill Caroline, or by what that will mean to the vote. Audience chatter dies away. Very few delegates clap, and those that do quickly sense they are out on a limb, and cease. The booing begins. At first one or two delegates, then more join in. It gets louder and louder.

Initially, Nguyen seems not to notice. He stands in front of the lectern, ready to make his opening address. Delegates shout. Some stand. 'Liar!', 'Poacher!', 'Rhino killer!' Nguyen runs his hand over his widow's peak and leans closer to the microphone.

'Welcome to Johannesburg and the seventeenth GROWT convention,' he begins.

'Killer!' somebody shouts.

'How can you live with yourself? Hypocrite!'

'Arrest him!' another yells.

'Murderer!'

'What's going on?' Caroline asks.

'Every delegate was emailed a link to my video. Nguyen's rah-rah speech to his syndicate, telling them how he plans to rig the vote. It's gone viral.'

Wolfe starts recording Nguyen and the angry audience.

From stage right, two SAPS officers walk onto the podium, and two other officers enter from stage left. Nguyen is handcuffed, but he keeps his composure.

'You're making a terrible mistake,' he says as he's led away.

The crowd cheers and whistles and applauds.

As Nguyen is led down the aisle, a following of hecklers forms behind him. Nguyen spies Wolfe. He lunges at her. 'You'll pay. Remember that.'

He's dragged away, but by now an angry crowd blocks their exit. Nguyen and the four officers are surrounded. A woman thumps her fist into Nguyen's chest. He's shoved from behind. 'Get back,' shouts a cop, and draws his weapon. Another calls for backup on his radio. The crowd around Nguyen surges, their anger swelling, fast turning into fury. Shouting drowns out the SAPS officers' warnings. Hands grab at Nguyen and he becomes a rag doll in a tug of war between the crowd and the officers.

A scream. Then another. People panic, back away. Run for the exits. But he's still surrounded by a whirlwind of confused and angry people. Wolfe can't see Nguyen anymore. Where did he go? More officers arrive, batons raised and they force the crowd to move back.

Nguyen lies on the floor motionless, a hunting knife protruding from his back.

102

Wolfe and Caroline sit in a quiet corner of the hotel bar, flanked by two SO1 officers. Wolfe throws back a much-needed gin and tonic. Caroline sips a sparkling mineral water.

'Who killed him?' Caroline asks.

'No idea.'

'Does his threat worry you?'

'Not now he's dead.' Wolfe has checked that Butcher and Ponnappa are alive and well and told them about Nguyen's arrest and murder. 'But I can't believe the conference went ahead anyway.'

'And the vote, too,' Caroline says. 'I'm just glad it's over. All I want to do now is get on a plane home.'

'After what Nguyen did to try to rig it, I'm surprised at the result,' says Wolfe.

Of the 143 member countries that voted on the motion to lift the ban on the international trade in rhino horn, twenty-two abstained, sixty voted to lift it, and sixty-one in favour of upholding it.

'I changed my mind,' says Caroline. 'I voted to uphold the ban.'

'Your vote tipped the balance. Can I ask you why?'

'I know what you're thinking. I did what Nguyen wanted. But this isn't about what that evil man wanted. It's about what I believe is the right way to tackle the issue.'

'You weren't–'

'Intimidated? No. I changed my mind long before Nguyen tried to kill me.'

'Why?'

'A briefing paper from the International Consortium on Combating Wildlife Crime. In their view, a legal trade sends a message that it's okay to buy horn. It undoes all the good work done by conservation charities to change attitudes in places like Vietnam.'

Wolfe hears her name called, looks up and sees Hannah Venter waving at her from the other side of the bar. Hannah makes her way to them. A nose-guard covers her broken nose. Her face is swollen, and she has eggplant coloured bruises under both eyes. Samuel had given her quite a beating.

Wolfe gives Hannah a hug and introduces Caroline.

'I can't believe you made it,' Wolfe says. 'I thought you were consigned to bed.'

'Nothing was going to stop me voting,' Hannah says, wincing. Moving her jaw even a fraction is clearly painful. She takes Wolfe's hands. 'You saved my life. I can't thank you enough.'

'You'd have done the same for me. Any news on Dan?' Wolfe asks her. 'I phoned the hospital, but they won't tell me anything.'

'I won't lie, Olivia. He's pretty bad. But he's conscious. He's asked after you.'

'Me?'

'Yes. He's insisted your name is on his visitors' list.'

'He has a list?'

'He's protected around the clock by a British police officer. He's a key witness in Sackville's trial. As you are.'

Wolfe falls silent. She doesn't want to think about the months, even years, it will take to get somebody as powerful as Harold Sackville to trial and then having to relive it all on a witness stand.

Caroline steps in to fill the hiatus in the conversation.

'Hannah, I'm so sorry to hear about your father.'

'At least now I know what happened and that those responsible have been dealt with. My wounds will heal. I'll survive. Sadly, my rhinos probably won't.' Hannah's face creases and her eyes grow watery. 'I'd better leave before I embarrass myself. I need an early night.'

They watch Hannah go.

'I need to get some sleep too,' says Caroline, standing awkwardly, one hand under her belly. 'I fly back to London in the morning.'

Caroline takes Wolfe's arm and they leave the bar. 'Liv, I know I haven't been a good friend recently.'

'Don't be daft.'

'No please. Let me say this. When the media went after you because of your relationship with Yushkov, I turned my back on you. I feel ashamed. I'm sorry.'

'Forget about it.'

'I was wrong about Yushkov,' Caroline adds.

'I'm not sure you were. I really don't know who he is anymore. I suppose I should be happy he did the right thing in the end–'

'In the end?' asks Caroline.

'Yes, shooting Blunt. He must have had a last-minute change of heart.'

Caroline stops, takes Wolfe's hands. 'My dear friend, you've got it all wrong. Remember when he bent down at the pool's edge and spoke to me?'

'Yes. You looked terrified.'

'I *was* terrified. But not because he threatened me.'

'I don't understand.'

'He told me he was your friend. That a man had been sent to kill me. And he was going to help me.'

'But he tried to kill Agent Stone.'

'No, he incapacitated Agent Stone, then used his gun to kill Blunt.'

'You're saying he never intended to kill you?'

'He never intended to kill me,' says Caroline emphatically. 'I am eternally in his debt. My baby too.'

103

Hospitals always smell of cooked cabbage and disinfectant, and shoes seem to squeak loudest on their floors. It's late. Visiting time is about to end, but Wolfe hopes they'll make an exception. Too wired to sleep, she's decided to visit Casburn.

Above the double swing doors of Johannesburg Hospital's Trauma Unit, a sign directs visitors to use the antiseptic handwash in a pump on the wall. Wolfe does so and enquires at a desk for Dan Casburn. She's asked for proof of ID. The nurse makes a phone call. Wolfe gets the okay.

'ICU, Room 8,' the nurse says. 'I'll take you, I'm going that way.'

Wolfe is led through the emergency ward. Doctors and nurses scuttle around a man with a hole in his stomach so big she can see his intestines. She passes a gurney: a teenager's leg is shattered and bloody. The ward is crowded and noisy: the beds, monitoring screens, respiratory and other equipment separated by a flimsy blue curtain.

'Gang war,' the nurse says.

'How is Dan doing?'

'Stable. He's a lucky man. The bullet missed his heart by a few millimetres. But he was in deep haemorrhagic shock when he was admitted.'

Through a set of swing doors and down a long corridor, they arrive at a small unit of eight intensive care cubicles for patients that need a dedicated round-the-clock nurse. The front wall is glass. Four are occupied. A patient and a nurse in each.

'He's in the one at the end.'

A police officer in casual dress sees her and stands, affording her a glimpse of his gun and holster beneath his open jacket.

'ID?' the officer demands. He checks it, then pats her down, removing her phone. 'I'll hang on to this.' He pockets it. 'You're the only journalist on the list, so don't push it. Everything's off the record, right?' His Glaswegian accent is pronounced.

'Right.'

Casburn is in a pale blue hospital gown, eyes shut. There is a drip in his arm, an oxygen tube in his nose, and so many other tubes attached to him and beeping machines behind him, she wonders how he can sleep. A nurse sits in a chair to the right of the bed. Her name tag says Evelyn. She smiles at Wolfe. A wall-mounted TV is on, tuned to a SATV news channel.

'How is he?' Wolfe asks her.

'Alive,' Casburn answers, before the nurse can. He opens his eyes.

'Doing well,' says the nurse. 'Don't tire him.'

There is a chair near the bed. Wolfe takes it.

'I never thought I'd see you in a dress,' says Wolfe mischievously, eyeing his hospital gown.

'I never thought you'd visit me in hospital,' Casburn replies.

'Got this for you,' Wolfe says, opening up her new go-bag and pulling out a daffodil in a yellow ceramic pot with a smiley face on the side. Miraculously the hospital shop was still open when she arrived. She places it proudly on the over-bed table. 'Ta-dah!'

'No, no,' says the nurse. 'Not in here. No flowers.' She opens the door and hands the smiling daffodil to the officer outside.

'A smiley face?' Casburn says, clearly amused.

'Thought it would cheer you up.'

'I'm not a good patient.'

'I can imagine.' She grins. 'Have you heard about Nguyen?'

'Yeah, his murder really pissed me off. As far as I'm concerned, death was too good for him.'

'Look on the bright side. His syndicate is finished.'

'It's an international shitstorm, that's for sure. Every law enforcement agency under the sun is trying to muscle in on this.'

'Wish I'd been there to see Sackville arrested.'

'You and me both. Sorry you never got to publish the story.'

'Moz isn't happy.'

'You're a key witness, Olivia.'

'I know. It kind of limits what I can print. But once I've testified, I can tell my story. I've just got to be patient, which isn't my strong point.'

'We worked out why Nguyen wanted Venter, the Russian woman, the Fin, and the lad from Swaziland to disappear.'

'It's something to do with the vote?'

'Yes. They were all relatives of the convention delegates. None of them had the delegates' surnames, which is why no one connected the dots. The lad from Swaziland was a grandson. The Russian woman was a sister. The Finnish man, a brother. Venter was the only one whose name was on the delegates list. Nguyen was blackmailing the delegates to force them to vote the way he wanted. They were told their relatives were alive and would be returned unharmed once the vote was over, as long as they did what he said.'

'And Caroline's death was going to look like accidental drowning?'

'Yeah, it was.' Casburn glances at the nurse. She's watching the TV. 'Can we have a moment in private, Evelyn?'

'Sorry. You have to have a nurse with you at all times.' Evelyn resumes watching the TV news, at least pretending she's not listening to their conversation.

'It's coming back to me,' Casburn says, his voice hushed. 'In flashes. Samuel. What he did to you. I'm sorry.'

The mention of Samuel makes her skin creep. 'I'm not the one full of bullet holes.'

'I'd be dead if it wasn't for you. The way you handled him was...'

remarkable. Kept him talking. Controlled your fear, your pain. Played him at his own game. You're wasted in journalism.'

Wolfe breaks the eye contact. She doesn't feel proud. Far from it. 'I lost it, Dan. At the end, after all he had done to me. I wanted to kill him.'

'You killed him in self-defence. End of story.'

As Wolfe leaves the Trauma ward, her phone beeps. Owethu has returned her call and left a voicemail. She wanted to know that he and Mama Gcina were safe. She listens to Owethu's voice message:

I have Mr Ximba's laptop. I kept it hidden from the police. Now that Msiza's been arrested, what do I do with it?

She phones him back. Despite the late hour, Owethu answers.

'I'll meet you in the morning,' Wolfe says. 'I'll hand it in. That way, nobody need know you took it.'

'Thank you, Olivia,' Owethu says. 'Now my father can die in peace.'

104

She hears a whimper and opens her eyes. Covered in sweat, Wolfe has no idea where she is. The room is dark. She's lying on her side, curled up, the sheet gripped so tightly that her fingernails have left dark pink indentations in her palms. Ahead, a gap in the curtains reveals a slice of a cityscape at night, the orange glow of sodium-vapor lights painting the underside of an overcast sky a sickly brown. Johannesburg. Her own whimper woke her. A nightmare. Samuel peeling skin off her body, piece by piece.

She blinks at the clock: 3.53am. Straightening her legs sends a spasm of pain through her abdomen. The painkillers have worn off. There's a glass of water on the bedside table. The painkillers are in the bathroom. She is loath to sit up and go and get them, anticipating the throbbing agony that would accompany the effort. A ribbon of light under the hotel room door refracts in rainbow shades through a cut-glass tumbler on her bedside table.

Wolfe freezes.

Reflected in the mirror on the opposite wall is a solid shape. A person. Sitting on the bed, behind her.

Groggy, she racks her brain for a weapon to use. She has none. Last night, close to collapse, it had been all she could do to pop some pills, undress and get into bed. She fell asleep immediately. She hadn't considered she might still be in danger.

'Olivia?'

She catches her breath.

'I had to see you,' Yushkov says.

Wolfe struggles to sit up, wincing. She lets out a small groan with the effort.

'Put the light on, will you?' she asks, panting softly. 'You're creeping me out in the dark.'

The sudden glare of the bedside light makes her blink. Yushkov smiles.

'When you sleep, you are so beautiful.'

'Don't do that.'

'Do what?'

'That thing where you put me off my guard.'

Yushkov gets up, his movements stiff.

'Where are you going?'

'We both need painkillers. Bathroom?'

'Yes.'

He stoops slightly. Returning with a sachet of ibuprofen, he gives her two tablets and takes two for himself, which he swallows without water.

'Can I sit with you?'

Her mind yells *tell him to leave*, but her heart says otherwise.

Yushkov sees her confusion. 'I'm sorry you were caught up in this.'

'I know you saved Caroline's life. And I thank you for that. But tell me one thing. Why work for a man like Nguyen?'

Yushkov looks away. Silent.

'Do you know what Samuel did to me?' she peels back the dressing on her arm. The skin either side of the sutures is inflamed. 'He cut me. Here, and here.' She lifts her T-shirt so he can see the dressing on her stomach. 'He was skinning me. Alive.'

He tries to take her hand. She snatches it away.

'Do you know what I had to do to stop him?' Her face is screwed up. Not with rage. With self-loathing. 'I had to seduce that sick fuck. Offer myself to him. Do you have any idea how filthy that makes me feel? How disgusting? I swear to God, if I'd had to go through with it... I don't think I could ever...' She hugs her knees to her chest and rocks back and forth.

Yushkov has turned his head away. 'I am so sorry, Olivia.'

'Look at me!' She takes his chin and turns his face towards her. He will not make eye contact. 'Please, Vitaly, look at me.' His are wet. 'Why, Vitaly? Why protect Nguyen?'

'Do you know what it is like to desire one life and be forced to live another?'

'How could someone *force* you to work for Nguyen?'

'If I tell you, I'm a dead man.'

'No, you're a survivor. You'll find a way. Tell me.'

His jaw tightens. 'What about Casburn?'

'I won't tell him.'

There is doubt in his eyes. 'I see the way he is with you. He wants you.'

'You saw that? When?'

He reaches out his hand and lays his palm over her heart. 'He wants this.'

Wolfe pushes his hand away. 'You're not making any sense.'

'Casburn tortured me. Let my sister die. Accused me of something I did not do. Destroyed my life. And now he wants to take from me the only person I have left. You.'

'That's crazy. He couldn't stop the Russians killing your sister. He cleared your name. Let you leave England a free man.'

'He wants you to think this. Do not trust Casburn, Olivia.'

'I don't think you have a right to tell me what I can or cannot do. You chose to work for Nguyen. And you kept doing it, even when you knew he'd sent that monster after me. You have no right to criticise a man who almost died bringing Nguyen to justice.'

'I want you to be happy. But not with Casburn. Anybody but Casburn.'

'Stop this, Vitaly. I just can't do this anymore. It tears me apart. Please, just go.'

In three angry strides Yushkov is at the door. She thinks he will yank it open. Instead, he leans his brow against it. 'You struck a deal with Casburn, remember?'

'Yes, I remember. You got a pardon and a new life.'

'There was more to that deal.'

'Go on.'

'My pardon came at a price.'

'Yes. Never return to England. I know.'

'No, you don't know,' he says, bitterly. He turns to face her, his back to the door. 'There was more. I am forever bound to your country.'

'What does that mean?'

He looks down. Wolfe gets out of bed.

'Tell me, please.'

'I am controlled by your Secret Intelligence Service. Your MI6. Casburn set it up. He said if I didn't want to spend the rest of my life being tortured in an Egyptian prison, I must work for them.'

Wolfe shakes her head. 'That can't be right. We agreed you would be free, to do as you like.'

Yushkov shakes his head. 'Casburn was very clear on one thing. You must never know. He said if I told you, I will be terminated.'

'He wouldn't do that.'

'I did not choose to come to South Africa. I was sent here. MI6, they gave me a new identity, Dmitry Lazarev. They wanted to take down Nguyen and the syndicate. MI6 needed proof. Two British spies tried and failed to infiltrate his syndicate. They were killed. I was sent undercover. I am Russian, so I am expendable.'

Wolfe's mind is a whir of questions. 'Why didn't Casburn use you to capture Samuel?'

'He did not know I was embedded with Nguyen. MI6 and SO24 do not talk. You must know this, Olivia.'

'Okay, the spooks don't like sharing. I get that. But show me something, anything that proves Casburn set you up.'

'There is no proof. All I have is a phone number. A woman. She is MI5. Tells me what to do. Tomorrow, I get a new assignment. With a new identity. You must decide, Olivia, if you believe me, or Casburn.'

Wolfe takes him in her arms. 'I was wrong to doubt you,' she says.

'I am tired of living, Olivia.'

'We'll find a way. Come to bed. Sleep. We'll work this out in the morning.'

Yushkov climbs into bed beside her, his body tucked into the back of hers, their fingers entwined. They sleep.

She wakes. It's 8.11am. There is no weight on the mattress next to her. Just a dent left in a pillow.

105

LONDON, UK, SIX WEEKS LATER

The Balham pub is heaving. Wolfe weaves through the throng searching for Butcher, whose birthday she has come to celebrate. The crowd at the bar is four deep. She spies Butcher and Ponnappa at a far corner table, both with already half-drunk pints in front of them. She gives Butcher a kiss on the cheek, then Ponnappa a big hug.

'Emma not coming?' Wolfe asks. Emma is Butcher's wife.

'She's got a surprise party organised.' Butcher grimaces as if sucking on a lemon. 'I have to be home by seven thirty and act surprised when I find people I hardly know in ridiculous party hats pretending to like me.' He smiles at Wolfe. 'I guess you're in on it too?'

Wolfe glances at Ponnappa and they both burst out laughing.

'It's impossible to keep anything from you,' says Wolfe. 'Now, who wants another drink?'

'A Past Masters, thanks,' says Butcher.

'Brew Dog for me,' says Ponnappa, her bangles clanking on the tabletop. 'And cheese and onion crisps. I'm famished.'

'If I don't make it back from the bar in the next ten minutes, send out a search party,' says Wolfe.

She joins the jostling crowd waiting to be served. Ahead, a

twenty-something office worker orders a round of cocktails for five female colleagues. She sighs. It's going to be a long wait. To her left, she realises there are only two people waiting for drinks and the man at the bar has just paid. She takes a moment to register the familiar flat-top haircut, shaved close at the back, and his jaw chewing gum. Casburn turns, a beer in hand.

'Dan!' Wolfe waves to get his attention. 'Can you order some drinks for me?' she calls out.

'Sure,' he replies. 'What are you having?'

Wolfe gives him the order, ignoring the groans from the people waiting. Casburn manoeuvres the tray of drinks through the crowd like a wide load through city traffic. But he moves slowly, his back slightly bent.

'Let me take that.' Wolfe carries the tray. 'Come join us. It's Jerry's birthday.'

'Hold up a moment.' Casburn leans against a pillar. 'I just need to catch my breath.'

He's lost weight and has the pinched look of somebody in pain.

'I'm guessing you're back at work, despite doctor's orders?'

'Yes. And you? I hear you're moving back to Balham.'

'Yup. It was time.'

'Nothing from your old stalker?'

'Seems he's given up. Maybe now my life can go back to normal.'

'Normal? You?'

'Yeah, yeah. So, what are you doing here? This isn't your neck of the woods...' Her voice trails away. 'Ah, I get it. This isn't a coincidence, is it?'

'Not exactly. I wanted to talk to you.'

Butcher and Ponnappa watch them from their corner table, clearly as fascinated as she is as to why Casburn would go out of his way to find her.

'Fine. I need to ask you something first,' Wolfe says.

'Go ahead.'

'It would mean a lot to me if you answered honestly.'

Casburn frowns. 'I have a feeling I'm not going to like this question.'

'Is Vitaly working for MI6?'

'I don't know. I doubt it. Why do you ask?'

He doesn't lift his chin, which is his 'tell' that he's lying. Yet, he doesn't appear surprised by the question either.

Wolfe shrugs. 'Just a theory. It might explain why he was working for a monster like Nguyen. You know, undercover. I could understand something like that.'

'Six doesn't tell me what they are doing, and I don't tell them what we're doing, either. So, I have no idea. Look, I didn't come here to talk about Yushkov, but I did want to ask you something.'

'Fire away.'

'I want you to join SO24.'

Wolfe blinks several times. She can't have heard him right. 'Say that again?'

'Come and work with me.'

She laughs. 'Join the Police? You're joking, right?'

Casburn shakes his head, his expression serious.

He's winding me up. 'They'd never have me.'

'Specialist units like mine can take on non-police officers with desirable skills.'

'I'm the last person you'd want.'

'I disagree. You're exactly what SO24 needs.'

Later that evening, Casburn buys a burner phone and calls a contact in the Russian SVR. There is no exchange of greetings.

'Vitaly Yushkov is in Turkey,' Casburn says, giving an address.

'Why you do this?'

'He's become a problem.'

ACKNOWLEDGEMENTS

I consider myself incredibly lucky. Not only do I love making up stories for a living, I also meet the most incredible people. Dr Lynne MacTavish is one such person. Lynne has spent the last eighteen years running a private wildlife reserve in South Africa. Her most formidable task is defending her rhinos from poachers. She is an incredibly brave woman and an inspiration. Until I spent time with her, I had no idea that the battle to save South Africa's rhinos is just that – a battle. The poachers are well-armed and brutal, funded by criminal cartels in Vietnam and China. There are many conflicting views on how rhinos can be saved from extinction. In *Prey* I've created characters with varying views on this emotionally charged topic. My novel does not try to come up with an answer as I'm ill-equipped to offer one. But my greatest wish is that an answer is found soon.

I would also like to thank Dougal MacTavish for taking me on night-time perimeter patrols, teaching me how to use a rifle (for research purposes only!) and for the wonderful tales he shared with me. These experiences have enabled me to create an imaginary wildlife reserve populated with imaginary people who bear no resemblance to Lynne or Dougal. The Global Regulation of Wildlife

Trade convention in this novel is fabricated. Any errors relating to rhino conservation and the trade in horn is of my doing.

Thank you, Lara James, for introducing me to Lynne and for your friendship. I am indebted to Peter James for his words of wisdom on all things publishing and his support over the years. Thanks also to Mary, Anneliese and Scotty Stewart for trying your best to educate me in South African dialects and slang. Any mistakes are my own. Thanks also to Damien Mander, founder of the International Anti-Poaching Foundation, and to Fiona Macleod, director of Oxpeckers, for taking the time to answer my questions, and to science journalist and broadcaster, Robyn Williams, and documentary maker, Jonica Newby, for cheering me on.

A big thank you also goes to authors Tony Park, Paul Mendelson, Caroline Carver and Kimberley Howe for your words of encouragement, and to my literary agent, Phil Patterson, for your guidance and patience, and of course a huge thanks to everyone at Bloodhound Books. Betsy Reavley, Fred Freeman, Tara Lyons and Loulou Brown, you guys rock!

My first readers gave me fantastic feedback on an early draft. They are my husband Michael Larkin, Caroline Kennedy-Roach, Carolyn Tate, cyber security expert Ray Packham, PR guru Tony Mulliken, and retired Detective Chief Superintendent of Sussex CID, David Gaylor, and his wonderful wife, Lyn. Thank you for your honesty and helping me see the wood for the trees.

Printed by Amazon Italia Logistica S.r.l.
Torrazza Piemonte (TO), Italy